RAZOR GIRL

Razor Girl

CARL HIAASEN

ALFRED A. KNOPF

NEW YORK

2016

THIS IS A BORZOI BOOK
PUBLISHED BY ALFRED A. KNOPF

Copyright © 2016 by Carl Hiaasen

All rights reserved. Published in the United States by
Alfred A. Knopf, a division of Penguin Random House LLC, New York,
and distributed in Canada by Random House of Canada, a division of
Penguin Random House Limited, Toronto.
www.aaknopf.com

Knopf, Borzoi Books, and the colophon are registered trademarks of
Penguin Random House LLC.

Library of Congress Cataloging-in-Publication Data
Names: Hiaasen, Carl, author.
Title: Razor girl : a novel / Carl Hiaasen.
Description: First United States edition. | New York:
Alfred A. Knopf, 2016. | "2015 | "This is a borzoi book."
Identifiers: LCCN 2016007926 | ISBN 9780385349741 (hardcover)
ISBN 9780385349758 (ebook)
ISBN 9780451494269 (open market)
Subjects: LCSH: Swindlers and swindling—Fiction. | Traffic accident victims—Fiction.
| BISAC: FICTION / Mystery & Detective / General. |
FICTION / Suspense. | FICTION / Thrillers. | GSAFD: Mystery fiction.
Classification: LLC PS8558.I217 R89 2016 | DDC 813/.54—dc23
LC record available at http://lccn.loc.gov/2016007926

Jacket design by Mark Matcho
Manufactured in the United States of America
First United States Edition

For Fenia, always dancing

RAZOR GIRL

ONE

On the first day of February, sunny but cold as a frog's balls, a man named Lane Coolman stepped off a flight at Miami International, rented a mainstream Buick and headed south to meet a man in Key West. He nearly made it.

Twenty-seven miles from Coolman's destination, an old green Firebird bashed his car from behind. The impact failed to trigger the Buick's airbags, but Coolman heard the rear bumper dragging. He steered off the highway and dialed 911. In the mirror he saw the Firebird, its grille crimped and steaming, pull onto the shoulder. Ahead stood a sign that read: "Ramrod Key."

Coolman went to check on the other driver, a woman in her mid-thirties with red hair.

"Super-duper sorry," she said.

"What the hell happened?"

"Just a nick. Barely bleeding." She held her phone in one hand and a disposable razor in the other.

"Are you out of your mind?" said Coolman.

The driver's jeans and panties were bunched around her knees. She'd been shaving herself when she smashed Coolman's rental car.

"I got a date," she explained.

"You couldn't take care of that at home?"

"No way! My husband would get so pissed."

"Unreal," said Coolman.

The woman was wearing a maroon fleece jacket and rhinestone flip-flops. On her pale thigh was the razor mark.

"How about a little privacy?" she said. "I'm not quite done here."

Coolman walked back to the Buick and called the man he was supposed to meet in Key West. "I'll be a few minutes late. You're not gonna believe what just happened," he said on the man's voicemail, leaving it at that.

The cops arrived and wrote up the red-haired pube shaver for careless driving. Naturally, she had no collision insurance; that would be Avis's problem, not Lane Coolman's. A tow truck hauled away the Firebird, which needed a new front end including a radiator. The woman approached Coolman and asked for a ride.

"Tell your 'date' to come get you," he said. One of the police officers had pried the damaged bumper from the Buick, and Coolman was trying to fit it into the backseat.

"He doesn't have a car," said the woman, who'd buttoned her jeans. She was attractive in a loose and scattered way. Coolman had a weakness for redheads.

"See, I work for an escort service. We go to where the client's at," she said.

"Yes, I understand the concept."

The woman's fleece was unzipped and beneath it she wore a black sequined top. Her toes must be freezing in those flip-flops, Coolman thought; the temperature was 55 degrees with a biting north wind, arctic conditions for the Florida Keys.

"My name's Merry," she said, "spelled like Merry Christmas."

"My name's Bob," said Coolman, "spelled like Bob."

"Does that mean you'll give me a lift?"

"Why not," Coolman said, the worst mistake he would ever make.

At Mile Marker 22, Merry told him her last name was Mansfield, like the bombshell actress of the Fifties. Coolman stopped at a Circle K where he got a cup of coffee and Merry bought three eight-hour energy drinks, chugging the little purple bottles one after the other.

"You running a marathon?" Coolman asked.

"I'm all about performance."

At Mile Marker 17, she told him she didn't really work for an escort service.

"Wild guess—you're a dancer," he said.

"On my own time," she replied. "Not one of *those*."

"I didn't mean it in a bad way."

"Why didn't you just say stripper? The games you guys play, I swear." Her eyelashes were a paler shade of red than her hair.

Coolman said, "Why would you make up a lie about being an escort?"

"'Cause I needed a ride, *Bob*. If I said I was an artifacts appraiser you would've left me standing in the road."

"What is it you appraise?"

"Sunken treasure. Doubloons and cannonballs and so forth. Business is slow right now. I'm an expert on eighteenth-century Spanish maritime."

"Do you have a real date, or did you make up that part, too?"

Merry laughed. "He's an Air Force pilot based at Boca Chica. Why else would I be doin' my trim at sixty-five miles per hour?"

At Mile Marker 8, she blurted, "Did I say Air Force? I meant Navy." She was buzzing like a flagpole in a lightning storm. "His name's Rocky."

"What about your husband?"

"He's a Rocky, too."

"Stop," said Coolman.

"Don't be judging me. I go for men with strong names."

The closer they got to Key West, the more Southern her accent became. Coolman was foolishly intrigued.

"What about you?" she said. "What's your field, Bob? Your expertise."

"I'm in the entertainment business. I manage talent."

"Your own, or somebody else's?"

"Ever seen the show *Bayou Brethren*?" Coolman asked.

"Little Rocky watches it all the time."

"That's your son? Little Rocky?"

"No, it's what I call my husband. Don't make me spell out why."

"Anyway, I manage Buck. You know—the family patriarch? Buck Nance."

"No shit?"

"Leader of the clan," said Coolman.

"Yeah, Bob, I know what a fucking patriarch is."

The show was taped in the Florida Panhandle at a swampy location that somewhat resembled a Louisiana bayou. Buck Nance and his brothers were actually from Wisconsin, but the network paid for a Cajun dialogue coach.

Merry said, "So what brings you all the way down here?"

"Buck has a personal appearance."

"Where?"

"Parched Pirate."

"Doing what?"

"Just being Buck."

Coolman hoped the guitar player had found the bar. Buck Nance had trouble speaking in public unless he was accompanied by a live musician. For his road gigs the writers at the network had come up with eight or nine amusing redneck stories, what you might call a monologue, and afterward Buck would take questions for ten minutes or so. The questions were printed on index cards distributed in advance to random fuckwits in the crowd.

Coolman offered to take Merry to the show. "We'll hang backstage," he added. Like there *was* a backstage.

"What about my date?" she asked.

"Bail," Coolman said. "Tell him the truth—you had car trouble."

"But then I shaved down there for no reason."

"Not necessarily."

The redhead smiled and shook her head. "For the Zac Brown Band I'd ditch my Navy boy in a heartbeat, but not for some yahoo from the bayou."

"It's only the top-rated cable program in the whole country."

"I prefer the nature channels. You know—penguins and cheetahs. Shit like that."

"Buck converted his Bentley to an ATV with rifle racks."

"Why would a grown man do something so ridiculous?"

"America worships the guy. You should come hear him tonight."

"Another time," said Merry.

At Mile Marker 5, she made a call on her cell phone. All she said was, "Don't wet yourself, sugar. I'm almost there."

At Mile Marker 4, after they'd crossed the bridge into Key West, she flipped open the visor mirror and checked her makeup. Freshened her lipstick. Brushed her hair.

"You look terrific," said Coolman.

"Damn right, Bob."

At Mile Marker 3, she exclaimed, "Okay, pull in here!"

It was a small shopping center with a Sears as the high point. Merry directed Coolman where to park. He was surprised when a white Tesla rolled up beside them.

"That's your boyfriend?" Coolman knew a couple of CAA agents back in L.A. who drove jet-black Teslas. The white model looked pretty sweet. Coolman himself leased a corpuscle-red Mercedes SLK 350 that required no electric outlet.

"I thought you said he didn't have wheels."

Merry shrugged. "Must be a loaner."

The young man who got out of the Tesla was wearing a leather bomber jacket. If not for the gold earring and oily long hair he could have been a Navy pilot.

"It was nice meeting you," Coolman said to the redhead.

"Oh, you're coming with."

"Me? What for?"

The man in the bomber jacket yanked open Coolman's door and put a pistol to his neck.

"Let's go, dipshit."

"Just take my wallet," Coolman said, breathless. "The Rolex, too, whatever you want."

"You're adorable, Bob," the woman whispered. "Now get out of the fucking car."

Bayou Brethren had been conceived as a reality show about moonshiners, but another network snatched that idea first. Next on the concept list was pig farming, the unsavory auditions dragging on for months. Eventually Buck Nance and his three younger brothers were chosen to star in the program, though they knew nothing about swine husbandry. They got the nod because of their exquisite beards, rough-edged banter and punctuality.

The pilot episode of *Bayou Brethren* was a major disappointment, the visual appeal of high-def hog shit having been overestimated by a network vice president who was summarily promoted to a more harmless position. The new network vice president in charge of the project felt the brothers needed a more esoteric vocation to distract from their unappealing personalities, a view shared by potential advertisers who'd screened the off-putting pilot. Specialty chicken breeding was chosen as the alternate milieu—Buck and his brothers would raise prize roosters whose multi-hued hackle feathers would be crafted into beautiful flies for catching gamefish such as trout and tarpon.

Midway through the first season Buck got pecked in the eye while chasing one of the birds, which he vanquished indecorously with a Babolat tennis racket. The show's ratings soared, and the Nances made the cover of *People* magazine. Currently Lane Coolman's agency was negotiating preposterous new contracts for the clan, and during a short break in taping it was decided to put Buck on the road in a few soft markets, South Florida being one of the softest due to its diversity.

The Parched Pirate was packed, so Buck was on edge. Coolman hadn't arrived yet, which meant no pep talk, no wild stories about the hot babe (or babes) Lane had banged the night before. Even though there were direct flights to Key West, Lane had insisted on driving down from Miami because he said he wanted to see the islands. Now he was late for the event, something that had never before happened.

Buck and Lane had a certain way of getting ready, and Buck faltered if their routine was altered. Plus the guitar player was nowhere in sight—some cow-eyed slacker from Pasadena, all he had to do was pick a few notes while Buck told humorous redneck yarns. Buck had lobbied for a banjo player but Lane said they cost too much, which made no fucking sense to Buck because a banjo's got fewer strings than a damn guitar.

Before the show, Buck waited alone in a small room that had a card table and a couple of folding chairs. He would have preferred to park himself at the bar except he would have been mobbed by fans. The manager said several male customers had torn off their shirtsleeves in homage (Buck always wore a wifebeater on TV). Sometimes he'd stay after a gig and autograph the shirt fragments, but not tonight. No way.

The bartender poked his head in the door. "Ready, dude?"

"Born that way," said Buck Nance, though he was definitely *not* ready. Where the hell was Lane? The message he'd left on Buck's phone said something crazy had happened.

Everybody cheered and wooo-hooed when Buck ambled onto the small stage. Lane had assured him that the Parched Pirate drew a good biker crowd, and Buck was relieved to see lots of black leather mixed in with the cruise-ship garb.

He relaxed a little. Waved. Gave a fist pump. Somebody handed him a Jack-and-Coke, which he gulped, then somebody handed him another.

The first bit started out fine. It was the one about a good ole boy who comes home drunk and rolls into bed with what he thinks is his wife but it turns out to be a bear, only the man is too trashed to notice, and the two of them—him and the bear—are sleeping spoon-style when the wife walks in . . .

But storytelling wasn't the same for Buck Nance without the accompanying guitar, which set a laid-back mood. He started blanking—not stage fright exactly, just a few crucial gaps in the memory loop. It had happened two or three times before, but Lane Coolman had always been there, stage right, with a verbal cue to lead Buck back on track.

Not tonight. The microphone felt like a barbell in Buck's sweaty hand, and he wrapped up the bear-and-hairy-wife story as best he could. People chuckled, though it sounded to Buck like a communal politeness and not the genuine guffaws he'd come to expect in working-class sports bars. He wondered if he'd been given some faulty information about the Parched Pirate, and Key West in general.

He couldn't remember the second yarn on his set list. So, in an ill-considered burst of spontaneity, he decided to tell a joke he'd heard from one of his brothers.

"Hey, why can't homos drive faster than 68 miles an hour?" Buck Nance said. "'Cause at 69 they blow a rod!"

The barroom didn't go silent, but the walls weren't exactly shaking with riotous laughter. Buck wondered whether the joke worked better if you used "faggot" instead of "homo."

Next he told the one about four black guys in an Escalade arriving at the gates of Heaven, and this time not a living soul chuckled, not even the Caucasian drunks in sandals. A couple of heavyset individuals in the back of the room called Buck a racist asshole and began a sharp-elbowed charge toward the stage. Buck was unaccustomed to such naked hostility, and he'd prepared no clever comeback lines like real stand-up comedians do.

"Just chill out, sports fans," was what he said, desperately scanning the crowd for Lane's face. *Where the fuck was he?*

Soon enough it was explained to Buck Nance that Key West was a bad location to be making fun of homosexuals and also African Americans. This bulletin was delivered by a 275-pound biker who happened to be both gay and black, and owned a right hand that fit easily around Buck Nance's stringy hirsute neck.

Bouncers pulled the aggrieved patron away before the strangulation was complete, and Buck revived coughing and beet-faced. Angrily he began spewing down-home expletives that included the n-word, igniting a melee between a few diehard fans and the rest of the audience. Buck got walloped by flying fists and Budweiser bottles, and at one point a man costumed as Lady Gaga attempted to rip the beard from his chin. The man was surprisingly strong and wore just enough jasmine perfume to be distracting.

With the bar manager's assistance Buck shook loose and fled through a back door. In no particular direction he ran through the alleys of old Cayo Hueso fearing, not irrationally, that he was in mortal danger.

Yancy was bummed because Rosa couldn't drive down from Miami for the weekend. She had the night shift in the E.R. at Baptist. Selfishly he sometimes wished she still worked at the morgue; the hours were better because no urgent care was required.

He finished his glass of rum, grabbed his only sweater and went outside to stare at the stars. After a few chilly minutes he wished he'd put on some shoes and long pants. Somebody with a flashlight was walking back and forth in the vacant lot next door. The lot was blooming with weeds, and still littered with charred rubble from the arson that had leveled the previous owner's unfinished villa. Yancy hadn't set the fire though he bore indirect responsibility, and no remorse. Afterward the property had been surrendered in savage divorce litigation to the owner's wife, who'd recently sold it.

Yancy stepped down from his backyard deck, gingerly climbed the chain-link fence and made his way toward the stranger carrying the flashlight. It was a woman, and he startled her.

She aimed the bright beam at his eyeballs saying, "Hey, just back off!"

"Relax. I live in that house." Yancy reached out and repositioned her flashlight. "What are you looking for?" he asked.

"A ring."

"What kind of ring?"

"None of your business. I must've dropped it this morning."

"When you were here doing what exactly?" In the darkness Yancy couldn't see the angles of her face, but her skin looked glossy and her hair was light-colored. She sounded younger than he was.

"I was with our landscape architect," the woman said with a ludicrous air of importance. "And my fiancé."

"So it was your engagement ring you lost. That sucks."

"Hey, do you mind?"

It was an odd place to drop an expensive piece of jewelry. Obviously the woman hadn't told her future hubby; otherwise he would have been out there helping her search for it.

She said, "If you don't go away right now, I'm calling the cops."

Yancy tipped an imaginary cap. "At your service."

In the not-so-distant past he had been a real detective. Now he was stuck on the roach patrol, scouring local restaurants for threats to public hygiene. "My name's Andrew Yancy," he said.

"Let's see your badge."

"I'm in my boxer shorts, and crushed that you didn't notice. My badge is back at the house. You want some coffee? It's freezing out here."

"What I'd like is for you to leave me alone," the woman said, "unless you're planning to arrest me for something."

"How many karats?"

"What?"

"Your missing ring," Yancy said. "Karats as in diamonds, not bunny food."

"That's such a rude question."

"My specialty. Is your rock bigger than, say, a pistachio? I've got a cordless spotlight is the reason I ask. You want some help?"

"No," the woman replied. "I do not."

Yancy walked back to his place thinking she didn't believe he was a cop, or else she would have been more respectful. On the other hand, his nocturnal approach in underwear and bare feet might have made a sketchy first impression.

He was annoyed at himself for not asking the woman what she and her fiancé were planning to build next door. Yancy treasured his sunset view on Big Pine Key, and he hoped the new couple would honor the height restrictions in the building code. Nothing less than Yancy's own peace of mind was at stake. He didn't want more trouble on the street, now that Rosa was spending more time here.

In the kitchen he put on some Jack Johnson, fired up a joint and texted Rosa a photo of the two fresh lobster tails he was about to grill. Nearby he heard a car door slam extremely hard, suggesting that the woman with the flashlight had not located her lost engagement ring and was giving up for the night. There was an angry-sounding yelp of tires as she sped away in what sounded to Yancy like a high-powered European sportster.

After dinner he slipped on some jeans and, to spare his feet from the concrete shards and splintered lumber, a pair of thick-soled Rockports. Then he took the Q-Beam from his skiff on the trailer in the driveway, and returned to the empty lot.

The spotlight had a powerful halogen bulb, three million candle-power. From a hundred feet away Yancy spotted the glimmer of the diamond in a clump of weeds. It was a very large stone, which likely meant that the woman and her fiancé intended to build a very large house.

"Shit," said Yancy. He picked up the ring and shoved it into his pocket.

At half-past eleven he heard the phone chirping out on the couch, where he'd left it. He knew Rosa wasn't calling, because she was still at work in the E.R.

"You sleeping?" asked Tommy Lombardo.

"Yes," Yancy lied, "and I've got company."

Lombardo was his supervisor, not a bad guy. Mostly he left Yancy alone.

"It's an emergency, Andrew."

An "emergency" on roach patrol was code for an active infestation.

"Where?" Yancy asked.

"Clippy's."

"No way." Clippy's was one of the cleanest joints in Monroe County. Yancy had never found as much as a dead housefly on the premises. "Tommy, what manner of pest are we talking about?"

"No varmints, no insects."

"Screw it, then, I'm going back to bed."

"They're waiting for you, Andrew."

"Who?"

"Clippy and his partner. You understand?"

Yancy did understand. "Tell me what we're dealing with, Tommy. It's almost midnight, for Christ's sake."

"You know this already from your cop days," said Lombardo. "There's some fucked-up people in the world. Is that front-page news? I don't think so."

TWO

The man with the long oily hair wasn't named Rocky, and he wasn't Merry Mansfield's boyfriend. Zeto is what she called him. He and Merry had been hired to kidnap a swindler who'd pissed off a short-fused individual in the borough of Queens, New York. The swindler's name was Martin Trebeaux, and he was driving from Miami to Key West in a late-model four-door Buick painted quicksilver metallic, a factory job virtually indistinguishable at dusk from champagne silver, another standard color in rental fleets.

"You hit the wrong fucking car," Zeto informed Merry.

"Hey, you said silver Buick, did you not?"

"Wrong fucking car. Wrong fucking guy." Zeto halfheartedly kicked Lane Coolman, who lay hogtied on the floor.

"Maybe it's him and he's just carrying fake ID," Merry said hopefully.

"No, this is definitely not Trebeaux." Zeto had pawed through Coolman's wallet. The photograph on the California driver's license matched Coolman's face, which did not match the pictures of Martin Trebeaux that had been texted to Zeto.

Trebeaux was sandy-haired, jowly, and had the pursed countenance of a feeding carp. Coolman's features were more angular, and he owned standard hominid lips.

"You fucked up. End of story," Zeto said to Merry.

"No, dear, *we* fucked up."

From Coolman: "Just let me go and we'll forget all about it."

"Hush now, Bob," said Merry.

Coolman didn't believe the oily guy with the gun would actually kill him, reflecting an insufficient concern for his own well-being. That he was more worried about Buck Nance bombing at the Parched Pirate underscored Coolman's laser focus on his career. Buck and his brothers were the agency's hottest clients, a galactic media phenomenon, but they required round-the-clock supervision. Buck in particular could be a runaway train.

"There's two grand cash in the wallet," Coolman said to Merry. "Take it all and let me walk."

"You told me your name was Bob. Don't I deserve better than that?"

Here Zeto cut in: "He wanted to bang you is all."

Coolman didn't bother to deny it. "Don't make this any worse than it already is. You got the wrong man, okay?"

Merry said, "Then prove it."

"Give me back my phone and I will."

Zeto said, "He's not Trebeaux, so shut up and let me think."

The floor was cold terrazzo. Merry unrolled a yoga mat and sat down beside Coolman. There was no furniture in the house; two bulbs in a recessed ceiling fixture provided the only light.

Zeto had forced Coolman at gunpoint through a back door after parking the Tesla in an alley. Now the gun peeked from a shoulder holster beneath Zeto's leather jacket. Merry had offered to help tie up their prisoner but Zeto insisted on doing it himself, saying he didn't trust Merry's knots.

"I need to make a call," he grumped.

"God, no kidding you do." She rolled her eyes.

As soon as Zeto left the room, Coolman began lobbying Merry to be the reasonable one, the one wise enough to see that holding him captive would be a disastrous mistake. "You want to go to jail for the rest of your life," he said, "because of *that* guy?"

"Are you really a talent manager, or is that more bullshit?"

"No, it's the truth. Buck Nance is waiting for me right now at the gig."

"We'll see about that."

Merry took Coolman's cell phone out of her handbag where it had been tooting and humming every couple of minutes. This was pure torture for Coolman, who, like all agents, hated missing a call.

"What's Mr. Buck Bayou's number?" Merry asked.

"Jesus, I don't remember off the top of my head. Speed-dial it from my Favorites."

"Woo-hoo, look at this! Mark Wahlberg. Reese Witherspoon. Denzel—are you kidding me?"

"Scroll to the N's," said Coolman.

Merry found Buck Nance's name and touched the number. A woman answered. Merry had difficulty hearing her because of a grinding roar on the other end. The woman said she was on the back of a motorcycle cruising Duval Street. Her boyfriend had found the phone on the floor of a bar—somebody had crunched it with a boot heel, but it still worked. The woman asked Merry to tell the owner of the phone to swing by Blue Heaven later and pick it up.

"Just keep it, honey," Merry said, and hung up.

Coolman was unsettled by the news that Buck Nance had lost his phone. He pleaded with Merry to redial and find out if the woman had attended Buck's show. Merry said, "What—now I'm your secretary? No, sir."

She zipped the fleece up to her neck. "It's cold in here, right? My nips are basically icicles."

"I'm guessing you're not really married," Coolman said. "There are no Rockys in your life, right? And you know nothing about sunken treasure."

"More than you do, I bet."

"What's your real name?"

She laughed. "Merry Mansfield!"

The ropes on Coolman's wrists were strung so tight that he'd given up trying to squirm out of them. "Really, this is what you do for a living? Crash into strangers on the highway?"

"There's a trick to it," Merry said, "especially holding a razor."

She had done fourteen solo bump jobs, eight hundred bucks each, never once injuring herself or the target. Her preferred speed at impact was six miles per hour faster than the car she was hitting. She'd learned the technique from a guy in South Beach, her boyfriend at the time, an insurance fraudster and confirmed shitweasel. Now Merry worked totally freelance off her reputation. The bikini-shave aspect of the scam was her signature, pure genius because the targets were always men. Often she wasn't told who had ordered the crash, but the why never changed: Somebody was dodging a debt. The objective of the abduction was money, not murder. Merry viewed herself as an independent contractor in the collection process. Zeto provided the bump vehicles. Merry kept a brick of fake IDs for when the cops arrived to write up the "accident."

This was the first time she'd taken down the wrong car, and she blamed Zeto for fuzzy intel. His text had said: "Southbound silver late-model Buick Lacrosse w/white male driving, early 30s." No tag number, no specificity on the precise shade of silver—and, by the way, who could tell the freaking difference between quicksilver and champagne?

"Trebeaux's here in Key West," Zeto announced upon his return.

"So the job's still on? We can set up the crash on a side street, easy peasy," said Merry.

Zeto snorted. "What makes you think we'd use *you* again?"

Merry let the insult pass because she needed the money. "So, meantime, what should we do with mister hot-shit talent manager?"

"Dump him in the ocean was my orders."

"You mean kill him?" Merry said.

"You're a quick one, babe." Zeto took out his gun.

Coolman was thunderstruck.

"Don't be a fucking idiot!" he bleated at Zeto. Then, less excitedly, to the redheaded woman: "This would be the all-time, worst-ever dumbest thing you could ever possibly do. They'll lock you up for life."

He thought the scared-straight approach would be more effective than weeping.

Zeto said, "Lock us up for what, dipshit? Your body won't never be found. Twenty miles out at sea in the belly of a goddamn tiger shark is where you'll be at. No victim, no crime scene, no evidence. Arrest us for what, Einstein?"

Merry gave Coolman's head a commiserative pat. "His mind's made up, Bob. Sorry."

"No, wait, wait please," said Coolman, and without further delay began to beg. "You want money? Because the people I work for will pay big bucks to get me back safe and sound."

Zeto seemed mildly interested.

Merry said, "Define big bucks." She dialed another number on Lane's phone, and he heard her say, "Hello, is this Mr. Mark Wahlberg? You're shitting me! Mark freaking Wahlberg?"

A shark attack might be less painful, Coolman thought despairingly.

"Sir, a speed-dial *compadre* of yours is in major trouble," Merry went on. "Mr. Lane Coolman, okay? The talent agent. There's bodily harm in his future unless somebody comes up with, I don't know—half a million dollars by noon tomorrow? I see . . . well, yes . . . allrighty then. Sorry to trouble you, sir. By the way, you were amazing in *Boogie Nights.* That last scene at the mirror? Fucking awesome!"

Coolman's chin was on his chest by the time Merry hung up. That was some heavy number—five hundred thousand—to pull out of her ass.

"It was really him?" Zeto asked. "*The* Marky Mark?"

"It was," said Merry.

"So, what's the story?"

"First he said, 'Lane Coolman's *not* my friend.'"

"Figures." Zeto glared at his captive.

"He said Mr. Coolman is a worthless douche bag, his exact words," Merry related, "and we'd be lucky to get five fucking cents for a ransom."

Zeto cackled and put a round into the chamber. "This is from the movie star, right? Unbelievable. A worthless douche bag, he says."

"Hold on, just wait! Please!" Coolman cried. "Scroll up to the A's and I'll tell you which name to call."

Merry said, "Now we're getting somewhere, sugar."

Clippy was Irv Clipowski. His partner was Neil Gluckman, who happened to be the mayor. That's why Lombardo had summoned Yancy so late at night—nothing turns you into a responsive civil servant faster than a phone call from the mayor. Hop in your car and go.

Neil and Clippy weren't downhome island bubbas but rather New Yorkers who'd hit a home run on Wall Street and then semi-retired to Key West. At first they were distrusted because of their sobriety and competence, but in time the locals accepted them. Clippy was a long-distance runner who had a goatee that he dyed goose-white. Neil narrowly won the mayor's race after his opponent got busted in the Marquesas cramming two thousand Mollies into a SCUBA tank.

The restaurant they owned was only a few blocks from the Hemingway House. Lunch and dinner were offered, brunch on Sundays. The designated cuisine was "heart healthy," a menu gimmick designed to ward off the cruise-ship crowd. Clippy could be a snob at times.

He led Yancy to a stainless-steel vat in the back of the kitchen.

"That's quinoa, Andrew. Please don't tell me you've never had it."

"I eat it twice a day, sprinkled with kale." There must have been twenty-five pounds of the stuff, which to Yancy resembled bullfrog eggs.

"They call it a supergrain," Clippy said dully. "It's got lysine, B_2 and manganese, the mortal enemy of free radicals. Not to mention it's a natural laxative—"

"So is rum."

"—and totally gluten free."

"I love gluten. I always order extra."

"This is in no way funny, Andrew."

Yancy pointed at something in the vat. "That's your emergency, correct?"

Clippy nodded somberly. "We were slammed tonight. He must've snuck in the back door when the chef was busy. You need a bag?"

"I brought my own, thanks." Yancy donned a pair of latex medical gloves. Rosa had smuggled him two boxes from the E.R.

"What kind of monster would do something like this?" Clippy said with a world-weary groan. "Neil took one look and got ill. I sent him straight home."

Yancy handed a Ziploc baggie to Clippy. "Hold this open for me, please."

"He used our herb scissors, too! You'll need those for evidence."

"Oh, absolutely." The shears were a top-of-the-line German brand. Yancy set them aside, thinking Rosa might need a pair.

Then he reached into the vat and began to remove the offending adulterant—damp clumps of wiry hair. The strands were silvery gray flecked with black, and they smelled of stale booze. Yancy ended up filling three baggies.

Clippy whispered, "Please tell me it's from a human."

"That, or an alcoholic opossum."

"God, this is so revolting."

Yancy was sympathetic but firm. "You've got to eighty-six all the quinoa for tomorrow."

"Well, certainly."

"Then spray down your countertops and nuke this tub at, like, a zillion degrees."

"Done and done," Clippy said. "Neil told me to tell you we definitely want to prosecute. Your lab people can get the DNA from the hair, right?"

Yancy suspected that the Division of Hotels and Restaurants employed no laboratory techs, and had zero budget for genetic testing.

"You can nail him for trespassing, obviously," Clippy was saying, "tampering with food products, malicious whatever they call it . . . 'misbehavior.' Throw the book at this perv."

"I'll let you know if we come up with an ID."

"Dust the shears for fingerprints!"

"Of course," Yancy said, knowing it wasn't going to happen.

Clippy, who apparently watched every CSI show on television, would have been crestfallen to learn that the roach patrol held no police authority. Yancy could shut down a restaurant for gross health-code violations, but he couldn't throw anybody in jail. Nor was forensic work part of his job description, unless counting mouse turds qualified.

"You should probably file a police report," he suggested to Clippy.

"What—and see it all over the news? Neil would never forgive me, Andrew. It would devastate our business."

By the time Yancy drove back to Big Pine it was two in the morning. He placed the bags of vandal hair in his refrigerator and drifted off to sleep. At some point Rosa called to tell him about her night in the E.R., another rough one. For months he'd been trying to persuade her to relocate to the Keys, where assault-rifle wounds and spousal eviscerations were rare.

But Rosa was a city girl.

"I miss your legs," Yancy said.

"Are you behaving?"

"Some moron dumped like a kilo of dirty hair in the kitchen at Clippy's."

"Thanks for the visual," Rosa said.

"He used the steel bowl as a mirror while he gave himself a trim. Hey, you need some herb scissors?"

"Night, Andrew."

He fell asleep while writing his report. He dreamed of tarpon rolling in Pearl Basin until he was awakened by a knock. It was a harsh intrusion, so soon after sunrise. He stalked cursing to the front door and flung it open.

The woman who'd lost her diamond engagement ring was standing there. Her eyes crawled up and down Yancy, who was nude except for his reading glasses.

"I'll take that cup of coffee now," she said.

It was assumed by locals that Buck Nance had made his way to the airport, hopped a chartered jet and fled the island. Everybody figured that, like all celebrities, he employed savvy handlers to whisk him away whenever a crisis occurred.

The incident at the Parched Pirate didn't make the morning print edition of the Key West *Citizen*, but a headline was bannered on the newspaper's website along with two videos of Buck's brief performance, provided by disgruntled bikers with iPhones. Soon the whole Internet was crackling. What Buck had considered harmless saloon jokes were now being denounced as racial and homophobic slurs. The network vice president in charge of *Bayou Brethren* told the vice president in charge of corporate relations to release a statement expressing dismay at Buck's crude remarks. An overcooked apology was made to gays, African Americans, women and anyone else who might have been offended.

Meanwhile, the show's prime-time advertisers were under attack in the blogosphere, and by midday the ACLU had called for a boycott of all fishing flies tied with rooster feathers from the Nance farm. Word of the backlash sent the network vice president in charge of *Bayou Brethren* lunging for a pre-lunch Xanax. He couldn't fathom why neither Buck nor his manager, Lane Coolman, would answer their cell phones.

The whereabouts of the other Nance brothers—Clee Roy, Buddy and Junior—had been ascertained. They were chilling at the forty-acre Pensacola estate leased by the network and used as an outdoor set for the fractious family barbecue scenes that closed each episode. Down the road a stretch was the rooster farm, which the clan avoided except during taping days because of the stench. The writers had decided that Buck Nance's brothers should refer to him as "Captain Cock" when quarreling on the show, and inevitably the sleeveless tee-shirt bearing that nickname became the top seller of all *Bayou Brethren* merchandise.

Buck had been wearing one onstage at the Parched Pirate, but now the shirt was in a dumpster on Whitehead Street and the remains of his famous beard were in a bowl of ricey gunk at some restaurant he'd ducked into while fleeing the imaginary lynch mob. The puny kitchen scissors had left him with nappy bristles exposing a weak jawline that he hadn't seen in years. His bare face looked pasty and shrunken, and in no way resembled the imposing Moses-like visage on his TV show.

Which was good, in a way. Buck Nance feared that if he were recognized on the streets of Key West, he would be set upon and sodomized by militant homos, Negroes and other socialist-leaning minorities, a rioting of godless heathens.

His survival plan was to blend with the common civilians until he could be safely extricated by Lane. The night was spent in a banyan tree listening to stray cats scrap and screw. Buck didn't sleep a wink. At dawn he climbed down shivering and walked to Mallory Square, where he dozed off on a public bench. Soon he was jarred awake by the horn of an arriving cruise ship. The sun felt warm on his shoulders, promising a better day.

Having lost his phone in the fray at the Parched Pirate, Buck entered a shop on Duval Street to purchase a disposable. There he learned that, despite the island's laid-back reputation, shirtless men with fresh scrapes and bruises aren't welcome in all establishments. He also discovered that his engraved sterling money clip had apparently fallen from his trousers when he scrambled up the banyan tree, meaning he had no cash or even credit cards, which he always tucked between the hundred-dollar bills.

Somewhere on Simonton he shoplifted a random tee-shirt that bore a nonsense caption: WHERE IS BUM FARTO? He darted into a bougainvillea-fringed courtyard to put on the shirt, and out of habit he tore off the sleeves. An artist sitting languidly before an easel offered

Buck fifty bucks to pose nude, and Buck's response was to punch a fist through the blank canvas and stomp off. The artist considered calling the police but decided on a nap instead.

Florida's beaches erode pitilessly, the unstoppable rise of sea level presenting a nightmare scenario for waterfront hotels, coastal developers and real-estate agents. Once upon a time you could get away with selling submerged land to faraway rubes, but those days were over. Now buyers wanted to visit the property first, and not by paddleboard. Likewise, high-end vacationers to the Sunshine State derived no tropical enchantment from the sight of waves crashing through their hotel's lobby.

Climate change created a boom for a hurricane-spawned industry known as "beach renourishment," a process by which thousands of tons of sand are dredged from the sea shallows and dumped onshore to replace the acreage washed away by nature. The enterprise is as costly as it is futile, though for a few glorious months the shoreline appears authentic if not pristine. This fluffing of public beaches is funded by helpless taxpayers, while privately held oceanfront is often augmented at the expense of the property owners. Either way, beach-renourishment deals are fabulously profitable for the contractors because the job never expires—every grain of sand you dump gets washed away.

Martin Trebeaux had purchased a fleet of marine barges using the proceeds from a poshly falsified BP oil-spill claim. He named the new dredge company Sedimental Journeys, and before long he'd locked up the replenishment rights for eroding beachfront in five Florida counties, ninety-seven miles in all. Flagrantly generous to local politicians at election time, Trebeaux was repaid by the hundredfold when the bids fell his way.

As a cutter of corners he soon got in trouble for dredging too near the shore. The bulky equipment and piping were unsightly, and the pumping method churned the surf to a murky hue that offended tourists, who came to Florida expecting the Atlantic Ocean to be somewhat blue. Trebeaux's heedless bottom-sucking technique also killed catfish, littering the newly buffed beach with bloated whiskered corpses that deterred all but the hardiest of sunbathers.

Over time, companies such as Sedimental Journeys vacuumed so much sand from Florida's coastal seabeds that Trebeaux and his competitors were forced to search elsewhere for product. The Bahamas seemed the obvious choice because the sand there was of superb quality, and the barge trip across the Gulf Stream was short.

Trebeaux rented a plane and scouted digging locations along the Bahama Banks, less than eighty nautical miles from fast-sinking Palm Beach. A lawyer in Freeport obtained the necessary permits in exchange for a modest commission based on the tonnage shipped.

Everybody involved was rolling in dough until the commonwealth abruptly terminated its arrangement with Sedimental Journeys. An international enviro group had produced a scientific study showing that the sand collection operation had silted the reefs, suffocating the coral and dispersing the tropical marine life that tourists paid so dearly to see. Disheartening underwater footage was provided to all major media outlets, including the BBC. The Bahamian government, which is sensitive to negative publicity in the same way kittens are sensitive to firecrackers, immediately shut down Trebeaux's dredging rigs.

With orders backing up, he turned to a Miami rock-mining proprietor who assured him that a credible approximation of telegenic beach sand was abundant in a borrow pit being excavated on the eastern edge of the Everglades. This claim turned out to be spurious. The texture of the load delivered to Trebeaux more closely resembled shrapnel than sugar granules. He spread it anyway.

Among his disgruntled clients were the municipality of Boynton Beach and the Royal Pyrenees Hotel and Resort, whose guests in unmanageable numbers were complaining of lacerated feet and—among small children making sand castles—shredded fingers. Martin Trebeaux could safely ignore the half-assed threat of litigation from the city's attorney, but he was foolhardy to brush off the outcry from the proprietors of the Royal Pyrenees.

The hotel had been built with union pension funds controlled by the Calzone crime family, which continued to manage the property and take an avid interest in the cash flow. Viral videos of bloodied tourists with their wailing toddlers were bad for business, and the Calzone organization believed that Martin Trebeaux was obligated to replace the defective beach behind the Royal Pyrenees immediately. This view hardened after a geologist hired by the hotel reported that the newly deposited sand was actually a slapdash mixture of crushed limestone, recycled asphalt fragments and broken glass. The whitish gleam of the grit was attributed to industrial bleaching.

While the mobsters appreciated a novel fraud when they saw one, they did not enjoy being its victims. A *capo* named Dominick "Big Noogie" Aeola left a message on Martin Trebeaux's phone instructing him to appear at the Royal Pyrenees on a certain morning at ten sharp. Trebeaux, who was partying on South Beach with a decertified yoga instructor, listened to the voicemail but opted not to call back. Instead he sent a text saying he had to leave town on a family emergency.

Big Noogie was doubtful, and an experienced stakeout man was dispatched to Trebeaux's condominium building on Collins Avenue. Once Trebeaux's lie was verified, a plan was devised to snatch his ass and reorder his priorities. For a sawbuck the doorman at the high-rise offered up the information that Trebeaux would be departing the next day for Key West in a rented silver Buick, due to the fact that his Lexus coupe was in the shop.

From a safe phone Big Noogie placed a call to a person known as Zeto, who agreed to arrange a bump-and-grab on the Overseas Highway. Zeto bragged that he used a chick driver who was the best in the business.

Yet somehow the job got screwed up, and the sand man remained at large. Big Noogie was irate. The county had roped off the beach behind the Royal Pyrenees as a public health menace, and droves of limping guests were checking out of the hotel. The bosses in New York demanded an explanation.

Meanwhile, Martin Trebeaux was lapping a Bloody Mary on the

deck at Louie's Backyard in Key West, pondering his next move. From across the straits beckoned Havana, or rather a romanticized vision of Havana, for Trebeaux had never been there. He'd heard the music scene was sensational, the women heart-stoppingly beautiful. It was said that Cuba's beaches put all others in the Caribbean to shame, and Trebeaux didn't doubt that.

Perhaps the Castro brothers would sell him some of their sand.

THREE

The bride-to-be said her name was Deb. She wore pressed white slacks, designer sandals and a swipe of liver-colored lipstick that matched her toenails. She said she preferred her coffee with almond milk, which Yancy didn't stock, so she settled for cream. This was after he'd put on some clothes.

"You're definitely not a cop," she said, eyeing a half-smoked joint on the kitchen counter.

"It's medicinal."

"For what—sunburn?"

"Okay, it's evidence," he said. "I was field-testing for purity."

Deb pointed at the Remington twelve-gauge in the corner. "What do you need *that* for? Is it loaded?"

"Of course. You know what they call an *un*loaded shotgun?"

"What?"

"A stick," he said.

"Are you the lunatic that killed the drone?"

"Was that yours?"

"Our realtor's," Deb said. "He was making a video of the property and somebody shot his little toy out of the sky. Two grand, boom."

"I've still got the pieces somewhere."

The real-estate agent's drone had hovered too closely one afternoon while Rosa was sunbathing topless behind the house. With a single blast Yancy had demolished the craft and its tiny camera. It was way more fun than shooting clay pigeons. Afterward the realtor had hysterically called the sheriff's office, which determined Yancy had broken no laws.

"The point is you don't want me for a neighbor," he said to Deb. "I'm a volatile individual."

She set down the coffee cup. "Will you help me find my engagement ring, or not? My fiancé doesn't know I lost it, and I don't want him to find out."

As she spoke she dragged theatrically on an electronic cigarette tipped with a neon-blue light. Yancy was aching to tell her how preposterous she looked.

He said, "So who's the lucky fellow? What's his story?"

"His name is Brock. We've been together almost a year. He's an attorney—product liability, pharmaceuticals mainly."

"Where?"

"Miami."

"Home sweet home," Yancy said.

"He was engaged to someone else when we met."

"Which explains why the rock fell off your finger."

"Yeah, she was a chunk-muffin," Deb said. "I was supposed to get the ring re-sized, but I've been too busy with the new-house stuff. Brock'll go ballistic if he finds out what happened. He told me the stone cost two hundred thousand—just the stone. I've looked all over the property and I can't find the damn thing anywhere. So, *officer*, can you please help me?"

Yancy said, "I offered last night and was coldly snubbed."

"Well, yeah, you scared the hell out of me."

"And what's changed? I answer the door naked and talk of firearms."

"We can reach an arrangement you'll be comfortable with, definitely."

"Like what?"

"Like the greatest blowjob you ever had," she said, the e-cig bobbing at the corner of her smile. "Seriously, you'll be cross-eyed for a month."

Yancy realized he'd fallen short of his objective, which was to exude menace, not sleaze.

"Don't take this personally," he said to Deb, "but I've reached a spiritual plateau where random sex needs to mean something."

"Are you some kind of freak?"

"Save your talents for Brett, I'll help you for free. But first tell me about the mansion you two are planning to build."

"His name's *Brock*," Deb snipped, exhaling whitish vapor. "Six thousand square feet under air. Two and a half floors, plus a Thai roof garden."

Foreseeing the loss of his uncluttered sunset view, Yancy fought an upwelling of anger. "Are you guys planning to live there full-time? Is he moving his practice to the Keys?"

"I'll be here. He'll come down weekends." Deb shrugged. "Summers we'll travel."

And this, Yancy thought, is how cruel stereotypes come to be.

For concealment he'd immersed her diamond ring in a bowl of fish dip. It was smoked king mackerel, Yancy being addicted to the stuff.

"Follow me," he said, and headed for the kitchen.

The bride-to-be was standing at his side as he opened the refrigerator door. Before he could reach for the mackerel dip, she grabbed his arm and said, "What is *that?*"

"Oh. Human hair." He held up one of the clear baggies.

"But . . . why?" Deb asked, backing up.

"Don't you worry, it's not mine."

"I mean, Jesus, where did . . . I mean, who . . . ?"

"Donor unknown," Yancy said.

Out she ran, leaving the front door ajar. Her mode of departure was a loud red Porsche.

Yancy sat on the front stoop thinking he might as well hang on to the diamond for a while. He opened his laptop to check the tides. The sky was bright, the breeze was getting warmer. He felt like going fishing.

. . .

Merry Mansfield held the phone to Lane Coolman's ear, because his hands were bound.

"Amp, it's me," he said.

"Where the fuck are you?"

Jon David Ampergrodt liked to be called Amp. He was the chairman-slash-director of Platinum Artists Management, the talent agency that employed Lane Coolman.

"Dude, I've been kidnapped!"

"Oh, that's original."

"I'm dead serious," Coolman said. "They snatched me in Key West. Broad daylight!"

"Snatched, as in *Taken*?"

"Totally."

"Jesus Christ, what about Buck? Did they hurt him? How much money do they want?"

"They don't have Buck. Just me."

Amp sighed irritably. "Then where the fuck is Buck?"

"They're asking for five hundred grand cash," said Coolman. "All fifties and twenties."

"This is a joke, right? You're pranking my ass."

"Amp, they're gonna kill me deader than the last Nic Cage movie they don't get paid by sunset tomorrow. Understand? Five hundred grand in a gray Balenciaga—hang on a sec . . ."

"The new ostrich one," Merry clarified.

"You heard that, right? The ostrich Balenciaga," Coolman relayed to Amp. "They said to leave it on the third to the last car of the five p.m. Conch Train. Some corny tourist trolley—"

"Lane!"

"What?"

"One more time: Where the fuck is Buck Nance?"

"I don't have a clue. I've been tied up, literally."

"You weren't with him?"

"No, I got taken hostage," Coolman said. "I thought I mentioned that."

"FYI, the gig was a motherfucking disaster. Buck got chased out of the bar," Amp said. "It's all over social media."

"Well, I can't go searching for him right this minute because, see, there's a loaded gun aimed at my head."

"That's just great."

"Can you get working on the ransom, ASAP?"

"We'll talk later."

Amp clicked off. Coolman stared at the phone.

"Doesn't sound too promising," Merry said.

Zeto shrugged. "He's a douche, just like Marky Mark said. Nobody gives a shit if he gets whacked. Let's go to the boat."

The Tesla had no trunk, so Coolman was permitted to ride in the backseat. This slender bit of good fortune allowed him to press his case for mercy. Zeto remained cold to his pleas, but Merry seemed open to the idea of giving Coolman more time to raise some funds.

"Say nobody comes through. How much you got in the bank?" she said.

"It's all frozen. I'm in the middle of a divorce."

"Because you cheated on her, right?"

He said, "Listen, the agency will definitely pay the five hundred. I mean guaranteed. Amp's got a lot on his plate right now but, once he focuses, it's a done deal."

Zeto, over his shoulder: "No, asswipe, *you* are the done deal."

At the dock they hustled Coolman aboard an old lobster boat. Zeto ordered Merry to go back and wait in the Tesla while he took Coolman out to sea. Merry said she wanted to ride along, and lingered in the wheelhouse until Zeto ran her off.

What saved Coolman from ending up as shark bait was a damaged wire that made it impossible to start the boat's engine. Zeto failed to diagnose the problem, and in any case possessed minimal skills with a toolbox. After half an hour he gave up in a funk that had been aggravated by Merry, repeatedly winking the high-beams of the Tesla to pester him.

Zeto shoved Coolman into the forward cabin of the boat, taped his mouth, re-cinched the ropes and left him there. The cramped space reeked of sweat, black mold and decomposed shellfish, though Coolman wouldn't have slept a wink on rose-scented linens at a Four Seasons. He remained shaken by his phone conversation with Amp, who either hadn't grasped the gravity of Coolman's situation or had decided he was dispensable.

That the agency's most promising curator of talent had been kidnapped by murderous lowlifes should have upset Amp more than the fact that some redneck chicken-plucker had disappeared on a bender. For the moment Buck Nance was a mega-client—but Lane Coolman was the shining future of Platinum Artists. Amp himself had said so many times.

As he lay in the rank darkness contemplating the prospect of a watery death, Coolman found his thoughts inchworming toward Rachel, his future ex-wife. The cause of their pending disunion was, as Merry Mansfield had surmised, his own uncountable infidelities. These had sparked a series of retaliatory flings by Rachel. If she'd been doing only the Comcast guy, the marriage might have been saved. However, it was her vindictive nature to arrange indiscreet sex with Lane's rival agents from CAA or ICM, and always at the Beverly Wilshire. Worse, she delighted in paying for the suite with his credit card. He recalled his outrage after one such tryst when the hotel billed him for a room-service delivery that included five cans of Reddi-wip, a single Maraschino cherry and a quad-pack of D batteries.

Rachel was the undisputed queen of the revenge fuck in a town with many contenders for the title. Another memorable hosing: Coolman had foolishly taken a late-ish Friday lunch with one of his hot girlfriends at the Ivy, where he was spotted by a junior turd fondler from William Morris Endeavor named Kane Drucker. Before Coolman had even touched his calamari app, Drucker was on the phone with Rachel. The two of them lay in a sweaty tangle by the time Coolman and his girlfriend had finished their huckleberry sorbets.

And now Rachel's attorneys were doing to Lane in divorce court what she'd done to Drucker and all the others at the Wilshire. The judge had granted Coolman a living allowance (pitiable by Hollywood standards) while Rachel's hawk-eyed forensic accountant pored through his bank records and brokerage statements. Such was the desolate state of Coolman's liquidity that, by his own calculations, he had at most $21,300 to contribute to his own ransom.

"Let me call Amp again," he begged Merry the next morning, after she peeled off the duct tape.

"You lucked out for now, Bob. The mechanic's too stoned to fix the boat."

She didn't tell him that she was the one who'd mangled the ignition wire, foiling Zeto's plan to kill him at sea.

"Where's your psycho partner?" Coolman asked.

"Finding me a crash car. We've got a job this morning." Merry was wearing a denim jacket and a long cotton skirt with an imitation Seminole bead pattern. Her hair was in a saucy ponytail. To Coolman, who'd spent the night huffing lobster fumes, she smelled heavenly.

She'd brought him a banana smoothie, put the straw to his lips.

"Suck," she commanded.

After downing the whole cup, he told Merry he had to relieve himself.

"Do you see a restroom, Bob? This is not a fucking Carnival cruise."

"Cut me a break, okay? I've been holding it all night."

"Make it fast." She stood him up, unzipped his pants and aimed his cock at a random bucket left by the lobster crew. "And if you get hard," she warned, "I'll push you overboard myself."

Coolman was too unnerved by the grab to become aroused.

"I used to be a nurse," said Merry.

"No, you didn't."

"Okay, I worked in a nursing home for a summer. Same deal. I had to handle lots of dicks."

"Welcome to my world," Coolman said.

While waiting for his bladder to unseize, he pitched an idea.

"Tell Zeto I got out of the ropes and overpowered you," he said to Merry. "Knocked you down, jumped off the boat and ran away. What's he gonna say? Tell him it's all his fault because his lame knots came loose."

"Would you pee already? We've got a big day."

"You don't want to go to prison for a murder. That would be insane."

"Swear to God, you jiggle one drop on me, Bob—I just did my nails!"

Her watch said eight a.m. It was three hours earlier in Los Angeles, a bad time for engaging Amp.

"Is there a Bank of America down here?" Coolman asked. "I've got like twenty-one grand in a checking account, plus the two in my wallet."

"Oh, Zeto already took that."

"Twenty-one isn't so terrible, right? It's all yours if you take me to the bank and let me go. Screw Zeto."

Merry flicked Coolman's penis back into his pants and dumped the bucket of piss overboard. "You're losing traction with me," she said.

As expected, Amp didn't answer his phone. When Coolman blamed the time-zone difference, Merry just shrugged.

Zeto arrived, untied Coolman and led him to the Tesla. This time he let Merry take the wheel while he sat in the backseat pressing the gun to Coolman's ribs.

"We're going to Bob's bank," Merry announced.

Zeto scowled. "Says who?"

"God, everything's a power play with you. Take a fucking chill pill. The man's in the middle of a soul-crushing divorce, yet he's generously offered to give us every dime he's got left."

"You're shitting me, right?" Coolman said. Again he felt like a moron.

In the rearview he saw Merry wink at him.

"Damn, I just remembered," she said. "The banks don't open for an hour."

"Forget it. We ain't got an hour," Zeto muttered. "Let's go get the car."

Merry wanted to stop at a CVS so she could wash her hands and buy a fresh razor. Zeto told her to use the one she had.

"The one I cut myself with yesterday? No thank you."

Coolman became conscious of the fact that he was the only occupant of the vehicle who hadn't showered the night before, one drawback of being a hostage. He braced for a low comment about his body odor.

"You don't need a new razor," Zeto carped at Merry.

"Now you're an expert on grooming vaginas. Amazing," she said, parking at a drugstore on Truman.

While she was inside, Coolman tried to talk some sense into Zeto, who shut him up with a sharp twist of the gun barrel. Up close Coolman noticed that Zeto had a thin pinkish scar circling his neck. He decided not to ask about it.

The new crash car was an '05 four-door Honda Civic that Zeto had bought for nine hundred cash and stashed behind a Wendy's. Merry gave the Civic a round-the-block spin and pronounced it a death trap.

"Like you got a choice," Zeto said.

"The brakes are totally fried, dude."

"Trebeaux's staying at the Reach. I sent a chick to his room. She's gonna make sure he's outbound on Roosevelt at noon sharp."

Merry said, "Men. I swear."

"Past the stop light at Kennedy, that's where you hit him. This time no cops—just stall him for a minute till I get there."

"Dazzle him, you mean."

Zeto said, "Don't fuck it up again."

They went to scout the intersection, the Tesla following the Honda. Merry pulled off at a strip mall and Zeto turned in beside her, steering with his gun hand free. She got out and walked up to his window.

"I see no problems. This'll be short and sweet," she said.

"Fifteen minutes he'll be coming by with the girl. Meanwhile, this sorry fucker"—referring to Coolman—"is stinkin' up my interior."

"Then let him ride with me."

"For the bump?" Zeto snickered.

"Why not?" Merry said. "The kiddie-proof locks on that junker still work."

Coolman spoke up. "Seriously, guys? I don't want to be involved in this."

"Go," Zeto said. "Make one wrong move, say one wrong word, I'll shoot your phony California ass. Just sit still with your mouth shut and let the lady do the talkin'."

Merry practically skipped around the car to open Coolman's door, saying, "Come on, Bob. It'll be something different!"

Sheriff Sonny Summers had never watched *Bayou Brethren*, but he knew who Buck Nance was, and of course he'd already heard about the incident at the Parched Pirate. Now some fast-talking shaker named Jon David Ampergrodt was on the phone explaining that his company—make that his "agency"—represented Mr. Nance.

"We haven't heard from him, and frankly we're concerned for his safety," Ampergrodt said.

The sheriff said the protocol on missing persons required at least twenty-four hours without contact before a report could be filed.

"The last thing we want is a missing person's report, okay? Not happening. Nothing in writing."

"But that's the only way we can start looking for him—after somebody makes a report."

"Oh, come on, sheriff."

"Has it been twenty-four hours?"

"No, but Mr. Nance isn't just some homeless tweaker. We're talking about the most popular television personality in the whole damn country, and he's disappeared in your little tourist town. Is that really the kind of publicity you want?"

Sonny Summers wasn't the sharpest tack on the corkboard but he recognized a condescending asshole when he heard one. Still, Jon David what's-his-face had a point. If Buck Nance came to a sordid end in Key West, the headlines might adversely affect the city's latest multimillion-dollar advertising push to attract the elusive non-drunk segment of the tourist trade, specifically couples with children. The island was aggressively marketing itself as a safe and carefree family destination, and Sonny Summers well understood his role as a steward of that myth.

"Maybe Mr. Nance is just partying with some young lady he met," the sheriff said. "It's been known to happen down here."

"He's happily married for twenty-nine years!" exclaimed Jon David Shithead. "Don't you follow the show? He's a lay minister at his church, for fuck's sake."

Sonny Summers said he didn't watch *Bayou Brethren* because it aired the same night he coached Little League, which was untrue.

"I'll FedEx you a box set of the first season," declared Mr. Nance's obnoxious representative. "In the meantime, on behalf of the family, I'd like you to green-light a major manhunt. Discreetly, of course."

"That would basically be impossible in a town this small. Everybody'll know about it in five minutes."

"Nothing's impossible, sheriff. When are you up for re-election?"

"This year."

"And I don't suppose you could use a fifty-thousand-dollar campaign donation? No strings attached."

Unlike some officeholders in South Florida, Sonny Summers owned a healthy fear of criminal indictment. "The limit on individual contributions is a thousand bucks," he informed Jon David Douche Bag.

"You don't think I've got fifty friends in Hollywood who can write a check that big? Make it fifty-one, including me. Do the math."

Sonny Summers did the math, on his pocket calculator. Fifty-one grand worked out to roughly $1.33 for every registered voter from Duval Street to Key Largo. It was enough money to buy truckloads of "Keep Sonny" yard signs and bumper stickers, money he'd no longer have to pry from local merchants, who in return often demanded favors such as free passes on future DUIs.

Except for the political demands of the job, Sonny Summers enjoyed being the sheriff of the Keys. He didn't mind occasionally wearing a blazer or shaking hands at the Elks Lodge or flying off to law-enforcement conventions in Vegas. Physically he was far more active now than he'd been as a deputy, and as a bonus the pernicious hemorrhoids he'd acquired during all those nights on road patrol were finally deflating. Even at the height of the season, not much happened on the long chain of islands that required Sonny Summers's undivided attention. He could count on one hand the number of press conferences he'd had. That was because serious crimes in Monroe County were usually overshadowed in the news cycle by some ghastly carnage up in Miami.

Colorful, hard-charging sheriffs historically end up squirming in front of grand juries, so civic leaders appreciated Sonny Summers's low profile, aversion to bold ideas and instinct for ducking controversies. At his wife's urging he'd once explored the notion of running for state attorney general, only to discover that a law degree was required. Sonny Summers was privately relieved by this deficiency on his résumé. He would have been content to remain sheriff forever.

Unfortunately, getting re-elected was expensive.

"Send the check to my campaign committee," he said to Jon David Dickbrain. "My assistant will give you the address."

"And you'll get your best people out looking for Mr. Nance?"

"Right away."

Sonny Summers felt sure the missing man would turn up soon in a stewed daze, as other wayward celebrities did, shambling with a venereal sting down Duval Street. His handlers would spirit him away, and that would be the end of his raunchy misadventure in Key West.

It was purely wishful thinking by the sheriff.

FOUR

"You seem a little nervous, Bob."

"No shit," said Coolman. "It's my second car crash in two days."

"Rule number one: Relax your body." Merry Mansfield elevated her skirt as she settled behind the steering wheel. "Stay as limp as possible. That's why so many drunk drivers walk away from bad wrecks, they're like rag dolls. Tensing up is what causes your major neck and spine issues. Also, keep your seat belt snug."

In one hand she held a travel can of Edge gel with aloe; poised in the other hand was the new Gillette disposable that she'd bought at the drugstore.

"I don't really need to shave again," she said, "but it's gotta look legit for Monsieur Trebeaux."

"This is nuts," Coolman grumbled from the rear seat.

"Well, does it work, or not?"

"I would've given you a ride anyway, without the free peek."

"Maybe so," Merry said. "But that's what iced the deal, and don't pretend otherwise."

She had locked the rear doors with a switch that disabled the interior handles, meaning Coolman was trapped. He could have reached around Merry's headrest and seized her by the neck, but he feared she would lay open his wrists with the razor. He also knew Zeto was somewhere nearby, watching from the Tesla.

Merry said, "Now cover your eyes while I do this."

"Really? You're about to flash a perfect stranger."

"That's business, Bob. You and I are practically dating."

He saw her tilt the shaving-gel can, and heard a squirt. He turned away, trying not to think about the skimming sound of the blade.

She said, "Keep your eyes peeled for that silver Buick."

"Can I say something? The whole Mark Wahlberg thing—it was an honest disagreement. Also, we weren't a good fit. Sometimes that happens in my business."

"So you're not really a douche."

"Not with clients." This was true. Coolman was loyal and fair, relative to the Hollywood norm. "Mark got an offer to do a voice-over commercial and, yeah, I talked him out of it. The money was insane but the material wasn't right for him. Trust me."

"Who cares. It's just TV."

"See, no, you're wrong. A megastar like Mark, everybody would recognize his voice and then word gets all over town he'll do anything for a buck. The product, get this—was a combination deodorant and testosterone wipe. For men only—"

"Duh."

"—some greasy goop you smear in your armpits. I told Mark it would hurt his brand and, see, branding is what we do best at Platinum Artists. So he turned down the voice-over gig and then that slut Affleck said yes for two mil. Ben, not Casey. A week later Mark fires me! But then it turns out I was right—that stuff's got some freaky-ass side effects, and major, *major* PR challenges. But instead of thanking me, Mark, the ingrate, he's still pissed."

"It doesn't work?" Merry asked.

"What?"

"The jelly. It doesn't give you a titanium hard-on?"

"You're missing the point," Coolman said. "The only reason for the story—I wanted to explain why he and I parted ways. It was a professional difference of opinion, that's all."

"The armpit thing makes no sense to me. I mean, why not just smear the stuff right on your knob?"

"Okay, forget I mentioned it."

Merry capped the can of Edge and placed it in a cup holder. "Hey, there's our merry traveler!"

"Where?"

"Remember what I told you, Bob. Go limp."

Coolman grabbed the edge of the seat with both hands as the Civic snaked into the traffic on Roosevelt. Merry weaved between two cars and a city bus, then cut in tightly behind the Buick and goosed the accelerator. The force of the crash jolted Coolman but nothing popped or snapped. He heard Merry swear, and saw that the airbag on the steering column had blown open. Snowy powder speckled her cheeks and hair, and she was groping on the floor for the razor, her key prop, which had been knocked from her hand.

"That lazy fucking Zeto!" she said. "He's supposed to take out the damn airbags before we do the bump—I've only told him like a hundred times."

The deflated fabric obstructed her view, yet Merry managed to hold the Civic on course, trailing the damaged Buick into the same strip mall lot from which Coolman had been abducted. A woman wearing Kermit-green spandex and four-inch clogs hopped out of the target car and beelined for the mall. She never looked back.

A man that could only have been Trebeaux emerged from the driver's side, stalked up to the Civic and froze at the sight of Merry Mansfield—pretty much all of Merry, who had dusted off the airbag residue and composed herself. Trebeaux's eyes widened and he swallowed three times, by Coolman's count.

With a faint French accent Merry apologized for the smashup. Sheepishly she displayed the razor as she lowered her skirt. "I'm on my way to a really big date."

Trebeaux struggled to maintain his outrage. "What the hell were you thinking? I mean, who *does* that while they're driving? You could kill somebody!"

"Please don't call the police. I'll give you cash to fix your car—can you take me to the Hampton Inn? That's where I left my money."

Coolman, who considered himself an expert on deception and doubletalk, marveled at Trebeaux's transformation from irate motorist to lustful schemer. Trebeaux stooped to peer at Coolman in the backseat.

"Who's that?"

"Some hitchhiker," Merry said. "He looked so lonely and pitiful I had to give him a lift."

"Well, Jesus, he got quite a show."

"No, that's why I made him sit in the back."

"How do you know he's not a rapist or a serial killer?"

"Because I can read men. He's totally harmless." She lowered her voice. "I think he's brain damaged. Ask the simplest question, all he does is grunt."

Coolman tried to establish eye contact with Trebeaux, but Trebeaux had already refocused on the redhead behind the wheel.

She said, "I'm super-duper sorry I scared your girlfriend away."

"Hell, she's not my girlfriend. Where's the Hampton?"

"Just up the road. I'm Merry, by the way. Spelled like Merry Christmas." She put down the Gillette and shook his hand.

"I'm Bill," he said. "Where are you from?"

She laughed. "Nice to meet you, *Bill.*"

"I'll give you a ride to the hotel, but first let's stop somewhere for a margarita. Then maybe afterward we can call it even. No police reports, no insurance companies."

"Deal," she said.

"What about the hot date you're meeting?"

"No worries. He's used to waiting."

Coolman perceived that he'd become invisible, or at least superfluous. It seemed like a good time to make a move. He dove over the front seat toward the passenger door, which failed to yield to his shoulder.

"Simmer down," Merry advised him. Then to Trebeaux: "I told you he wasn't right in the head."

Through the windshield Coolman helplessly watched the gliding-ghost arrival of the white Tesla. Merry feigned alarm. "Oh God, it's him!"

"Who?" Trebeaux asked.

"The guy I was supposed to meet! How'd he find me here?"

Trebeaux guessed that the swarthy young man in the bomber jacket was either a Russian gangster or some empty-headed poser from South Beach. When he saw the man's handgun all he said was: "Oh fuck."

"Exactly, Bill." Merry swung her long legs out of the Civic, smoothing her dress. "Now be smart."

While she and Zeto escorted Trebeaux to the Tesla, Coolman remained muddled and motionless in the crash car. He didn't notice that Merry had remotely rolled down his window until she flung him an over-the-shoulder glance that said, *What are you waiting for, numbnuts?*

He wriggled headfirst out of the Civic and hit the ground running.

Every morning Yancy woke up amazed that Dr. Rosa Campesino still cared about him. On paper the match wasn't ideal. She was sharp, beautiful, single, sane, and saved at least two or three lives per day in the E.R. He was a banished cop consigned to probing the grim hot kitchens of funky restaurants, bringing home vile stories of insects amok in the cornbread mix.

Rosa's initial attraction to him wasn't entirely baffling because Yancy was good at making first impressions. He could be funny and semi-charming, though with smart women that carried you only so far. It didn't take them long to unpeel your true personality. Yancy was prone to an acid bluntness that produced poor results career-wise and also on the domestic front. While he wasn't one of those loudmouthed fools who uttered every thought that entered their heads, his idea of self-editing often fell shy of the societal norm. Rosa said she tolerated his sharp tongue, preoccupied moods and impulsive detours because there was old-fashioned nobility in his heart, and his social missteps were made with good intentions. Yancy hoped she truly believed that and wasn't just trying to convince herself he was worth the effort.

When he returned from fishing she was waiting at the house, still wearing her hospital scrubs which drove him wild as she well knew.

"Catch anything?" she called out as he backed the boat trailer into the driveway.

"*Nada.* The water's still too cold."

"But it's a gorgeous day, no?"

"Breathtaking," Yancy said. She was.

While he rinsed the skiff and wiped down his fly rods, Rosa fixed Cuban sandwiches and warmed some black beans with rice. He walked inside and caught her eyeing the container of fish dip, which he snatched from her fingers. After spooning out the engagement ring he told her the story of Deb and Britt (or Brad, or whatever the hell it was), his potential new neighbors.

"Please tell me you're not holding on to her diamond," Rosa said, "for leverage."

"That would be wrong?"

"So wrong. Also illegal, no?"

"But the way she described the house they're planning, it's a bona fide atrocity. I'm not kidding, baby—maybe worse than the last one."

An unspooled ex-girlfriend of Yancy's had torched the previous offending structure in a bid to win back Yancy's affections. Rosa's devotion stopped well shy of felonious melodrama.

Yancy wiped off the ring and handed it to her. "Her boyfriend told her it cost two hundred grand. What do you think, doctor?"

"I think it's quite large." Rosa tossed it back.

"Come on, try it on."

"Really? Here's how my delicate fingers spent the afternoon: Groping for lead slugs inside the intestines of a three-hundred-pound heroin dealer who'd shorted the wrong customer. So I'll pass on the hand modeling today, if that's okay."

"A man can dream," Yancy said. He mushed the ring back into the fish dip.

"The dealer survived, by the way. Shot five times, and he'll be back on the street in time for Easter." Rosa bowed. "My service to the human race."

"See, this is exactly why you should move down here. Our E.R. isn't so demoralizing."

"Promise you'll return the diamond to this Deb person, no matter what kind of architectural monstrosity she and her scuzzy boyfriend want to build next door. You get busted for grand theft, mister, that's pretty much a career killer."

"How did I ever live without you?"

"How can you not have a decent imported beer in this house?"

Rogelio Burton stopped by and had a plate of black beans. He'd been Yancy's best friend and calming influence in the detective bureau, and they were still close. That didn't mean Yancy listened to his advice. Rosa changed into a devastating swimsuit and went out on the deck to catch some sun.

"The sheriff sent me," Burton said to Yancy.

"Where's my badge?"

"Don't start again."

"Then you know what? Sonny and I have nothing to talk about."

The problem was election-year politics. Although Yancy had single-handedly solved a major murder case—a first for the roach patrol—Sonny Summers had postponed reinstating him due to the controversy it might stir.

"You watch much TV?" Burton asked.

"Weather Channel. *MythBusters* reruns. That's about it," Yancy said. "They gouge you for the porn on pay-per-view, so I'm boycotting."

"There's a reality show called *Bayou Brethren*. It's about a family of redneck chicken farmers in Louisiana."

"Somehow that one slipped past me."

"It's actually funnier than it sounds."

"Do-it-yourself liposuction would be funnier than chicken farming."

"Being a fisherman you'll like this: They sell the damn rooster feathers for trout flies. The star's a guy named Buck Nance. They call him Captain Cock, because cock roosters is what they raise." Burton summarized Nance's catastrophic stand-up appearance at the Parched Pirate.

"The dumbass told a gay joke?" Yancy said incredulously. "On Duval Street?"

Burton took out his smart phone and showed one of the YouTube videos taken at the bar. Yancy wondered aloud if Mr. Nance had a death wish.

"They ran him off, and now he's gone missing," Burton said. "That's why Sonny sent me to see you. He heard what happened at Clippy's—all that hair they found in the cobbler."

"It was the quinoa."

"I want recipes I'll call Rachael Ray. Just hang with me on this, Andrew. The AWOL reality dude, he's famous for his long beard. We're thinkin' maybe he chopped it off in a panic so people wouldn't recognize him. That stuff you picked up at the restaurant, Sonny wants it sent to Miami for a DNA test."

Yancy stiffened. "The sheriff's got no jurisdiction over health inspections."

"It's the height of the season, man. It would be epically shitty PR for the Keys if something bad happened to this moron while he was here. That's Sonny talkin'. Drop whatever you're doing and go find Buck Nasty is what he tells me this morning. You think I signed up for this?"

"Tell Sonny I'll trade him a hair sample for my detective badge."

"Listen, he's the one who cut the sweet deal that kept your ass out of jail, and he's the one who got you another job. Or did you forget already?" Burton was getting aggravated. "Swear to God, Andrew, your own worst enemy is you."

It was not Yancy's first exposure to the concept. He said, "You're lucky I sleep with a forensic expert."

He removed one of the collection baggies from the refrigerator, walked outside and presented it to Rosa on the sundeck. She looked up from the chaise lounge and said, "For me? This is more romantic than roses."

"Please? We need to know if it's beard hair."

"If you weren't so earnest, I'd pop you in the balls."

From the doorway Burton said, "Rosa, I swear, this wasn't my idea."

She opened the bag and gingerly lifted a salt-and-pepper tuft. "I would say it's from a white male, middle-aged. My guess is facial, but you'll need to put it under a microscope to make certain. Beard hairs are grooved and they look triangular in cross-section. By the way, I don't want to hear the story behind this disgusting little treasure. I'm serious."

Rosa had been a rising star with the Miami-Dade Medical Examiner's Office until she burned out on autopsies and quit to go work on live patients.

She returned the mystery follicles to the bag and said, "Do you have some Purell, Andrew? You've got exactly thirty seconds."

He sprinted for the medicine cabinet in the bathroom, handing the baggie to Burton as he flew past.

Buck Nance's mistress wasn't part of the TV show. He'd been faithfully married to the same woman for almost thirty years is what America had been told. Krystal Nance was hefty and hardspoken and loved Buck truly, but she didn't put up with any BS from him or any of the brothers. It had all been laid out in the script for the pilot. Krystal Nance was tough as nails.

Buck's girlfriend went by the porny name of Miracle though she had a master's in computer science from Florida State. Buck had met her at a popular Pensacola oyster bar, where she worked as a second-string shucker. A month later he bought her a condominium overlooking Escambia Bay, a transaction opposed by Jon David Ampergrodt, Lane Coolman and the entire management team at Platinum Artists. However, they stood powerless against Miracle's allure, which was exclusively sexual. Her favorite position was called "The Wet Wolverine," which played deviously to Buck's Wisconsin roots. One night he shredded an ACL attempting to carry her mid-coitus from the ironing board in the condo's pantry to the futon in the living room. The injury—portrayed to Krystal as a post-hole-digging accident—forced a hasty rewrite of a *Brethren* segment that had called for Buck to kick in the door of Clee Roy's brand-new Durango.

Miracle was needy and also short of patience. She reacted melodramatically when feeling ignored by Buck, and her tantrums were a source of peptic anxiety for his handlers. With trepidation Jon David Ampergrodt had phoned her to ask if she'd heard from Buck in Key West.

"Not for thirty-seven hours," Miracle replied with homicidal chill.

Amp told her what happened at the Parched Pirate, and encouraged her for verification to check out the YouTube clips. "We're all a bit concerned for the big guy," he added, hoping to dilute her anger with worry.

"Why? He's just off chasin' pussy."

"No, he's not. He probably got scared shitless by the crowd, and now he's hiding in a dive somewhere."

"Deep in strange pussy is where he's hiding," she said.

"Miracle, listen to me. Nobody's heard a word from him—not his brothers, not his mom, not Krystal, nobody."

"That's because he and Lane are too busy whorehopping."

"No, no, Buck would never—"

"Hey, he whorehopped me, didn't he?"

The line went silent. Twenty minutes later somebody hacked the official *Bayou Brethren* Facebook page and posted a close-up photo of Osama bin Laden side-by-side with a head shot of Buck. The caption said: "Two epic beards! Yo, maybe I should join the Taliban!"

By lunchtime, the bin Laden item had galvanized a horde of patriotic bloggers who didn't know the difference between the Taliban and al Qaeda but were nonetheless infuriated by Buck's apparent flippancy. One even accused him of sculpting his facial hair in homage to the dead terrorist.

Informed of the crisis, Jon David Ampergrodt became so engrossed in damage control that he was answering his private lines without checking the caller ID, which is how he ended up speaking to an unrecognized number in the 305 area code. It turned out to be a rare pay phone in Key West, with Lane Coolman on the line.

"Amp, I escaped!" he shouted. "I got away from those crazy fuckers!"

"Got away from who?"

"You're kidding, right?"

"Oh . . . shit, yeah, I almost forgot. Sorry, dude, it's been manic around here today. You won't believe what—"

"You forgot I was kidnapped?" said Coolman.

"No . . . I mean, of course not. It was at the top of my to-do list. The ransom, et cetera—we were putting together a totally solid counter offer. But then, dude, Miracle pulled one of her bipolar freak-outs—"

"Unbelievable."

"Yeah, she's a major thundercunt."

"I'm not talking about *her*, Amp."

"Point is you got away from the shitheads who snatched you, which, nice work, double-oh-seven. You saved the agency some serious bank. Plus you're okay, which is the most important thing."

Well, not really the *most* important thing, but Jon David Ampergrodt perceived that Lane Coolman needed to feel some love.

"I'm just totally stoked to hear your voice," he said. "Tell me everything that happened, blow by blow, but not right now. The *Brethren* Facebook page is basically in flames, thanks to Buck's bimbo."

"Yeah, well, I spent my morning as a fucking crash-test dummy," Coolman said. "Now I'm standing in a phone booth that doubles as a public urinal. No cash, no credit cards, just the stinking shirt on my back. Get me on a plane back to L.A., okay?"

"Absolutely, buddy. Soon as Buck turns up, we'll send the G5."

"No, I want out of here now!"

A message from Amp's assistant flashed on his desktop: A reporter from Al Jazeera was on line two seeking reaction to a Taliban statement condemning Buck Nance for mocking Islamic custom. Mother-fuckers!

"Lane, I gotta grab this call. We'll book you a suite at the best hotel on the island. Have a shot of tequila, take a hot shower. I'll send money and plastic."

"Seriously, Amp. Bring me home."

"I *am* serious. Buck's your ticket."

FIVE

The next morning they ate breakfast at a diner on Sugarloaf where Rosa broke the news. She was going to Europe for a couple of weeks—Stockholm, Düsseldorf and Oslo.

"Why Oslo?" Yancy asked.

"The rain forest, of course."

"Be serious. It's freezing cold there."

"Winter, yes," said Rosa. "But at least nobody's getting shot."

"Is that even true?"

"They've got actual laws against walking around with loaded guns on the street. Same in Sweden and Germany."

The proprietor of the diner approached to ask if their meals were all right. Yancy had once written him up for an eggs Benedict infraction (under-refrigerated Hollandaise sauce), but overall he felt he'd been treated fairly. Yancy told him the food was excellent, and the man happily headed back to the kitchen.

To Rosa, Yancy said: "Sometimes I'm dead slow on the uptake. Are you inviting me to come along on your trip?"

"I need a break from all the blood, Andrew."

He'd traveled a few times to the Bahamas and once long ago to Canada on a walleye expedition with his father, but he'd never been overseas. He asked Rosa when she was leaving.

"Tomorrow."

"Aw, come on."

"The travel agent got me a great package. I know it's last-minute, I'm sorry."

"But my passport—it's expired, remember?"

"Still?" She didn't look up from her omelet.

It was impossible to get a passport renewed in twenty-four hours. The other obstacle was Yancy's job; during the high season Tommy Lombardo never let roach-patrol inspectors take vacations, only funeral leaves.

"The hospital's cool with your leaving on such short notice?"

"Not at all," Rosa said. "I resigned yesterday."

"Boom. Okay."

"Andrew, could you please pass the Tabasco?"

Later at his house they made love, though the moves seemed mechanical. Yancy had no intuition about the fragile arc of relationships, so he was accustomed to being blindsided. Still it always hurt. He was fairly sure that Rosa was dumping him, whether she was aware of it or not.

Obviously she'd planned her trip knowing he couldn't accompany her. His lapsed passport was the reason they'd canceled a dive outing to Eleuthera a few weeks earlier.

She said, "I'd better go home and start packing."

"When you get back from Europe, you should move down here and open a practice. There's a critical shortage of sultry, multi-orgasmic doctors."

"I bet."

"This sucks," Yancy said as he walked her to the car.

"It's got absolutely nothing to do with you."

"Gosh, I've never heard *that* one."

"Be good," she said, and kissed him.

After watching her drive away, Yancy went inside and poured a tall glass of Haitian rum. While searching for limes in the refrigerator he encountered the fish dip concealing the diamond belonging to naughty Deb. Soon the dip would go bad and he'd have to find a clever new hiding place. Another option was to quietly give it up. Pretend he'd never seen the damn ring—just toss it over the fence. Eventually Deb or one of the construction workers would find it on the scorched lot.

From his backyard deck Yancy observed activity on the property—two men conferring as they walked the property lines. The older of them wore a trucker's cap, jeans and work boots, and he carried a set of cardboard tubes. A builder, Yancy concluded glumly. The other man appeared to be in his early forties, like Yancy. He wore tailored camel slacks and a shiny shirt undone perhaps one too many buttonholes. His face was supernaturally tan, his blowfly sunglasses were ultramarine, and his hair glistened like barbecue. Yancy made the shallow but accurate assumption that this person was the Miami lawyer to whom Deb was engaged.

Liberated by the rum, Yancy hurried inside and from the recycle bin in the pantry he pulled three empty bottles of Stella, the import he'd bought for Rosa. Then he snatched his twelve-gauge and hurried back to the deck. The first toss was too low, and his shot missed the bottle. On the second toss, which was perfect, he blew the neck off. The third beer bottle he blasted into granular rain that harmlessly peppered his skiff, parked in the driveway.

By now, on the other side of the fence, Brock and his builder were retreating toward their respective vehicles—a Ford pickup for the builder, a sports car for the lawyer. Yancy waved amiably at the men but failed to elicit a response. They sped off without even tooting their horns.

Yancy picked up the shotgun shells and every piece of broken glass, a time-consuming chore. After refreshing his drink he stretched out on the sofa, opened his laptop and committed himself to three back-to-back episodes of *Bayou Brethren*. He wasn't too drunk to comprehend the show's appeal, and found himself wondering about the secret to Buck and Krystal's long marriage. She plainly wasn't enchanted by life on the rooster farm, barely tolerated the other brothers, and complained constantly about Buck's aversion to slow dancing, seat belts and Hank Williams. Nonetheless she remained devoted to her man, which touched Yancy in his maudlin swoon.

He pressed the Pause button freezing a close-up as Buck challenged Krystal on the subject of free-range chicken facilities, which Buck proclaimed were exorbitant and also underappreciated by the chickens. Yancy took out one of the evidence bags to compare the silver-gray wads plucked from Clippy's quinoa to Buck's long, lushly tended beard. Holding the baggie next to the laptop screen, Yancy decided the shorn hair was identical in coloration. It wasn't as definitive as the DNA test in progress, but why wait? Rosa was flying away to Europe and he needed a distraction.

Tomorrow he would go searching for Captain Cock.

Matthew Morgan Romberg and his brothers were born in Milwaukee and raised in the suburb of Whitefish Bay. They were not authentic shit-kickers, although Wisconsin has its share. Their father was a successful commodities trader and their mother bred prize English setters which she sold to wealthy bird hunters. The Romberg household was politically divided to the extreme, Kathleen Romberg being a Hubert Humphrey Democrat while her husband parroted the views of Alabama's incendiary governor, George Corley Wallace. The tension was too much for the marriage, and one day Mrs. Romberg ran off with a snowmobile mechanic who reminded her of Cat Stevens.

The Romberg boys fell under the strident sway of their father, although they grew up displaying little of his vehemence and none of his business savvy. Matthew, who would one day become "Buck Nance," attended the University of Minnesota and dropped out six credits shy of a finance degree. Bradley ("Junior"), Henry ("Buddy") and Todd ("Clee Roy") all went to Madison, joined the same Greek fraternity and entered the music program, which impressed a certain dreamy type of coed but somewhat narrowed their prospects for secure employment. One by one they returned to their father's house in Whitefish Bay and reoccupied their childhood bedrooms.

While mulling options the younger brothers started a band that performed accordion covers of popular rock songs. Matthew joined up after being fired under cloudy circumstances from a hard-won management position at Florsheim Shoes. He blamed reverse racial discrimination when in fact the company had caught him stealing cordovan wingtips by the gross and hawking them at a flea market near Eau Claire. It was there he'd connected with Krystal Nordval, his future spouse, who presided over a booth offering hand-blown bongs and bootleg eight-tracks.

The name of the brothers' accordion band was GFR, which stood for Grand Funk Romberg, and they kept it rolling even as they grew older, married and settled into undemanding day jobs. Mostly they played weekends at county fairs and chili cook-offs, but every once in a while they scored a wedding. The idea to grow out their beards came one summer night from Matthew while they were rehearsing a raucous polka-fied rendition of "Tube Snake Boogie." He suggested that they work up a four-song medley of ZZ Top hits, which soon became the centerpiece of their act. Todd taught himself the bass guitar and Henry bought a drum kit at a pawn shop in Green Bay. At first their beards grew unevenly, so the Rombergs wore fakes borrowed from a local theater troupe that specialized in Nativity plays. The beards, used by Joseph and two of the Wise Men, had to be returned in time for Christmas rehearsals. By then the brothers' natural facial bloom was in full glory.

Out of nowhere, GFR received an offer to play a rodeo down in Little Rock, Arkansas. Matthew saw this as a portal to stardom, and after researching the demographics he proposed that the group change its name to "Buck Nance and the Brawlers." The other brothers had no objections because Matthew deserved top billing, serving the triple-threat roles of lead accordion, promoter and business manager. The Rombergs were eager to gain a following in the South, as they'd become increasingly disenchanted with the so-called progressive elements on the rise in Wisconsin politics. They looked forward to reaching a wholesome, simpleminded audience that would appreciate their anti-government patter between songs. Also, they'd never been to a real rodeo.

Buck Nance and the Brawlers performed eight songs and were well-received, their barbed commentary drawing laughs and even some applause. After the gig Bradley dislocated a shoulder when one of the cowboys let him throw a rope on a calf, but the other brothers bought him a sling at Walgreens and dosed him with painkillers. Two nights later they opened at a shrimp festival in Biloxi, and two nights after that they were playing a Masonic lodge near Stone Mountain, Georgia.

Matthew's bold prediction was coming true: The band caught fire on the biker-and-Bible circuit. The Rombergs traded their Dodge mini-van for a second-hand Winnebago, and said goodbye to Whitefish Bay. During the next twenty years they returned only once, to attend the funeral of their father. The old man had suffered a massive heart attack during an ice storm while covertly trying to scrape an "Obama for President" bumper sticker from a smug neighbor's Audi.

The election of a black president brought a boom in TV reality shows featuring feisty rednecks, and talent scouts began scouring the Dixie belt in a fevered search for the next *Duck Dynasty* franchise. Buck Nance and the Brawlers were discovered at a Howard Johnson's off the interstate near Chattanooga, playing a toned-down set for a Catholic bachelorette party. They were flown business-class to Los Angeles for a meeting at Platinum Artists with Jon David Ampergrodt, who pronounced the Romberg brothers "perfect" except for their superior dental work. He promised them fame and wealth, presented a two-year management contract and sent them by limousine to a Malibu orthodontist to get their front teeth darkened and chipped. Matthew was allowed to keep the stage name of Buck while his brothers chose their own from a list of homespun monikers provided by the agency.

The transition from obscure regional musicians to wildly popular television stars put a strain on the brothers' fraternal bond. From the beginning, the creators of *Bayou Brethren* felt the show should revolve around the colorful Buck character and the iron-willed Krystal. Inevitably resentment took root among the other family members—Junior, Buddy and Clee Roy also had wives who enjoyed being recognized in the supermarket, and they wanted their own story lines. Tension between the younger brothers and Buck began to worsen during the tapings, a situation which elated the director, a pragmatic Brit named Damien Poe. Soon he began placing fungo bats at strategic locations throughout the Nance compound in hopes that one of the siblings would snap while the cameras were rolling.

Buck's dalliance with sex-crazed Miracle exacerbated his brothers' jealousy while making their lives more wretched at home. Among the Nance spouses only Krystal seemed unaware that Buck was fucking around; the other wives cracked down preemptively, grilling their husbands on a nightly basis while dropping the names of notorious divorce lawyers.

Because of the family discord, the news of Buck's disappearance in Key West was not received with the utmost consternation by Junior, Buddy or Clee Roy. Like Miracle, they assumed Buck had been seduced by a female fan and was probably holed up in some nasty doublewide, waiting for his hangover to abate. In the meantime, his absence presented an opportunity for the other Nances to carve larger roles for themselves on the television show.

"What the hell. Let's just tape the next episode without him," Clee Roy suggested to Jon David Ampergrodt during a conference call.

"Let me think on that."

"Tell the writers to stick all this shit into the script. That Buck went and disappeared? Talk about monster ratings!" It was either Junior or Buddy speaking; Amp couldn't tell them apart over the phone.

The idea itself wasn't terrible. After a few weeks Buck could return after a staged rehab, blaming booze and pills for his coarse behavior at the Parched Pirate and apologizing tearfully to all the minorities he'd defamed.

Amp said, "That's an interesting concept, boys. I'll run it by Damien."

Next on the agenda was Miracle's insidious online stunt using the bin Laden photo. The brothers agreed that a full-time keeper should be hired to supervise the loony bitch until Buck resurfaced. Amp said he'd already sent out a blast tweet saying the *Brethren* website had been sabotaged by Chinese intelligence agents, who feared the growing global influence of the Nances now that Netflix was streaming the show.

"By the way," said Amp. "Can any of you guys get me Buck's tooth-brush? I'd ask Krystal except her head's not in a great place right now."

Clee Roy said, "Damien told us not to brush again till we go on hiatus."

"But flossing's okay," either Junior or Buddy cut in. "Right?"

"A comb of Buck's would work just as well," Jon David Ampergrodt said. "Toenail clippings. Snotty handkerchief. Hey, a cigar butt would be spectacular."

"What the fuck, Amp?"

"They've asked for a DNA sample."

"Who?" demanded Clee Roy.

"The sheriff down in the Keys. Standard procedure, guys. They want some of Buck's DNA just in case, God forbid."

For several moments no faux Cajun voices came from the phone speaker on Amp's desk, and he wondered if he'd upset the three brothers.

Then either Buddy or Junior piped up: "I got somethin' of Buck's, but they need to send somebody with a bag. I ain't touchin' the damn thing."

Merry Mansfield and Zeto weren't interested in Martin Trebeaux's gran-diose plan to barge beach sand from Cuba across the Gulf Stream to Florida. Merry scoffed when he offered them a piece of the action in exchange for his freedom. Zeto's response was an elbow to the larynx, which caused Martin Trebeaux to black out choking. He awoke gagged and bound on the bare floor of a bare house, where he overheard some-one's future being discussed.

It was his future, and the outlook was poor.

The house was almost dark when Dominick "Big Noogie" Aeola

arrived with a shorter man who stood at his side mouthing an ivory toothpick. Big Noogie paid Zeto with cash, and Zeto paid Merry, who counted the bills by the light of her iPhone.

"What about the other guy you grabbed? The first guy?" Big Noogie asked.

Zeto looked tightly at Merry.

"The mistake," Big Noogie elaborated.

"Oh, him. He's gone," Merry said.

"So that's all took care of?"

"Like it never happened."

"Good," said Big Noogie. "You two can go now."

They did.

The moment the duct tape was removed from Trebeaux's Trump-ish lips he blurted the story about the redheaded crash driver and her sexy shaving ploy. "It's fucking brilliant!" the swindler gushed to Big Noogie. "Was that your idea?"

Big Noogie said, "No, *this* is my idea."

He took out a pair of ten-inch surgical hemostats, which he clamped onto the crotch of Martin Trebeaux's linen pants.

"Not my nut sack!" wailed the sand man.

"What'd you expect?" said Big Noogie.

The Tesla was still in the alley beside the house, but Merry didn't hear any of Trebeaux's screams because Zeto was blasting Pit Bull on the radio. When she asked Zeto for a lift back to Miami, he said the car didn't have enough juice for the trip. The charging station in Key West was still under construction, so he drove down Simonton until he found a house with hurricane shutters on the windows. After backing into the driveway, he hopped out and plugged the Tesla's cord into a socket on the outside wall.

"How long will this take?" Merry asked.

"I'm gonna get a room at the La Concha. Two beds."

"No, thank you."

"Then you're on your own, babe."

Merry was too tired to deal with Zeto sneaking his hairy ass between the sheets in the middle of the night. She had a strict rule against cuddling with potential co-defendants.

"What do you think's going to happen to Martin?"

"Ever see *The Godfather*?" Zeto asked.

"Nope."

"You're shitting me. Not even Part One? Okay, then Tony Soprano."

"Who?" said Merry.

"Do you live in a cave on Mars, or what?"

"Don't be a dick. I know about the Mafia. All I asked you is what're they going to do to Martin, since you're the expert on everything."

"Go rent the movie," Zeto said, and walked away.

While Merry waited to cross the street, three tow trucks rumbled past one after the other. The first two were hauling the same type of cars, late-model, silverish Buicks with rear-end damage. The third truck was hauling a Honda Civic with a mangled front fender. Merry smiled at her handiwork.

She walked back to the bread-and-breakfast on Catherine Street where she'd booked a room. The place was packed with milky-limbed Austrians who innocently plodded around town in black nylon socks and sandals. Merry found it endearing, for the twenty-first century. She had the same reaction to Mennonites, who made no wardrobe concessions despite Florida's heartless humidity.

The next morning she checked out and headed toward Truman Avenue with the thought of hitching a ride, thereby avoiding four hours in a car with Zeto. Yielding to a procession of Duval-bound tourists she spotted a familiar face.

"Yo, Bob!" she called out.

Lane Coolman leaped sideways, landing with both shoes in the road. Merry yanked him clear of an oncoming moped and told him to chill, for God's sake.

"Have you been following me?" he asked shakily.

"Don't flatter yourself. It's a small island."

"I'm going straight to the police!"

She said, "Cool, I'll come with you. Let's see whose story they believe. You want to hear mine? All the perverted stuff you made me do after you tricked me into getting in your car? The ropes, the hot glue, the roller blades."

"Know what? You're a terrible human being. I mean a total sociopath."

"And you'd be dead if it wasn't for me, don't forget. What are you still doing here is the question."

"Where's your thug boyfriend?" Coolman glanced in both directions, then over his shoulder.

"I took care of all that," said Merry. "The mob guys think you're at the bottom of the sea, and Zeto doesn't give a shit either way. So let's go grab a bite."

"Are you kidding?"

"Here you are, all showered and peppy. I approve this new look."

Self-consciously Coolman reappraised the orchid print shirt and cantaloupe-colored Bermuda shorts that he'd paid for with the money that Amp had wired him.

"Just leave me the fuck alone," he said to Merry Mansfield.

"Don't you want your phone back? I've still got it."

"Then give it here!"

When Coolman reached for her handbag, she grabbed his arm and twisted it behind him, spinning him on the sidewalk. The tourists, unfazed, trudged past like zombies.

"Let's get a basket of conch fritters," said Merry. "I want to hear what you're up to—a day in the life of a big-time Hollywood talent manager, whatever."

She let go of his arm. Coolman tried to act like it was nothing, like they were just fooling around, but he was shaken by how tough and ballsy she was. Dropping his voice: "Just let me have my phone, please. I've gotta find Buck Nance."

"Want some help?"

"No!"

"Oh yes you do, Bob."

She took his hand, nudged him with her hip, and that was that.

SIX

An artist friend met Yancy for lunch at Clippy's and, working from photographs, penciled a sketch of what a clean-shaven Buck Nance might look like. Clippy said the face on the napkin resembled Keith Urban twenty years down the road, while Neil the mayor said no, the chin was totally David Duchovny.

Neither Clippy nor Neil admitted to watching *Bayou Brethren,* but Yancy's straight artist friend said it was his second-favorite reality show after *Mud-Wrestling Supermodels: Cancún.* Buck's celebrity status didn't impress Neil and Clippy, who vowed to prosecute him for shearing his gnarly growth into their acclaimed quinoa, if the DNA test proved positive. They also hinted at the possibility of a civil lawsuit, citing "mental anguish."

Yancy stopped by the city police department, where a detective who'd once helped him catch an albino ATM robber told him that all the road officers were on the lookout for Buck Nance. Sheriff Sonny Summers had made a call to the chief. Yancy skimmed the latest incident reports to see if Buck had committed any more crimes against hygiene. Most of the night log was routine Key West turpitude—drunken fistfights, inept dope deals, a handful of auto burglaries, one halfhearted domestic assault (the husband was struck with a bag of frozen snapper chum) and seven unsolved cases of public urination.

A spate of shopliftings caught Yancy's attention because of their exceptional pettiness—an $11 tee-shirt filched from a store on Simonton, a pair of black board shorts taken from a dive shop off of Caroline Street and a Panama-style hat snatched from a window mannequin at Fastbuck Freddie's. In each instance the theft had been witnessed by other customers who described the shoplifter as a white middle-aged male with a choppy facial burr.

If Buck Nance was the perpetrator, such smallish crimes indicated he was roaming the streets dead broke. A second thumbing of the police reports turned up a break-in at a motel room where the only articles stolen were a pair of size 12 flip-flops, a score that would pretty much complete Captain Cock's island wardrobe.

Yancy spent the rest of the afternoon walking around Old Town. He spied several crisp Panama hats though none of the noggins belonged to Buck Nance. At an upscale guesthouse Yancy interviewed one of the shoplifting witnesses, a soft-spoken widow from Philadelphia. She addressed him as "detective," making him pine for the days when he carried a real badge. The widow said the napkin sketch "sort of" resembled the person she'd seen swiping the surf shorts except there were dark bags under the thief's eyes. "He looked more homeless," she said.

It mystified Yancy why Buck hadn't already fled the Keys. Possibly he'd lost a screw and turned paranoid after the uprising at the Parched Pirate. Nor could a drunken jag be ruled out, though it wouldn't explain the shoplifting spree. Another possibility was that Buck's "disappearance" had been a manufactured drama, a fake breakdown meant to mitigate his controversial performance at the bar. TV psychiatrists would be happy to theorize that poor Buck had cracked under the pressure of starring in a hit show, that his self-destructive outburst was the proverbial cry for help. Later he would be found in calculated dishevelment, a squinting haggard figure hustled away by family members in a cortege of anthracite SUVs. A hushed period of rehab would be followed by a weepy public contrition, always a ratings booster.

It was all speculation because, at this point, Yancy knew nothing about the man's motives or his state of mind. Over beers at Pepe's, Rogelio Burton informed him that Buck's real name was Matthew Romberg.

"Fantastic!" Yancy exclaimed. "I love it."

"He and the brethren are from Wisconsin, of all places. They had an accordion band, I swear to God. Nobody's supposed to know. There were some videos on the Internet but they all got yanked, once the boys signed their TV contract."

"But I watched the show. They all talk Cajun, sort of."

"Big deal. You should hear my Ringo Starr, and I've never set foot in Liverpool."

Yancy told Burton about the string of lame shopliftings, and the witnesses' description of the suspect.

"That could be half the bums on the island," the detective remarked.

The waitress brought an order of fried plantains. While eating, Burton delivered a mild lecture about Yancy firing a twelve-gauge shotgun in front of civilians.

"Hey, it's perfectly legal," Yancy asserted. "Guy down the street from me has a pistol range in his backyard! All I did was murder a few beer bottles."

"Sonny found out. He's not thrilled."

"Who the hell told him?" Yancy feared that the Stella massacre would be added to the file of perceived fuckups that the sheriff unsheathed whenever Yancy came pleading for reinstatement.

Burton said, "One of the dudes you scared shitless is a lawyer from Miami named Brock Richardson. He's got ads all over TV, which doesn't mean anything except that Sonny's heard of him."

"He bought the lot next door. Wants to build a McMansion for his girlfriend who, by the way, offered me a BJ."

Burton nodded. "I get that all the time."

"No, she really did. You'll be proud to know I declined."

"Why?"

"Because I want to stay faithful to Rosa," said Yancy.

"No, asshole, I meant why did this total stranger offer you sex?"

"Who knows. Maybe it's just her way of being neighborly."

"A carrot cake is neighborly," Burton said. "A blowjob is a plan."

Yancy didn't tell his friend that Deb wanted him to help find her lost diamond, which happened to be hidden inside his refrigerator. He knew that, like Rosa, Burton would advise him to return the ring as soon as possible.

"Tell me about this ace attorney," Yancy said.

"He's way too important to dial 911, so he calls up Sonny's office direct, screaming that some crazy bastard's shootin' up Big Pine Key."

"How did this jackoff pass the bar if he doesn't even know the firearms statutes?"

"As usual, you're missing the point."

"Well, guess what? This is Florida, the land of batshit, trigger-happy motherfuckers. Love it or leave it is what I say."

"Dial it down, Andrew, if you want your badge back. That's the takeaway." Burton ate the last plantain, pushed the plate to the side and ordered a cup of coffee.

Yancy said, "Does he really want to live next door to a whack job like me? That's what this guy ought to be asking himself."

"Or he could just go to a gun show and buy a bigger cannon than yours. It *is* Florida, like you say." Burton smiled.

He was a good cop and a solid guy, still married to his college sweetheart. They had three kids, all soccer players, and drove them all over the state for tournaments. Rogelio didn't screw around on his wife, never stayed out late with the hard chargers. His was a life conducted with clear boundaries and deep commitments. Yancy envied his steadiness. If Burton had been mad at Yancy for getting booted from the detective bureau, he'd kept it to himself. Throughout their friendship he'd always been the grownup.

"Rog, I think Rosa's leaving me."

Burton sat back and slapped his hands on the tabletop. "What the fuck did you do now?"

"I've got no idea, but she quit her job and she's off to Europe for a couple of weeks. We've all seen that movie. Weeks turn into months, and months turn into forever."

"For Christ's sake, Andrew, you always assume the worst."

"That's my motto. Put it on my tombstone: 'Assume the worst.'"

"What tombstone? You said you're getting cremated. You said you want your ashes scattered at high tide in Pearl Basin. See? I remember all this shit. The rum talking."

"Fine, then write it on my urn: *Assume the fucking worst.*" Yancy paid the tab and followed his friend out the door.

Burton was meeting a source, a call girl who lived on Olivia down by the cemetery. He asked Yancy to tag along. Smart cops never went alone to interview prostitutes, because that's how rumors and occasionally true drama got started.

"Sonny's all over me to shake some trees, so I'd appreciate a little support," Burton said. "Other words, let me do the talkin', okay?"

"So you think Buck Nance got waylaid by a hooker."

"Probably not Giselle, but it's possible she's heard something."

"'Giselle,' is it? My goodness, Rog."

"Try to control yourself."

Giselle had a neat wooden house with canary-yellow shutters and a spice garden in the front yard. She was getting ready for a date, hurrying between the bathroom and bedroom wearing dark hose, black panties and a matching bra. It looked like her closet had detonated, clothes flung all over the place. Burton and Yancy weren't sure where to sit down, so they didn't. Out of habit Yancy scanned the baseboards for rodent scat, but he saw nothing.

After Giselle finally picked out a dress to wear, she was shown the napkin sketch of Buck Nance, along with a photograph of him fully bearded. She stated without pause that she'd never laid eyes on the man.

Burton explained that Buck and his brothers had a popular cable television show. "Any of your girlfriends say anything about hookin' up with a famous john?"

Giselle smiled as she put on her lipstick in front of the hallway mirror. "That's what we're all waiting for, right? The Brad Pitt call."

"So the answer's no?"

"I'll ask around," she said. "Are we done? Because I gotta run."

Burton laid a fifty-dollar bill on the kitchen counter (which, Yancy noted, was cleaner than some of the restaurants on his beat) and signaled that they should leave.

"Hang on," Yancy said.

Next to the bagel toaster was an empty silver money clip. He picked it up and showed Burton the ornate engraving: *Captain Cock.*

"Isn't that the nickname of our missing shitkicker?" he said.

Giselle turned from the mirror. "No offense, tiger, but who the hell are you? Rog, is this nosy prick your new partner?"

"He works for the state. Officially it's Inspector Yancy—but everyone calls him Andrew."

"Inspecting what—thongs?"

It wasn't Yancy's fault. The furniture was strewn with lingerie that Giselle had tried on and rejected.

"The dude who gave me that silver clip isn't the one you're looking for," she said. "I took it 'cause he only had seventy-three bucks in his pocket and my price is one-fifty. He tried to give me a hard time but I said, 'Listen, Captain Cockhead, you play, you pay.' I told him he's got three business days to bring me the rest of the cash he owes, otherwise I'm totally pawning that thing."

Burton said, "You're positive that it's not the person in the sketch or photograph?"

Giselle cackled. "Not unless he fell asleep on a tanning bed for about six months."

"Your gentleman acquaintance was of dark complexion?"

"Very much so. He said he found the money clip just layin' in the dirt under one of those big trees on Whitehead, which I'm so sure."

"Ever seen him before?" Yancy asked.

"He buses tables at the Bull. Name's Winchell."

Yancy slipped the silver clip into his pocket. "Police evidence," he said to Giselle. "Sorry."

"Yo, wait—how do you even know it's the same Captain Cock?" She glared indignantly at Burton, who laid down another fifty.

"If Winchell comes back," he said, "tell him I need to speak with him right away. Give him my cell number."

"Oh right, he'll be so chatty." Giselle stooped to put on a pair of nosebleed heels. She glanced up at Yancy and said, "Quit starin' at my tits, Inspector."

"I'm not staring." And he wasn't, either. He was practically a hundred percent certain.

"Make him stop," Giselle said to Burton, who laughed.

"Don't you be flirtin' with my boy. He's got enough problems."

Back in the car Burton told Yancy to give him the money clip.

"Don't worry, Rog, I'm not gonna lose it."

"Hand it over. I need something to show the sheriff."

"So he'll think you're hot on the trail, right?"

"Just give me the damn thing," Burton said.

Yancy reached over and attached the silver piece to the driver's-side visor so that the inscription was visible.

"What if winsome Giselle is right?"

Burton, who was wrestling a balky seat belt, said, "You mean if there's more than one Captain Cock?"

"It's Key West, Rog. There might be a franchise."

"I'm gonna drop by Sonny's office and fill him in on what we've got. What *I've* got."

"Good old Sonny," Yancy said. "It'll be nice to see him."

"You're not coming."

"What could it hurt? Just a quick hello."

Burton cut the wheel hard and pulled away from the curb in a manner that ended the conversation.

"Then drop me on Duval," said Yancy. "Now that Rosa's bid farewell, Buck Nance is my new obsession."

"Why don't you go home and lie around feeling sorry for yourself until she comes back? Tell Lombardo you can't work because you caught hantavirus from breathing all those rat hairs. Drink heavily. Smoke too much dope. Sleep late and don't bathe. I'll swing by to check your pulse every few days."

"The human bloodhound is what they call me."

"A pain in the sphincter is what they call you. Please don't screw up my case."

Yancy stepped out of the car at the corner. "You'll be the first to know when I track down this character," he said to Burton. "Keep your ringer on, amigo."

Winchell wasn't working at the Bull that night, but the barmaid gave Yancy an address in Bahama Village. It was Winchell's wife who answered the door. In a clamorous scrum behind her Yancy counted four small kids. Winchell emerged from a back room wearing a towel and a frown. He looked much older than his wife and stood at least six-two, though his arms were thin and his gut was flabby.

"Who are you, man? Get outta my house."

"Police business," said Yancy, which was true enough. It was police business to which he was contributing his expertise, solicited or not. "Put on some clothes and let's take a walk."

Winchell did what he was told and never asked to see a badge, so convincing was Yancy's cop-like comportment. Nor did Mrs. Winchell raise a challenge as her husband was led out the door, instead scalding him with a glare that made clear she presumed him guilty of any and all accusations.

Yancy waited until they were a block from the house before asking Winchell about the money clip he gave to Giselle.

"I didn't give her nuthin'. She took it."

"Where'd you get it from?"

"That bitch say I stole it? She be a damn liar!" Winchell wanted Yancy to understand how insulted he felt.

"She didn't say you stole it, Winchell."

"Well, she still be a damn bitch for takin' it away from me."

"Is your wife aware you slept with a prostitute?"

Winchell looked away muttering.

Yancy said, "Forget Giselle. Tell me about the silver clip."

"Nuthin' to tell. I found it."

"Where? Show me."

They turned and walked north along Whitehead. Winchell stopped beneath an immense banyan tree as old as the pirate town. The tree's peripatetic roots had tunneled a hump in the sidewalk and disfigured a nearby brick wall.

Winchell pointed to a spot on the ground and said, "Right here."

"You just happened to look down and there it was? Lucky you."

"I was just chillin' in the shade, man, havin' a smoke."

For some reason Yancy believed him. On the tree were fresh bark scrapes that could have been made by the toe of a heavy shoe. It was possible that Buck scrambled up the banyan to hide, causing the money clip to fall out of his pocket. It was also possible that Winchell had mugged him, although a forty-five-year-old busboy was not your prototypical Key West street predator.

Yancy asked Winchell how much cash he'd found in the clip.

Again he puffed up, indignant. "Man, there wasn't no cash! What're you sayin'?"

"I don't give a damn whether you kept it or not. I just want to know how much was there."

"Do I gotta give it back? 'Cause we been havin' some expenses."

"You don't have to give back any of it."

"All right, then. I counted six hundred even," Winchell said.

Yancy felt confident doubling the sum in his head. "Any credit cards? ATMs?"

"Naw."

"I knew you were too smart for that rookie shit," Yancy said. "Stolen plastic leaves a trail. Plus every time you swipe it through a machine there's a camera snapping your picture."

Winchell managed a nod, though his face was clouding with unease.

"Did you see anybody else around?" Yancy asked. "Someone sleeping on the sidewalk, or maybe passed out in the bushes?" He took out the artist's drawing of the shaved Buck Nance and a photo of the bearded version. Winchell said neither face looked familiar. Yancy thanked him and told him he could go.

"I 'preciate that," said Winchell. "But listen here, my wife . . . she don't know 'bout the cash money I found and so forth."

"What'd you spend it on?"

"They's a poker game over on Seminary."

"Let me guess how that worked out," Yancy said.

"Man, you can't never win if you don't take a chance. Even the Good Book says so."

"I'm pretty sure it doesn't."

The breeze brought a jumble of music and cheers from Mallory Square, where the crowd was assembling for sunset.

Winchell was in no rush to go home. He said, "Yo, the man lost that money clip—he must be hung like a horse they be callin' him 'Captain Cock.'"

"He got that name because he's in the rooster business."

Winchell seemed let down. "We got too many goddamn roosters, you ask me."

Key West was overrun with chickens, an issue that had long divided the community. The birds were loud and messy, yet some locals thought they were cute. Winchell did not agree, nor did Yancy, who'd been dispatched to more than one outdoor café after patrons complained about the bold, loose-boweled fowl.

When Yancy asked him about *Bayou Brethren,* Winchell said he'd never watched the show, and complained that his wife maintained a Baptist's iron fist on the TV remote.

"Listen, she'll kill me she finds out I's with another woman. I mean she'll kill me, cut off my fuckin' jewels and then kill me all over again. Understand what I'm sayin'?"

"Then you'd better pay Giselle what you owe. Otherwise she'll be knockin' at your front door."

Winchell said, "I'll pay up soon as I can. She knows I'm good for it."

"Go tell your wife we're cool. I'm not taking you to jail tonight."

"I 'preciate that. I do."

Yancy put a hand on his shoulder. "Now, here's what happens next. I'm going to stroll very casually up the street, pretend I thought of one more question to ask, turn around and hurry back. But you'll already be gone."

"Yes, sir."

"Then I'm going to stop at this very same spot under this very same tree, where I will unexpectedly see something important lying on the ground, something I missed the first time."

"You just might," Winchell said quietly.

"I thought so."

SEVEN

"Bottom line, it wasn't even your idea," Lane Coolman said.

"It was my idea to do it *on purpose,* absolutely." Merry Mansfield was explaining the inspiration for the razor scam. "I was up in Miami, doing these boring insurance crashes, when I read about a chick who rammed a carful of tourists while she was shaving her bikini area. That's what the newspaper called it—'her bikini area.' She told the cops she was tidying up down there to meet a boyfriend and took her eyes off the road, which was too good *not* to be true. The accident was totally legit, but the *visual* is what got me thinking. The concept of staging it that way. I knew I could turn it into something that would pay way better than those scumbag claim runners.

"So a friend put me in touch with Zeto, who was doing routine bump-and-grabs for dopers and loan sharks. First he thought I was full of shit but then I rented a Caprice and set up a random crash, to prove my plan would work. My presentation, let's say. I did the bump right on Biscayne and 36th at rush hour—some schoolteacher in a Saab older than my mom. He was so mad when he got out of his car! But then he saw me sittin' there with a razor in my hand and my pink undies all bunched up, and swear to God he almost asked me to marry him. He ends up giving me five hundred cash to get my rental fixed—and the wreck was all my fault! I totally plowed into the dude at a stop light, okay? Men are so pitiful."

Coolman said: "You need to lay off the energy drinks."

"I know, right? Ever since I quit smokin'. They say coffee's healthier but I hate the taste."

"Why not just wear a super-short skirt for the crash? The snatch-shaving thing, that's pretty twisted."

"These days you need more than a great pair of legs, Bob. You need to boggle their little minds. A performance artist is what I am, basically. Not just a stunt driver."

"I've never heard of anyone running a game like this, not even in L.A."

Merry said, "I could definitely rock it there. No doubt."

"And everything else you told me about yourself . . . ?"

"All lies. Pretty much, yeah."

They were sitting at an umbrella table poolside at the Casa Marina, where Platinum Artists Management had booked a top-floor room for Coolman.

"Can I have my phone now?" he asked.

Merry took it from her purse. "Battery's dead as a doornail."

The charger was in his travel bag, which was still in the crumpled trunk of the Buick, locked in an impound lot somewhere on the island.

"Use mine," Merry offered.

It was the same model iPhone as his. He got on YouTube and looked at the video clips from the Parched Pirate. Merry scooted her chair closer to watch.

"So that's your man? The 'talent' you manage."

"He had a bad night," Coolman said tightly. What he saw and heard made him heartsick.

Merry cackled. "A bad night? The dude's a total homophobe. Also, a bigot!"

"There's a culture gap, that's all."

"No, it's a decency gap, Bob. Your client's a flaming a-hole. What's the matter with you? I'm so disappointed."

Coolman had received other morality lectures, though never from a professional criminal. Even more depressing than the bar videos were the comments flooding the *Bayou Brethren*'s Facebook fan page. The condemnations of Buck's tasteless performance were to be expected, but the ranting responses of his defenders (including an unnervingly literate covey of white supremacists) were so loathsome that Coolman was taken aback. He hoped Amp was working to have the offending posts deleted.

"I need to call California. In private, if you don't mind."

"Ah. What's her name?"

"No, it's strictly business," Coolman said.

"You're such a dog, Bob. Wanna drink?" She didn't wait for his answer and headed for the pool bar.

Lane Coolman *was* a dog. His gaze locked on Merry's butt as he dialed Amp's number. Would it be wrong to seduce your own kidnapper? Coolman wondered. Not after all the grief she'd caused him. She was probably a sociopath, but so were half the women he screwed in Hollywood. He wished she'd use his real name and stop calling him Bob.

When Amp finally got on the line they commiserated about the Internet mudfest, which Amp characterized as a "primitive character assassination" of Buck Nance.

"Has anybody heard from him yet?" Coolman asked.

"You mean like kinfolk? No, sir, not Krystal or the brothers."

"What about the kids?"

"Negative."

Buck and Krystal had two grown sons, both private equity managers, who declined to participate in *Bayou Brethren* and therefore went unmentioned on the show.

"You're his go-to guy," Amp said. "Manager, confidant, pimp, shepherd—you're the one we assumed he'd be calling."

"What about Miracle? He usually talks to her every day. He's terrified not to."

"Don't mention that psychotic witch." Amp told him about the twisted bin Laden photo prank. "She's convinced Buck ran off with a groupie. He's the only one that can calm her crazy ass down."

"Amp, I don't even know where to start looking."

"The whole damn island of Key West is only four square miles."

Then send SEAL Team 6, Coolman wanted to say. He was still smarting from his boss's phlegmatic reaction to the six-figure ransom demand from Zeto and Merry. What other agent had come so close to sacrificing his life for Platinum Artists? Amp didn't seem to care.

"What are the cops saying?" Coolman asked.

"We're wiring some dough to the sheriff's re-election, so he's keepin' me in the loop. They've got a few decent leads."

"Like what?"

"Buck hacked off his beard," Amp reported. "A food inspector's got the remains, or whatever you call it. The DNA test came back positive."

"A food inspector? Jesus Christ."

"I know. If the cops find Buck before you do, they've promised to hold him in a safe place. By then the jet'll be on the way."

Coolman was trying to picture his famous client clean-shaven.

"How's the family dynamic?" he asked Amp.

"I've been on the horn with the network all morning. They like Clee Roy's idea of doing a show about Buck's vanishing act, the whole clan gathered anxiously at the rooster farm waiting for news."

"Rolling up on their Harleys, right?"

"Absolutely," Amp said. "Product placement never sleeps."

In their transformation from Rombergs to Cajuns, the brothers had been schooled in certain rural skills as prioritized by the program's Manhattan-born set designer. At the top of the list was dipping tobacco, shooting firearms and mastering motorcycles. Buck had destroyed his first Harley within an hour of delivery, fracturing both ankles when he slid into the rear axle of a sod truck. While confined to a wheelchair he employed a shotgun to herd the roosters, a gruesome panorama that caused the Beretta Corporation to withdraw its sponsorship of the show.

Buck was mended completely from his accident, but a stunt double now performed most of his motorcycle scenes, and Buck's twenty-gauge was loaded only with rock salt.

"We're taping a new episode tomorrow," Amp said.

"You're joking." Coolman sensed his influence was eroding in Buck's absence. The other brothers previously had been lobbying for more face time on camera—Clee Roy, in particular, who was spurred by his wife, a shrill blond fireplug with a fondness for Bergdorf's.

"No time to waste," said Amp. "We expect Kardashian Nielsens."

The tabloid shows and websites were hot on the story. In the hotel lobby Coolman and Merry had passed a crew from *ET* interviewing some sunburned goober who claimed to have seen Buck lighting out for the Marquesas on a lemon-yellow Jet Ski.

"On the show each of the other brothers will be given a theory to push," Amp explained. "Did Buck have a mental breakdown? Was it foul play? Maybe he fell on his head while running from the bar, and now he's got amnesia. It's all good stuff. Krystal doesn't cry easy but we've got somebody working with her."

"And what if Buck shows up tomorrow?"

"Then he makes a grand entrance!" A laugh came from Amp's end of the call. "We'll rewrite on the fly."

Merry had returned to Coolman's table with two frosty rum drinks. She'd also changed into a sleek one-piece swimsuit that undoubtedly had been charged to his room, which was fine with him.

"We're even doing a prayer vigil scene at the church," Amp went on, recapturing Coolman's attention.

The church was a creation of the *Brethren* writers. They called it the First Chickapaw Tabernacle of Hope and Holiness. Buck had demanded the title of deacon, while the other three brothers settled for being elders. A chapel-like structure was erected on the site of an old sawmill, four miles south of the cock farm. Several fevered worship scenes had been taped there, Buck sermonizing on the traditional Christian values of country life. The small congregation was comprised of community-theater actors and drama students bused from FSU; all were paid in cash and required to sign confidentiality agreements.

"You know Buck better than anyone outside the immediate gene pool," Amp was saying to Coolman. "This is not a complicated organism we're dealing with. Put yourself inside this fuckwhistle's head. If you were him, where would you go to hide out?"

Not this town, Coolman said to himself.

Back in the hotel room he plugged his dead phone into Merry Mansfield's charger while she took a bath with the door locked. When the phone's touch screen finally flashed to life, he found no texts or voice messages from the missing Nance patriarch. It was beyond peculiar. Buck normally called when he was drunk, when he was high, when he was bored, when he was scared, when he was with a woman, when he didn't know *what* he was with, or where he was. For almost two years Buck had reached out to his manager multiple times a day, at any hour and for the flimsiest of reasons. Now: nothing.

Coolman briefly considered—then chased from his thoughts—the crushing possibility that his most important client, his friend and meal ticket, the prime reason for his meteoric ascent at Platinum Artists, had dumped him for another agent.

A second scenario, not quite as unbearable as the first: Buck Nance was dead.

The third and most likely story line: He was lying low in a state of fear, exhaustion or petulance.

Merry emerged, wringing her hair with a towel.

"Cheer up, Bob," she said. "I bet I can find that idiot."

The next day Yancy called Burton to say he'd recovered Buck Nance's credit cards—a gold Amex and a black Visa.

"Excellent. Where?"

"Under the same tree Winchell found the money clip."

"Go figure."

"Call it a pang of conscience," Yancy said. "He's already spent the cash."

"This is good, though, finding the plastic. I'll let Sonny know."

"Be sure to tell him how I worked the old magic on my witness."

"Small steps, Andrew."

"Any news on your end?"

Burton disclosed that the hair in Clippy's quinoa definitely came from Buck Nance's beard. "The DNA matched a big gob of tobacco he'd hawked into one of his brothers' golf bags. Episode Eighteen, case you missed it. 'Road Trip to Augusta.' Anyway, they overnighted the chaw to a lab in Miami, and bingo on the saliva."

"No surprise there," Yancy said.

"You know the wine shop where that model worked? The one who was in *Sports Illustrated.*"

"That snob. It was like ten years ago she made the swimsuit issue. At least ten years."

"Right. Because she wouldn't have a drink with you, that makes her a snob. I remember. Anyway the shop has security video of a guy entering a side courtyard who resembles our missing shitkicker. He puts on a Bum Farto tee-shirt and rips off the sleeves," Burton said, "then for reasons unknown he punches out some artist dude's easel."

"Maybe the painting was really awful."

"No, man, the canvas was blank."

"On the plus side," said Yancy, "this means Buck's still alive, alert and ambulatory."

Burton said he went to speak with the artist but it was a waste of time. "He offered me fifty dollars to sit for a nude portrait. You believe that shit?"

"Totally. You've got the body of a Greek god. Who lives on pasta."

"Bite me."

Yancy got distracted by something he saw through the back window. He hung up on Burton, hurried outside, jumped the fence and jogged across the empty lot toward Deb, the frantic fiancée. She was waggling a long-handled metal detector, which upon seeing Yancy she raised at a defensive angle.

"Easy, neighbor," he said. "I came to apologize for grossing you out the other day."

"Stay the hell away from me."

"Honest, there's no corpse buried under my house. The hair in the baggies is evidence in a missing persons case."

Deb had the look of a spooked mare, confirming to Yancy that he was successfully establishing himself as an eccentric.

"Brock says you nearly shot him the other day!" she said.

"What a crybaby. It was target practice with beer bottles, perfectly legal recreation."

"Not in a residential neighborhood."

"The sad song of a deluded liberal. Never once did I point that gun in Brent's direction, you have my word."

"It's *Brock*," Deb snapped. "He made some calls. He says you're not really a cop."

"In what sense? Because I could argue the point."

"Just stay back!"

Today's ensemble was skinny jeans, a pale rose blouse and matching tennis shoes. Her ash-blond hair was cinched with a white scrunchie. The shades were Chanel, naturally, non-polarized and therefore useless against the tropic glare.

Yancy took her metal detector and demonstrated a better search technique, vectoring between the red survey flags while sweeping the wedge-headed device back and forth above the ground. He thought of Rosa's sound admonition to return the lost diamond ring, but he couldn't bring himself to do it. Not just yet.

Fuming, Deb followed him at what she perceived was a safe distance. She said, "I can't believe I almost blew you."

"I can't believe I said no. There might be sainthood in my future." Yancy stooped to pick up a rusty flathead nail that the detector had revealed with a warble. He put the nail in his pants pocket thinking of the Key deer, which sometimes browsed the open lot at dusk. A punctured hoof pad could cause a nasty infection.

He asked Deb if she'd finally informed her future husband that she'd lost the engagement ring on the site of their dream home. "Brock doesn't need to know," she said. "I'll find it myself."

"And if you don't? What happens when the backhoes show up to clear the property? They'll bury that rock forever."

She dragged sourly on her e-cig. The metal detector cheeped again. Yancy picked up a tarnished dime, minted in 1973. "Back then we were both in Snuggies," he said. "I still wear one on special occasions."

"You. Are. Disgusting."

"At a minimum." When he handed the coin to Deb, she slapped it out of his hand.

He said, "I were you, I'd stall Brad as long as possible—"

"*Brock*, you dick. Brock, Brock, Brock."

"Don't let him bring in the heavy machinery until you've searched every square inch of this property. I'll help you, Deb, but you've got to stay strong."

"How do I stall him? He wants the slab poured by next week."

Not happening, thought Yancy. "Isn't the ring insured?"

Her answer was a bitter no. "If it was insured, he could get his money back and buy me a new one. Which is what I deserve, instead of wearing some other tramp's diamond."

"He hasn't noticed it's not on your finger?"

"I told him it's at the jeweler, getting sized. That's what makes me so mad—this is actually his fuckup, not mine. If he'd given me a ring that fit, my *own* ring instead of hers, it wouldn't have fallen off."

Because Richardson had been too lazy (or too cheap) to insure the two-hundred-thousand dollar pebble, the search for it was bound to continue, delaying construction and buying Yancy some time. He fully intended to surrender the diamond once Deb and her beau split up, scrapped their vulgar house plans, and put the lot up for sale. In Yancy's mind he hadn't stolen the gem; he was holding it in protective custody.

When the time came, he would return it in anonymous, untraceable packaging.

The metal detector led Yancy to two more nails, a bent stub of rebar and a size 7/0 fishing hook. Deb warned that Brock was having him investigated by professionals, which Yancy saw as a positive development. The details of his personal history would only heighten Richardson's doubts about Yancy's fitness as a neighbor.

"Tell me something," he said to Deb. "Why do you lovebirds need to build such a huge place? What's wrong with a classic four/three ranch-style? That's plenty roomy for a vacation home—and you'd have space in the yard for a pool."

Deb said, "Nobody in Florida with Brock's kind of money builds a one-story house. I can't believe you'd say that."

"What is Brock's kind of money?"

"Enough to fill a Bounce House and roll around in naked. Haven't you seen the ads on TV? He's got all the Pitrolux lawsuits, a gi-mongous class-action."

Pitrolux was a deodorant armpit gel that also boosted testosterone. The target market segment was middle-aged men with slack penises and gagging body odor, but the refreshing juniper scent had attracted teenage girls who failed to read the warning label while rifling their parents' medicine cabinets. Among the jarring side effects of Pitrolux were volcanic acne, yam-sized larynxes and goatees as lush as any in the NBA. Scores of young plaintiffs, including a squad of misfortunate high-school cheerleaders from Austin, went after the drug manufacturer, the labs, the retailers and even Ben Affleck, the famed actor who was the voice on the Pitrolux commercials. Affleck had been quickly dropped from the lawsuit and held blameless by a judge who happened to be a diehard fan of *Gigli*.

"Your fiancé must be quite the busy beaver at the courthouse," Yancy said.

Deb laughed. "Brock doesn't do any trial work. He farms all the cases to other lawyers who specialize."

"So he's basically an 800 number, a referral switchboard. What's his split of the settlements? Or does he take a flat fee?"

She nodded toward her Porsche. "However he collects it works just dandy for me."

"What a country," said Yancy.

"Grow up."

She asked if she could leave the metal detector so that Yancy could keep searching in his spare time. He played along, waving as she roared off. After lunch (a sardine-and-tomato sandwich), he went online to locate Rosa on Flight Tracker. According to the miniature jet icon on the map, the plane hadn't yet departed from Miami. He sent a pining note in the hope she was checking her emails.

Tommy Lombardo called asking Yancy to rush to a new seafood joint in Marathon called the Reef Raff.

"Maybe tomorrow," said Yancy. "Today I've got a McDonald's, a Checkers and Stoney's, of course, which'll take all afternoon." The owner of Stoney's Crab Palace, a man named Brennan, was a serial offender of the health codes. Roaches were so plentiful at his restaurant that Yancy used an improvised suction device to expedite the roundups.

Lombardo told him to forget Stoney's and proceed at full speed to the Reef Raff. "Somethin's moving in their mango salsa," he reported gravely.

"Yum."

When Yancy first went on roach patrol he'd dropped thirty pounds in a haze of constant revulsion. These days almost nothing bothered him. "Exactly what type of movement was observed?" he asked Lombardo.

"Wiggling is what they said."

"Wiggling, or wriggling?"

"What the fuck's the difference? They got a lady fainted face-first into the salad bar. Fire rescue's on the way. So is freakin' Channel 7."

"Then I'll shut the place down right away." Yancy knew his boss dreaded emergency closures, which generated reams of paperwork in addition to unwanted publicity. Among restaurant inspectors it was considered the nuclear option.

"Now hold on, Andrew—don't do a damn thing till you find out what you're dealin' with up there. Maybe it's not so bad."

"And what kind of life-form would be acceptable in a platter of salsa, regulation-wise?"

"Work with the man," Lombardo implored. "That's all I'm sayin'."

Yancy got dressed in his inspector clothes, including a semi-clean necktie, and organized the contents of his briefcase. Halfway down Key Deer Boulevard he decided he wasn't up for a maggot inquiry; it was simply too nice a day. A stern phone call to the Reef Raff insured that the condiment in question would be sealed and preserved for Yancy's future scrutiny. Upon reaching the Overseas Highway he aimed his car in the opposite direction of Marathon, back toward Key West.

The supermodel who'd rejected Yancy was long gone from the wine shop, but the college-age woman behind the counter was happy to help. She left him alone in the broom-closet office where a desktop computer cycled black-and-white loops from the shop's security cameras. Although the courtyard video lasted only thirty seconds, the quality was crisp enough for Yancy to see that the unbearded man donning the Bum Farto shirt closely resembled the sketch of Buck Nance. His assault on the artist's canvas seemed like the spontaneous act of a batty street person, but without any audio it was impossible to know if Buck and the aspiring Renoir had exchanged harsh words beforehand.

"Is Bum Farto a real person? I see those tee-shirts all over town."

The young clerk was watching the video clip over Yancy's shoulder. Like a heron she'd stepped silently into the cubby.

"Bum was the fire chief here a long time ago," Yancy said. "He got busted for dealing blow from the station house but he disappeared before they could put him in jail. The locals say he ran off to Costa Rica and lived like a king. By now he's dead from old age, but the legend lives on in casual wear."

The woman leaned in for a closer look. "So, what's the deal with the skanky dude?"

"That's Buck Nance. The other detectives didn't tell you? He's on *Bayou Brethren*."

"Never heard of it."

"Darling, you just made my day," Yancy said.

"Why're you guys lookin' for him?"

"There's a fear he might endanger himself."

The shop clerk shrugged. "Isn't that why people come here?"

Yancy walked out thinking he was wasting his time. Sonny Summers probably wouldn't rehire him even if he personally delivered Buck Nance. It was an election year and Yancy's name was still toxic, or so the sheriff would claim.

The search for Captain Cock offered therapeutic diversion from the Rosa setback, but a selfless act of public service it wasn't. If the cops didn't find the bogus Cajun chicken farmer, the tabloids would. On the drive to Marathon Yancy unilaterally took himself off the case, vowing to save his meddling for serious true crimes.

He was elbow-deep in mango salsa when Burton called to tell him about the dead body.

EIGHT

The old Bahia Honda Bridge was chosen for its altitude, scenic vista and lack of bystanders. It had been built for Henry Flagler's train and was later paved for automobile use. Dominick "Big Noogie" Aeola was mildly afraid of heights, a condition ameliorated by three screwdrivers and three milligrams of Niravam. His toothpick-chewing companion did most of the strenuous work, the stripping and binding of Martin Trebeaux. They hung him from the abandoned bridge using his own belt, cinched with authority around his puffy marbled ankles. The belt was teal green with festive little whales on it. Big Noogie said he wouldn't last five minutes in Ozone Park wearing shit like that. Trebeaux was gagged with his tartan boxer shorts, and dangled naked except for the surgical hemostats still clamped to his scrotum. Their polished steel reflected a soft salmon glow from the sunset sky.

Big Noogie's plan was to terrorize the scammer and then give him two weeks to replace the defective sand behind the Royal Pyrenees hotel. But Trebeaux kept trying to talk his way out of the jam. He wouldn't shut up about Cuba, the fantastic beaches ripe for export. Claimed he had an inside track to Raúl Castro. It's the most gorgeous tuff in the Caribbean, Trebeaux kept burbling. Sand so soft and tan you want to strip down and hump it.

The visual was more than Big Noogie could abide, so now Trebeaux was dangling from the Bahia Honda Bridge, his gay whale belt knotted around a spike of rusted girder. Below, on the newer four-lane span, traffic swept along in both directions. Occasionally a car would slow, the occupants peering up curiously at the old truss structure.

"Somebody with good eyes might call us in," the man with the toothpick said.

"Yeah, maybe."

"Would the cocksucker die if we just cut him loose? What I mean is, is the fall down to the water far enough to snap his neck?"

"Good question," said Big Noogie.

Martin Trebeaux was flapping like a spastic fruit bat.

"Because if he don't die," the toothpick man went on, "and the sharks don't get him, we could be fucked."

"I understand."

"He'll tell the cops everything. You know he goddamn will."

"The man never shuts up," Big Noogie agreed.

He was ready to get off the bridge, which was spackled with bird shit and stunk acridly.

"So, Noog, want me to pull him up or what?"

"Yeah, pull him up. You need some help?"

"Better not. Your back's still hurt, 'member?"

Big Noogie had popped a lumbar disk while burying a body in the Meadowlands. The dead guy weighed like two-eighty and they'd had a bitch of a time rolling him into the hole. What had ruptured was Big Noogie's L5-S1, right above his butt bone. He got the same surgery as Tiger Woods, yet his lower back continued to ache and now his right foot was permanently asleep. Golf was out of the question.

"Aw, fuck it," he said, and grabbed one of Trebeaux's legs.

Back in the car, they allowed their captive to remove the hemostats from his ball sack and put on some clothes. The toothpick nibbler was driving; Big Noogie stayed in the back with the sand man.

"I want a new beach, a real beach," Big Noogie told him, "or you're dead."

"Absolutely! I'm on it," Trebeaux promised. He noticed the mobster was holding his cell phone.

"Guess who's on your voicemail, Marty? The Key West cops."

"I didn't call 'em! Swear on my mother's grave!"

Big Noogie grinned, his teeth shaded brown from all the coffee and cigars. "I know you didn't call 'em. Otherwise we'd have thrown you off that bridge and the sharks'd be chewin' on your fat ass." He wiggled the phone. "The cops want to know about that car you rented."

"The Buick?"

"They towed it from where you left it. Now they got a few questions," Big Noogie said. "Questions you ain't gonna answer."

"Of course not. How could I?" Trebeaux cupped his crotch protectively. "I'm not a rat. I'm not a squealer. I'm not suicidal, either."

"Prove it."

"How?"

"By shutting the fuck up," said Big Noogie.

Turning to look out the window, he thought: *Once we get our new sand, I'm done with this shitsucker.*

The Tesla had come into Zeto's possession after its owner, a man called Escambrine, fled the United States to avoid a prison hitch. A smuggler of exotic bromeliads, Escambrine had asked Zeto to care for the car until he could secure a forged passport and return to Florida for another illicit orchid raid in the Everglades.

Zeto had never driven an electric vehicle, and he'd heard mixed reviews. But with its racy lines, whiplash acceleration and high-tech interior, the Tesla proved to be a hit with the babes. Zeto also liked the novelty of gas-less motoring, although there were few car-charging stations in South Florida. Using a standard outlet was annoyingly slow; to speed the process Escambrine had advised using 240-volt sockets instead of a standard 110. Zeto could never make himself wait long enough before unplugging, and consequently the Tesla's mileage range was reduced to that of your average golf cart.

It didn't matter in a little town like Key West, but soon Zeto would be heading back to Miami, a drive he preferred not to interrupt with power-up pit stops. On Eaton Street he cased out a two-story guest-house where a young Latin man wearing neon-blue Beats was clearing the sidewalk using a jumbo electric leaf blower. Zeto attempted to inquire about the power source but the leaf blower was too loud, and the man declined to turn it off or remove his headphones. To signify the number 240, Zeto held up two fingers, then four fingers followed by a circle made with his thumb and an index finger. The man nodded vaguely and stepped around him.

Zeto followed the cord of the leaf-blowing machine to an external outlet on the shady side of the house. He whipped the Tesla into a side driveway, uncoiled the charging apparatus and connected the cable to the car. The problem arose when he attempted to plug the other end into the wall outlet. That it didn't fit properly would have been obvious to your average six-year-old. A simple adaptor lay unnoticed on the floor of the Tesla's backseat. Also available and untouched: an instruction manual.

Using a pair of side-cutter pliers Zeto unwisely endeavored to reconfigure the prongs on the recharge plug. A licensed electrician later summoned to the scene would determine that Zeto's brute effort not only damaged the prongs but also inflicted a one-inch slice in the cord, exposing wires that Zeto was inadvertently touching when he jammed the plug for the last time into the wall. It was not beneficial to be kneeling in a water puddle at the moment of contact.

The socket blew out with a champagne-cork pop that flattened Zeto, his face forever a mask of puzzlement. A dime-sized burn on his right wrist emitted a tendril of smoke that was dissipating by the time his body got discovered by the landscape attendant, who'd stalked up the driveway to find out why his leaf blower had suddenly crapped out.

Juan Zeto-Fernández was identified by fingerprints and also by the prison scar encircling his neck, a failed garroting plainly visible on a recent mug shot. A medical examiner would later rule the cause of death to be heart failure caused by electrocution. The report would also note the presence of coronary artery disease and cocaine in the bloodstream, two factors that didn't improve Zeto's chances of surviving high voltage. His gold earring was eventually claimed by a cousin who declined to pay for the funeral.

The Key West policeman who searched the Tesla found a loaded handgun under the driver's seat. In the rear of the vehicle, among the ripe Wendy's wrappers and fry cartons, was a wrinkled paper upon which an unusual list had been printed. It was immediately turned over to the office of Sheriff Sonny Summers.

Detective Rogelio Burton texted a screenshot to Yancy:

Green Room Rider for MR. BUCK NANCE

Four 24 oz. cans of Pabst Blue Ribbon beer on chipped ice

Two bottles of Jack Daniel's whiskey

Six large bags of Fritos original corn chips

100 M & M's (green only)

10 Reese's peanut butter cups (refrigerated at 46 degrees F)

Two Bose speakers with Bluetooth

One 8 oz. wedge of Grand Cru Gruyère Surchoix cheese from Emmi Roth's in Monroe, Wisconsin

No fucking veggie platters!

Yancy texted back: "Your missing shitkicker is a total diva."

He arrived at the impound lot still wearing his medical gloves from the Reef Raff condiment probe. No larval intruders had been detected in the mango salsa; the wriggling culprit turned out to be a juvenile ring-necked snake, harmless as a guppy and quite lovely with its coral-colored belly. Still, Yancy had no choice except to write up the bistro for violating section 35-a of the health statutes, an unfairly broad prohibition of animals in food-prep areas. The docile reptile now lay curled inside Yancy's shirt pocket, for future release.

The blue exam gloves made Yancy look official, so the watchman at the impound lot let him enter with no questions. Yancy combed the Tesla but didn't find any other traces of Buck Nance. Afterward he tracked Burton to the Casa Marina where the detective had gone to interview Buck's manager, a man named Lane Coolman.

"What did he have to say?" Yancy asked Burton in the lobby.

"Coolman's not in his room. Or at the pool. Or the bar."

"What about the flash-fried felon?"

"Nance's talent agency says they've never heard of the late Señor Zeto, and have no idea how the Green Room list ended up in that car."

"It takes a special kind of moron to electrocute yourself with a Tesla."

"A Darwin finalist," Burton agreed.

"I'm done with this case, by the way."

"That's a heartbreaker."

As they walked to the parking lot, Yancy noticed that the coconut palms along the driveway were rustling. A fresh breeze had kicked up from the northwest, signaling another cold front. He breathed in the spice of night-blooming jasmine and said, "Who leaves Florida for Sweden in the dead of winter? Somebody who's dumping a boyfriend, that's who."

"Have some faith," Burton said.

"I got a bad feeling, Rog."

"When she sends the first picture, what you want is a selfie."

"Suggesting she's alone," Yancy said.

"Right. Because if it's not a selfie, that means somebody else took the photo."

"Yeah, I get that."

"Her new ski instructor, for example. Six two, long blond hair and a schlong like a cobra."

"I'm glad you find this amusing."

"Be an optimist for once."

"Not me," said Yancy.

"A Buick rented to Coolman was found near the Sears. Matter of fact, it was one of two Buicks towed the same night from the same parking lot. Both had been struck from behind by other cars. They found one of those, too, in the same Sears lot—an '05 Civic with a mashed front end. Paint scrapes match up with Buick number two."

"Basically a demolition derby on Roosevelt. Weird."

"We'll sort it all out, don't worry," Burton said. "I know you're a busy man."

"Who rented the second Buick?"

"Guy named Martin Trebeaux. He's got a condo in Miami Beach. We're in the process of locating him. Hey, don't you have a contaminated meat locker somewhere to inspect? A horde of marauding earwigs or whatever?"

Yancy pulled off each of his gloves with a snap. "Just come out and say it, Rog. You're gonna miss me."

They walked out of the La Concha just as a tow truck rumbled by with the Tesla on the hook. The doors of the car had been sealed with yellow police tape.

Merry Mansfield said, "Looks like they busted my boy Zeto."

"Good! One less psychopath." Lane Coolman put on his sunglasses. "He better not rat me out, swear to God."

It was their second day together, and still no leads on Buck Nance. They'd hit all the island's top hotel bars and pool scenes, Merry's theory being that Buck would tire of slumming and gravitate back toward high-end accommodations.

She caught Coolman peeping down her blouse and said, "FYI, the last three guys I went to bed with couldn't get it up."

Her words were like salt on a slug.

"What's the matter, Bob?"

"I'm fine. And it's *Lane,* okay?"

"Some men are intimidated because I expect a marathon performance. But you aren't scared of me, are you?"

"That's very funny," Coolman said, still shriveling.

"You'll get maybe one shot, so make it your best. There's a strict protocol."

"I seriously cannot wait."

"Just be ready," said Merry. "The mood hits me, watch out."

She'd come up with a stopper like that every time Coolman thought about driving to the airport and catching the next flight out. He was fairly sure Buck had already fled Key West, but he didn't want to leave until he screwed Merry, just once. It was ego. It was revenge. It was unhinged carnal curiosity.

What on earth did she mean by "protocol"?

They ate lunch at Clippy's, where Buck Nance had deposited his beard shavings as a garnish. Afterward they tried to reconstruct his route on foot. The farther they walked, the more certain Coolman became that Buck was gone. Wild chickens were roaming all over the streets.

"Your pal ought to feel right at home," Merry said.

"You kidding? He hates the damn things. Says they're filthy and crawling with lice."

"Chickens get lice?"

"I work hard not to think about it," said Coolman.

Midway through the second season of *Bayou Brethren*, Buck had developed a loathing for the birds his family was supposed to be raising. Nobody knew whether it was triggered by some bad incident, or simply too much time on the cock farm. Krystal said it was the incessant crowing that upset her husband, who, like his brothers, had naively believed roosters vocalize only at dawn. At Coolman's insistence, the show's producers had agreed to cut back Buck's scenes with live fowl, and utilize a green screen whenever possible.

"Point is," said Coolman, "he'd never hang around a place like this."

Merry kept walking. "But where could Bucky Boy go? Based on his so-called comedy act, Miami's definitely not his scene. The Hispanic milieu, and all," she said. "Lauderdale might be more his speed."

Coolman shook his head. "Buck's not a beach person."

Merry eyed him over the rims of her oversized shades. "Of course we're assuming the best-case scenario—that he hasn't been murdered and dumped in a ditch somewhere, right? That he's still alive and making his own decisions, not rotting somewhere with multiple ice-pick wounds to the torso."

"Jesus, what a ray of fucking sunshine you are."

Back in L.A., Amp had issued a statement on behalf of the Nance family announcing that Buck was in rehab at an undisclosed location. The subject of his alcoholism would be dealt with "frankly and openly" in future installments of *Brethren*. In the meantime, retail sales of the popular Buck Nance action figure, mud flaps, gun racks, spittoons, rattlesnake vests and other patriarch-related merchandise would be suspended until Buck's recovery, when he returned to the show. Most of the ugly online tumult was already ebbing, except for a few nutty tweeters obsessed with the rumor that Buck was a Taliban sympathizer. To avert more trouble on that front, Platinum Artists had dispatched a "personal assistant" to move in with the half-cocked Miracle, take her shopping and sabotage her Internet connections.

Coolman didn't want to think Buck was a victim of foul play. In the absence of a corpse he remained hopeful that his star client's disappearance was caused by a drunken binge, a contract-related tantrum, or an exploitable emotional breakdown. In any case there wasn't much that Coolman could accomplish traipsing the streets of old Key West.

"Let's go back to the room," he said to Merry.

"And do what?"

"Watch a movie. Wait for the phone to ring."

"I could use a massage," she said.

"That's an outstanding idea."

"From a deep-tissue professional, Bob. You may observe, not participate."

In the lobby they were cornered by a perspiring crew from TMZ. Coolman acted miffed though he was secretly pleased that the tabloids knew he was Buck Nance's manager, and had gone to the trouble of tracking him down.

"No comment," he chirped, hoping Amp would see the clip on TV and appreciate his coolness under fire.

Merry covered her face as they elbowed past the cameraman. When Coolman asked her why, she whispered, "Practice, sugar. For when I'm famous."

In the hotel suite they drank watery mimosas until the arrival of the masseuse, a matron with bowling-ball shoulders and an Eastern European accent. She unfolded a table and asked Coolman to leave the room. Merry said it was all right if he stayed.

"Bob just quit the monastery," she told the masseuse. "We're easing him into the secular life. What do you say? His poor little pecker looks like a baby sparrow, waiting to fly."

"Then of course," said the masseuse.

Coolman turned crimson. Merry peeled down to nothing and stretched out on her tummy with her face turned away, her hair tumbling like a waterfall off the edge of the table. She held her long legs straight, tapping the heels of her feet together like Judy Garland in the ruby slippers. The masseuse began kneading Merry's bottom and hummed a harsh Slavic lullaby that killed Coolman's lust.

He went into the bathroom, shut the door and called his divorce attorney, Smegg, who demanded to know why he'd missed the mediation hearing that morning.

"Shit, I totally forgot about it," Coolman said. "I'm seriously stuck in Florida."

"No biggie. Rachel never showed, either."

"Really?"

"She's in Tahoe with Drucker," said Smegg, "fellating him dawn to dusk."

"What? I thought that was over."

"She friended me on Facebook."

"Classic," said Coolman.

"It's all to your ultimate benefit, this licentious taunting. A poor reflection on your wife's character, most judges would agree. Having said that, I hope you're getting laid down there in Margaritaville. Discreetly, please."

"Yeah, I can hardly walk, my dick's so sore."

Drucker, the priapic toad from William Morris, would be gleefully following the Buck Nance fiasco in the media. Coolman suspected that Drucker was angling to steal Buck away from Platinum, and milking

Rachel for intel in the sack. Lately her legal team had been dogging Coolman to produce a roster of his clients and the commissions they'd paid, but so far the deft Smegg had been able to stonewall.

The mediation session had been reset for the following week. Coolman assured Smegg that he'd be back in L.A. before then.

When he emerged from the bathroom, Merry Mansfield looked up from the massage table and said, "So, Padre, did you take care of your little bird?"

"I'll be down at the tiki bar."

Slowly she rolled on her side. "You sure about that, Bob?"

On her sleek thigh he spied the pink razor knick from the fateful crash on Ramrod Key. His hungering gaze rose to one of her cinnamon-freckled breasts, where in lieu of a standard nipple ring Merry had opted for a bronzed pop-tab from a beer can, or possibly a soft drink.

"Diet Fresca," she confirmed. "Don't give me that look, because you are totally digging it. Tell me I'm wrong."

Oiling her palms, the masseuse spoke up. "Father, do you still hear confessions?"

Coolman shook his head vehemently and made for the door. "I'm not a goddamn priest," he snapped.

The masseuse, a reconfirmed Catholic, whirled and decked him with a slippery right hook. He awoke sometime later sprawled across one of the king-sized comforters, Merry pressing an ice-filled towel to his jaw.

"Time to get up, sugar," she said. "The police are waiting downstairs."

"What for?"

"A man's been killed on the Conch Train. They need you to look at the body."

NINE

Yancy took Deb's metal detector and walked the neighborhood collecting bottle caps, loose change and the odd brass bullet jacket. He was thinking about the bumblefuck who'd electrocuted himself with the Tesla. How did Buck Nance's Green Room demands end up in that car? The list probably belonged to Lane Coolman, Buck's manager, though Yancy couldn't imagine a scenario in which Coolman would willingly ride around with a goon like Zeto. Maybe it was he who'd crashed into Coolman's rented Buick, but then why was there no damage to the Tesla? Only Coolman could fill in the blanks; Yancy hoped he'd be easier to find than Buck.

There remained the additional mystery of Martin Trebeaux, the driver of the second crunched Buick—where did he fit into this rolling clusterfuck?

Back at the house Yancy tried to FaceTime Rosa so she could share the sunset over his shoulder. Then he remembered she was still airborne, and unreachable.

The cold front had chased away the bugs and energized the little Key deer; two does and a buck friskily crossed the empty lot next door. Yancy went indoors, put on some Stevie Ray and lit a fat one. When

Deb and her boyfriend appeared on the front steps, he flung open the door and spread his arms.

"Back the fuck off!" yeeped the lawyer, his muskrat eyes darting fearfully to Yancy's Remington, at rest in the corner.

"Relax, counselor. Who wants a hit?"

"I'm here to tell you—*order* you—to leave my fiancée alone."

"My heart crumbles," said Yancy. Then, spinning toward Deb: "So, then, it's over?"

"Real funny," she said.

He hung his head. "You're one lucky bastard, Brandon. Among her myriad charms, she can suck the husk off a coconut."

Yancy dodged Brock Richardson's right cross and dropped him with a knee. Deb called Yancy a prick, though instead of tending to her whimpering spouse-to-be she took a long smokeless toke from her e-cig. Richardson wobbled upright like a newborn calf while Yancy re-fired his joint.

The lawyer panted, "For that I'm gonna sue your ass."

"If only you could find the courthouse."

"I know all about you, Yancy, everything—like why you're not a detective anymore. My people have a file *this* thick"—thrusting a liberally spaced thumb and forefinger—"about your felony arrest." For Deb's benefit he added: "For assaulting a highly respected doctor whose wife you were screwing."

"Not my finest moment. However, I thought he was hurting her."

"I've seen the police report," Richardson sneered. "You used a goddamn—"

"Handheld appliance. It's true." Yancy turned to Deb. "Which reminds me, darling. Do you want your metal detector back?"

"Wait—what?" said Richardson.

Yancy's eyebrows danced. "She's a kinky one, Brad."

"Oh shut up," Deb snapped. "This little visit wasn't my idea."

"Well, it's a good time to clear the air. Sit down," Yancy said to the lawyer. "Or don't. You should be aware that your attractive though hard-edged future bride approached *me,* not the other way around. She managed to lose her expensive engagement ring somewhere on your property, and enlisted my help to find it."

Richardson seemed to teeter on his heels.

Yancy went on: "She offered a reward, which I declined. A substantial reward."

He winked, prompting this from Deb: "I hate your guts."

It wasn't easy to pity a woman who wore Lilly Pulitzer on Big Pine Key. "Wait here," Yancy instructed the twosome, "and try not to dismember each other."

Carefully he navigated to the carport and returned with the metal detector and a plastic bait bucket, which he placed on the floor for Richardson's inspection. "Here's all I found so far. Bottle caps, ammo, but no diamond, sad to say." Yancy had earlier pocketed the coins.

Richardson was aghast. "You lost the fucking ring and didn't tell me?" he screaked at Deb. "And now you're trusting this sociopath to give it back if he finds it? Have you lost your goddamn mind? Seriously, am I engaged to a mental defective?"

"Maybe you should've bought me my own rock, you cheap sonofabitch, instead of giving me your fat ex-girlfriend's!"

The shouting went on for a while. Yancy was grateful to be stoned. He picked up the twelve-gauge and reclined on the sofa, trying to maintain focus. Using his phone he clicked the stereo to his Mudcrutch playlist.

When the couple in his living room ran dry of taunts, he said, "Listen up, Brick. The diamond ring? It can be found."

"It's *Brock.* And guess what, they're set to clear the damn lot in two days."

"Then never mind. Once the bulldozers get here, ha, it's over. The slab gets poured, you'll never see that stone again. How much did it set you back? Two hundred grand's the number Deb mentioned. And no insurance, for some reason." Yancy yawned. "Now refresh my memory. Who's the mental defective?"

When the lawyer took a step toward him, Yancy raised the shotgun barrel to waist level. Richardson wore a crocodile belt befitting a class-action ace. Deb grabbed his arm warning, "Just stay cool. He's crazy."

"You told him how much the ring cost? Seriously?" Richardson hissed. "Unfuckingbelievable! You don't think he's gonna run straight to a pawnshop if he finds it?" He glowered at Yancy. "I bet he already did."

Yancy clicked his teeth. "Deborah, my little spitfire, you never told me your beloved was a high-stakes gambler."

Richardson raised his palms. "I'm just sayin'—"

"No, no, by all means, summon your contractor and tell him to crank up the heavy equipment pronto. Clear your precious lot and pour the concrete, you really think I've got the ring. Oh, and good fucking luck getting a warrant to search my house. You do recall from law school what a warrant requires? Probable cause, which you don't have. But go ahead and roll the dice—or, as an alternative . . ."

"What now? What's the alternative?" Deb said dully.

"Don't let your crew disturb so much as a twig on that land. We'll keep on searching for your overpriced jewel night and day until we recover it." When Yancy stood up with the Remington, Richardson crow-hopped backwards a step.

"Fine. Brilliant. Now would you please tell him," Deb said, "that we never had sex."

"That's true, sir. Not even a covert grope." Yancy spoke solemnly.

The lawyer said, "I don't trust a goddamn word you say."

"Of course not. You'd have to be a fool."

"God, what's in your shirt?" Deb was staring at Yancy's breast pocket, which had begun to twitch.

He'd forgotten about the ring-necked snake he had rescued from the mango salsa at the Reef Raff. He took out the little reptile to show his visitors, who hastily departed without a civil goodbye. The Porsche was a cherry speck by the time Yancy emerged to release the squirming snake in his front yard. The text from Rogelio Burton arrived soon thereafter. Yancy was too baked to drive so he cabbed it back to town.

Burton was waiting at the crime scene.

. . .

Abdul-Halim Shamoon had been born in Syria and raised in Brook-lyn Heights, where he still resided. He owned a prosperous discount electronics shop in midtown Manhattan, half of a taxi medallion and a dozen refrigerated freight units near LaGuardia. Twice a year he treated himself to a cruise, always alone, because his children were grown and his wife of three decades got seasick. Abdul-Halim looked forward to these solitary trips. He was free to do whatever he wished, and no one tried to steer him away from the fun. The ship that brought him from Miami to Key West was called the *Carib Vagabond,* and it would continue on to San Juan, St. Thomas and Nassau. Unfortunately, Abdul-Halim never got to explore those scenic ports of call.

After debarking with twenty-three hundred other passengers, Abdul-Halim stopped at a kiosk in Mallory Square where he purchased a ceramic seahorse and a smallish watercolor of a blue-faced parrotfish. Then he went to Captain Tony's and ordered a rum-and-Coke because it looked like straight Coke, in case a more devout Muslim might see him drinking. He nearly fell off his barstool trying to count all the bras stapled to the ceiling; some were so astoundingly large that they con-jured shameful parachute fantasies. After downing another drink (it *was* Key West), Abdul-Halim walked outside and actually shivered in the wind. Florida wasn't supposed to get so cold. With guidebook in hand he trekked down Duval Street to the Southernmost Point. There he took a cheerful selfie and sent it to his wife, who texted back: "Have fun. The downstairs toilet is backed up."

Thirty-three minutes later Abdul-Halim boarded one of the mustard-yellow Conch Trains, which were actually jointed trams that puttered through the island's quainter streets. Abdul-Halim wasn't wearing his kufi or any traditional garb that would have advertised his Arab heritage. The other passengers said he was approached by a shirt-less, middle-aged white man wearing a banded Panama hat. There were differing accounts of what happened next. A couple from England told the police that Abdul-Halim jumped from the moving tram car when the white man began shrieking at him. Another passenger said there was a struggle first. Still another said the shirtless rider cold-bloodedly shoved Abdul-Halim off the Conch Train.

In any event, the accosted man sacrificed himself to protect his souvenirs, locking both arms around his shopping bags. Having no way to break his own fall, he smacked the pavement facedown at full force. The impact drove the pointy snout of the ceramic seahorse into the soft cleft beneath his sternum, where it snapped off, puncturing his aorta. Blood spurts ruined the pretty parrotfish painting, as well.

"God Almighty," said Yancy when he looked at the body.

Burton motioned for him to lower the tarp. "You smell like cheap weed, by the way."

"Oh, it's not cheap." Yancy had pulled on a pair of medical gloves but somehow he couldn't fit his left pinkie into the proper finger holder. "Who is this poor guy?"

"A tourist. The suspect would be our missing shitkicker." The detective summarized what the other Conch Train riders had said.

"Motive, Rog?"

"The victim was a Muslim. Nance hates Muslims."

"And we know that . . . how?"

"I'll show you," said Burton.

Yancy followed him to his car, where he took out an iPad and opened an amateur video of Buck preaching to a small congregation at a church called the First Chickapaw Tabernacle of Hope and Holiness.

"This went up on YouTube for about seven seconds," said the detective, "which apparently was long enough."

"Brothers and sisters, let's stop kiddin' ourselves. The Muslim ain't our friend. He ain't our comrade. The Muslim, deep down they all want the same thing Al Katie wants—"

"He means al Qaeda," Burton translated.

"—which is the total destruction of white Christianity. The Muslim, now, you might actually know one or two of 'em personally. You might even think, 'Oh, he seems friendly enough. I like that wife of his, too.' And maybe

their kids are on the same soccer team as yours, and every Saturday you see this happy Muslim family out at the county fairgrounds, cheerin' and handin' out grape Gatorades and so forth. And you might think, 'Well, they're decent folks. Nuthin' t'all like those cold-blooded heathens who hijacked our airplanes and flew 'em into the World Trade headquarters or whatever.'

"But I'm here to tell you, the Muslim can't never be trusted, no matter how kindly and normal he acts. They ain't no true peace or love in his soul because his religion decrees his sworn enemy to be Jesus Christ, our Lord 'n' Savior. Also the United States of America, which will fall only when white Christianity succumbs. So, brothers and sisters, all I'm sayin' is don't let your guard down. Stay vigilant and suspicious, and we will prevail. To be weak and softhearted is to be doomed. Oh, and all these things I'm warnin' you about? Same goes for the homosexual crowd and the Negroes.

"Now, lay your right hand on your neighbor's knee, and let us pray . . ."

"Possibly the lamest Cajun accent ever," Yancy said.

Burton agreed. "More hillbilly than swamp rat."

"The hand on the knee is a clever touch."

"Yeah, literally. He makes 'em sit boy-girl-boy-girl."

The detective put away his iPad and locked the car. He and Yancy made their way through the rubberneckers, ducked under the perimeter ribbon and returned to the lake of blood surrounding Abdul-Halim Shamoon. A crime-scene tech was enumerating the fragments of the lethal seahorse figurine.

Yancy said he was mystified about why Buck Nance had begun assaulting strangers—first the artist in the courtyard, now a cruise-ship passenger.

"People do come unglued," Burton said.

"Was he wearing a hat?"

"One of those Panama jobs. How'd you know?"

"What else you got?"

"Ink," Burton said. "Our witnesses saw a fresh tat on his back, right across the shoulder blades. Know what it says?"

"Hit me, Rog."

"'HAIL CAPTAIN COCK.' Roman script, all capital letters."

"Gotta love the spirit," said Yancy. "I'm putting myself back on the case, by the way."

"Uh, no, you're not."

"He killed a guy, which changes everything. You wouldn't have called if you didn't want my help."

Burton said, "Don't get carried away. This is strictly under the radar."

"Where I do my best work."

"Andrew, we're not having this conversation."

"Of course not. And we're not standing next to a body tarp, either."

They stepped back to make way for the coroner's crew.

It was Lane Coolman's first ride in a squad car since college. Merry Mansfield sat in the caged backseat and downed two eight-hour energy drinks. The cop kept checking her out in the rearview; she still wore a sexy sheen from the massage oil.

"How's your jaw?" she asked Coolman.

"I'm fine," he said, though speaking was painful.

When the cop asked what had happened, Merry cut in, "I clocked him, okay? I've got jealousy issues, he's got fidelity issues. You know that tune. Truth? He's lucky I didn't chop off his pecker and feed it to the pelicans."

"Don't say anything more," the officer said, "or I'll have to arrest you."

"Oh, he won't press charges."

"Under state law it doesn't matter. So do us all a favor and hit the Mute button."

Coolman piped angrily: "She didn't lay a hand on me! I don't know why she'd say such a sick thing. Swear on the Bible, she never touched me."

Merry tapped a cardinal fingernail on the steel grid separating the cop from his passengers. "See how he's trying to protect me, officer? That's more than loyalty. It's true love."

"I barely know this chick," Coolman protested through clamped teeth.

The cop's slack expression established that he didn't give a shit. His job was to drive them to a corpse, period.

Frances Street had been blocked off on each side of the parked Conch Train. There were five open trolley-style cars hooked to a tractor dolled up like an old-time locomotive. The restless passengers were being interviewed by Key West city detectives, one of whom peeled off to greet Coolman and Merry. As they were led toward the bright yellow body tarp, Coolman's stomach clenched and he tasted sherry-doused chowder on the rebound from lunch.

He felt sure he was going to see the body of Buck Nance, which was sad and shocking, yes, but also it pissed him off. Self-destruction was acceptable in show business when your career was tanking, but not while you're starring in America's hottest cable show. *Bayou Brethren* was still a monster hit, generating monster revenues. The other Nance brothers would carry on for a season or two, but without Buck's crusty presence the ratings would slide and the network would lose enthusiasm. Meanwhile, facing the dark freeze of agent purgatory at Platinum Artists, Coolman would be forced to dredge, poach and beg for a new top-name client.

"You folks ready?" asked the Key West detective.

Coolman said, "Yeah, let's do this." Like he'd viewed a hundred stiffs.

The tarp was tugged aside, and there lay a slightly built Mideastern-looking man with a wispy coal-black beard. His open eyes were glazed, his shirt front was drenched with blood—and he was a complete stranger.

Coolman made no effort to conceal his relief. He tried to high-five Merry, who backed away muttering, "Jesus, Bob, dial it down."

"That's not him!" Coolman whooped to the detective.

"Who?"

"Buck Nance!"

"We know that, sir. We believe Mr. Nance was the assailant."

Coolman was stunned. "You think Buck did this? That's insane."

"Do you know the victim? Or maybe your client knew him." The detective pointed with the toe of his shoe.

"I've never ever seen the guy before. You can't be serious." Coolman wished somebody would close the dead man's eyes.

The city detective asked him to please notify the department as soon as he heard from Mr. Nance. Coolman was then passed along to a different detective—Burton was his name—on special assignment from the sheriff.

"Buck did *not* murder anybody," Coolman repeated.

Burton nodded agreeably. "It's a manslaughter all the way. Argument turns to punches or maybe just a shove, and poor Mr. Shamoon tumbles off the Conch Train. All that blood you saw? The unlucky bastard impaled himself on some knick-knack he bought for like nine bucks. So, you're right, it's definitely not murder. They'll file it as manslaughter one but they'll let him plead to a lesser. Anyway, you and I need to talk."

Coolman said he had to make a phone call right away.

"He's quite the big shot," Merry said to Burton. "A mover and shaker. Can't you tell?"

"What's your connection here, ma'am? Are you with the same talent agency as Mr. Coolman? Do you know Mr. Nance?"

Merry laughed and laughed. "No, no, I've never even watched that stupid rooster show. Mr. Coolman and I just recently met. He bought me a swimsuit and a so-so lunch, which he thinks entitles him to a courtesy fuck. It does not."

"Don't forget the massage," Coolman added acidly.

"You men!"

"Go make your phone call," Burton said to Coolman. "I'll expect you back here in five minutes."

For privacy Coolman hustled halfway down the block. He tried Amp's super-secret cell number, but there was no answer. Coolman left a long message relating what he knew about the death on the Conch Train, adding: "Buck's in the deepest of shit, dude. He's gonna need a lawyer, so call me back ASAP."

Burton was huddling with his Key West counterparts, so Coolman went looking for Merry. He found her speaking to a tall, lean man with a baked-in Florida tan.

"Say hello to Inspector Yancy," Merry said.

Except for the blue hospital gloves, Yancy was dressed more like a bartender than a detective. And he smelled like grass.

"Are you in Homicide?" Coolman asked doubtfully.

"No, I'm on loan from another agency."

"Buck Nance didn't kill anyone, okay? The whole idea is ludicrous. You've seen his TV show, right?"

"Indeed I have."

"Well, then, you know," said Coolman, "he couldn't hurt a flea."

"Still it doesn't look good. Let's be honest." Yancy swung a saddish gaze toward the body tarp. "Mr. Nance doesn't have a reputation for cultural tolerance. I watched one of the videos from the Parched Pirate. Talk about making a poor impression."

"Andrew wants to take us to dinner," Merry said. "He knows an oyster bar we can walk to from here."

So it's Andrew already? thought Coolman. *Jesus, she doesn't waste any time.*

He told Yancy he didn't do shellfish because he was hyper-allergic.

Merry sighed. "Then order a freaking cheeseburger, Bob. Let's just get out of here, okay?"

Yancy looked amused. "'Bob'? I thought your name was Lane."

"Inside joke," Coolman growled.

"Tell me what happened to that car you rented. The silver Buick—the one they towed from the Sears lot."

"What? Oh." Coolman glanced anxiously at Merry, who was unfazed and in his opinion standing too close to Yancy. "I, uh, backed into a tree."

"At about forty miles an hour, from the looks of it."

"I don't . . . who do you work for, Inspector?"

Coolman was saved from Yancy by Detective Burton, who led him to a quiet area and asked too many questions. He tried to hide his surprise when Burton brought up Zeto's name, and he asserted he'd never met the man. Likewise he played dumb when the detective mentioned Buck's Green Room manifesto. Coolman guessed it had fallen from his pocket during the kidnapping, but to Burton he feigned bafflement.

When the subject of the damaged rental car arose, Coolman stuck with the lie about hitting a tree. He didn't wish to complicate his mission, which was to find Buck and bring him back to Los Angeles. Burton undoubtedly would have been entertained by a truthful account of the crash, especially Merry Mansfield's razor antics, but with lust on his mind Coolman decided to shield her from the authorities. Later he could have kicked himself for being such a sucker.

Because after the detective finished interviewing him, Coolman went looking for his redheaded companion—and she was gone. She'd waltzed off to dine with her new friend, Inspector Yancy.

Just the two of them, of course.

TEN

On the fourteenth of February, unseasonably hot and calm, Martin Trebeaux and Dominick "Big Noogie" Aeola boarded a New York–bound flight at Miami International. Trebeaux was dragged down the concourse by an inbred Irish setter wearing a blaze-orange vest stamped: "Working Service Dog." The setter had no special training whatsoever; in fact, it barely responded to its own name, which was "John." Trebeaux had purchased the official-looking vest for thirty-four dollars online, no documentation required. A shrink who lived in Trebeaux's building had composed a letter for the airlines saying Trebeaux was emotionally unfit to travel unless accompanied by a "comfort animal," specifically John.

"They gotta let him on the plane," Trebeaux explained to Big Noogie. "It's an FAA rule."

"You are the scum of the scum."

"No, it's the hot new thing. Everybody's doing it."

"Like who?"

"Like half the Hamptons, that's who. Know how much Delta charges to fly a full-grown dog in cargo? Look how happy John is here with us."

"Make him lie down," said Big Noogie, who was as large as his nickname suggested. Even in a bulkhead row he felt cramped.

"I can't make him lie down. I can't make him do anything," Trebeaux confessed. "He doesn't really pay attention."

Big Noogie wrapped a hand around the setter's silky snout and bent over until they were nose to nose. "Yo, John," he said. "Lie the fuck down."

The dog flopped onto the floor.

"Now *that* is respect," Trebeaux said, neatly coiling the leash in his lap.

"Get him off my feet or he's goin' in the overhead."

"Sure, Dominick. Absolutely."

Trebeaux understood he was still alive only because a bright new beach was being born behind the mob's Royal Pyrenees Hotel and Resort—a flawless white crescent that was the envy of neighboring hoteliers. Trebeaux had told Big Noogie that all thirty-eight thousand cubic yards had come from the northeastern coastline of Cuba. In truth the pristine crystals had been pirated from the Canaveral National Seashore, vacuumed from the shallows at night by high-volume dredges and then barged south to the Royal Pyrenees. The glistening booty was being fanned over the cheap gritty fill that Trebeaux's crews had initially deposited behind the hotel. Big Noogie found the new mantle so rich and velvety that he set aside his low opinion of Trebeaux and asked his associates in Queens to consider a shareholder role in Sedimental Journeys.

In other words, grab the whole goddamn company.

Trebeaux wasn't yet aware that he might be surrendering his beach-renourishing operation to the Calzone crime family, and the Calzone crime family wasn't yet aware that Trebeaux had no high-level connections in Havana, no secret source of fine Caribbean sand.

Somewhere over the Carolinas, Trebeaux offered to sell forty-nine percent of his company, but only if he remained chairman and CEO—that was the deal breaker. Big Noogie chuckled and said they'd sort out the details over lunch. For the rest of the flight he played Sudoku and exchanged no words with Trebeaux. During the bumpy descent to JFK,

Big Noogie looked out the window and saw rough waves on Jamaica Bay. The pilot came on the intercom and said the temperature was thirty-three degrees, have a wonderful day in the tri-state area.

A dingy Town Car picked up the men at the airport. They pulled over along the Van Wyck so that John the fake service dog could take a leak. The sight of the fluorescently garbed setter slowed traffic, New York motorists assuming it was a police K-9 sniffing for corpses.

The meeting was in Oceanside at a small joint called Crisco's— red-checked tablecloths, red lampshades, red walls. While waiting for the other mobsters to show up, Trebeaux ordered spaghetti, meatballs and prosciutto lasagna. John was ejected from the dining area after slurping a sausage from Big Noogie's plate. The owner of the place, Crisco himself, led the dog out the front door and placed it in the backseat of the Town Car.

Soon two men in long winter coats arrived. They were introduced to Trebeaux as "Joey" and "Vin," straight out of the movies. Joey was slender and going gray at the temples; Vin was younger and broad as a dumpster.

"You must be the sand man," said Joey.

Trebeaux bowed. Vin and Joey sat down and listened to his pitch. Surprisingly, they asked few questions.

"So, the demand for restored beaches is, literally, eternal," Trebeaux said in summary. "Soon as you lay one down it starts washing out to sea. Next thing you know, these suckers are back on the phone, begging for more sand."

Vin said, "We get it."

"As I told Dominick, I'm willing to sell forty-nine percent."

"How 'bout dis? We take a hundred percent, you get to fly home with your dick in one piece."

Trebeaux was silent for a few moments. Then: "At least can I keep the title of chairman? I just bought a shitload of letterhead."

Big Noogie chuckled. So did Vin and Joey and even Crisco, who was uncorking a bottle of Chianti for the table.

"You can call yourself El Fuckstick Supremo for all I care," said Joey, "but you still work for us."

"Can I ask about my salary?"

Big Noogie said, "It was me, I wouldn't."

After lunch they all walked outside and shook hands. Joey and Vin departed in a Suburban with tinted windows and mismatched tires. Big Noogie and Trebeaux got into the Town Car.

"Hey, where's John?" Trebeaux held up the empty orange vest.

The driver said, "I walked down to Starbucks for like five minutes. Came back he was gone."

"What kind of creep would steal a service dog?"

Big Noogie said, "You got a brother?"

Usually Crisco's was safer than the police precinct house. Everyone in the neighborhood knew who ate there; the regulars never even locked their cars. Whoever swiped Trebeaux's Irish setter had to be from somewhere else, Big Noogie said. He told the driver to put the word out: Bring back that goddamn mutt, or else.

Trebeaux said, "Don't worry about it, guys. Let's roll."

"But he's your pet dog, for Christ's sake."

"No big deal, Dominick. I'll pick up another one for the flight home."

"You're serious."

"Why not? We can hit a shelter on the way to Kennedy. I'll get directions off my phone."

The driver looked at Big Noogie, who said, "Unbelievable, right?"

Trebeaux was already scrolling through a list of animal adoption facilities in Queens. "But we've got to call the new one John, too," he explained, "because that's the name the shrink put on his letter, and that letter is what gets us bulkhead."

"Plus early boarding," said Big Noogie.

Thinking: *Scum of the scum.*

Jon David Ampergrodt couldn't believe the sheriff of Monroe County, Florida, wouldn't take his calls. *Everybody* took his calls. The sheriff's assistant said Sonny Summers was very busy. Jon David Ampergrodt replied that nobody could possibly be busier than himself, and he would greatly appreciate five precious minutes of the sheriff's time. The sheriff's assistant didn't sound particularly young or fuckable, like Jon David Ampergrodt's assistant, but her stance was loyal and unwavering. Jon David Ampergrodt came to admire her during the time he was being jerked around.

"Call me Amp," he'd say.

"No, Mr. Ampergrodt."

"Well, may I call you Jessie?"

"'Mrs. Kunkle' is fine."

Finally, one morning, a breakthrough. When Amp reached the sheriff's assistant, he said, "Please tell your boss I'm interested in donating another pile of money to his re-election."

Minutes later, the phone rang. It was Sonny Summers in Key West.

"I understand you've got a homicide on your hands," Amp said.

"Unfortunately. Tragically. A passenger from a cruise ship."

"And Buck Nance is your prime suspect? I must tell you that's totally absurd."

"Officially he's a person of interest," the sheriff said. "Mrs. Kunkle mentioned something about campaign donations?"

"You received the first bundle, I believe."

"Yes, and thank you."

"However, I'd been left with the impression that in exchange for our generous support, you'd make it a priority to track down Mr. Nance."

"Oh, we tried," said Sonny Summers. "Now we're trying even harder. His silver money clip and credit cards have been recovered. Those are solid leads."

"Outside of your department and the city police, who knows he's your main guy in this choo-choo train killing?"

"Not a soul. No one. Well, hardly anyone."

"Can you keep it quiet as long as possible?" Amp asked.

"I don't like press conferences. Actually, I don't *believe* in press conferences. We run a tight ship around here. No leaks."

"That's good to hear. I've got fifty other friends that are thinking of giving to your re-election committee." As before, these would be names collected at a soup kitchen near the Staples Center. Amp's assistant would arrange for the cutting of all the cashier's checks, drawn from a special company bank account.

"I'd be real grateful for the help," said the sheriff. "Just a reminder—"

"The max is a thousand dollars per customer. I remember."

Amp was no longer in a panic to get Buck Nance back on the cock farm. The first episode of *Bayou Brethren* completed after his disappearance had absolutely *killed* in the ratings. It had been written as a somber family discussion of Buck's recently fabricated struggle with booze and pills, setting the stage for his eventual return from fake rehab. During the taping, however, each of the brothers wandered off-script to share unflattering anecdotes meant to document Buck's disintegration and also sabotage his popularity with viewers. Krystal Nance had chimed in with an uncharacteristic tirade, having received revelatory correspondence (with photos attached) from a woman claiming to be Buck's secret mistress. Despite around-the-clock supervision, Miracle had somehow gained access to a laptop, and also to Krystal's personal email. As a result, the crying coach hired for Krystal faced an impossible task, and was sent back to L.A.

The success of the Buck-less *Brethren* thrilled Poe, the director. He persuaded the producers to accelerate the season's shooting schedule to two episodes per week, and shave the editing time by half. The mission: Exploit the domestic turbulence among the Nances to lure an even larger audience. Amp had been informed via conference call that Buck's phony rehab period should be extended until further notice; his presence in Pensacola was unneeded.

Amp wasn't sure if it would help or hurt the show if Buck was jailed for attacking an innocent Muslim. The malicious Internet chatter had mostly abated since YouTube had pulled the videos of Buck's bar monologue in Key West, but floating somewhere around cyberspace was another incendiary clip from a stridently anti-Islamic "sermon" that he'd delivered at the fake church. Amp had told no one in the Nance family or on the *Brethren* production team that Buck was now a murder suspect. So far, the only ones who knew were Amp, Lane Coolman and a high-powered Malibu defense lawyer—and, once more, Coolman had fallen off the planet.

He hadn't been heard from since he'd left the voicemail on the night of the Conch Train killing, two weeks earlier. It made Amp wonder if his protégé was wigging out because of the divorce. Coolman's first kidnap story had seemed shaky; maybe he'd made up the whole thing. Maybe he'd needed the "ransom" to cover his legal fees. Had Amp owned a fully formed conscience he would have experienced at least a tickle of guilt for boning Rachel Coolman on the sly, but he'd lost not a minute of sleep. It had been her idea, after all, and Amp was but one of many to meet her for a quick one at the Wilshire. That she would pauperize her future ex-husband in court was a given—it was California, right? And hadn't Coolman, a scheming hound himself, put the moves on every babe on the tenth floor, including Amp's own not-too-swift assistant, who'd almost said yes?

"I'm also concerned about Buck's manager," Amp said to the sheriff. "We haven't heard from him in a while. Could your people ask around?"

Sonny Summers said his people were pretty darn busy. Amp suspected they might hunt harder for Coolman if Amp offered to further fatten the next bundle of checks for the sheriff's re-election committee. Amp briefly considered making such a proposition, yet he couldn't summon a sense of urgency. The truth was, Coolman's absence at Platinum Artists had created no discernible void.

"Never mind," Amp told Sonny Summers. "He'll surface eventually."

"They usually do."

"But please let me know if you arrest Mr. Nance? Before I see it on the news."

"Don't worry. We'll do it low-key," the sheriff said.

"Low-key would be lovely."

Amp said goodbye and speed-dialed Rachel Coolman's number. He was free for lunch, and she ate fast. She did everything fast.

Yancy's situation worsened soon after the Conch Train killing, when Burton reversed field and told him to forget about the Buck Nance case. The sheriff had heard Yancy was poking around, and was threatening to leave him on roach patrol for eternity unless he backed off. Yancy accepted the news maturely and went bonefishing until the tide ran out. When he returned, his would-be neighbor Deb was sitting on the doorstep. Her nose was elaborately bandaged due to a vaping mishap—after too many cocktails she'd touched a vintage Ronson to the tip of her e-cig as if it was a Marlboro, sparking a minor detonation. Yancy withheld sympathy due to her sarcastic appraisal of his landscaping.

He invited her inside and went to fetch the metal detector. Naturally that's when Rosa happened to FaceTime him from overseas, Deb answering on his behalf. The two women were having an improbably civil chat when Yancy re-entered the living room. Deb handed him the phone on her way out the door.

"She drop by often?" Rosa asked in what Yancy prayed was a teasing tone.

"That's the future next-door neighbor I told you about."

"So you finally returned her diamond?"

"I will, I will."

"Andrew!"

"The mackerel dip aged aromatically so I switched to hummus." He told her of his plan to safekeep the ring until Deb and Brock the P.I. lawyer parted ways, their unbuilt villa a casualty of fractured romance.

Rosa said, "I cannot believe what I'm hearing."

"It'll never last. They're tragically mismatched."

"This is crazy. You're gonna get caught."

"Hey, is it snowing over there?"

Days passed before Rosa FaceTimed him again. Against all odds the call was answered by another unexpected female visitor, a worldly redhead who went by the name of Merry Mansfield. Yancy had met her at the scene of the Conch Train assault and harmlessly taken her for fried oysters while Burton interviewed her male companion, Buck Nance's manager. Over dinner Merry had downplayed her relationship with Lane Coolman, saying he was a mere diversion from her tedious day job as an appraiser of sunken treasure and maritime artifacts. Yancy found her to be a delightfully entertaining liar, but at the end of the evening he said goodbye with no thought of seeing her again.

Yet somehow she'd ferreted out his address and presented herself with no warning. She said Coolman had failed to return to the Casa Marina the night Yancy took her out. The man she playfully called "Bob" was staging a jealous sulk, she said, and not responding to her texts or voicemails. For days she'd continued to occupy the hotel room until being summoned to the front desk and informed that Platinum Artists was no longer picking up the tab—would Ms. Mansfield be paying with an Amex, MasterCard or Visa?

"Bottom line, I've got no place else to go," she said to Yancy after the taxi delivered her to his driveway.

"This is a phenomenally bad idea."

"Where's your spare bedroom, sugar?"

"It's uninhabitable at the moment."

"You've got a couch, right? Don't pretend you're not going to let me in, because we both know you will."

That afternoon as Yancy stood in the shower—having positioned his phone carefully on the countertop, between the floss and toothpaste—Merry breezed into the bathroom and sat down to pee. Moments later Yancy heard the dreaded chiming of FaceTime, and hollered for Merry not to answer. She did anyway.

Pawing shampoo suds from his eyes, he flung aside the shower curtain and vaulted dripping wet out of the tub. He slipped, no surprise, windmilling through the steam until his forehead smacked the tile. It was his sorry fate not to be knocked unconscious.

Merry placed the phone in his fingers, flushed the toilet and glided out the door. Yancy smiled wanly at Rosa, whose gaze was as frosty as the Oslo twilight.

"Are you naked, Andrew?"

"This is *not* a date, I swear to God. She just showed up at the door."

"A Jehovah's Witness in a tube top," said Rosa. "What a lucky fellow you are."

"It looks bad, I know. Two calls, two different women pick up my phone. But I haven't laid a lip on any of them—"

"Andrew, I'm not mad."

"You should be. *I* would be."

"I'm just disappointed."

"Christ, that's worse," Yancy said. "Anger cools. Disappointment only festers."

"I've decided to stay abroad a bit longer."

"Aw, don't do this. Please?" Thinking: *Did she really say "abroad"?*

"I want to see more of Norway."

"In the middle of winter. Norway."

"Honestly, I'm not angry," Rosa said.

"But you don't even ski."

"I can take lessons. Hello? I learned to paddleboard in like five minutes, remember?"

"Not the same," said Yancy. "Not even close."

"From now on—here's the new rule, okay? You listening? In the future, instead of me calling you, you call me. Preferably when you're not having company."

After the phone went dark Yancy wrapped a towel around his waist and threw himself on the couch. Merry prepared a bag of ice for his head. She apologized for pissing off his girlfriend. He said she definitely needed to find another place to crash.

That night he grilled bison burgers from Montana. For a beverage he stuck with iced tea because he knew he'd be driving. Merry was drinking Land Sharks and getting relaxed. She changed into a Guy Harvey leaping-marlin tee-shirt that she'd found folded inside a drawer—Rosa's Sunday morning wardrobe.

When they were done eating Merry helped clear the table and load the dishwasher. When she asked if Buck Nance had really clobbered that Muslim guy on the Conch Train, Yancy said he honestly didn't know. He told her he was working on a different case, one that required a different skill set.

It was the truth, too—a Code Red crisis at Clippy's, worse than beard remnants in the quinoa. This one was a bona fide onslaught, a furry monster's ball.

"Why'd you come find me?" he asked Merry.

"Not to have wild upside-down-in-the-mirror sex, if that's what you're thinking."

"Tell me your real name."

"The reason I'm here, I had a really good time that night at the oyster bar. You made me laugh—and not accidentally, like most guys. How lame is *that*? Because you're lookin' at the last girl in the world who should be chasing after a cop."

Yancy said, "I was once a kickass detective, that's true, but I've been ingloriously reassigned."

"Because you screwed up, right? There's a shocker."

"Her name was Bonnie, and she was married."

"That's it? Your big slip?"

"Her husband was a doctor, not a good man," Yancy went on. "One day I saw them together and mistakenly thought he was hurting her. I happened to be cleaning my car at the time so I went after him with my DustBuster. A case could be made that I got carried away. There was a proctological aspect to the encounter."

Merry howled. "You did him with a vacuum?"

"A cordless 12-volt. This was at Mallory Square, with swarms of tourists watching. The doctor pressed charges, I took a plea, lost my badge," said Yancy, "and terminated my torrid affair with Bonnie. Who turned out to be a fugitive, by the way, and torched the spec house that once stood right there." He pointed through a window at the empty lot next door. "She was trying to win me back, which didn't work. Still I confess I wasn't sad to see the place go up in flames. It was an abomination."

Merry uncrossed her fine legs. "Andrew, that's a fantastic story on such short notice."

"It's all true."

"Well, I can't wait to hear about the new job. What is it you do?"

"Inspect local eateries for evidence of filth, spoilage and unwanted fauna."

"No way!" she said.

"In fact, I've got to work tonight."

"Where? Can I come with?"

"A fancy joint in Key West," Yancy said, "and the answer is a hard no. Put on some underwear. I'll drop you at the Hyatt."

"Is it like an emergency?"

"Moving you to a hotel? Absolutely."

"Don't be a smartass. The restaurant call is what I'm talkin' about."

"Depends on your definition of emergency," said Yancy. "Does a galloping infestation qualify?"

Merry cringed. "You mean like in the Bible?"

"That would be a pestilence, though you're in the ballpark." Yancy reached beneath the sink and took out a pair of sky-blue medical gloves.

"Duty calls, darling," he said with the darkest of smiles.

ELEVEN

In the heyday of South Florida's exotic animal trade, niche-seeking entrepreneurs began importing an unusual creature called the giant Gambian pouched rat. In nature it can be found from Senegal to Mozambique, although like most rodents it hardily adapts to any environment. The tropicality of the Keys would prove ideal.

Weighing up to nine pounds, *Cricetomys gambianus* is the world's largest rat, a dubious selling point for pet stores. Its body coloration appears dark gray or brown, the belly fur is pale, and the tip of its long tail looks milky white, a trait that breeders hoped would add a cuteness factor. The animal's bat-like ears seem cartoonishly proportioned, while its tapered snout is lushly wreathed with probing whiskers. The term "pouched" doesn't refer to a kangaroo-style tummy pocket, but rather to grotesque cheek cavities with enough stretching capacity to hold a pork chop. Ravenous ground foragers, the supersized rodents will also scale trees and trellises in search of snacks. They are nocturnal, restless and perpetually fertile.

Not surprisingly, they never caught on as house pets. What limited market there was evaporated completely when U.S. health officials blamed the species for a harrowing outbreak of monkeypox, a fiercely contagious virus. The government reacted by banning importation of the African behemoths, but by then a breeder on Grassy Key had already set free his unwanted collection, which was thriving in the wild. All attempts to extirpate the wily invaders failed.

The breathless call from Clippy's came midway through the night's final seating. Tommy Lombardo immediately phoned Yancy and ordered him to get moving. "And no guns!" he added.

When Yancy got there he saw Mayor Neil Gluckman pacing outside the evacuated restaurant. Irv Clipowski stood by the front entrance holding a pitchfork. Meanwhile a sallow envoy from County Animal Control was examining the broken hinges of a live-catch trap that was large enough to hold a full-grown badger.

Yancy approached the mayor, who said, "He busted the damn trap! I mean, we had the cocksucker cold!"

"How the hell did it get out?"

The man from Animal Control spoke up: "Brains and brute fucking force. That's how." He loaded the damaged device into the back of his truck and drove away.

Clippy stepped forward saying, "One of the busboys opened the fire exit—it wasn't his fault, Andrew—and this godawful monster bolts straight into the dining area."

"Which was packed," added Neil.

"Neil was there. He saw it all," Clippy said.

"Night. Mare." Neil closed his eyes. "There was an older couple from Brisbane, they called it in as a rabid wallaby. I mean, dear God, they've already posted it on TripSwami."

"Even though we comped their drinks and dinner." Clippy sighed bitterly. "Heartless, Andrew, some people in this world."

Yancy felt badly for Clippy and the mayor. Weeks after the initial sighting, not a single pouched rat had been killed or captured on the property. Traditional rodent baits lay untouched in prime corners and crevices. Traps were found sprung or disabled, always empty. Exterminators from as far as Detroit had come and gone, each more vexed than the last.

"What did you tell your customers?" Yancy asked.

Clippy mumbled at his shoes. "We said it was a stray cat."

"One of the Hemingway cats," added Neil.

"Guys, come on."

"You got anything better?" Clippy snapped. "Under pressure, I don't think so."

Neil asserted their patrons never got a clear look at the animal because it was moving too fast. Yancy took the pitchfork from Clippy and said, "All right. Open the door."

He anticipated this inspection would repeat the pattern of previous visits. There would be clear evidence of occupation by mega-fauna—gnawed baseboards, shredded batts of insulation (the Gambies showing an appetite for R-19 fiberglass), territorial urine smears on the PVC, and a daunting abundance of bullet-sized pellets—but no visual confirmation. Yancy had yet to lay eyes on a pouchie, so he was at the mercy of his imagination. In his dreams the buck-toothed bastards charged at him like bull rhinos.

"Could you kill the lights?" he asked Clippy.

Gambian pouchies had poor vision, a weakness Yancy aimed to exploit. He'd brought a blinding, high-lumen Rayovac that in close quarters could double as a bludgeon.

Neil jerked a thumb over his shoulder. "I'll be hanging outside."

Clippy hesitated.

"You go, too," Yancy told him. "I'll yell if I need backup."

Unstated among the three men was the fact that a live rat sighting would trigger an emergency closure. Yancy liked Clippy and the mayor, and he had good memories of dining at their place with Rosa. Still he was bound by the health codes, which said that roaming *rodentia* of any size were a menace to hygiene.

He let his eyes adjust to the dim conditions, then kicked off his shoes and started slowly through the main room. The tables were positioned cozily; Clippy's being a popular joint, every square foot of dining space was utilized. As Yancy advanced he became aware of the beer cooler's droning hum and his own shallow exhalations.

After taking a few steps he heard scurrying above him. He aimed the beam of the Rayovac at the drop ceiling where pocked tiles quivered under the tread of an unseen commuter. Stillness followed and Yancy moved forward, poking the handle of the pitchfork at random overhead panels. A sharp clatter made him whirl toward the bar. His flashlight fixed on wide-set ember eyes glowing behind a tipped green fifth of Tanqueray. It was a well-fed, fully mature *Cricetomys gambianus,* nosing the air and flexing its gin-soaked haunches. Drawing closer Yancy saw that the tawny trespasser had stuffed its springy cheeks with Neil's special gourmet mix, which featured dwarf almonds imported from Catalonia.

Yancy heaved the pitchfork javelin-style but missed, taking down a row of top-end liquor bottles. The spooked intruder leapt in a full stretch from the bar counter to the wall, where it dangled by two legs from a frame displaying Clippy's treasured three-star certificate from Michelin. Yancy swung the heavy Rayovac, the blunt end cracking the glass but failing to make contact with the *über* vermin, which dropped to the floor, defeated daintily and dashed away.

"Are you shutting us down?" Clippy asked wretchedly when Yancy emerged moments later. "Don't, Andrew, please. Can't you see I'm begging?"

Neil the mayor waved both hands. "Stop, Irv. The man's only doing his job. Imagine if it ever got out that we interfered."

"I would suggest a voluntary closure," Yancy said hoarsely. "Say, for renovations?"

Clippy's shoulders drooped. "But it's the height of the season."

"Hey, he's doing us a favor," Neil said. "You all right, Andrew? You look shaky."

"No, I'm not all right."

"How many did you see?"

"Just the one," said Yancy. "But holy fuck."

"Were you not able to . . . ?"

"Kill it?" Yancy shook his head and ripped the gloves from his hands.

"Jesus, next we'll be all over Yelp," Clippy groaned. "Those bloody

Australians. Once we're viral, we're dead. D-e-a-d. It's only a matter of time."

"Go get Andrew some water," the mayor said.

Clippy made a bit of a scene, backpedaling down the sidewalk. "I'm not going back in *there*. No freaking way, Neil! Not alone, I'm not."

Yancy said, "Don't bother. I'll be fine."

But fine was the opposite of how he felt on the drive home. He needed a break after his face-off with the pouched fiend, quiet time to steady his nerves and reassess his fast-dwindling role in the universe. Sleep came slowly, but free of dreams.

The next morning he shuffled out of his bedroom and saw that Merry Mansfield had returned. She was wearing camo yoga tights and doing cartwheels on the deck, her long hair whisking the cedar planks like a ginger broom. Instead of running her off, Yancy asked her to ride along while he checked out some funky tattoo parlors in Old Town. She seemed tickled by the invitation.

Over the moon, as a matter of fact.

"The dog's name is really John?"

Martin Trebeaux said, "I don't see the problem. He's a service companion."

The detective said there was absolutely no problem. "What's the nature of your disability, Martin?"

"Chronic anxiety."

The pickings were lean at the adoption shelter in Rego Park. Trebeaux had ended up with a skinny half-beagle half-whippet that looked odd in the large orange vest. Since the dog was too young to be neutered, the shelter made Trebeaux sign a paper promising to arrange the surgery before the animal reached the age of two. The sand man had brought his new companion to the interview at the sheriff's headquarters in Key West hoping to soften the detective, whose name was Burton.

"Tell me about the Buick," he said.

"No biggie—it was a hit-and-run, like I said on the phone." Trebeaux wasn't about to admit what really happened, especially now that he was business partners with Dominick "Big Noogie" Aeola, the man who'd paid that nutty redhead to crash into him.

Burton said, "So you just abandon the car in the Sears parking lot."

"I figured the rental company wouldn't care."

"Actually, they did. Why didn't you call the police?"

"Nobody got hurt," Trebeaux said, "and I was late for a meeting."

"But the Buick was drivable." Burton shrugged. "So why'd you ditch it? That's what I'm getting at."

"Because I was meeting some important people—it wouldn't look good for me to roll up in some dented piece-of-crap. That's the reason I parked it and called for a limo." Trebeaux had already explained to the detective that he owned Sedimental Journeys, a leading provider of beach renourishment services.

"Describe the vehicle that hit you," Burton went on.

"Some old Jap sedan—Toyota, Honda, whatever. I wasn't looking in the rearview when it happened. A loud boom is all I remember. Guy took off right away." Trebeaux couldn't understand why the cops were wasting time investigating a damaged rental car. Who could possibly give a shit? Burton wasn't even taking notes.

The dog began loudly lapping its outsized balls. "Stop it!" Trebeaux snapped. "Bad boy!"

John the Second ignored him.

The detective said, "When you pulled in at the Sears, did you happen to notice another car like yours?"

"I wasn't paying attention. All I wanted to do is get off the road as quick as possible."

"There was a second Buick with rear-end damage abandoned in the same lot. Pretty damn strange."

"What's this all about?" Trebeaux asked.

Burton showed him a photograph of a shaggy yahoo called Buck Nance, who starred in a cable show that Trebeaux had watched only once. The detective asked if he'd seen Nance on the night of the accident.

"Is that the moron who hit my car?"

"He went missing in Key West a couple weeks ago."

Burton handed Trebeaux a picture of a younger man with slickened black hair and a studio tan. "That's Lane Coolman, Nance's manager."

Trebeaux stated that he'd never laid eyes on either Coolman or Nance. It felt peculiar to be telling the truth.

The detective said, "All right, then. Thanks for coming in."

John the Second had contorted into a writhing ampersand, trying to shed the service vest. Trebeaux jerked the dog to its feet. "He's still in training," he said to Burton.

Burton reached down and petted the mutt. "Martin, I was hoping you could give me the name of that limo company—the one that picked you up after the accident."

Trebeaux was caught off guard. "Uh . . . I don't think I saved the receipt."

"Where you stayin'?"

"At the La Concha."

"I'm pretty sure they got phone books in the rooms. Check the yellow pages and see if any of those car services ring a bell."

"Do you not believe me? Seriously?" His fake indignation flopped, so Trebeaux tacked south. "Okay, what if it wasn't a limousine that picked me up? What if maybe it was a woman, and what if she's married and doesn't want the whole town to know what she's doing while her husband's on a shrimp boat in the middle of the Gulf?"

The detective smiled and placed a firm hand on Trebeaux's shoulder. "Martin, even if all that was true—hell, if only *half* of it was *half*-true—I'd still need a name. You understand? Don't leave the island without giving me a call."

When Trebeaux stepped from the building, the low rays of the winter sun caught him square in the face. He walked all the way to Louie's hoping for an open bar stool. A hostess posted in the foyer said he wasn't allowed to bring John the Second into the restaurant.

"But this is a bona fide comfort animal!" Trebeaux objected.

The young woman came out from behind the podium and dubiously studied the dog. "His vest doesn't even fit. Do you have some documentation?"

"So this isn't your first rodeo."

The hostess shook her head. "We get this a lot. It's the new thing."

"You know what? Never mind."

"There's a two-for-one on piña coladas."

"Be back in a sec." Trebeaux marched out the front door and down the wooden steps, where he removed the dog's collar and unsnapped the orange vest.

"This isn't working out," he said to John the Second. "You're free to go."

Joyously the mutt galloped off down Waddell, its great ripe balls swinging like Georgia peaches.

The romance of Brock Richardson and Deborah had hit a bumpy stretch, due partly to Deborah losing her expensive engagement ring and partly to Brock's secret experimentation with Pitrolux, the same product whose frightful side effects he recited so ominously on television.

No one should have known better than Richardson that Pitrolux was dangerous, that the male body couldn't safely absorb and metabolize thrice-daily applications of strong deodorizing chemicals juiced with male hormones. Yet because he merely farmed out product-liability cases and had never actually litigated one, Richardson assumed the allegations against Pitrolux were hyped, a common tactic in his field. He would have spared himself much misery by studying the victims' sworn statements or just scanning a summary of the expert testimony, but he'd never done that before—not in the Ambrosia flammable diaper lawsuit, not in the Ram-Vigor Vitamin contamination case, not even in the Lamb-Gland Injectibles class-action.

Richardson's only role was to troll for fresh plaintiffs using slick TV spots in which he starred as the pin-striped, doom-faced messenger of gruesome manifestations. The diverse Pitrolux litany included excessive hair growth (facial and torso), elongated larynxes, unwanted testicular enlargement (often bilateral), suppurating acne, random tissue deformities and life-threatening erections, to name a few.

Long before the ninety seconds of infomercial horror was over, Richardson's 800 lines would light up. Sympathetic-sounding paralegals would interview the callers, winnow the whack jobs and hook up the others with a legitimate law practice. When the claims got settled, as such cases usually did, Richardson would receive a very sweet slice of the pie. It was a system that had already made him a multimillionaire. He couldn't remember the last time a live client had walked through his door—and what would be the purpose of such a visit? Except for the wall of uncracked legal books that served as the backdrop for Richardson's TV ads, his law office looked more like a Calcutta call center.

Over a decade he'd done so many commercials about so many supposedly harmful pharmaceutical products that he had grown numb to the possibility that some of it might actually be bad shit. He assumed Pitrolux was just another worthless dick-stiffening potion that had been carelessly packaged and clumsily marketed. Whose brilliant idea was the juniper fragrance? And all those Texas cheerleaders who tried it—where the hell were Mom and Dad while their medicine cabinets were being pillaged?

Concealed in Richardson's suit closet was a twelve-pack of Pitrolux that had been sent as a TV prop by one of the seven law firms to which he funneled future plaintiffs. One day he'd curiously opened a box and thus began a furtive ritual, buttering the sticky purple gel under his arms using the patented Soft-Glide applicator. A week later he awoke with a hard-on that endured two cold showers and all three hours of the *Today* show. He surprised Deb with it when she returned from a pedicure. Afterward she said the sex was the best she'd ever had.

These extended romps continued until suddenly, late one Sunday afternoon, Richardson was unable to perform. He doubled down on testosterone squirts and within days he returned to turgid glory. Unfortunately, his bedroom exertions revealed another disconcerting product flaw, namely that Pitrolux wasn't a particularly effective deodorant. Worse, the tang of juniper began to overpower not only Richardson's effluvial perspiration but also other emissions. He shaved off his thickening body hair, yet still he reeked. Soon Deb declared an end to all intimacies, and demanded that he consult a personal groomer.

It was at about this time, while visiting their future home site on Big Pine Key, when she dropped the diamond engagement ring, a two-hundred-thousand-dollar fuckup that enraged Richardson and temporarily chilled his animal ardor. Still he continued his covert use of Pitrolux, testing different dosages behind locked doors inside his bay-front house on Miami Beach. Manic wanking sessions found him self-gagged with a towel to muffle the deep-jungle roars that accompanied every climax.

Meanwhile he and Deb were barely speaking, except for a nightly exchange of barbs on the topic of the missing rock. Richardson saw no choice but to postpone construction of the Keys villa while the bare lot was searched for the ring. For that important task he recruited professionals, three out-of-work treasure salvors who shared a house trailer on Summerland. So far they'd spent a hundred fruitless man-hours combing the property with metal detectors, shovels and sifting buckets. Richardson was beginning to wonder if his fiancée had concocted the story about losing the diamond. What if she'd gone and hocked it herself? Maybe she had a drug habit, or a gambling problem. Or a secret boyfriend with a drug habit *and* a gambling problem.

Richardson's mind squirmed with such ugly doubts while he lathered himself in the shower. He was distracted by a tweak of pain when his loofah snagged on something in the cleft of his left armpit. He explored the site with a forefinger, making a strange discovery. His exclamation was loud enough to echo off the polished walls. Deb entered the bathroom and found him in front of the mirror naked and wet, one soapy arm held upward.

"What now?" she asked.

"Nothing!" The arm snapped down.

"What were you looking at, Brock? Let me see, come on. Don't be such a baby."

Remembering her uncle was a dermatologist, Richardson lifted his arm. Deb stepped closer and peered at the shorn pit.

"Whoa," she said with a sickly wince. "Not good."

"It's just a skin tag. Don't touch it."

"Are you serious? You couldn't *pay* me to touch it."

"I'll get it zapped off at the doctor's. No big deal."

"Jesus, it sort of looks like—"

"I *know* what it looks like." Richardson spun away grabbing for a towel.

"Let me text a picture to Uncle Rob, in case it's something serious," Deb said.

"It's nothing, okay?"

Hurriedly he dried off, bounded across the bedroom and locked himself in the walk-in closet. There he took out an unopened dispenser of Pitrolux and re-read the warning label, which wasn't nearly as frightening as his TV script.

In the car he caught himself steering with his knees while he fingered the pink twig of flesh sprouting beneath his arm. By the time he got to Big Pine his mood was low, and it didn't improve during his meeting with the treasure hunters. They had failed to recover the two-hundred-thousand-dollar diamond, but were keen to show him something else they'd unearthed.

A molar, they said. Possibly human.

TWELVE

Merry Mansfield told Yancy a version of her life so far-fetched that he bit his lower lip, trying not to laugh.

"That's so rude," she said.

"You've got a charming imagination. I could listen to you go on all day."

"What did I say that you don't believe?"

"Basically every word."

"See, I'm just testing you. So far, so good."

They were waiting outside Tramp City Ink & Piercing for the owner to return from a late lunch. It was the third stop on their tour of tattoo parlors.

"Technically, I'm not a maritime artifacts appraiser," Merry admitted. "Also, I didn't really go to boarding school in Switzerland. My mom wasn't a consular attaché in Morocco. My dad never had a thing with Sigourney Weaver. I wasn't the youngest of six sisters, all master equestrians. I *did* get married when I was eighteen, except my husband wasn't pulped to death at an orange-juice factory. What really happened, he went to prison for counterfeiting food stamps and I divorced his ass. No kids from the marriage, thank God—that part's true. What else? Oh yeah, I didn't lose a three-million-dollar bauxite inheritance to Bernie Madoff. My folks are still alive, and they're not leaving me a nickel."

"So I know who you're not," said Yancy. "Now tell me who you are."

"Aren't you the smooth one?" She laughed.

"Then at least your real name. Come on."

"Merry Mansfield. And even if it wasn't, you're still going to ask me for crazy hot sex."

"I doubt that," Yancy said. "No offense."

"You men, I swear. Look at me."

"I am."

"No, right here." Merry, pointing two fingers at her eyes. "Now I dare you to tell me with absolute, one thousand percent certainty that you're never, ever gonna try to get in my pants, that there are no earthly circumstances that would ever put that notion in your head. Lemme hear those words. Come on, Andrew."

"You know I'm in a relationship."

"Just say it: 'Merry, you're a phenomenally attractive woman, but we are never, ever going to have crazy hot sex. It's totally out of the realm of possibility. No chance whatsoever.'"

"Not on this planet, not in this lifetime," Yancy said. "How's that for categorical?"

Merry stuck out her tongue. "Dick."

"That's my point. I'm nothing but trouble."

"Me, too!" She whacked him on the arm. "Don't you get it?"

"The answer, again, would be no."

"I feel like you're in denial. Something in your voice."

"It's called spiritual fatigue. Last night I went one-on-one with a rat the size of a Corvette. This isn't the career I envisioned for myself."

She said, "Know what I'm gonna do for you, sugar? I'm gonna get a tattoo."

"That's flattering, and also insane, but we're here on business."

The owner of Tramp City was called Wikky, anemic and heavy-lidded. Oddly, he bore no visible body ink or hardware.

When Yancy flashed his roach-patrol ID, Wikky slapped shut a Jack Reacher paperback and said, "What's the problem, man? I run a sanitary premise."

Yancy said he wasn't there to do an inspection. "I'm looking for a certain customer."

"Privacy is important to our clientele," said Wikky. "You don't have a warrant, I can't help you."

"Then maybe I'll take a peek at those needles, after all. You disinfect 'em after each tat, right? The machine, no doubt, also spotlessly maintained."

Wikky surrendered in a blink. "Tell me the dude's name."

"Buck Nance."

"The bayou brother from TV? I thought he was in treatment after what went down at the Pirate. They said on TMZ he's in Malibu."

Yancy said, "It's possible he's still in Key West. He got rid of his beard, so you might not recognize him."

Merry Mansfield sidled ahead of Yancy and introduced herself. "Sir, I would very much like to get inked," she said.

Wikky frowned. "This some kinda trick?"

"I was thinking of a little bumblebee."

"Please don't make a scene," Yancy said to her.

Wikky opened a fat three-ring binder full of vivid templates. "You want a standard honeybee, or one of the Mexican hybrids?"

"Just a honey, honey." Merry twirled around and lifted her skirt. "Right there."

Yancy hustled her outside, stepped back into the shop and bolted the door behind him. Wikky looked disappointed. Merry waved to him sadly from the other side of the window.

When Yancy held up the sketch of a beardless Buck Nance, the tattoo artist shook his head and said, "I never seen that guy."

"Maybe he came in on your day off."

"I don't take any days off. Long as the bars on Duval stay open, I'm open."

"So, you remember every single tat you've ever done?" Yancy asked.

"Plus I save all the paperwork for the state, if that's what you mean. I'm strictly legal."

"Ever do one that said 'Hail Captain Cock'?"

Wikky folded his arms. "Run that past me again."

"'Hail Captain Cock,'" Yancy repeated. "Capital letters, straight across the shoulder blades. Roman script?"

With a wary nod Wikky said, "Yeah, but he wasn't the same dude you showed me in the drawing."

"Then who was it? I'll need the name."

The tattoo man dug through a dented file cabinet until he found it. "Krill," he said to Yancy. "With a K. First name Benjamin."

The address was an apartment house on Petronia. Yancy wrote down the number, unit 277, though he didn't expect to find anybody named Benjamin Krill. More likely the mystery customer was Buck Nance, giving a fake name and address. Wikky probably hadn't recognized him; a pencil sketch wasn't as reliable as a photograph, for ID purposes.

"And you saw this guy when?" Yancy asked.

"The second time was February fourth. See, I got it logged right here. The Captain Cock."

"And the first time he came in?"

"Two nights before." Wikky had the customer's file in his hands. "I get lots of repeats 'cause I'm the best in town. It ain't braggin' if it's fact."

"What kind of tattoo did you give Mr. Krill on the 2nd?" Yancy asked.

"A badass Chantecler rooster, in profile. Custom job."

"Where?"

"On his stomach. For the bird's eyeball I inked the dude's navel. He had an innie, so it hurt like a mother. But, hey, he asked for it."

Yancy took out his phone and found a publicity shot of Buck Nance on the *Bayou Brethren* website. Wikky studied the photo but said he couldn't be sure. "Every skinny old white fart with one of them ZZ beards looks the same to me."

When Yancy left the shop Merry called him a prick for locking her out. Then she took his hand and declared there might still be hope. The sensible thing for him to do was say goodbye and walk away, but he didn't. He enjoyed her company. She was a trip.

When they got to the apartment building on Petronia he asked her to wait out front. The door of unit 277 was opened by a stout woman who could have been forty, or sixty. Yancy presented a lightning glimpse of his roach-patrol credentials hoping she'd mistake him for a regular detective, which she did. He told her he was looking for Benjamin Krill.

"Nobody calls him that," the woman said. "He ain't here anyhow."

Yancy was surprised to learn that Krill existed. Buck Nance must have known him, or at least heard of him, in order to use that name at the tattoo shop.

"Are you his wife?" Yancy asked the woman.

"Common-law, but not on paper. Lemme guess—he ain't paid the damn rent again. Or is it worse than that?"

"What do they call him?"

"I call him Benny but he goes by Blister. You come to throw his ass in jail?"

In the background Yancy heard chittering sounds and a blaring television. He asked the woman if he could look around. She yawned and motioned him inside. Dirty laundry was strewn all over the place. The high-pitched barking emanated from a full-grown mongoose leashed on a rope triple-knotted to a leg of the dining table. When the animal spied Yancy it flattened its ears and lunged wildly on the rope. The woman hurled an ashtray yelling, "Shut the fuck up, Clee Roy!"

Yancy withdrew straightaway.

Back in the doorway the woman said, "Wouldn't break my heart, you had to shoot that thing. Say it got loose and come chasin' after you."

Yancy informed her that he didn't have his gun.

"What! Whoever heard of a cop that didn't carry."

"I'm not here to arrest anybody, Mrs. Krill. This is an administrative visit."

"Oh well." She plucked a bent cigarette from the pocket of her housecoat and lit it. "You can call me Mona."

Yancy said, "I have one more question about your husband."

"No, I *don't* know where he's at. You find that bastard, tell him to drag his scrawny ass home, so I can kick it."

"I was wondering if he's got any tattoos."

"Benny?" Mona clucked. "No, sir—and I'd be the best one to know." She winked and flicked an ash on the floor.

When Yancy emerged from the apartment building, Merry Mansfield was thumbing an old newspaper she'd picked up from somebody's front lawn. "Check this out," she said, and showed him a headline on page 3:

ELECTROCUTION VICTIM IDENTIFIED AS MIAMI EX-CON

It was a story about Juan Zeto-Fernández frying himself while recharging his Tesla.

"Did you know this genius?" Yancy asked.

"We were partners, Andrew."

Oh, this ought to be good, he thought. "Partners in what?"

And, for once, Merry told him the truth. She didn't know what had come over her.

Lane Coolman was sure nobody had ever been kidnapped twice on the same trip to Key West. In his mind he was working up an outline for the script, a miniseries for HBO or possibly Netflix. He knew plenty of writers who'd kill for the job.

Working title: "Hell Island."

It was the redhead's fault that he'd been snatched a second time. Had she not pranced off with that sketch cop Yancy, Coolman wouldn't have been walking from the scene of the Conch Train homicide alone in the dark; he would've been side-by-side with Merry Mansfield, and the kidnapper likely would have left them alone. It was exponentially way more difficult to abduct two persons at knifepoint than one. This was a known fact even among the stupidest criminals.

Coolman longed to be back in L.A., reclaiming his turf at Platinum Artists and demolishing his future ex-wife in divorce court. Rachel's attorney was probably pitching a fit, complaining that Coolman was staying out of California as a stall tactic. Coolman wondered what Amp thought about his disappearance, if Amp thought about it at all. The man had the attention span (and conscience) of a mosquito.

Once again Coolman found himself imprisoned on a vessel—not a lobster boat, this time, but a weather-beaten cabin cruiser called *Wet Nurse*. The kidnapper said the previous owner was a playboy obstetrician. For days Coolman had been shackled to one of four small berths in the bow. After dark he could see the lights of Key West, and sometimes hear applause from the crowds at Mallory Square. During the day other boats would pass nearby, but he'd given up shouting for help. His asshole kidnapper blasted music 24/7 from portable speakers on the deck, a relentless loop of hard Southern rock—Skynyrd, 38 Special, Marshall Tucker, the Allman Brothers. One afternoon, "Ramblin' Man" played seventeen times. Coolman kept count. When he pleaded for an updated playlist, his reward was a slap to the back of his head.

The kidnapper used an inflatable dinghy to travel back and forth to the island. Coolman was given food twice a day, and the menu didn't change: cheeseburgers, tater tots and lukewarm lime Gatorade. The narrow berths on the cabin cruiser featured spore-covered mattresses and thin woolen blankets. A plastic bucket served as the toilet. Soapless bathing was permitted on occasion, thirty-second dousings from a deck hose spewing seawater. A salty crust had thickened on Coolman's skin; his hair was grimy, and his unshaved stubble itched constantly.

Early on he'd tried to initiate a discussion of ransom, but the kidnapper showed no interest. A scornful grunt had been the response when Coolman announced he had twenty-one grand in the bank that he was willing to pay for his release. Still, except for the "Ramblin' Man" blowup, the kidnapper didn't seem particularly violent. His knife stayed out of sight, and threats were kept to a minimum. He seldom spoke to Coolman and treated him as more or less invisible, which was irritating though understandable. The man had bigger fish to fry. Some days he'd be gone for a long time, and Coolman would bloody himself trying to squirm out of the handcuffs. Unfortunately, it was impossible to lose weight on a cheeseburger-and-taters diet; if anything, Coolman's wrists were getting chubbier. The truth was he had no willpower. Every time a bag of junk food was placed in front of him, he went at it like a wolf on a fawn. It was a scene that wouldn't appear in Coolman's script. To portray him a hot young actor would be cast, someone who could do stoicism and also drop thirty pounds during the shoot.

Coolman envisioned "Hell Island" as a career-saving parachute, in case Amp axed him from Platinum Artists. The money from a mini-series could be semi-decent, especially if Coolman started the ball rolling with a bestselling book about his back-to-back hostage ordeals. Hire some slick ghostwriter and spend a week at the W yakking into a tape recorder. How tough could *that* be?

Dwelling on this vainglorious project was mental therapy, for Coolman had no logical reason to be upbeat. Mornings on the boat were pierced by the basso horns of cruise ships in the harbor and the high whine of passenger jets on final approach to the airport—melancholy reminders of how close he was to freedom. Whenever the wind clocked out of the north, the temperature plummeted, the old boat pitched, and the windows whistled. Coolman had never been an avid sailor, never understood the so-called romance of the high seas. Yachts were tolerable, yachts he could do, but anything under a hundred feet—forget it. Although he didn't get seasick, he was miserable in other ways. The kidnapper had thrown his cell phone overboard, a traumatizing blow for any agent. It made Coolman feel small and helplessly out of touch with his world. The *Wet Nurse* was cramped, rank, gloomy. When the seas got rough he couldn't fall sleep, unlike the other hostage, who was cuffed to the opposite bunk. The all-night snoring and fart-fest drove Coolman batshit, though he didn't complain. The mood down below already was sour and tense.

"You're useless," the other captive would bark, upon waking.

"You told me about a hundred times."

"I'm tellin' you again. You suck at your job."

"Take it easy—"

"No, man, I'm done with you. You are *motherfuckin' fired*!"

Then Lane Coolman would patiently say, "Chill out, Buck. We're in this together."

THIRTEEN

Brock Richardson interrupted with a question: "What the hell's a Calusa?"

"An extinct Native American tribe," the state archeologist replied. In one hand he cupped the molar at issue. "I would say this find dates from about 3,500 BC."

"Which means . . . ?"

"Your property might be an ancient settlement. Or even a burial ground."

"Oh, terrific." Richardson wanted to strangle this fucking pinhead and also the three salvors who'd let him on the property. The men said they'd had no choice but to cooperate. Human teeth are bones, they'd said, and bones are body parts. You can go to jail for concealing the discovery of a body part, they had explained, no matter how tiny.

"Bottom line," the archeologist said to Richardson, "this site must be preserved until we can determine if the Calusa once lived here."

"Whoa there—what about my house? They're pouring the slab next week."

"I'm afraid not."

"Are you kidding me? Where do you get off?"

The archeologist's name was Dr. Whitmore. He put up a "Posted" sign while Richardson paid off the salvors saying, "Thanks for nothing, shitheads."

Dr. Whitmore took photographs and jotted studiously in his notebook. Richardson phoned his real-estate lawyer and told him about the potential Calusa problem. The lawyer said, "You might be screwed, buddy boy."

"That's helpful. Remind me again how much I'm paying you."

"Want my advice? Bribe somebody."

Richardson had been mulling the same approach. He walked up to the archeologist and offered him five hundred dollars to forget he ever laid eyes on the dead Indian's tooth.

"Oh, I could never do that," Dr. Whitmore said.

"Say you found it somewhere else. I'll give you a thousand bucks, cash."

"Keep your money, Mr. Richardson. There's important work to be done here."

"At least can I see the damn thing?"

Dr. Whitmore wouldn't allow Richardson to touch the molar but he held it up for viewing. The crown portion was chipped and brown-stained. "Probably from wild coffee beans," the archeologist surmised. "The Calusas chewed them for energy."

"Fascinating," muttered Richardson. "Let's call National Geographic."

"Check out the root prong. Notice the decay?"

"So somehow it's my fault they didn't floss. Guy's tooth falls out and five thousand years later I'm not allowed to build my house?"

"In the event we don't find any more bones or artifacts on your land," said Dr. Whitmore, "you'll be free to proceed."

"And how long will it take you dweebs to finish?"

"The site's been disturbed by previous construction, so we'll need to do some excavating. Still I can't imagine the project lasting more than two years. Three tops."

Richardson cursed hotly. "This is unfuckingbelievable! It looks like an ordinary goddamn molar."

"Oh no, Mr. Richardson."

Yet in fact it was an ordinary molar. It had been yanked from the gums of a taxi driver named Kupnick and provided to Andrew Yancy by Kupnick's dentist, who also happened to be Yancy's dentist and occasional fishing companion. Yancy had strategically positioned the Kupnick extraction on Richardson's property shortly before the hired salvors began their diamond hunt.

The molar's discoloration came from twenty-eight years of chewing tobacco, not wild coffee beans. This would have been evident to a legitimate archeologist, which "Doctor" Jimmy Whitmore was not. In real life he was a drama teacher at Key West High and a weekend boat mechanic. He'd done all the rigging on Yancy's bonefish skiff, and he was glad to volunteer when Yancy called up looking for an actor. The coffee-bean line that Whitmore lobbed at Brock Richardson was pure improv, for Whitmore knew essentially nothing about the ancient Calusan diet. Likewise he was winging it when he dated the molar at 3,500 BC, though he'd found an article online saying Paleo-Indian tribes had settled South Florida long before then.

"One more thing," said Richardson, watching Whitmore deposit the molar in a square brown envelope. "When you start digging, could you keep an eye out for something my girlfriend lost? I mean my fiancée. It was her engagement ring—not cheap, either."

Whitmore nodded. "I'll be sure to alert my team. Can you describe it for me?"

"A humongous diamond mounted on a platinum band, okay? A gigantic mo-fo diamond. Impossible to mistake for an Indian trinket. But what I'm wondering is can I trust your people not to keep it? Because, swear to Christ, if that happens—"

"You've got my word, Mr. Richardson. Our only interest is preserving the remnants of a lost native culture. Anything else we might find here belongs to you," said Whitmore, "or, in this case, your fiancée."

Like she was the one who paid for that rock, thought Richardson.

"Call me right away if it turns up," he said. "Did I mention I'm an attorney? Because you should be aware, I don't intend to eat this mortgage for two or three years while you pick over my property with goddamn tweezers. I'll be calling your boss in Tallahassee first thing tomorrow."

Whitmore said, "I truly appreciate your frustration."

"No, you truly do not."

Richardson boiled and grumbled all the way to Key West, where he had an appointment with a cosmetic surgeon to discuss the odd penis-shaped growth under his left arm. At the office he learned the surgeon had been summoned to the hospital to remove a treble hook from a tourist's eyelid, so Richardson drove to Louie's for an early cocktail. At the bar he sat next to a gregarious light-haired man with flushed cheeks and prehensile lips. The man said he owned a company called Sedimental Journeys, which supposedly rebuilt entire beachfronts that had been lost to erosion. He gave his name as Martin Trebeaux and said, "I recognize you from somewhere, don't I?"

"My law firm does lots of advertising."

"You're the Pitrolux guy from TV!"

"Guilty," said Richardson. It was a topic he normally didn't mind discussing, but not now. Not with delicate skin-tag surgery on his mind.

Trebeaux said, "I tried that stuff, but it gave me a rash that smelled like rotten burritos."

Richardson handed him a business card. "Call my office tomorrow, Martin. We'll sign you up for the class-action."

They raised a toast to the American justice system, and then bought each other several rounds. Richardson was the first to get drunk and blab too much. Martin Trebeaux seemed sincerely outraged by what he heard.

"All because your fiancée dropped her engagement ring?" he said. "Let me get this straight: You hire some pro treasure hunters but all they come up with is a moldy old tooth. Then the government marches in and says your property is a sacred burial ground, so now you can't build your island dream house. Friend, that's just wrong. There's no other word for it. Wrong, wrong, wrong. How much did you lay out for that diamond?"

"Two hundred K. It just fell off her damn finger, so she says. I think the asshole who lives next door might've ganked it. If he wasn't an ex-cop, I'd send some guys down to turn his house inside-out."

"You have guys like that?"

"I know some people, yeah," said Richardson.

"Me, too. That's funny."

"My guys are club bouncers on South Beach. Ex-NFL."

Martin Trebeaux raised his martini glass. "My guys are Mafia."

"Do not even joke about that shit."

"Friend, I'm not joking. I gave 'em a piece of my beach business, but I'm still the head honcho. Google the Calzone crime family, you want some cozy bedtime reading. Look up a gentleman named Dominick Aeola, AKA Big Noogie. I'm dead serious."

Richardson had heard of the Calzone organization, but that didn't mean Trebeaux wasn't blowing smoke. Richardson asked him how he got connected.

"Long story. Not important." The sand man's words were a bit slurred but his brain was clicking. "Hey, were you serious about cutting me in on the Pitrolux case, or was that just the usual Miami bullshit?"

"No bull, Martin. You still got the rash?"

"Naw. Went away in like a day and a half."

"Tell me you got some pictures," Richardson said.

"On my phone, sure."

"Good enough. You're in."

"Brilliant!" Trebeaux pinky-fingered the bright olive out of his drink and flicked it into his mouth. "Listen, maybe I can return the favor. Your situation? It's very possible I can help."

"Nobody can help," mumbled Richardson.

"What would it hurt—I'm just saying—if I sent my guys to visit your asshole neighbor?"

"But I told you, he's an ex-cop."

"So what?" Trebeaux said. "Now, if he's ex-FBI then I see your point, because that's like a blood fraternity. But ex-cops lose their juice about ten seconds after giving up the badge. Your sweetheart—what's her name again. Donna?"

"It's Deborah. Deb."

"So Deb's got her heart set on a house in the Keys, right? For now you can't touch your land, but what if your ex-cop neighbor suddenly decided to sell his place? What if he's willing to go low? I mean insanely low."

"His house is a fucking shoebox."

"So bulldoze the damn thing and build whatever you want. You can unload your other lot for a profit, soon as they're done scooping up all the Indian dentures."

Richardson turned to gaze at the ocean, which was blurry. So were the birds on the shore and the clouds in the sky. Had he and Deb been on more intimate terms, buying out Yancy would have been an appealing option—same quiet neighborhood, same amazing sunset views. Deb would have been impressed by her future husband's resourcefulness, rewarding him with silky favors. Given the current chill in their relationship, though, Richardson wasn't sure he wanted to sink another nickel into Big Pine real estate.

Trebeaux scribbled a phone number on a cocktail napkin. "Think about it, and let me know. Here's my private line."

"Yancy won't sell cheap," Richardson said. "He'll play the hardass."

"Well, my guys can make miracles happen." The sand man called for his check.

Richardson paid his own tab at the same time. Checking the phone he saw that he'd missed a couple calls from the surgeon's office. There was nothing from Deb.

Outside Louie's, Trebeaux hovered uncertainly, peering up and down the street. "You hear a dog bark?" he whispered to Richardson.

"That was a rooster, I'm pretty sure."

A pink cab cruised by and Richardson waved it down. He was too bombed to drive himself to the hotel.

"Want a lift?" he asked Trebeaux, who said sure and practically dove into the backseat.

On the ride through Old Town Richardson thought it would be polite to ask Trebeaux about his business. "Where do you get all the sand for your projects, Martin? How does that work?"

"Mega-dredges and barges, friend. Mother Nature provides the product. Right now I'm lining up an epic deal in Havana. It's all on the hush."

"*Viva* Coo-ba," said Richardson, touching a finger to his lips. He'd done his part; he'd pretended to be interested.

Trebeaux climbed out of the taxi across from the La Concha. "We'll talk soon, friend," he said, and walked off swaying among the throngs. He didn't look like a man who was tight with hardcore New York mobsters, but the possibility couldn't be ruled out.

"Hey!" Richardson called after him. "Don't forget to send me those pictures of your rash!"

Only on Duval Street would such a line fail to turn any heads.

Yancy elected to believe Merry Mansfield's story about the car-crashing scam. It was too richly layered to be one of her lies. The fact she was a con artist didn't concern him that much. At least she wasn't a killer, bank robber, or (like his girlfriend before Rosa) an arsonist. The pride with which she described the precision of her collisions was oddly touching. Yancy couldn't resist being impressed by the audacity of the razor ploy, and also by the dexterity required to groom between one's legs while operating a motor vehicle at high speed. Merry was a most uncommon criminal.

The proper thing was to hand her over to Rogelio Burton, but that would be wasting the detective's time. Merry would deny everything she'd told Yancy, and there was slim chance of prosecution, with Zeto deceased and the "victims" so shady.

So, when Burton stopped by the next morning, Yancy kept quiet about Merry's unusual occupation. Burton remembered her—who wouldn't?—from the scene of the Conch Train attack, where she'd appeared at the side of Buck Nance's manager.

"Where is Mr. Coolman these days? I need to speak with him," the detective said.

"Who knows." Merry smiled coolly. "Not my circus, not my monkey."

Yancy felt that Burton deserved an explanation for Merry's presence. "She's staying here for a few days—in the guest room, Rog. We're just friends."

"The guest room's disgusting. There's not even a mattress," said Burton.

"On the couch, I meant."

"That's the story you should stick with."

Yancy said he had a solid lead on the Conch Train homicide. "A man using the name Krill got a 'Captain Cock' ink job shortly before that tourist was killed. There's a Benjamin Krill on Petronia, but he wasn't home when I went by. His wife didn't have much to say."

Burton crossed his arms. "First, goddammit, you're not supposed to be working the case. Sonny made that crystal clear. So, as your life coach, I'm telling you to cease and desist."

"Objection noted, and overruled."

"Second, Homicide still sees Buck Nance as the main suspect on account of his extreme anti-Muslim sentiments and recent sketchy behavior."

"I'm not so sure he did it," said Yancy. "You should—"

Burton cut him off. "Third, I know Krill. On the street he's Benny the Blister, which fits his personality. Lifelong burglar, hopelessly incompetent, nothing violent on his rap sheet—I can't see him going after a total stranger."

Yancy said, "For what it's worth, he keeps a pet mongoose."

"Yes, generating numerous complaints and citations. The damn thing tried to eat a psychic's cockatiel on Whitehead."

Merry whistled. "This parallel universe of yours, Andrew, I love it."

Burton said Benny Krill was unexceptional for Key West. "Also, as I say, a terrible burglar. Last time we busted him he was climbing out the window of an art gallery. He didn't break in to steal the art, he went to steal cash. Know how much cash they keep at art galleries? Basically zero dollars, since everybody pays for paintings with plastic or personal checks. So Blister's basically an idiot."

"Still, I bet the sheriff would prefer for a career felon and not Buck Nance to be the Conch Train killer," said Yancy. "He'd be eternally relieved if I cleared Captain Cock's name."

"The sheriff would prefer that you continue to excel on roach patrol."

"Rog, this would be the second homicide I've solved in my spare time since leaving the department. There's no way Sonny could *not* give me my badge back."

"It's sad, really, this detachment from reality."

Merry said, "You guys are like two old married people."

Burton headed for the door. "Andrew suffers from these wild delusions. Maybe you can talk some sense into him."

Later that afternoon Irv Clipowski called to say he was flying in an exterminator from Marrakesh who claimed to have unparalleled experience battling Gambian pouched rats. "Soldier on, Clippy," said Yancy, who planned to avoid the besieged restaurant until the invasives were vanquished.

For privacy he locked himself in a bathroom and unsuccessfully tried to FaceTime Rosa. Next he attempted regular dialing, with the same result.

Merry tapped sympathetically on the door. "Let me talk to her," she said.

"Thanks, but I got this." Yancy wasn't even sure where Rosa was. Text after text traveled nowhere, undelivered.

The door handle turned and in walked Merry, having picked the lock with a fondue fork that was a relic from Yancy's first and only marriage. He reported to Merry that Dr. Rosa Campesino wasn't taking his calls.

"She's still pissed because I answered your phone," Merry said. "Give her some time, Andrew. Meanwhile try not to think about you and me in the shower together, all slick and soapy. Not that I'd ever let that happen, but just try not to think about it."

"Let's take another ride," he said.

Half an hour later they were parked down the street from Blister's place. Merry said it was her first stakeout in a 1993 Subaru. She was less fidgety since Yancy had imposed a cutoff on the energy drinks. Two per day was the new limit, which she honored mainly because the rhubarb-flavored mix (her favorite) was staining her teeth. She appraised her smile in the side mirror while arranging herself cross-legged on the seat.

"Why are you so quiet, Andrew? What's on your mind? Like I don't know."

"That mongoose is what's on my mind. The woman called it Clee Roy." Yancy was aggravated because he hadn't picked up on it at the time. "I think Buck Nance has a brother with that name."

Merry said that wasn't something a normal person, much less a detective, would forget. "No wonder the sheriff canned your ass."

Yancy tinkered with his phone until he pulled up the *Bayou Brethren* web page, confirming the connection. He couldn't have been expected to memorize all of Buck's TV kinfolk, but a Dogpatch moniker such as Clee Roy should have stuck in his head. Merry was right: He was off his game. Lax and distracted.

Obviously the Nance family had an extreme fan in Mr. Benjamin Krill. That would explain the Clee Roy tribute and both of his recent tats.

"What do we do when this freak shows up?" Merry asked.

"Let's see what happens."

"Ha! And I thought you weren't the spontaneous type."

A car rolled down Petronia and parked at the opposite end. It was a charcoal Taurus, a model used by plainclothes city detectives. Yancy could only assume that Rogelio Burton, despite his purported skepticism, had passed along the tip about Blister.

"Traitor," Yancy mumbled.

If Krill appeared now, the cops would snatch him like a bug off the sidewalk. By dinnertime they'd have a signed confession—and Yancy would get no credit for cracking the Conch Train case, no redemptive brownie points with the sheriff. Yancy wasn't proud of his selfishness, yet he couldn't change how he felt. The roach patrol was sapping his spirits, one wriggling baggie at a time. He had to fight his way out.

Merry said she had an idea. It wasn't terrible. At least no razor-play was involved.

"What the hell. Give it a shot," Yancy said.

She got out and headed toward the unmarked cop car. Her stylish walk warmed Yancy with an impure fantasy. It evaporated when he received a lengthy text from Rosa abroad. "This has nothing to do with you," she began, and went on to say that working in morgues and emergency rooms had wrecked her in ways she'd never realized until spending time in civilized places where children never, ever die from gunfire. "Andrew, I'm not sure I can come back to Miami," she wrote.

"Then don't," he texted back. "Move down to the Keys and live with me. You can open a boutique practice! I'd break my own leg just to be your first patient."

No immediate response from Dr. Campesino. Yancy understood too well what she was experiencing. He remembered how good it felt to be liberated from that city. The berserk-o side of the place was basically all you saw, if you were a cop or a coroner.

Down the street, Merry Mansfield was chatting up the detectives in the Taurus. Her jeans weren't too tight and her sweater wasn't cut too low, but her hair was killer. She would be telling them that a sketchy-bearded dude with "Hail Captain Cock" inked on his back had nearly knocked her down on a bicycle moments earlier. She'd be telling them that the tattooed man said something obscene as he flew past, and that he looked crazed in the eyes. When the detectives asked which way the man had been riding, she would point toward downtown.

Yancy grinned at the sight of the Taurus peeling out. Merry returned and sat down beside him giving a cheeky toss of her head.

He said, "Yeah, I know. Us men—we're pitiful."

"Totally, Andrew."

"They ask for your number?"

"Of course," Merry said. "Luckily, I got a hundred of 'em."

Minutes later a person who could only be Benny the Blister materialized in the neighborhood. Barefoot and solo, he wore a dirty tee-shirt, reflector shades and a scarlet biker bandanna. Each sunburned arm lugged a grocery sack.

Yancy waited until he entered the apartment building before easing out of the car. "Stay right here," he said to Merry.

"Not this time, sugar."

Quietly she trailed Yancy up the stairs. The door to unit 277 was cracked open, and they could hear a man and woman arguing. The background track was a TV game show—somebody had just won three days in Tahoe. When Yancy slipped inside the apartment, the first weird thing he saw was Clee Roy the mongoose buttoned in a plum tunic. The animal stood on the kitchen table holding a chicken drumstick.

The next thing Yancy noticed was the printing on Benny Krill's grubby sleeveless shirt: WHERE IS BUM FARTO?

Benny the Blister squared off, both hands jammed in his cutoffs. He glowered at Yancy, snapping, "Who the fuck are you?"

"He's the law, dumbass," said Blister's wife, rooting like a half-starved bear through the grocery bags. "Goddammit, you forgot my fuckin' Tostitos again!"

Yancy never had time to take out his roach-patrol ID.

"Benny, where'd you get that shirt?" he managed to say, and two seconds later he was bleeding all over his shoes.

FOURTEEN

Merry made it to the hospital in six minutes flat. She was sharp behind the wheel, the best Yancy had ever seen.

He told the E.R. nurses he'd fallen on a rake. If he'd given the truth, the police would have been called, and a report would have landed on the desk of Sonny Summers, who didn't want Yancy near the Conch Train case, the Buck Nance case, or any other case that was making news. The sheriff wanted Yancy offstage, counting cockroaches.

Merry said, "What a whack job. I didn't see the knife until too late."

"This is all on me."

Benny Krill had made one spazzy swing with the blade and sliced Yancy's belly.

"How are you feeling?" Merry asked.

"Stupid and mortal."

No vital organs nicked, but nineteen stitches. The doctor wanted Yancy to remain in the hospital for a few days. He promptly bolted. Merry took him back to Big Pine and helped him into the house. Collapsing on the sofa he tore off the paper gown to examine his bandages.

"Blood is seriously not my thing," Merry said, losing color.

"You've done more than enough for me. I'll call you a cab."

"I don't want to go. I mean I do, but I don't. You're in rough shape, Andrew."

"Mainly my ego."

"Full disclosure: I suck at the nurturing thing. One summer I worked at a nursing home and it was a disaster."

Queasily she untied his bloody sneakers and tossed them in the trash can. Through the window she saw a small shiny sedan idling on the street.

"Doesn't look like a cop car," she said.

Yancy swallowed two Percocets. "Whoever it is, we're not in the mood for company."

"Then I'll let them know."

She was out the door before Yancy could object. He tried to rise, but his roaring skull weighed him down. The numerals on his phone were shimmying beneath his fingertips. He detected a fresh text from Tommy Lombardo, something about Clippy's, but the words smeared together on the screen. Yancy lay shaky and exhausted. He eyed the Remington, which he was too weak to reach. After a few moments he floated free, forgetting about the raw wound in his gut and the strange car parked in front of his house. When he opened his eyes, Merry Mansfield was gazing down at him.

"I figured out who you remind me of," he said. "Susan Sarandon. I've had a crush on her since *Thelma & Louise.*"

"That's the nicest thing you ever said. Must be the hair."

"Also the laugh. I'm a sucker for throaty laughs."

Merry stroked his cheek and said, "Can you sit up? These gentlemen want to talk to you."

"Guess what. I think Blister snatched Buck Nance!" Some people got plastered on heavy painkillers but Yancy found himself cogitating with marvelous clarity. "Two birds with one stone! Let's go get 'em!" he burbled.

"Andrew, listen to me," said Merry.

"Who are those guys?" he inquired, finally noticing the strangers.

"They said they're looking for a diamond ring."

Yancy sagged. "Not tonight, fellas. Go away."

But they didn't.

Big Noogie couldn't care less that Martin Trebeaux's new friend was having problems with his ex-cop neighbor. What spiked the *capo*'s interest was the missing two-hundred-thousand-dollar engagement ring. It was worth sending Jelly and Nick down to the Keys to poke around. Hell, the boys were due for a vacation.

Jelly and Nick worked in downtown Miami for a document-shredding service that Big Noogie had acquired by coercion and immediately converted to an identity-theft operation. The shredding machines were sold as scrap but not the company's armored truck, which Jelly and Nick drove from one glass office tower to the next. Their corporate clients would scrupulously insert all sensitive papers into locked plastic tubs, which Nick and Jelly lugged down the service elevators and placed in their steel-plated vehicle. The tubs then were transported to a warehouse in Hialeah Gardens, to be opened with a master key. A team of recently paroled stockbrokers and accountants waited at folding card tables to sift through the tonnage, sniffing out payroll records, bank statements, credit-card summaries, 1099s, K-1s, transfer receipts, inventory reports and other promising material. Executives who used their firm's shredding tub as a repository for intimate correspondence were at especially high risk, for Big Noogie encouraged freelance blackmail by team members.

Jelly and Nick were being sent to search the house of a man named Andrew Yancy. If they found a diamond ring they were supposed to hand-deliver it to Big Noogie so he could gift it to Dom Jr., his eldest son, who would soon propose marriage to an assistant deli manager from Staten Island. An ample brassy girl, full of life—Big Noogie was fond of her. She'd go nuts when she laid her big chocolate eyes on that rock.

Grateful for a break from the stuffy armored car, Nick and Jelly considered it an honor to be chosen by their boss for a personal mission. Nick was only twenty-five and since arriving in Miami had never been south of the landfill at Black Point. Jelly was a few years older and had twice gone to Key Largo stealing outboards. For the trip to Big Pine, Big Noogie had rented Jelly and Nick a plain Kia compact, which was all right. They didn't require a full-sized sedan because they weren't hulking, thick-necked men in the usual mold of mob legbreakers. Both were on the shorter side, with lean faces and narrow shoulders. Although capable of inflicting severe bodily harm, they preferred verbal intimidation and hair-raising gunplay.

Parked in wait outside Yancy's house, Nick and Jelly had not expected to be approached by the curvy red-haired woman who'd come out the front door. Both men understood this would test their professionalism.

The redhead approached the Kia and nonchalantly addressed Nick, who was riding shotgun: "Are you two rascals here to see Andrew? Honestly, there's no need for rough stuff—he got knifed this afternoon, so he won't give you any trouble. My name's Merry, by the way. Merry Mansfield, like the actress."

"We gotta toss the place," Jelly said. "Or, he can just tell us where he put the fuckin' ring and save on the mess."

"What ring?" asked Merry.

Nick was curious about the stabbing. "How come he ain't at the hospital?"

"Because he's a stubborn fool, that's why. Come see for yourselves."

Jelly pointed. "Zat his blood on your top?"

"Thanks for noticing. Follow me."

Jelly and Nick wondered if it might be a trap. They drew their weapons as they got out of the Kia. The hottie named Merry smiled and said, "Fine. If that makes you feel better."

They trailed her into the house and found Yancy sprawled on a frayed old couch, his midsection heavily taped with white gauze. He looked like hell. When the redhead informed him that the men were searching for a ring, Yancy's head fell back and he said, "Not tonight, fellas."

"Who stabbed you?" Jelly asked him. "Was it her?"

Referring to the woman, who zapped him with a glare.

Yancy said, "You came a long way for nothing. I don't have the damn diamond."

"Then I guess we gotta wreck your crib." Jelly turned to Nick. "You heard the man. Time to remodel."

Merry asked the legbreakers to please put away their guns. "Look at the poor bastard—he's a mess."

They agreed that Yancy posed no threat.

"Who sent you?" Yancy asked. "I bet I know—the dick lawyer that owns the lot next door, his fiancée is the one who lost the ring you're looking for."

"We don't work for no lawyer," said Jelly, and instructed Nick to begin with the sofa.

Nick got a steak knife from the kitchen and Jelly rolled Yancy onto the floor. While the two toughs gutted the cushions, Merry stood there shaking her head. "He's not *that* dumb," she said.

The stuffing yielded no ring. Nick said to Jelly: "It'll take all fuckin' night to toss the whole place. We should torch his boat and maybe then he'll talk."

"I dunno. Ain't much of a boat." Jelly was eyeing the skiff through the window.

"They still blow up good, bro. Drop a rag in the gas tank and touch it off—all that fuckin' fiberglass, you kiddin' me?"

Yancy was gray-faced, on his knees. "Don't burn my boat," he rasped. "Go look in the refrigerator."

"We ain't thirsty." Jelly was screwing with him now.

"I hid the diamond in the hummus," Yancy told them.

Nick grimaced. "That's so fuckin' gross. I'm glad you got stabbed."

Both thugs refused to touch the hummus. They made the redhead scoop out the engagement ring and rinse it under the faucet.

Before leaving, Jelly approached Yancy, who was still on the floor. "Also, we're supposed to tell you it'd be a real smart move to sell this fuckin' house. Other words, someone makes an offer I'd jump on it."

Nick said, "Yeah, like tomorrow."

Yancy looked up and said, "Aren't you guys late for the *Jersey Boys* audition?"

On the way out Jelly kicked him in the side. Nick kicked him in the ass. Afterward they drove to Key West, checked into the Reach and went looking for fresh stone crabs. Nick phoned Big Noogie from the restaurant to tell him the good news.

"So where's the rock now?" Big Noogie asked.

"Jelly's pocket."

"I hope that's a joke. Ha fuckin' ha."

"Whaddya mean?"

Big Noogie explained, "If the ring don't make it back to Miami, you're both dead. Just pick out a fuckin' dumpster for me to throw your body parts."

Nick and Jelly ran to the Kia and hightailed it back to their room, where they locked Big Noogie's diamond in the safe. Then they walked to a titty bar counting eleven roosters along the way, and also the biggest motherfucking rat they'd ever seen.

Benny the Blister's fanatic passion for *Bayou Brethren* sprang from an induced sense of kinship with Buck and his rowdy family. The show's producers had strategically cultivated a fandom with two distinct segments: those who were cynically amused by the boorish culture of the Nance clan, and those who identified with it. Each week the writers strived to portray the brothers on a social bandwidth halfway between harmless rednecks and odious white trash. It was a precarious tightwire.

From the very first episode Blister Krill could imagine the brothers' severe opinions about homos, transgenders, blacks, Muslims, Hispanics and probably Jews. Although the show's scripts steered away from touchy political messaging, Buck's bootleg YouTube rants had convinced Blister that he and Buck were on the same righteous page, ideologically. (The patriarch's tirades were mostly outtakes from the weekly TV tapings that had been leaked to the Internet by disgruntled crew members, much to the rapture of hardcore *Brethren* cultists.)

The abduction of Buck Nance had unfolded spontaneously, with no criminal intent. Of course Blister had been front and center at the Parched Pirate when Buck fled the angry mob. Blister had tried to catch up, running as fast as a nearsighted half-drunk imbecile could run, but Buck had vanished in the maze of fragrant alleys that crisscrossed Old Town.

All night Blister had stayed up searching, and he didn't let up at daybreak. It was mid-afternoon when he'd spotted a haggard figure huddled by the seawall at the Southernmost Point. The man wore the standard Panama hat, board shorts and Bum Farto tee-shirt, yet his demeanor made him stand out from the other tourists who were posing for group selfies in front of the famous red-topped sea buoy.

Blister had sidled closer to study the loner, who paced restively and scratched at his pale bristled jaw. It was a testament to the depth of Blister's worship that he recognized Buck without the hallmark beard. Perhaps the bow-legged gait and lopsided slope of the shoulders would have been recognizable to anyone who'd watched every *Brethren* episode no less than fifty times.

"Yo, Captain Cock!" Blister had sung out.

The huddler's head had snapped around, the wary pale eyes sizing up this brazen intruder. There was no place to run. Nor was escape by water an option, because, as Blister well knew, Buck was a terrible swimmer. During one show he'd nearly drowned trying to spring a dead muskrat from a snare his brothers had submerged in the family bayou; Buddy Nance (or maybe it was Junior) had dived in and hauled Buck by the suspenders back to the pirogue.

On the southernmost seawall Blister Krill stepped up and introduced himself as Buck's all-time number one fan in the world.

"I'm not Buck Nance," the man had said.

"Are too. You shaved your face is all."

"No, my name's Romberg. Matt Romberg."

"Now quit that," Blister had said firmly. "With me there's no cause to be skeert."

Buck didn't look bad without a beard, just thinner and older.

"Go away. Get lost," he'd snapped, the melodic Cajun accent supplanted by a pinched flat cadence that hinted at a sinus infection. Blister figured this was part of Buck's effort at self-disguise, in case factions of the angry Parched Pirate mob were still stalking him.

"I was there at the bar last night," Blister had confided. "It was shameful how you's mistreated. I thought your jokes was real funny and who cares what them fags say. Don't worry, Buck, I won't let nobody hurt ya."

"I don't know what the hell you're talkin' about," Buck had insisted in a heated whisper. "Leave me be!"

All Blister had wanted was some one-on-one, yet Buck had remained standoffish and curt. So Blister had pressed a fishing knife to his ribs and led him down the waterfront to where the dinghy was tied. It had been a choppy white-knuckle ride out to the *Wet Nurse*, a patched-up old cabin cruiser that Blister had won in a dart game and kept secret from Mona, his common-law wife, who would have nagged him into selling it to pay off their bills.

As a captive Buck was slow to soften, refusing to drop the stupid Romberg routine. Until that happened, Blister warned, they could never be best friends. It was important that Buck Nance own his Buckness.

"But, dude, it's just a fucking act!" Buck would plead.

"Really? So, you sayin' it's cool for two homos to marry?"

"No! No! Of course that ain't natural. Same with whites and blacks hookin' up. Sin is sin, okay? But the guy you see on the TV show, that's not actually me. They were casting for a major hick, you understand, someone to eat grits and preach hellfire. Me and my brothers, we're just musicians from Milwaukee."

Blister said, "Nice try, Coon Ass."

Buck remained cuffed to his bunk though well fed and sufficiently hydrated. Blister took away his Panama hat and later the Bum Farto tee-shirt. As a show of support he chopped his own beard and got an ornate rooster tattoo on his belly. Buck wasn't as moved by those gestures as Blister had hoped, so Blister went the extra mile and had his back emblazoned with the words "Hail Captain Cock."

Buck's reaction: "You're scaring me, man."

Aboard the *Wet Nurse* Blister kept a small cedar box of trout flies made with feathers from the fancy fowl on the Nance farm. There were midges, woolly buggers, stimulators, caddises, parachute Adamses and even yellow humpies. Blister, who wasn't a fisherman, had purchased the flies from a collector on eBay and memorized their names. He opened the box to show Buck, who said he didn't care much for trout; pike and muskies were his favorites. He also let slip his hatred of chickens, which hurt Blister's feelings in light of his new tummy tat.

Most days, after his cheeseburger run, Blister would spend time hanging with Buck on the boat. Occasionally he'd stay the night before returning to the apartment to deal with Mona and the unruly mongoose, which a crabber had falsely sold him as a prize mink. Mona was the only one who called it Clee Roy, a caustic dig at Blister's obsession with the Nance brothers. The pungent critter would snooze on his lap while he watched his game shows or Maury. In the evenings Blister leaned toward Fox News, which was doing a thorough job of covering Buck's disappearance. That was how Blister learned that the producers of *Bayou Brethren* were continuing to tape the series despite the absence of the venerable patriarch. When Blister excitedly tuned in to the first of the new episodes, he was dismayed to hear the other brothers (not to mention Krystal, Buck's once-adoring wife) present a callous cover story saying Buck was in rehab, Buck was a mess. How could they talk that way about him?

Owning no vehicle, not even a bike, Blister traveled back and forth from his apartment to the harbor by jumping the last car of the Conch Train. The day after getting his Captain Cock tattoo he spied an obvious Muslim sitting alone, pretending to be a harmless tourist. As a disciple of Buck's YouTube diatribes, Blister felt intellectually equipped to confront the dark-skinned passenger, who tried to act peace-loving and puzzled by the intrusion. Blister wasn't fooled. All those bastards had jihad in their bones, like Buck said.

So Blister got up in the little Muslim's face and began unloading some major white Christian truths, when all of a sudden the dude spun around and leaped off the tram. His face hit the street so hard that it sounded like brick on brick. Blister ran away knowing the man was hurt, though he didn't learn he was dead until later. The story came on the Channel 10 news while he and Mona ate supper. Blister freaked and ran straight to the toilet, where he barfed up his Hot Pockets.

Cop cars were still blocking the intersection when Blister crept back to the scene. It was there he spotted Lane Coolman, Buck's manager, whom he'd seen interviewed on either TMZ or E! Blister waited until Coolman was alone on a side street before rushing him from the shadows, brandishing the knife.

Later, after delivering his new captive by dinghy to the *Wet Nurse*, Blister felt as though he'd fallen short again. Buck was the polar opposite of joyful upon seeing his friend and career advisor. He ripped angrily into Coolman, calling him—among other things—a useless Hollywood shitstick.

"This is all your fault!" Buck yelled. "You're the dumbass who booked a stand-up in Key fucking West—and then you bailed on me!"

The shouting hurt Blister's eardrums, so he slapped strips of duct tape across each of his prisoners' mouths. To Buck he said, "You won't believe what happened, brother. I think I kilt me a ISIS!"

Buck's pupils widened, and his head shook back and forth so violently as to launch the Panama hat, which Blister had removed from his own head and placed at a festive slant upon Buck's.

"Ain't no lie," Blister said, trying to sound cold. "Man was sittin' in broad daylight on the damn Conch Train. I 'spect he was gonna blow the motherfucker up. But not now he ain't! Now he gone to meet all them horny virgins."

A low moan escaped from beneath the tape on Buck's lips. He looked at Coolman, who gravely lowered his head.

In the following days Blister came to regard Buck's manager as clutter, a piece of unused furniture that kept getting in the way. Aboard the *Wet Nurse* Blister focused on bonding with Buck, and there were moments when he seemed to be gaining headway. Other times Buck was sulky and peevish.

Blister would be rambling on about which of all the *Brethren* shows were his favorites, about Krystal's new Miranda Lambert haircut or Junior's drunken ATV rollover or Clee Roy's lame moonshine or Buddy's secret recipe for sautéed gator jowls when suddenly Buck would start thrashing in his handcuffs and burst out:

"But I'm just a Romberg, don't you get it? Swear to God I'm just a Romberg from Wisconsin!"

Blister was in no mood for Buck's outbursts when he returned to the cabin cruiser after stabbing the stranger in his apartment. He jumped bare-chested off the dinghy and stomped down to the bottom deck and threw the crumpled Bum Farto tee-shirt at Buck's feet.

"Please tell me that's barbecue sauce on it," Coolman said, craning forward on his bunk.

Blister shook his head. "That be blood, Mr. Hollywood Boy."

"Are you hurt?"

"Hell, do I look hurt?" He thumped his bony chest and pointed down at the tattoo rooster, whose luminous navel-eye seemed fixed on Buck's forehead.

"Then whose blood's that?" Buck asked.

Blister was pleased that his hero was finally showing some interest. He said, "I just put a knife in a cop."

"You did not."

"Yessir. And it's for you I done it."

Buck said, "Have you lost your goddamn mind?"

"Did he die?" Coolman interrupted in a trembling voice.

"That I can't say. Some chick dragged him off, left a spatter trail like a gut-shot hog so maybe yeah he's dead. Leakin' real bad if he ain't." Blister sat down on the end of Buck's mattress and licked the salty rime from his lips. He felt tired, jumbled. "Point is," he said, "I can't wear that damn shirt no more 'cause they both seen it on me."

Coolman said he'd need more than a new wardrobe if he really killed a policeman. "Like plastic surgery, a fake passport and a suitcase full of cash."

Blister revised that part of the story. "He told Mona he's a cop but I never saw no badge. He was trespassin' on my homestead is my position as a citizen. And a man's homestead is his righteous castle under the law. Ya said so y'self, Buck Nance. Season two, episode six."

"Aw, come on." Buck raised his arms, rattling the cuffs. "Man, what is it you want from me? If not cash money, then what?"

That's when the idea struck Blister like a thunderbolt from the heavens.

"I want to be on your show," he said to Buck Nance. "I want to be one of your brothers."

FIFTEEN

"What parts did I leave out before, Andrew? Besides the best."

Merry thought he was sleeping, so she opened up.

"I was a super-normal kid, believe it or not—an only child, B-plus student, girls' softball. I played second and shortstop. This was suburban Orlando, my reality. Mom and Dad couldn't stand each other, so after high school I married a guy to get out of the house. Paul was his name. Paul, the food-stamp scammer, I found out later. He was in prison when the divorce went through, and I took that a-hole for everything he had—$274 and a set of golf clubs. Then comes a gap, as they say, in the narrrative. Several years of me figuring out how the big bad world works."

Yancy wasn't asleep, just neutralized by pain pills. He kept his eyes shut so Merry would keep talking.

"Waiting tables, bartending, selling ladies' shoes, even patio furniture," said Merry. "One time—you'll love this—I took a job at Disney as a backup Snow White. And guess what—the seven dwarves? They're all chicks! After that, let's see, TGI Friday's, Ruby Tuesday, Red Lobster. I drew the line at Denny's, though. Not a morning person."

She was sitting beside him on the edge of the bed. Her hair was pinned up, and she was wearing her tube top and jeweled flips. She touched Yancy's arm but he didn't stir.

"Fast forward to South Beach and my life of crime," she said. "His name was Chip. Said he was in the insurance business, and he sure *looked* like an insurance man. Of course I believed him. His name was fucking 'Chip'! Turned out his real deal was ripping off insurance companies—crashing into cars on purpose, faking whiplash and then suing. It was a big operation. They had their own doctors, lawyers, chiropractors. I looked around and didn't see any good guys. Chip was making decent money, so one day I said, hey, let me drive the bump car. And it was a *major* rush, Andrew, gotta be honest. The point of impact was, like, the best sex ever. Total control. Total power. And nobody ever got hurt, not even a bruise. So I was basically all in."

Yancy opened his eyes. Merry said, "You little shit! You were faking it!"

"Why tell your life story to an unconscious person?"

"Because then technically it won't be a lie when I say I've told you everything."

That almost made sense. Yancy credited the pain meds. He asked Merry what had happened to good old Chip.

She said, "I caught him boning the Geico adjuster. A bottle redhead!"

"There was fallout, I assume."

"Here's what I've decided, Andrew. I'll stay and take care of you until your precious Rosa comes back—but no rehab nookie."

"There's nineteen sutures in my gut," he reminded her.

"That won't stop you from trying. It's only a matter of time. You could be in a body cast and I'd still make you pop a tent."

Yancy squinted at his watch. "Oh no. I was supposed to be at Clippy's an hour ago."

Merry offered to drive. She grabbed her fleece, threw on some jeans, and helped him into the Subaru. The Percocets were wearing off. He put on his sunglasses and probed the cupholders in search of a joint, with no luck. As soon as they reached the main highway, Merry stomped on the gas pedal. She encouraged him to call Rosa and tell her he got stabbed. "I bet she'll jump on the first plane home."

"She's started a new job in Oslo," Yancy said. "I don't want to wreck her plans."

"Why not? Lovers wreck each other's plans all the time." Merry was flying past an eighteen-wheeler, Yancy digging his fingernails into the armrest. He refused to peek at the speedometer.

"Is it a legit doctor job she's got," Merry was asking, "or a bullshit job, just to jerk your chain?"

"Rosa's not a chain jerker."

She was working in a butcher shop until she passed the Norwegian medical boards. First she had to learn the language, so she'd moved in with the butcher's family.

Merry said, "And that's it—you're just letting her go? Don't give me that look, Andrew. I know that look."

"It's just terror. Please keep your eyes on the road, I'm begging you."

When they arrived at the restaurant, Merry said, "I'm snaggin' that handicap spot, so be sure to limp when you get out of the car. Make it good."

A buoyant Irv Clipowski was waiting in the dining room. "We nailed the last one!" he announced. "You ready for champagne?"

On rubbery legs Yancy followed him to the freezer, where the remains were sealed in Tupperware. Clippy said the sous chef had dropped a sack of basmati on the fleet intruder.

Yancy borrowed salad tongs to lift the corpse. His verdict: "It's not a pouchie."

"No way! Check out the balls on that mother."

Merry, standing behind Yancy, said, "They're whoppers, Andrew."

"Sorry, but this isn't a *gambianus*. Cheeks are too small. Tail's not white. It's just a standard, well-nourished rat."

Clippy drooped. "Stomp on my heart while you're at it."

Yancy did a quick walk-through and found, besides three bottle-fly wings, only one reportable violation: spoiled meringue.

"Dump it," he told Clippy, and "you're back in business tonight."

"I love, love, *love* you, Andrew!"

"But, listen, I can't cut you another break if more pouchies show up. Not to mention you'll get slaughtered on TripSwami."

"Destroyed," Clippy agreed. "Don't worry, Neil and I won't let that happen. Would you like a crabcake for the road?"

Martin Trebeaux remained in leisure mode. He'd heard nothing more from Detective Burton, which meant that the Case of the Two Crashed Buicks was no longer a priority.

The view from the La Concha's rooftop had kindled Trebeaux's daydream of movable Cuban beaches. It was a blustery afternoon, always good for business. High winds meant brutal erosion along Florida's Atlantic coast, a godsend for companies like Sedimental Journeys. The unstoppable sea was once again inhaling priceless waterfront, and soon Sedimental's phones would be chiming off the hook.

Trebeaux had first become intrigued with the possibilities of sand trafficking during the BP oil spill, when lush Gulf beaches were smeared by green-black tar and dotted with sick sea birds, flapping to exhaustion in the goo. Panic took hold in seaside communities, soiled beachfront and dying marine life being lethal to the tourist trade. Even the Spring Breakers, normally unfazed by stench, were fleeing the coast. The thought occurred to Trebeaux that all those beleaguered municipalities would pay outlandish sums to get their beaches restored, the gunk and gull corpses buried safely from view under tons of clean, white, blindingly photogenic sand.

At the time, however, Trebeaux had been unable to capitalize on the crisis. He was tied up on another lucrative project—filing false claims for massive financial losses that he never actually incurred due to the drilling accident. The businesses he owned were three virtual massage parlors, a unisex waxing salon and the obligatory strip joint. All were located in Kissimmee, Florida, ninety-seven miles inland from the Gulf of Mexico and therefore untouched by the oil spill. No one was more happily surprised than Trebeaux when a compensatory check for 1.6 million dollars arrived from BP. It was doubly satisfying because Trebeaux didn't have to split his windfall with any lawyers, salivating hordes of whom had been trolling for fake victims up and down the Sunshine State. Instead of signing with a shyster firm, Trebeaux had hunkered alone in his condo and personally filled out every claim form, diligently documenting a non-existent plunge in tourist traffic at his Kissimmee establishments following the Deepwater Horizon blowout. His meticulous fraud paid off, the BP payout being large enough to seed his current sand-dredging enterprise.

The Pitrolux case he would leave to Brock Richardson. Trebeaux emailed photos of his unsightly though long-healed rash to the lawyer, then he returned his focus to the Cuba project. A political shift in Washington was panning out in his favor; soon he'd be able to travel to Havana with no troublesome scrutiny from the State Department. Because cultural visits were being encouraged, Trebeaux had decided to present himself as a sculptor. He was already busy composing phony letters of acclaim. There was no free time to pursue Pitrolux over its defective hard-on gel, so he welcomed Richardson's offer to include him in the class-action gangbang.

The lawyer's newest TV commercial had begun airing on ESPN, strategically slotted between ads for Cialis and Flomax. Trebeaux was back in his hotel room, watching the Miami Heat blow a twenty-point lead to the Bulls when Richardson's Pitrolux pitch came on, ending with a killer tag line: *"And remember, I'm not just your lawyer, I'm a fellow victim!"*

Trebeaux immediately called to congratulate him. "Where'd you come up with that one?"

"It just hit me one night," Richardson replied without elaboration. "I'm glad you called. I've been waiting to hear how it went with your guys."

"My guys? Oh, yeah. *Those* guys."

"Did they go visit my asshole neighbor?"

"Yeah, but bad news. They didn't find your pretty lady's diamond,"

Trebeaux said. One of Big Noogie's crew had phoned to tell him the rock wasn't there.

Richardson groaned and said, "Shit."

"They turned the whole house inside-out. These were pros."

"Was Yancy there when they showed up?"

"You bet. That was the whole point, right? Let him know who he's messin' with."

"For sure," said the lawyer. "Did they say he's ready to sell?"

"You should go see him. Bring a contract."

"Get this: The geek-ass archeologist dug up another fucking tooth on my lot. He's all stoked because this one's an incisor."

"Also from a dead Indian? That sucks." Trebeaux stood in his boxers at the window, watching a mammoth cruise liner leave the port. Illuminated from bow to stern, it looked like a floating shopping mall. Destination: San Juan, Negril, or maybe the BVI. One thing was certain—all those passengers, thousands of sun-seeking zombies, had paid good money to go somewhere that had a beach.

"Thanks just the same," Richardson was saying, "for making that phone call. Your guys—when they went to see Yancy, how'd they get the message across? I'm just curious."

"These things I don't ask. For all I know it was a calm, friendly chat."

"Right." Richardson chuckled dryly on the other end. "I'll keep you up to speed on the Pitrolux litigation. They'll never risk a jury trial, so we'll get a lump-sum settlement, for sure."

"Any guess on how much?"

"Eight figures at least."

"Nice," Trebeaux said. "Split how many ways?"

"Depends on the number of plaintiffs. No worries, you'll be taken care of."

"Much appreciated, friend." Trebeaux cracked open the window. A sea breeze brought a sweet steel-drum version of "One Love." The sand man couldn't think of one good reason to drive back to Miami Beach in the morning.

"What'd the doc say?" he asked Richardson.

"Um . . ."

"When I saw you at Louie's, you were on your way to the proctologist."

"Dermatologist. And everything's fine," Richardson said brusquely.

"I get basal cells from time to time. It's the curse of living a sun-kissed life."

"This is just a little skin tag."

"Word to the wise. Keep an eye on it."

"Oh, I am," said the lawyer.

Merry took Yancy to Petronia Street where they found Blister's apartment cleaned out except for an untouchable queen mattress and a cracked hallway mirror. Yancy noticed half-scrubbed stains from his own blood on the floor, and mongoose tracks in the bathtub. The landlord said the Krills had moved out in the middle of the night. Other tenants had complained of a Ryder truck double-parked in front of the building.

Back in the car Yancy's phone began ringing. He saw it was Burton and let the call go to voicemail. Yancy had been dodging his friend in case he'd caught wind of Yancy's messy visit to the emergency room. Burton would never fall for the rake-mishap story.

Most criminals would have fled the county after knifing what they believed was a cop, but Benny the Blister seemed exceptionally thick. Yancy asked Merry to drive over to Stock Island, where the rents were lower. Sure enough, they came upon a Ryder truck parked at a duplex that hadn't seen a coat of fresh paint since Hurricane Donna. The truck's back door was rolled up and the cargo space had been emptied. There was no activity at the duplex.

Yancy told Merry to keep driving.

She said, "No disrespect, Andrew, but I don't get what's so fun about the cop life. You spend all day in the damn car. Where's the high?"

"When something big finally happens."

"Like getting stabbed by a random dirtbag. What am I missing here?"

"It's all about catching the bad guys. Very primal."

"Well, I'm primally hungry," Merry said.

"You want excitement? I know just where to go."

The nearest restaurant happened to be Stoney's Crab Palace, where Yancy had issued reams of gag-inducing citations. More than once he'd shut the place down. The owner, Brennan, darted for the kitchen as soon as he saw Yancy walk in the front door.

"Don't order the fish," Yancy advised Merry when they sat down.

"But it's a seafood joint."

"More like a petri dish with menus. When they say 'catch of the day,' they mean infection."

Brennan emerged wearing a hastily donned hair cap and two left-handed disposable gloves. With a taut smile he approached Yancy asking, "What brings you here, Inspector?"

"Lack of options. We'll both have the chicken, no gravy on the potatoes."

"So . . . this isn't official business?" Brennan glowed with relief. "How about a cup of conch chowder, on me?"

"That's exactly where it'll end up, if I eat it."

"Jesus, Andrew, not so loud."

"He got thirty-two stitches," Merry told Brennan, "so he's cranky today."

"What happened?"

"Nineteen stitches," said Yancy. He was eyeing the baseboard beneath the table, where a hale cockroach stood glossy and fearless. "Does that one have a name?"

"Aw, fuck." Brennan whipped off a shoe and began whaling at the insect, which escaped easily.

Merry excused herself and went to the ladies' room. After Brennan re-tied his shoe, he placed a greasy fifty-dollar bill beneath the spoon at Yancy's table setting. "Andrew, don't write me up for one lousy roach, 'kay?"

The bribe offer was a Stoney's ritual. Yancy made Brennan pick up the fifty and asked him if he knew a man called Blister. Brennan said no.

"Then where'd you get that thing?" Yancy pointed at a doll-sized tunic hanging on a wall hook.

"I bought it from some lady come in last night and tried to sell me a friggin' mink."

"That was a mongoose," said Yancy.

"I told her I had no use for such a varmint but I'd pay ten bucks for the purple jacket. She said okay, it's a deal."

"That's Blister's wife."

"The jacket's for my dog," Brennan seemed obliged to explain.

Yancy heard Merry calling from the restroom and he went to investigate, Brennan tight on his heels. Merry opened the door for them and said, with breezy satisfaction, "Gentlemen, look what I spied."

A trail of small dark pellets lined the dingy tile near a broken tampon machine.

"Capers!" Brennan squawked indignantly. "Some jackass from the kitchen must've spilled 'em there!"

Merry turned to Yancy and said, "This I find unacceptable."

They departed before their chicken entrées arrived. Yancy's midsection was on fire from the stitches; in the car he doubled over, arms tight across his waist. Merry fed him another pain pill.

Back at the duplex, the Ryder truck was gone. Yancy told Merry to park on the next block over. He selected a spot from which they could surveil Blister's new backyard, where the restless Clee Roy was tethered to a crooked swing set.

Merry said, "We should set it free, the poor thing." She grabbed one of her energy drinks and downed it like a shooter. "How'd I do back there at the restaurant? Spotting those teeny mouse poops all by myself."

"Great eyes. You're a natural," Yancy said. "Do me a favor."

"What—go down on you? I'm not sure that's proper stakeout procedure."

"Pin your hair, zip up the fleece and take a stroll past the duplex. See if anybody's home. And not a sexy walk, all right? A plain dull walk, like you're on your way to the post office."

Merry said, "What if I don't have a dull walk?"

"Try to blend in with the neighborhood is all I'm saying."

She clicked her teeth. "Challenging."

"Yes, I'm well aware."

She set off in a flat-footed stride, arms swinging, head down. Yancy would have laughed but his eyes were elsewhere, watching for Benny the Blister. He had a hunch that the man who stabbed him was the same one who fatally accosted the late Abdul-Halim Shamoon.

A gray bank of knife-edged clouds overtook the sun, flattening the afternoon light. Yancy got out and leaned against the car, waiting for the Percocet to kick in. He'd always loved the breeze from the Stock Island docks, the sharp tang of salt, iced fish and diesel. A pair of gray doves trilled from their perch on a telephone wire, and Yancy whistled back.

Looking between the houses he saw Merry coming down Blister's street—despite her best acting she still stood out, like most beautiful women when they try not to be noticed. Nearing the duplex she shortened her steps.

"No, no, keep going," Yancy coached under his breath.

Unexpectedly she slipped out of sight. He struggled back into the car and started the engine. Moments later the mongoose began yipping, and Yancy saw Merry sprint in her rhinestone flip-flops across the barren lawn. Somehow she climbed the fence hauling an object that looked like an oversized toilet seat. The instant she was back in the car, he hit the gas, heading for Highway 1.

"Nobody home," she reported breathlessly. "Boxes all over the place. Are you good to drive?"

As Yancy spun the steering wheel he experienced a bolt of pain just shy of agonizing. "Whatcha got there?" he asked.

Merry showed him. "It was lyin' on the ground near Clee Roy. I found it when I went to pet him."

"Did I not mention he was a fucking mongoose?"

"I felt super-sorry for him, Andrew, all lonely and tangled in his rope. Anyway, I thought this thing might be a clue."

"Looks more like Clee Roy's chew toy."

Merry made a snarky face. "You're welcome, *Inspector.*"

The item she'd taken from Blister's backyard was a lifebuoy of the donut style customarily hung on boat cabins. The Styrofoam was pocked with animal tooth marks, but the name on the lifebuoy was still legible:

Wet Nurse.

Yancy said, "Stop pouting. We'll check it out first thing tomorrow."

"Gosh, I feel so honored." Merry flung the life ring into the backseat, pulled off her flips and planted her bare feet on the dashboard.

Mona unpacked the rest of the boxes before walking to the Comcast office to sort out a credit issue. Blister expected full cable and Wi-Fi when he came back from wherever the hell he went every day. Mona wasn't in love with the duplex, but she was glad they weren't on the run from the law. Blister swore up and down that nobody had seen him spook the Muslim off the Conch Train. As for the dude he stabbed, Blister said it couldn't possibly have been a real cop or he'd already be locked up at county, no bail. That made sense to Mona; it also explained why the dude didn't have a gun. He probably got sent by somebody Blister owed money to, a list that included half the dirtbags in Monroe County. Mona didn't dwell on it; she was simply glad that Blister had decided to stay put. Island life suited her.

Upon returning from Comcast she peeked in the backyard hoping the mongoose had gnawed through the rope and run away—but no such luck. The night before, Blister had searched the apartment for the critter's silly purple jacket. Mona didn't tell him she'd sold it at Stoney's; her husband was aware she didn't adore his unusual housepet.

"Look on the bright side of the penny. We won't never have no snake problem with Clee Roy 'round," Blister would say.

"Hell, I'd rather have snakes," Mona would fire back. "Least a snake won't get into my fuckin' Froot Loops."

The Stock Island duplex was cheaper than the apartment on Petronia, though Blister had to burglarize a Dollar Store for the cash to cover their first, last and security. The Ryder truck he had hotwired at Trumbo Point. Mona had quit asking where he disappeared to all day long (sometimes even overnight). She wasn't the jealous type and, besides, he always came home salty and rank. No woman worth worrying about would go near such a man.

Mona had met Blister while working at a massage parlor in Central Florida where she drew the line at hand jobs and even then insisted on wearing an oven mitt. Blister had invited her to accompany him to Key West, his grand plan being to outrun a bench warrant for undisclosed felonies in St. Augustine. Halfway down the turnpike Blister had let on that he was driving a motorcycle that wasn't technically his, but Mona had been a good sport about it. They ditched the bike in the Aerojet Canal and hitchhiked the rest of the way.

Blister's first decent score in Key West was a 48-inch flat-screen that became their domestic epicenter. They shared an addiction to daytime game shows, Ellen, Maury, Steve Harvey, all the CSIs, beauty pageants, cage fights and documentaries about polar bears. However, their tastes diverged radically when it came to Blister's favorite reality program, *Bayou Brethren,* which Mona thought was bogus and stupid. She didn't care for Buck Nance and couldn't wait for Krystal to get wise and dump him. His shit-heel brothers were just as worthless, in Mona's sulfurous view. *Brethren* had triggered loud arguments in the apartment on Petronia because it was broadcast during the same time slot as *Learjet Vet,* Mona's beloved animal-rescue show, which they couldn't record because Blister had broken their DVR in the process of shoplifting it.

Mona hoped her husband's juvenile worship of the Nance clan had peaked with the idiotic tattoos, which he'd hidden from her by living for days in the same rancid shirt. One afternoon she'd peeled off the garment after Blister fell asleep during a Maury rerun, and was mortified to see the words "Hail Captain Cock" stenciled garishly across his grimy shoulder blades. In a fury she rolled him over, only to be confronted by the cycloptic rooster.

It was about the same time when Blister began spending more days at large. The main reason Mona didn't bust his balls for being away so much was that it left the TV under her sole control; she could catch up on all her missed episodes of *Learjet Vet.*

When Blister returned home on this night, she was watching the one where Dr. Zeke Nekrotos lands his surgically outfitted Lear 60 in foggy northern Greenland to set the fractured femur of a yearling caribou. Blister snatched up the remote and pressed the Mute button.

Mona rose up saying, "I will kick your ass, Benny Krill."

"Hold on now—this here's important. A game changer."

"Put the fuckin' sound back on."

"Baby Buns," he said, "listen to me. I'm gone be on TV!"

Mona rolled her eyes. "Lord, you're drunk. Gimme the damn remote."

"I ain't had one sip. You are lookin' at Buck Nance's new twin brother!"

"Oh. So you lost your mind is all."

"No, no, I'm joinin' the family. It's official."

"My ass," Mona said. "Not even a dog your age could get adopted."

"Tune in and see. We're gone be rich."

"That ain't funny, Benny. That's just mean."

He shivered with excitement. "It's the God's truth, Baby Buns. I even got me a agent."

SIXTEEN

Yancy heard the Porsche coming from a mile away. When it stopped in front of his house, he stood at the doorway beckoning.

Deb's bandage was gone though her beak was still scabby from the flaming e-cig. She had dressed low-key in a tailored dark pants suit and black flats. The lawyer boyfriend wore cream-colored slacks, a light blue golf shirt and a cranberry blazer. Yancy no longer had the energy to call him anything but Brock. For some reason he looked tenser than Deb.

The couple was under the impression their diamond engagement ring was still missing, which meant that the thugs who'd removed it from Yancy's kitchen had pocketed it. He shouldn't have been surprised, yet he was. He should have felt responsible, yet he didn't. The stone would still be safe in his refrigerator if Richardson hadn't sent the two Jersey boys.

Now the lawyer was bitterly recapping the discovery of tribal teeth on his property, and his travails with the pesky state archeologist. Yancy made a mental note to deliver a five-pound sack of stone crabs to his helpful dentist and also to "Dr. Whitmore," his teacher/actor friend.

"They're saying the excavation work might take years," Richardson said, "and we don't want to wait that long to build. Deb and I don't."

"That's right," Deb murmured, distracted by intimate articles of apparel scattered on the disemboweled sofa. Richardson noticed them, too.

"You have company?"

"She's at the gun range," Yancy said. "Practicing." In truth Merry had gone to the drugstore for more gauze and sterile tape. Yancy's swathed midsection was concealed by an XXL Florida Gators sweatshirt.

Richardson said, "Let's cut to the chase. I want to buy your house, Mr. Yancy."

"It's not for sale. You can call me Andrew."

"The offer is two-fifty."

Yancy crowed at the insult.

"Take the money," said Deb, "if you know what's good for you."

Richardson added: "We're going to bulldoze this shitbox and put up something fabulous."

Yancy was in a contemplative drift, possibly due to the medication. He said, "I'm curious—what on earth do you two see in each other?"

Deb's eyes flared and she looked away. Her fiancé frowned.

Yancy slipped another pill under his tongue. "Unless you come to your senses, prepare for a future of restlessness, disappointment and betrayal. One morning you wake up praying you're alone in bed, except you're not. Lying beside you is someone with whom you've exhausted all avenues of conversation."

The couple stood mute and rigid.

"Now's the time to reevaluate your commitment, before it's too late," Yancy continued. "Besides ritually overspending on jewelry and clothes, what do you lovebirds really have in common? This ridiculous villa you want to build, it's only a diversion from the brewing domestic shit storm. Clearly neither of you is enthralled by the other, or by this particular way of life. Brock thinks of the house as a foolproof real-estate investment. Deb, you think of it as a place to get away from Brock. Meanwhile the incompatibility question hangs—does it not?—like a toxic fog. My advice is to separate on good terms and bolt for the exit."

Deb was seething. "Don't you take this shit from him!" she cried at her fiancé, who wheeled on Yancy and said:

"Two-seventy-five is my final number. That's all cash, brother."

Yancy said, "It's not for sale, you poor doomed fuckwit."

"Hit him or something!" Deb whinnied.

The lawyer squared up and shook a finger in Yancy's face. "My friends from up North will be paying you another visit."

"They definitely aren't your friends," Yancy said. "Hey, can you guys help me haul this sofa to the road?"

Another unmannered departure followed, capped by a cliché of squealing rubber. Deb and her man were plainly a poor fit, although Yancy's interest in enlightening them was purely selfish. Once they broke up, the mansion-building project would be scotched and the lot would go back on the market. Yancy's transcendental sunset view would be preserved, at least for a while. With any luck, the next buyer would have a soul.

Yancy took his laptop out to the deck. There, hanging on a rail peg, was the pitted life buoy that Merry had swiped from Blister's yard. The *Wet Nurse* remained a mystery. In Florida, boat registrations list the owner but not the name of the vessel. According to the databases, no motorized watercrafts belonged to anybody named Benjamin Krill—hardly a shocker, given Blister's disdain for legalities. Yancy poked around the Internet long enough to find pictures of nine different boats named the *Wet Nurse*, at which point he gave up.

Merry returned wearing a white lab coat she said she bought at a thrift shop, to help put her in a nursing groove. The rest of her medical uniform was panties and sandals. As she tended Yancy's stitches one of her earrings dropped to the floor. When she bent to retrieve it, a bright little bumblebee peeked briefly from under her coat.

Yancy said, "You went back to Wikky? Please tell me that's just henna."

"No, it's real, because that's how I roll." Merry turned around to show off the tattoo, mid-slope on a heartbreaking butt cheek. "Am I the first girl to do this for you, Andrew?"

"Permanently scar themselves on a whim? Yes, I believe so."

"It's not a scar, buddy. It's a commitment."

"That would explain the 'A.Y.'"

"Know why I put your initials down there? So I'll never forget what a pain in the ass you were."

The sight of the bumblebee gave Yancy an erection that Merry taunted as proof of his lust-crazed intent. He shuffled to the kitchen on an imaginary errand. The point, as it were, couldn't be argued—he had begun to fantasize about diving under the sheets with his houseguest. Yancy worried that pain was all that stood between him and a fateful lapse of judgment. Thank God for the knife wound.

Merry drove him to the docks at Garrison Bight where he finally made headway. Captain Keith Fitzpatrick, a friend who ran deep-sea fishing charters, told Yancy he'd seen a cabin cruiser called the *Wet Nurse* anchored near Sunset Key. Fitzpatrick guessed the boat's length at thirty-one feet and described it as a crumbling mess, possibly abandoned.

"Can you take us to see it?" Yancy asked.

Fitzpatrick had to say no. He was up to his bloody elbows in a forty-pound cobia that he was filleting for his two clients, who hovered rapturously. Composite-flooring distributors from Chapel Hill, the men had invited Fitzpatrick to the Turtle Kraals for beers in hopes he would forgive them for arriving hungover that morning, vomiting into the bait tank and dozing through the only strike of the day. It was the captain himself who'd reeled in the fish with which the flooring executives had victoriously posed, the photos instantly zapped to their Anglergram pages. Fitzpatrick would have preferred the company of Yancy and his sweet-smelling companion, but he perceived that the defective Carolinians were withholding his tip until he showed up at the bar.

Yancy, who understood the grueling politesse of charter fishing, was sympathetic. Farther along the dock he and Merry approached a long-haired, part-time guide who for fifty bucks agreed to take them to Sunset Key. His nickname was Gack and he ran a 23-foot bay boat called *Marley's Ghost* in tribute to Bob, not Dickens. The clues were the knit Rasta cap and a scorched glass pipe on the console.

As they skimmed through a bracing chop past Trumbo Point, Merry slid closer to Yancy. For him there was nothing better than crossing open water with a woman at your side, and he was reminded of the warmth of Rosa's body on their morning rides in the skiff. He wondered again how she could trade such times for a butcher's block in Scandinavia.

The run to Sunset Key was short, and they found the *Wet Nurse* anchored exactly where Keith Fitzpatrick had seen it. The cabin cruiser indeed was in lousy shape, a faded, flaking live-aboard. Yancy asked Gack to circle slowly. They watched for movement but saw nothing but a lone seagull on the bow.

"She's too low in the water," Gack observed.

He was right. The *Wet Nurse* was squatting and stern-heavy.

Yancy said, "Let's go check it out."

"I can't put you on board, mister."

"Why's that?" asked Merry.

"'Cause it's not your damn boat. I won't abet an act of piracy."

Yancy was touched by the stoner's respect for maritime code. "Just get us a little closer, okay?"

Gack pulled parallel to the cabin cruiser but maintained a gap, in case Yancy was plotting to leap to the other boat. Merry had the same worry and tightened her hold on Yancy's arm. They called out several times but nobody stirred on the *Wet Nurse*. Rime on the hull's windows made it impossible to see inside, where the bunks would be located. Above deck there were no fishing rods, dive gear, not even a mop. A sloshing was audible as the boat rocked on its frayed anchor rope.

Merry asked, "Is that thing sinking, Andrew?"

"So it appears."

Gack stood up balancing on his seat, to gain a better view of the other boat's interior deck. He said, "Damn, there's a foot of water aft."

"What do we do?" Merry asked.

"Call the Coast Guard, then go home. Ain't nobody on that boat."

"You don't know for sure," said Yancy. "Let me jump aboard."

"Stay where you are." Gack hopped down and reached for his hand-held radio. "We'll give this another five minutes."

It didn't take that long. Before their eyes the *Wet Nurse* disappeared in a hushed blue-green swirl. The bird on the sinking bow didn't bother to fly. It waited for the sea to rise beneath it and then floated off, a whitish puff riding the wave crests.

When the roiling went calm, Gack said, "That was fucking impressive."

Merry could hardly believe it. The water wasn't deep, but the surface was choppy and churned. She couldn't see the shipwreck on the bottom, only formless dark patches. Gack was already on the phone with the Coast Guard providing GPS numbers and a description of the lost boat. Soon random items began floating up—Styrofoam fast-food containers, plastic cups, beer cans, seat cushions, moldy life preservers, a fire extinguisher.

"I need that," Yancy said, pointing at a smaller object, tan in color and crowned in shape.

Gack grunted. "What the hell for? You can buy a new one in town for like ten bucks."

"I don't want a new one."

Merry hung on to Yancy's belt loops while he painfully stretched over the gunwale to pick up what he'd spied amid the debris from the *Wet Nurse*. It was a banded Panama hat like the one reported stolen the day after Buck Nance went missing. Yancy placed the dripping hat in the front hatch of Gack's boat.

"You ain't even gonna put it on?" Gack said.

"It's evidence."

"Get out."

Merry said, "For real. He's a police inspector."

"Shhhh!" Yancy made a cutting gesture across his throat, as if it was supposed to be a secret. Merry acted mortified and said never mind.

Gack fell for it. In a low voice he asked Yancy, "So what's the deal? Are you, like, undercover?"

"Not anymore." Yancy threw a reproachful look at Merry.

"Is it a coke thing, or what? I won't tell anyone," Gack said. "You think there's a dead body on that fuckin' boat?"

"We're about to find out. You might want to hide that bong, captain."

"Oh, shit." Gack went into a scramble.

The flashing blue lights of a patrol vessel were approaching fast from the harbor. Gack pocketed the pipe, cinched his grotty hair into a ponytail and began tidying the deck. Merry asked him not to tell the Coast Guard officers that Yancy was a plainclothes detective.

"It'll screw up our whole case," she said.

"You a cop, too?" Gack whispered.

"Dude, I'm the informant. Without me, he's got nothin'."

Yancy couldn't get over what a pro she was when it came to this stuff. Absolutely stellar. He would miss the fun, when she was gone.

The Coast Guard crew was impossibly young and efficient. Within minutes a diver was in the water marking the site with bright buoys. Yancy studied the pattern on Gack's fish-finding sonar, which showed that the *Wet Nurse* had settled on its side, twenty-six feet down. The diver wasn't gone long. He surfaced with an upright thumb, lifted his mask and said, "All clear."

A petty officer told Gack that he and his passengers were free to go.

"Why'd she sink?" Yancy asked.

"Probably the bilge fittings went bad. Happens all the time."

Yancy didn't believe faulty bilge fittings sank the *Wet Nurse*. His doubts were confirmed when he overheard the Coast Guard diver telling the rest of the crew about the weird thing he'd seen on the sunken boat.

Two empty sets of handcuffs, locked to the bunks.

Jon David Ampergrodt gleefully thumbed a new sheaf of Nielsens showing that *Bayou Brethren* nailed a massive 23 percent share in its time slot. The show was hotter than ever. America did not miss Buck Nance.

More good news arrived via phone from Sheriff Sonny Summers in Key West: Buck was no longer a suspect in the Conch Train killing. Detectives had interviewed a local tattoo artist who'd recently inked

"Hail Captain Cock" across the shoulders of a two-bit career criminal named Benjamin Krill. The sheriff said Krill had moved out of his apartment and was on the lam.

"In other words," Amp said in a level tone, "your people aren't out looking for Buck anymore."

"They are not," the sheriff confirmed. "We've got a tight budget down here, Mr. Ampergrodt. Very limited resources."

"Yes, of course. I understand." Amp kicked off his Ferragamos and danced a jig in front of the window, fist-pumping for the wretches stuck in traffic down on Santa Monica.

"We believe Mr. Nance has left Monroe County," Sonny Summers continued, "and doesn't want to be found."

"It's very possible."

"You're better off hiring a private investigator."

"Already done," Amp lied.

"Just so you know—Benny Krill, the man that we believe killed our Muslim tourist, he's apparently a major fan of your TV show. That's why he got the tattoo. It'll all come out in the media once we catch him, which should be soon."

"I appreciate the heads-up."

"It's the least I can do, considering your generous donations to my re-election committee."

No shit, thought Amp. "Did you get the boxed set of the series I sent?"

Sonny Summers said, "Funny stuff. My wife thought so, too."

"Are you a fisherman?" Amp asked. "I'll FedEx some flies made with Buck's premium rooster feathers."

Sonny Summers said no thanks. "Blue water's my thing."

Amp had no clue what that meant. He said goodbye to the sheriff and took a call from the junior talent agent assigned to keep an eye on Buck's hotheaded mistress. To make sure Miracle wouldn't feel abandoned, the team at Platinum Artists had given her permission to seduce one of the other brothers. She selected Junior, who offered no resistance and was properly dazzled by her talents. As Amp had correctly calculated, allowing Buck's girlfriend to switch Nances had caused combustible rancor on the set, further boosting the ratings. Although the brothers' wives would never allow Miracle to appear on camera, she could still bloom into an important if unseen character—the ruthless mystery slut. Amp heard the new plot line was tracking strong in all market segments.

The young agent reported that Miracle was elated to be cheating on Buck, Junior was elated to have stolen his AWOL brother's girlfriend, and Junior's wife was threatening to put lighter fluid in his mouthwash.

"Would that kill him?" asked Jon David Ampergrodt.

"Not sure."

"Do some research, please. We don't need any more surprises."

"I'm on it," the agent said.

"And when you're done, for God's sake delete your search history."

Amp drove to the Wilshire where he met Rachel Coolman in a fourth-floor suite. His phone started ringing while his face was buried between her legs. She grabbed for his ears but he'd already veered away to peek at his caller ID.

"No way," he gasped.

"Get back down there."

"It's your husband calling."

Rachel said, "Tell him you can't talk now 'cause your mouth is full of me."

Amp retreated into a closet. "My man! Where the fuck are you?"

"I'm with Buck," Lane Coolman replied. "The where isn't important."

"So he's alive! Fantastic!" Amp strived for an approximation of relief.

"Buck's contract? Rip it up."

"The one we've been working so hard on? Why?"

"He wants a better deal, Amp. You'll need to take notes."

The connection was lousy, but the voice on the other end definitely belonged to Coolman. However, his tone was unfamiliar—frosty, subdued, curt. *Could he somehow know,* Amp wondered, *that I'm banging his future ex-wife?*

"Put Buck on the line, would you?"

"In a minute," was Lane's sharp reply, no deference whatsoever. Amp sensed that a very good day would soon be turning to shit. He wasn't wrong.

The deal presented by Lane was outrageous: Buck would return to *Bayou Brethren* at double his salary. He'd be bringing with him a long-lost twin named Spiro, for whom Buck had been searching far and wide. The stress from that heart-wrenching quest would be used to explain Buck's breakdown at the Parched Pirate and brief absence from the show. Fortunately, Buck was whole again—his brother Spiro would move to the chicken farm and acquaint himself with the rest of the family. The newfound sibling would receive $50,000 per episode; for reruns, scale plus twenty percent. If the producers refused those terms, Buck would quit and jump networks taking Spiro with him. Their new show would be called *Bayou Blood,* and it would be aired head-to-head against *Brethren.*

"And, oh, if that's how it goes down? I'll be moving to William Morris," Coolman warned Amp. "Buck and Spiro, they're coming with me."

Amp's brain was quaking. He had so hoped Buck would stay missing. The last thing the Nances needed was another brother, but the last thing the show needed was a competing spinoff.

"Lane, what is Spiro's real name?"

"Can't tell you."

"Backstory?"

"Think Elvis and Jesse Presley—except little Spiro didn't die at birth. He was kidnapped from the hospital nursery by Gypsies."

"No Gypsies," Amp said firmly.

"Then make it human traffickers. No, wait—a distraught woman who'd tragically lost her own child and was desperate to fill the void. That'll work. But then she turned out to be an amazing mom who adored little Spiro and made him the center of her life. When she died in a freak accident, he was devastated. Quit his job and ended up on the streets of Key West. That's where Buck finally tracked him down—homeless, grief-stricken and disoriented. That's our pitch."

"Okay. Tell me how the foster mother dies. What kind of accident?"

"She's hit by a runaway ice-cream truck," Coolman said.

"I like it. I really do."

"On the steps of a church."

"Too much," said Amp, scrambling to keep up. "You say Spiro was so heartbroken that he quit his job and moved to Key West. Why there?"

"Because it's the end of the great American highway, Amp. It's where the pavement runs out."

"Are you fucking with me? Because that's like pure poetry, man. We all end up at the end of the road with nothing but our dreams. Beautiful! Though I've gotta say, this lost-twin thing has sort of been overdone—"

Rachel rapped on the closet door to announce she was going home. "Tell Lane I'll see him in court. Tell him to lube up."

"What?" Lane said, his voice rising. "Who's that talking?"

"Just the waitress. I'm at Bouchon."

"I swear it sounded like Rachel."

Amp said, "Here's a question: Do they even look alike? Buck and his 'twin'?"

"When they grow out their beards, they will. Close enough, anyway."

"Lane, I've got to be honest—"

"No, Amp, you've got to be smart."

"Can I speak to Buck?"

"After the deal's done," Coolman said. "Did you think we'd disappear off the face of the earth, just to make your life easier? Seriously."

"Listen, you've got it all wrong. I am *totally* jazzed to hear your voice. I had every cop in the islands lookin' for you guys!"

Amp was rattled, off his game. Negotiating naked from a hotel closet had him at a disadvantage; normally he'd be manhandling Coolman via Bluetooth while gliding through the canyons in his Aston.

"I totally get the brother concept, Lane, but the problem is those shitbirds at the network. They're gonna want to know who is this Spiro guy, what's his angle, and so forth."

"Make the deal happen, or we're gone. I'm talking a cloud of dust."

"All right, you bet, absolutely," said Jon David Ampergrodt, jolted to the bone. "I'll have it iced by the next time we talk. That's a promise, man."

But nobody was on the end of the line.

The duplex was buzzing when Yancy and Merry arrived. Parked out front were two sheriff's cruisers, Rogelio Burton's unmarked sedan and a vented panel truck from Animal Control. Inside the apartment, Burton was attempting to interview Mona while the uniformed officers stood back watching the guy from Animal Control grapple with Benny Krill's mongoose. There was grunting and blood splatter.

When Mona saw Yancy, she said, "Shit, you *are* a cop. How bad did he cut ya?"

Yancy pulled up his shirt. Mona grimaced. "I never seen Benny like that before. He lost his goddamn mind is all," she said.

Burton led Yancy to the back bedroom and gave him a heated lecture ending with: "Andrew, this bullshit stops right now."

"Where's our suspect?"

"Like I would tell you."

"The wife claims she doesn't know, right?"

"We're still having that discussion," the detective said.

From the living room came a piercing cry. The mongoose had taken another bite out of the Animal Control officer.

"If it's any consolation," Yancy said to Burton, "Blister stabbed me."

"And still you didn't call. Unfuckingbelievable."

"Don't take it personally, Rog."

Yancy had known that either Burton or the Key West cops would eventually identify Krill from his tattoos and track him to Stock Island. It had been Yancy's hope that the hunt would take a few days, yet here they were already. He wondered if Mona would flip on her husband, assuming she knew where he went.

Another yowl arose, followed by more shouting and bedlam. Merry rushed into the bedroom to report that the mongoose had been Tased, with unsatisfactory results.

Burton threw his hands in the air, a gesture Yancy had seen many times; the two of them had had facing desks in the detective division. Yancy thought of how much he missed working with Burton; through all the low times Burton had stayed rock-solid and loyal, even when Yancy disappointed him.

"Rog, I'll tell you what I *think* I know."

"Just stick to the true parts, asshole."

"First, Blister's crazy as a shithouse rat. Second, he's got a major man-crush on Buck Nance because of that idiotic TV show. That's probably why he went after the Muslim on the Conch Train. I also think he kidnapped Buck to be his best buddy. He's been holding him captive on a derelict boat, which just happened to sink off Sunset Key this afternoon with no hands aboard. My guess is that Blister's still got Buck locked up somewhere."

"This time you're wrong, Andrew. I can't tell you how good it feels to say that." Burton was grinning. "Nobody's got Buck Nance. He's safe, sound and free as a bird."

The news jarred Yancy. "Where the hell is he?"

"The sheriff couldn't care less, and neither should you."

One of the uniformed cops knocked on the door saying the coast was clear, the mongoose having evaded capture and fled into the twilight. The officer from Animal Control was driving himself to the hospital to get his wounds treated.

Yancy asked Burton how he knew for certain that Buck Nance was safe.

"Because he called Sonny."

"Okay, wait—Sonny spoke directly with Captain Cock?"

"Less than an hour ago. Nance apologized for all the hassle he'd caused. Said he was going through a rough patch and took some time off for personal reasons, which is Hollywood for dope, booze or pussy." Burton caught himself, and turned sheepishly to Merry. "Sorry. 'Women' is what I meant to say. Dope, booze and women."

She smiled. "That's so sweet. Why can't I ever meet guys like you?"

Yancy pushed on. "How does Sonny know it was Buck on the phone?"

"Same voice from the TV show," said Burton. "Buck's agency sent Sonny a box of DVDs."

"Something's not right, Rog."

"You want to get off my shit list? Swear out a complaint against Benny the Blister for jamming that blade in your belly."

Merry piped up, "I was there. I saw everything."

"Outstanding. Then off we go." Burton drilled Yancy with an expectant stare. "That way, if this shithead skates on the Conch Train case, at least we can nail him for trying to murder you. It's your civic duty, Andrew, to press charges. Also, you fucking owe me."

"But Sonny'll go postal when he finds out what happened. I'll never get my badge back. The rest of my life I'll be swabbing meat racks for *E. coli.*"

"Let me handle the sheriff," said Burton.

Merry tugged Yancy toward the door. "Come on, sugar, time to roll."

"Rog, what you told me about Buck Nance—I'm not buying that story," Yancy said. "The pieces don't fit."

Burton said the pieces fit splendidly. "Andrew, listen to the lady. Go home, have a good night's sleep and tomorrow get your ass back on the job."

"Yes, Dad."

"Your *real* job," Burton added, as Merry pulled Yancy out the door.

SEVENTEEN

The furniture truck arrived with Yancy's new sofa—a seven-footer, slate-gray with white piping on the cushions. He lay down for a trial nap and awoke helplessly to the sound of Merry chatting on his phone.

"Why?" he croaked after she hung up.

"I called her because she has a right to know you got hurt."

"What'd she say? She coming back?"

"I promised her we hadn't slept together," Merry said. "Fifty-fifty, she believed me."

"But is she coming back?" Yancy sat up wincing. "She's not, is she?"

Merry stretched out, settling her head in his lap. "That gig at the morgue screwed her up big-time. Swear to God, *I* couldn't do it—working on stiffs all day, no way. She told me she's learning to ski. Cross-country, not downhill. She said she's getting used to the cold."

"I'm so glad you two got caught up. Want a pillow?"

"Don't tell me you're getting hard. Where's your famous manners, Andrew?"

Pinned to the sofa, he folded his arms to limit the mischief. Merry's hair was fanned exotically across his knees. Her throat featured dainty freckles in a pattern like the Little Dipper.

"Know what else Rosa told me?" she said. "They had only one

murder in all Norway last week! A couple drunk farmers arguing over a crossword puzzle, one guy smacks the other with a manure shovel. She said you hardly ever hear sirens at night, not like Miami where it's dawn to dusk. I think she really feels safe there. Much as she adores you, Andrew, she needs to be somewhere other than here. By the way, your cock's poking me in the ear."

"Do you not know anything about male hydraulics?"

Merry closed her eyes smiling. "I'm not worried. You're a hopeless gentleman."

"Tell me who you are."

"I did."

"I mean your real name."

"Who taught you how to nag?" Merry said.

Not wishing to involve Rogelio Burton, Yancy had contacted some cop friends in Miami. As he'd expected, they couldn't find anyone named Merry Mansfield in the state or federal computers. It was a relief, in a way, because there was no tawdry rap sheet to visualize.

He said, "I don't get why you're still here."

"Meaning with you? Because it's not too boring. Plus you got stabbed and need a driver. Relax, Andrew, I'll be gone soon."

"No rush."

"What are you going to do, now that the riddle of Buck the Missing Redneck is solved?"

Yancy said, "Blister's still out there."

"Your pal Burton'll find him."

"I need a project. You understand."

She drove him for a walk-through at a Wendy's, which checked out okay except for one chartreuse burger patty. The mortified manager sailed it out the rear door to a waiting raccoon, while Yancy looked the other way. The next stop was a Parisian-style bistro where an amber fleck on a cheese-cutting board turned out to be human ear wax. The laconic teenaged offender received a mild lecture on hygiene, and Yancy recorded the find as "noncritical."

Merry commented on his forgiving mood.

"Just wait," he said.

Two different customers at Stoney's Crab Palace had posted Instagram shots of "mystery meat" they'd been served as lamb kabobs. Tommy Lombardo said the photographs were inconclusive, and he asked Yancy to keep an open mind. After viewing the photos on his phone, Yancy told Merry to proceed straight to Stock Island. She dropped him in front of Stoney's, where he ambushed the owner in his office.

"Jesus, where'd *you* come from?" Brennan cried.

He was on his knees, tacking a rust-brown pelt to a bare pine plank.

Yancy said, "Is that what I think it is?"

"The mink I told you about. So what? The lady who owned it changed her mind."

"It's not a mink, you moron."

Brennan said, "Her old man's hyper-allergic, so she sold it to me for seventy-five cash. The fur is, like, a major score. I'm gonna sell it to Bergdorf's."

"What'd you do with the rest of it?"

Brennan wouldn't look him in the eye.

"The meat," Yancy said. "Shanks, loins, shoulders. Where is it?"

"Threw it all away."

"I can't decide what's worse, your lying or your cooking."

Brennan smoothed the edges of the pelt. "Show me in the code where it says you can't serve mink."

"First of all, it's a fucking mongoose. Second, you labeled it lamb, which is totally illegal."

"How bad illegal?"

Yancy anticipated another bribe offer and Brennan wasted no time, fishing a hundred-dollar bill from his back pocket. "Pitiful," said Yancy. "Put it away."

"Don't shut us down again, Andrew. I got a kid in college."

"Would that be the University of Cheech, or the University of Chong? I know your boy, Brennan. He runs a grow house on Big Coppitt."

"Cut me some slack, man."

In truth, food mislabeling wasn't a serious enough offense to justify closing down a restaurant, even Stoney's. Yancy suspected that the serving of mongoose meat wasn't specifically mentioned in the state health codes.

"Lucky you caught me on a busy day," he said to Brennan.

"I knew you was human."

Merry called Yancy from Fausto's grocery asking if he preferred Advil or Aleve. The night before, she'd flushed all his Percocets in an act of tough love.

When Yancy got off the phone, Brennan presented a platter featuring a purplish wedge of mammal flesh, scalded to the approximate texture of a roofing tile. "It's the last piece," Brennan said. "Try a bite."

"I'd rather slam my nuts in a screen door."

"It ain't half bad, Andrew. Even better would be fried cutlets."

Yancy slapped the platter from Brennan's hand and walked outside. He looked up at the bluebird sky wishing he'd worn his shades.

Spending time with Benny the Blister had shaken Buck Nance's confidence in the superiority of the white male. He and his brothers had clung to such views since their Romberg youth, warped by their father's fulminations. While redneck stardom had exposed Buck to many white fans who were poor advertisements for a master race, Blister stood out as one of the worst specimens he'd ever met—stupid, reckless, dirty and delusional.

And that's when he was stone sober.

"I can't believe we're in business with this maniac," Buck muttered to Coolman while Blister took a cacophonous dump, the bathroom door wide open.

"It's all good," said Coolman.

"He killed a dude."

"Keep it down."

"And stabbed a damn cop!"

"Ssshhhh."

"Where'd he come up with 'Spiro'? That's not a bayou name," Buck griped.

"Amp is properly freaked out, that's all that matters. A couple weeks from now, when the chopper I'm putting in your new contract lands at the rooster farm, you'll be making twice as much money as your back-stabbing brothers."

"And earning every damn dollar," said Buck.

Blister had warned them about the vicious new vibe on *Bayou Brethren*. Coolman wasn't surprised, but Buck refused to believe it until he saw for himself. They had screened the latest episode on a sixty-inch plasma in the conch house Coolman had rented for them on Fleming Street. It was the day of the rough dinghy ride back to the mainland, after Blister had sprung them from the handcuffs and sunk the *Wet Nurse* by disconnecting the seacock hoses.

Buck had grown furious watching Junior, Buddy and Clee Roy bad-mouth him on camera. He immediately gave Coolman permission to contact Jon David Ampergrodt and present the Spiro Ultimatum. Blister was soaring, too dim to foresee the obvious.

Coolman had no intention of casting a criminal on the show as his prize client's lost twin. Once Buck's rich new deal was finalized, Coolman planned to call Crime Stoppers and have Blister busted for the Conch Train killing. The network honchos wouldn't be upset; in fact, they'd be relieved because they wouldn't have to write an expensive new Nance into the story line. Meanwhile Coolman and Buck would stay mum about what happened on the boat. Putting Blister on trial for kidnapping would be counterproductive, keeping Buck in Key West at a time when his presence on the *Brethren* set would be crucial.

Now Coolman didn't need "Hell Island" or any other project in his back pocket; Buck's new deal was a lifetime score for both of them. The Nance patriarch's scrappy rebound from disgrace and scandal would be the hottest show-business story in America. At Lane's instruction Buck had already phoned the sheriff to say he was alive and well, and deeply sorry for all the fuss he'd caused. He promised to donate a truckload of *Brethren* swag to an auction benefiting the local kids' baseball league, which fully redeemed him in the eyes of Sheriff Summers.

Buck's return to television was guaranteed to rack up monster numbers in prime time and on streaming Internet. And, as the architect of the celebrity redneck's triumphal comeback, Coolman would be more valuable than ever to Platinum Artists, possibly even more valuable than Amp. The only cloud on the horizon was Rachel, and Coolman was now considering an expedited divorce settlement—before he got promoted, and the serious dough began rolling in.

"Oh no," he heard Buck say. "What the fuck?"

Blister was twirling a silver-plated semiautomatic that he'd stolen from a Mini Cooper outside the Pier House after docking the dinghy. Coolman was scared of firearms, and Buck's own limited experience came from the TV tapings, when he and his brothers would pepper whiskey bottles or beer cans under the off-screen supervision of a former Marine sniper.

"Is that thing loaded?" Coolman asked Blister.

"Not totally sure, dude."

Buck calmly told him to put the gun away. Blister instead aimed it at the plasma screen where one of the bad hairpieces on Fox News was offering insight on Ukraine.

"Just 'cause I don't have my own lawyer," Blister said, squinting one eye, "don't mean those Hollywood Jews can screw me over on this deal. You boys got my back, right?"

Buck roared, "Hell, yes, brother!"

Coolman, struggling to hide his fear, nodded devotedly.

Blister lowered the pistol. "Now on, call me Spiro."

"I'm proud to have you as a client, Spiro. Big changes are coming your way, good stuff, so get ready."

Coolman excelled at false enthusiasm, and Blister was swept along. That Coolman had persuaded the bonehead to uncuff them and abandon the *Wet Nurse* somewhat restored Buck Nance's faith in his agent. It had been Coolman who, upon learning of Blister's preposterous ambition to join the *Brethren,* conceived the lost-twin concept. Blister was so excited about becoming a Nance that he'd allowed Coolman to purchase a new cell phone for the ostensible purpose of accelerating negotiations. The rental house on Fleming, paid for with the same Platinum Artists Visa card, had been cleverly presented by Coolman as a luxury perk. Blister was ecstatic, even though the size of the place made it difficult to keep his eyeballs on Buck and his agent 24/7.

Coolman believed that Blister would come to treat them less as captives and more as fellow players in the TV deal. *Vanity always trumps common sense,* Coolman had whispered to Buck. *First rule of Hollywood.*

And, sure enough, Blister seemed to be letting down his guard. He assigned Buck and Coolman the same upstairs bedroom yet failed to secure the windows, so that escape via a Poinciana tree was available if necessary. While the presence of the handgun was unnerving, Buck reminded Coolman that Blister had acquired it by chance, not design. The dumbass had been snooping mainly for loose cash and jewelry in the Mini Cooper. His unfamiliarity with the basic mechanics of firearms confirmed his preference for knives; in addition to not knowing if the semiautomatic was loaded, Blister had no idea what caliber it was.

Buck hoped that, like most burglars, Blister would pawn the weapon at his first opportunity. Coolman was too jumpy to wait.

"You need to get rid of that thing ASAP," he told their kidnapper.

"How come? You're my agent, not my damn babysitter."

"Because if you get caught with a gun, our whole project's in the shitter. The network has a strict moral turpitude clause in every talent contract."

Blister sneered. "What the fuck is moral turpentine?"

Coolman smiled painfully. "*Turpitude.* It means bad behavior, Spiro. Such as drug use, sexual misconduct—or getting busted with a stolen firearm."

"I don't plan on gettin' busted."

"Still—"

"Listen here, I been thinkin' hard 'bout my contract," said Blister. "That man in California you been talkin' with—what's his name again?"

"Jon David Ampergrodt. He's the head of the whole agency."

"I wanna meet him."

Coolman sucked in a breath. Buck's expression turned grim.

"There's no need for a meeting," Coolman said to Blister. "Mr. Ampergrodt can overnight the paperwork directly to us."

"No, I wanna see the man. He thinks he's the shit, right? Well, *I* am the shit and I need a handshake."

Buck Nance spoke up. "Trust me, brother. That ain't how it works."

Blister waggled the semiautomatic. "It works however I say. How soon can he git here?"

Coolman cleared his throat. "I'll make a call."

"You do that." Blister flipped the gun around in his hand and casually peered into the barrel. "I can't tell if that's a damn bullet down there, or not."

Brock Richardson complained to the governor's office about the archeologist who was blocking construction of his house on Big Pine Key. The governor kept a team of smooth-talking aides who were trained to appease aggrieved campaign donors, and one of them referred Richardson to the Department of State, which referred him to the Division of Historical Resources, which referred him to the section on Compliance and Review, where nobody was answering the goddamn telephones. Richardson left an acid message warning of imminent litigation, naively presuming that anyone at that invisibly low level of government knew who he was, or gave a flying fuck.

Deb found him in the bathroom standing again with an upraised arm in front of the mirror. She said, "Don't tell me it grew back. Maybe you should go easy with that stuff."

"How about knocking first?"

"I'm not digging the visual, Brock."

"It didn't grow back. This is a new one," he said.

In fact, it was the third dangly stem to have budded in his armpits. The other pale intruders had been sliced off and biopsied, no evidence of malignancy. Richardson's doctor was, nonetheless, concerned. The tissue formations were uncanny in their resemblance to the male reproductive organ. Mini-dicks, the surgeon called them, eliciting a heartless chuckle from his nurse.

Brock had confessed his Pitrolux habit to Deb after she discovered a Soft-Glide applicator in his dopp kit. She didn't bitch him out too much because their sex life had reignited in a spectacular way. Fucking cosmic, in her words. One night, gleefully appraising his unbound erection, she exclaimed, "You could hang a rodeo saddle on that thing!"

The manufacturers of Pitrolux had replaced the product's pungent juniper infusion with a scent of "country apple," and discarded the original deodorant formula in favor of an additive that actually suppressed body reek. Deb wasn't merely approachable again, she was insatiable. Blinded by carnality, Richardson continued to slather on the dangerous hormone-infused goop several times a day—this, while his grave TV pitch with its scroll of loathsome side effects attracted more and more Pitrolux victims to the lawsuit.

"There's nothing to worry about," he told Deb in the bathroom. "They're harmless skin tags."

"Then how come they look like penises?"

"Because that's all you're thinking about these days." He managed a suggestive leer. "I'll take full credit, too."

They dropped to the floor and made love ferociously, cracking two of the travertines. Once again Richardson astounded himself. Afterward, in the shower, Deb returned to the subject of their dream-house dilemma. She implored him to reach out to Trebeaux. "Have him send those goons back to Yancy and *make* him sell his house to us."

Richardson said, "I already talked to Martin."

"You tell him we're in a hurry?"

"He knows, Deb." With soapy fingers Richardson probed his left pit, where the newest pygmy phallus had emerged.

She said, "I like Yancy's lot better than ours, anyway."

"Why? His is smaller."

"Something about the view. Can I borrow your conditioner?"

Richardson was still upset that Deb had lost the diamond ring, but the subject was no longer a constant flashpoint. This he attributed to his resurgent libido; nothing less than white-hot sex could soften a two-hundred-thousand-dollar grudge.

He toweled off, dressed for golf and called the sand man in Key West.

"What's the word, Martin?"

"Sorry, Big Noogie says no. He needs his guys to stay in Miami."

"Did you tell him I'll cover their gas, food, whatever? Yancy is balls-out refusing to sell. He basically laughed in my face."

Trebeaux said, "Those smartass types are hard to reason with. You've practically got to kill 'em."

"How much would that cost?" Richardson was startled by his own words—only a card-carrying nitwit would talk on the phone about hiring a hit man. He wondered if the Pitrolux was starting to impair his judgment. All the blood rushing to his cock might be starving his brain.

"Hey, it was just a joke," he told Trebeaux. "You know that, right?"

The sand man said, "Big Noogie's an important person. I don't want to take advantage of our friendship."

"So what the hell do I do about Yancy? For real, I mean."

Trebeaux could be heard sipping a beverage. "You told me you had guys of your own," he reminded the lawyer.

"Yeah, but they're not as good as your guys. The mob guys."

"Maybe they don't need to be. Surprise is key."

The sand man had a point, thought Richardson. Yancy wasn't hard-core; he was all talk. The club bouncers that Richardson occasionally employed might not be as experienced at assault as were seasoned Mafia goons, but years in the National Football League surely had taught them how to locate a kidney with their knees.

"I'm lining up my big Havana trip," Trebeaux was saying. "You wanna come? Bring your darling Deb."

"Some other time. We're still looking for that missing diamond."

"Bummer," said Trebeaux with a slurp. "I can probably get you a sweet deal on a new one. Just tell me how many karats. Every bride's gotta have a ring!"

"Only one to a customer," was Richardson's response.

Trebeaux switched to what he thought was a cheerier topic, the Pitrolux case. "Did you check out the photos of my rash? Gnarly, huh?"

On the other end of the call, Richardson was peering disconsolately up the sleeve of his shirt. "You got off easy," he said to the sand man.

EIGHTEEN

Yancy's passport arrived, the renewal expedited by an add-on fee he was happy to pay. He called Rosa in Norway to tell her he was coming. She said the temperature was fourteen degrees, minus-twenty counting the wind chill.

"I don't care if the fjords freeze," he said.

"Andrew, I'm not ready."

"Stay at the butcher's. I'll book my own room."

"This is a tranquil place," said Rosa. "I love you, but you're not a tranquil guy."

"I'll read Gandhi on the plane."

As Yancy was talking, Merry Mansfield appeared at the doorway, lifted her top, then danced away.

"Stabbing victims shouldn't travel," Rosa said.

"I'll be fine once I'm there. You're a doctor, remember?"

"Slow down."

"Tell me what's going on."

There was a discouraging pause. Yancy half-expected her to say she'd found a new boyfriend. He thought: *Please, God, anyone but the ski instructor.*

Rosa said, "You're right, it's got nothing to do with your damn stitches. I care about you—that's not up for debate—but I need to keep a distance from the turbulence you create. For example, getting stabbed the way you did—you could've died, okay? Died in a pool of blood on the floor of some dirtbag's apartment, and then someone like me gets to come to the scene and haul away your dumb, dead ass. I'm not trying to be cold, but it's totally your fault you ended up in that ridiculously dangerous situation with that ridiculously dangerous person—all because you wanted to prove something to the sheriff. Which, at this point . . . honestly?"

"Better spell it out. I specialize in clinging to false hope."

"A calm sea is the best place for me right now, Andrew. So hurry up and solve your case—then you can hop on that plane."

"The case is a muck pit. I'm not getting anywhere."

"You will. You always do. But don't come see me until you're finished, promise? I need you to be totally tuned in."

She said goodbye without interrogating him about Merry, another ominous sign. He'd been hoping for signs of jealousy.

Merry told him to quit moping. "For God's sake, I just showed you my tits."

"And adorable they are."

"Animal!" she snapped, then dissolved to a giggle when she saw his expression. "You don't know what to do with me, do you? I love that!"

Yancy suggested a trip to town for a late lunch. On Highway 1 they spotted Mona pedaling a child's bicycle across the Cow Key Channel Bridge. The tires were almost flat, and a sad-looking cloth purse swung from a chain around her neck.

Merry cruised ahead along South Roosevelt and pulled over at a motel to wait. As soon as Mona huffed past, Merry wheeled out and smoothly executed another leapfrog. In this way they were able to track Blister's wife all the way to Fleming Street without hovering close and drawing attention. Mona stopped at a pretty two-story conch house with lavender shutters, a rope swing on the front porch and a Royal

Poinciana in the yard. After an inelegant dismount, she propped the bike against a picket fence and approached the front door. From down the street Yancy and Merry could see her knocking with lumberjack vigor. The door opened and she stalked into the house.

Merry said, "Call Burton and tell him where we are."

"I probably should."

"Like, immediately."

"I hear you," Yancy said.

With Blister safely locked up, Yancy could be on a nonstop to Oslo tomorrow afternoon. Drop Merry in South Beach on his way to the airport.

He dialed Burton and got the voicemail. "Hey, Rog, call me back as soon as you get this. I believe I've found your Conch Train killer."

While they waited, Merry told Yancy about an item she'd seen on Page Six of the *New York Post*. "Katie Holmes went to Whole Foods, and they let her sneak in through a hidden passage. Isn't that fantastic? A grocery with a secret celebrity entrance! They should have one at Fausto's. Then, next time you send me for a gallon of milk and some Advil—except there probably won't be a next time—I could say, 'Sure, Andrew, I'll take the secret passageway.' That would be my dream. To just pop up like a genie in the produce aisle! Me and my Balenciaga."

Yancy said, "Who's Katie Holmes?"

"I will not let you burst my bubble. I refuse."

Mona came out of the conch house, mounted the bicycle and briskly began pedaling down the street, toward the spot where Yancy's car was parked. Merry said there wasn't enough room for a U-turn getaway.

"Pretend we're making out like lovers," she said, throwing both arms around Yancy's neck and kissing him in a way that didn't feel like she was pretending. He thought it would be impolite not to kiss back. Mona sneaked a sideways glance as she rode past; there was the naughty trace of a smirk, but no sign of recognition. She had turned down Grinnell Street and disappeared from sight by the time Merry sat back and started fixing her hair.

"You okay, sport?" she asked.

"I would have to say yes."

"Not a bad note to end on."

"Except we're not quite done," said Yancy.

"How dare you get bold with me!"

"No, look."

A black limousine was pulling up to the conch house. Merry identified it as the latest Cadillac stretch, with front-wheel drive and a large V-6. "You really need an 8," she added, "but these fleet companies, they want the better mileage."

"You drive limos, too?" Yancy asked.

"No, but I've done a few. Easy-peasy jobs—the chassis is so long that they don't fishtail when you hit the rear quarter panel. The chauffeurs are always super-polite, too. Some wild redhead with a razor in her hand, shaving cream all over her cooch—can you imagine what they must be thinking?"

"Only in Florida, is what they're thinking."

"I like to do limos," said Merry. "Nobody gets overexcited."

Three men walked out of the house and climbed into the stretch. First in line was Blister Krill. Next came Buck Nance, followed by his hotshot Hollywood manager, Lane Coolman.

Yancy said to Merry: "Please don't smash my poor little Subaru into that Caddy."

"Oh please. Your insurance'll cover it."

"Let's just follow them instead."

"The new Outbacks look super-sweet," she remarked. "Or you could get yourself a Forester."

"Burton's gonna call back any minute."

"Buckle up, Mario."

Yancy said, "That isn't funny. Not at all."

Dominick "Big Noogie" Aeola brought his girlfriend Juveline to Key West along with Martin Trebeaux's original bogus service dog, John.

The missing Irish setter had reappeared at Crisco's restaurant soon after word went out that Big Noogie intended to dismember whoever had taken the animal from his Town Car. Although he wasn't a pet lover, Big Noogie tolerated John the dog because his girlfriend insisted. Her given name was Lucinda but she'd called herself Juveline since age fifteen, when she'd been caught selling knockoff Burberry totes and a cop at the booking desk misspelled the word "juvenile."

Big Noogie got them first-class bulkhead on the flight to Florida. Wearing a new orange vest, John the First snoozed at their feet. Having set aside his scorn for the "comfort animal" scam, Big Noogie had persuaded a psychiatrist in Crown Heights to write a letter documenting Juveline's emotional need for canine companionship while flying. The shrink had a ruinous gambling habit so he leapt at the chance to assist Big Noogie, to whom he was monstrously in debt.

The sand man was waiting when Big Noogie got off the plane. He was surprised to see his ex–Irish setter leading the mobster down the jetway, and he felt a twinge of guilt about John the Second, the replacement fake service dog he'd set loose outside of Louie's. The feeling didn't last, for Martin Trebeaux's attention was dangerously diverted by a woman accompanying Big Noogie. She was taller, and owned many striking features—white-blond hair cropped like Annie Lennox's, full lips lacquered redder than Taylor Swift's, and a gravity-defying ass that was broad enough for a tray of mimosas. Trebeaux forced himself to look away lest Big Noogie catch him gawking.

When they arrived at the hotel, Juveline veered poolside with the dog while Trebeaux and Big Noogie discussed the Cuba deal over platters of fried seafood.

"So who's your Havana connection?" the mobster asked.

"Deputy Minister of Coastal Resources." Trebeaux had come up with that one while he was in the shower. He didn't know a soul in the Castro government.

"What's he asking for a cut?" Big Noogie said.

"Twenty-five percent."

"Fuck that in the ear. You tell him it's eighteen now on."

"I'll try, Dominick, but he's a hardass," Trebeaux said.

His plan was to hang out in Havana until he located the appropriate bureaucrat to bribe. He was confident he could get all the beach sand he wanted in exchange for twelve percent of gross resale. Big Noogie wouldn't know the true spread and had no way of finding out—he couldn't join Trebeaux on the trip because a judge was holding his passport pending resolution of a felony matter. *Alleged* felony.

"I'll fly one of my guys down there with you," Big Noogie said.

"Okay, but the Cubans got computers. Anybody with a rap sheet in the States is turned around at the airport and sent back."

Trebeaux didn't know if that was true, but it was worth a shot. He assumed every person in Big Noogie's inner circle had an arrest record, and Big Noogie's scowl seemed to confirm it.

"I can totally handle this alone," Trebeaux assured him. "It's what I do."

"Remember when you were hangin' upside-down offa that bridge? How fuckin' scared you were? Next time you're shark food, you don't play this straight."

"You think I'm out of my mind? I got the message loud and clear. Trust me, Dominick, we're gonna clean up big-time. Every tourist town on the Eastern seaboard will pay serious bank for this sand. It's like cocaine for your toes!"

Big Noogie chomped another conch fritter. "So, where's the best shit in Cuba?"

"Better than what I put down behind your hotel? My man Sergio— the deputy minister—says it's *mucho primo* on the northern shore. He says there's easy access for our barges, but I'll check it out while I'm down there."

Trebeaux ordered *mojitos,* and the two men raised a toast. Juveline appeared, body-turbaned in a flamingo beach towel. She said John the dog was chowing down on a room-service steak. Big Noogie passed his drink to her saying, "I could do without the fuckin' mint."

She said, "Noog, I just saw the biggest rat in the whole universe."

Trebeaux chuckled. "At the pool?"

"No, on the seawall. Chewin' a mango!" She placed a hand at knee-level to dramatize the creature's height.

Big Noogie looked doubtful. "Even Bronx rats ain't that big." Trebeaux said it was probably an opossum.

Juveline said, "I know what I saw. Both a you's can kiss my ass."

Trebeaux was covertly checking out her enormous bare feet, pink as boiled hams. Juveline appraised him over the rims of Gucci shades.

"When you leavin' for Havana?" Big Noogie asked.

"Soon as they okay my visa. I'll need some cash for expenses." Trebeaux didn't expect Big Noogie to say yes, but there was no harm in trying.

"Pay your own damn way. You'll get it back when the deal's done." Big Noogie handed a fritter to Juveline, who tore into it like a hyena.

Trebeaux thanked Big Noogie for sending his guys to rough up Brock Richardson's neighbor about the missing diamond ring. "Too bad they didn't find it," Trebeaux said.

"Yeah. Too bad."

"Can you believe that asshole won't sell his house? The neighbor I'm talking about. The ex-cop. Even after your guys totally trash his place, he tells my lawyer friend to fuck off, it's not for sale."

"Some balls," said Big Noogie.

Obviously the mobster didn't give a shit one way or the other, so Trebeaux dropped the subject. After lunch Juveline headed back to the seawall with a mission to photograph the mutant rat. Big Noogie was going deep-sea fishing though he extended no invitation. Trebeaux told him that Hemingway's marlin boat, the *Pilar*, was a popular tourist attraction in Cuba.

"You ain't a tourist. You're on business," Big Noogie reminded him, and went to change into sportsman garb he'd purchased online from Bass Pro.

An hour later, somebody knocked on the door of Trebeaux's hotel room. It was Juveline, wearing white short-shorts and a stressed tangerine halter. She asked Trebeaux if he was in the mood to be fucked into a coma. He said totally. She kicked off her sandals and began riding him so violently that he feared his hip sockets would crack. During the tumult a wooden slat succumbed beneath the box spring, yet somehow the bed frame remained intact. The sand man never lost consciousness and clearly heard Juveline say, before departing:

"Baby, you kiss like a blowfish on batteries."

For a long time he lay there sticky and sore, contemplating the foolishness of what he'd done. On the Death Wish scale of one-to-ten, screwing a Mafia *capo*'s girlfriend was like a seventeen. That the *capo* also happened to be your new business partner further magnified the risk. On a positive note, Trebeaux sensed it wasn't Juveline's first foray to a stranger's bed, which meant she was experienced at deceiving Big Noogie. If she weren't a skilled cheater, Trebeaux reasoned, she would already be dead.

Later he showered, shaved and walked to a restaurant called Clippy's, glowingly recommended by the hotel's rooftop bartender. While waiting to be seated, Trebeaux saw a man emerge from the women's restroom carrying an aluminum pole with a rubber snatch-noose attached to one end. The maître d' said there was a clogged pipe, which Trebeaux found amusing due to the indigo stitching on the so-called plumber's shirt: *Monroe County Animal Control*.

For wine Trebeaux selected a French Chardonnay, and for an entrée he chose poached yellowtail on a bed of quinoa. The server stopped by the table no less than a half-dozen times to ask if everything was all right.

It was Blister's first ride in a limousine. Giddily he lunged for the minibar.

Buck Nance used Lane Coolman's phone to call Krystal. "Baby, I'm coming home soon," he said.

"Who's this?"

"Aw, don't be like that."

"Wait . . . now I remember," said his wife. "You're the scumbag husband who keeps a whore on the side."

"She's just another stalker. I swear to Christ."

"Is Miracle her real name, or is that what her pimp tagged her with?"

"She's a total psycho, Krystal. You can't believe a word she—"

The line went dead. Buck tossed the phone back to his manager. His life was a war zone—first his mistress and now the entire family had turned against him. Krystal was the only one who had a legitimate cause for being mad. To Miracle he'd made no promises; she knew the score. It was the disloyalty of his three brothers that was so galling; Buck had been the steering force of their careers, from Grand Funk Romberg to the Brawlers to the *Brethren*. Without his guidance, those ungrateful jerkoffs would still be dragging their accordions to dairy festivals, opening for the bull-semen auction. Buck vowed to use his homecoming sermon at the Chickapaw Tabernacle to address in an evangelical context the betrayal by Junior, Buddy and Clee Roy. He told Lane Coolman to put a writer on the project ASAP.

The gun on Blister's lap reminded Buck that technically he was still a captive. Blister was finishing his second Jack-and-water, and he would have gulped a third had the drive to the airport not been so short. Blister fit the gun in the front of his waistband before they stepped out of the limo. The butt of the weapon was hidden by the white *guayabera* that Coolman had bought for Blister so he wouldn't look like some vagrant meth head loitering on the tarmac.

Buck got suspicious when he saw the plane taxi to a stop. It wasn't the jade-striped Gulfstream that Platinum Artists usually sent; this jet was somewhat smaller, and flat gray in color. Blister, however, was impressed. He tried to snap a picture with his phone but the battery had croaked.

The person who walked off of the aircraft was not Jon David Ampergrodt, another unsettling surprise for Buck. Coolman introduced the traveler as Cree Windsor, a senior vice president of Platinum.

"This is Spiro Nance," Coolman said to Cree Windsor.

"It's a pleasure to meet you, Spiro. I've heard good things." Cree Windsor held out his right hand, which Blister eyed as if it were a steaming cowpie.

"So you ain't the main man?"

"Mr. Ampergrodt really wanted to come, but unfortunately a personal matter came up at the last minute. He sent me instead, with his regrets. I brought the latest draft of the terms we'll be presenting to the network." Cree Windsor brandished an oxblood briefcase as evidence of his authority.

"What kinda personal matter?" Blister asked. "Death in the family?"

Cree Windsor glanced at Coolman for backup and said, "Well, yes, sadly."

"Was it his momma or daddy that passed?"

"Um . . . I believe it was an aunt."

Blister said, "That ain't good enough. He oughta be here, goddammit."

"Mr. Ampergrodt and his aunt were extremely close."

"You mean they was, like, doin' it?"

"What? No!"

Short, trim and soft-shouldered, Cree Windsor was preternaturally pale due to an exotic melanin imbalance that defied all tanning sprays. Often he had a hard time convincing clients that he lived in southern California.

Coolman assured Blister that Mr. Windsor was a major player at the agency, Amp's second-in-command. Blister stomped around in a huff but nobody heard what he was muttering because a 737 was rolling down the main runway.

When it was quiet again, Buck Nance asked Cree Windsor to show them the paperwork Amp had sent.

"Is your lawyer here to review it?" Cree Windsor asked.

"Not yet," Coolman interjected. "I'll do the first pass."

Blister fidgeted. "But this dude ain't even the top man!"

Cree Windsor balanced the briefcase on one knee and took out a three-page letter, which he handed to Coolman.

"What's the story with your hair?" Blister demanded.

Cree Windsor was rattled. "I'm not sure what you mean."

"It don't move."

Buck saw the situation disintegrating fast. "Okay, let's chill out. The guy flew all the way across the country to get this thing done."

"Windy as hell," Blister fumed, "and not one fuckin' hair on his head moves."

Plaintively from Cree Windsor: "It's just product, man."

"Product? Is that the same as jizz?"

Coolman said, "Why don't we go sit in the limo where it's quiet? Have a drink while I look over these deal points."

Buck said, "Liquor sounds like a damn fine idea."

"I got a better one," Blister sneered, raising his *guayabera* so that Cree Windsor could see the butt of the pistol. "Get back on that motherfuckin' airplane and go tell your boss I ain't doin' bidness with nobody but him. Tell him hurry up and plant his dead auntie and get his ass down to Key West."

Buck felt like grabbing the gun and plugging the moron. What held him back was the fear of blowing his lucrative new network contract; until the ink dried, Blister was Buck's negotiating leverage, his ace-in-the-hole. Where would Buck find another phony lost twin on short notice?

"Now, boys, this is gettin' a little craaaaazy," Lane Coolman said. "Let's not forget we're all on the same team." His dedication to the agency stopped short of stepping into the potential line of fire between Blister and the shaking Cree Windsor.

"I ain't crazy. All I want is respect." Blister plucked the letter from Coolman's hand, dropped his pants and wiped himself with the pages, which he then returned to Cree Windsor's briefcase.

"What the fuck?" said Buck Nance, clutching his head.

Cree Windsor kicked the briefcase away and loped toward the jet.

"Tell Amp we'll be waiting!" Coolman shouted after him.

None of this nonsense was witnessed by Andrew Yancy and Merry Mansfield because Yancy's car had been pulled over on White Street for running a red light, which Yancy agreed had been necessary to keep sight of the Cadillac limousine. Merry showed the cop one of her many driver's licenses, and he let her off with a warning and a wink. Yancy guessed that the limo had been heading to the airport, and he was correct. Unfortunately, by the time Merry pulled up to the private-aviation terminal, the big black stretch was already departing. Its tinted windows prevented Yancy from seeing that the passengers were still inside.

He and Merry stood at the chain-link fence watching a gray business jet take off and assuming that Buck Nance, Lane Coolman and Benny the Blister were on board. Yancy entered the terminal, where his roach-patrol laminate failed to impress the attractive silver-haired woman behind the desk. She pleasantly declined to tell him who owned the aircraft, or where it was going.

When they were back in Yancy's car, Merry said, "Let's you and me go celebrate."

"What would be the occasion?"

"Our last night together."

"Dinner's on me," said Yancy.

They stopped on Duval so Merry could buy some radical cutoffs that offered a crescent glimpse of her bumblebee tat. Yancy put on the Panama hat that he'd saved from the wreck of the *Wet Nurse.* They were walking hand-in-hand to Clippy's when Rogelio Burton finally called back. Yancy gave him the tail numbers of the gray jet. Having a real detective badge, Burton would have no problem obtaining the passenger list. Wherever the plane landed, cops would be waiting for Benjamin Krill.

Case closed, thought Yancy. *Back to the vermin beat for me.*

At the restaurant they were personally seated by Irv Clipowski, who thanked Yancy for allowing him and the mayor to reopen. They had decided not to sue Buck Nance over the beard clippings because his talent agency had spontaneously donated twenty-five thousand dollars to Neil and Clippy's butterfly preserve in Belize.

"Straight from the heart," said Yancy. "What's the pouchie situation?"

Clippy said there had been no new sightings of the Gambian goliaths on the premises. "Not one turd, Andrew!"

Yancy detected a tense hitch in the pronouncement. He ordered Barbancourt-and-Coke. Merry had a vodka tonic. At another table sat a light-haired, fleshy, fish-lipped fellow who was dining alone. Yancy noticed him eyeing Merry, though not in the way most men did.

"I know that guy," she said, and rolled a fingertip wave. "Hey, Martin!"

The fleshy patron turned away and called to get a server's attention.

"What's his story?" Yancy asked Merry.

"My last job. Obviously they didn't break his kneecaps, which is huge. The people who hired me, I mean. They were heavy dudes. Poor little Marty was slow to catch on."

"So that's the driver of the *second* Buick you bashed."

"He told me he deals beach sand, Andrew. He said you can call him up, order a whole freaking beach, and he delivers it on a great big boat. Who ever heard of a gig like that?"

Yancy said, "It's like printing money. I'm serious."

They watched the man named Martin pay his bill and scurry out of the restaurant. He didn't wave or say hello.

NINETEEN

Rick's career track to nightclub bouncer included Purdue University's football team, the Cleveland Browns, the Oakland Raiders and finally the Miami Dolphins. He was cut for the last time at age thirty-one, and decided he preferred the climate of South Beach to that of Pontiac, his hometown. It had been a similar path for his friend Rod—University of Iowa, the San Diego Chargers, the Dolphins, the Atlanta Falcons and then back to the Dolphins before blowing out a knee. Like Rick, Rod found no reason to leave Florida after his football days.

Both men ended up working at a club on Collins Avenue, where they connected with a wealthy weekend customer named Brock, who said he was a lawyer. The bouncers' first freelance assignment was to terrorize a landscape architect that Brock suspected of teaching Tantric techniques to his fiancée. Rick and Rod visisted the man, who soon afterward shut down his nursery, moved to Clearwater and took a job sculpting hedges for the Church of Scientology. The next time Brock contacted Rick and Rod, he asked them to go chat with the manager of a Hialeah impound lot, where one of Brock's pristine Porsches had been towed. The vehicle was released after a meeting that lasted barely long enough for Rick to demonstrate the versatility of a common crowbar.

A scenic drive to Big Pine Key would be the highlight of their third and final mission for the lawyer, a tune-up job for which they'd each been promised a grand. The bouncers had been sent to persuade some hardheaded fool to sell his house to Brock. They were unaware that the recalcitrant homeowner was an ex-cop, or that he might be reckless enough to take on two ex-NFL linemen whose combined weight was five hundred and twenty-five pounds. Through no fault of their own, Rick and Rod arrived unprepared for resistance.

Brock had supplied a for-sale sign to plant in the homeowner's front yard, which they did. Brock had explained that the sign was meant to galvanize the man's decision-making, which made sense to Rick and Rod. Visual aids were often helpful. They were seated on the man's comfortable new sofa when a car dropped him off and sped away. The man didn't come inside right away, which should have tipped off the bouncers to trouble. In their defense, it was extremely rare for anyone—even the drunkest jerks at the club—to do anything but wilt when facing Rick and Rod in tandem. As a result, their reflexes were rusty.

The man they'd been sent to rough up sneaked into his house through a rear door, sprinted yowling into the living room and whacked Rod from behind with the for-sale sign. The wood placard loudly broke apart, leaving Rod slumped unconscious and the attacker holding the sign's sturdy metal stems, one in each fist. Rick was struggling to elevate his heft from the sofa cushions when he received the first blow. Numerous others followed. He awoke sometime later on the floor, his thick wrists Zip-tied to those of his torpid partner. Their shiny South Beach trousers had been removed and knotted around their ankles.

Rick noticed that the man who'd overpowered them was tall though not very muscle-bound. He wondered how such a routine dude could have hit them so hard. Possibly the man was high on crystal meth or bath salts. That's what Rick intended to tell his friends at the gym, when they asked what the fuck had happened to his face.

The man, wearing a brimmed straw hat, said he was sick and tired of people breaking into his home. "By the way, that diamond ring you're looking for? It's gone," he said. "The first set of assholes took it."

"What diamond ring?" Rick asked. "What assholes?"

"Wiseguys from up North. They were pros, not like you. Ask Brad about 'em," the man said, "when you call him from jail."

"You mean Brock?"

"Tell him my house isn't for sale and he needs to get over it."

Rod awoke to the wail of approaching sirens and lifted his blood-caked head. "You called the law?"

"Paramedics, too."

Rick said, "What for? Shit, we're not hurt." Then: "*You* didn't hurt *us*. No way."

"Your friend is bleeding from the ears."

"*One* ear. Big fuckin' deal."

The sheriff's cars got there first, followed by a pair of ambulances. Rick and Rod were examined, EKG'd, bandaged, cuffed, questioned and gang-hoisted onto stretchers. As they were being lugged out of the house, a Subaru sedan squealed to a stop out front. The driver was a tall breezy redhead in short, short jeans.

"Andrew!" she cried, running toward the man who'd just tuned up Rick and Rod. The man's shirt was unbuttoned, and he was peeling a funky wrap of bandages from his midsection. The redhead kissed him so hard that she knocked off his hat.

"Wow," she said. "I thought you were dinner, but you were the show!"

The woman stood on her toes, exposing a vivid bug tattoo beneath her cutoffs, on the creamy curve of her ass. Rick fantasized about it all the way to the hospital, where he faded warmly into darkness following a jumbo dose of Demerol. Rod was already laid out inside an MRI tube, dozing through a scan of his jolted brain. Eight hours later both men were wide awake and eating breakfast, the only inmates in the medical wing of the Stock Island Detention Center. Together they invented an exculpatory version of the night's events to tell Brock. The other topic of discussion was their NFL retirement package—specifically, whether or not the league's insurance plan covered injuries sustained while committing a felony.

Benjamin Krill grew up in Palatka, on the St. Johns River in northern Florida. His mother attributed his lawless misbehavior to breathing fumes from the local pulp mills, though Benny's siblings had inhaled the same rancid air and grown up to be productive citizens with legitimate jobs. In fact, his brother worked deep inside the plant that manufactured scented maxi-pads, and he was healthy as a boar hog. Benny's sister owned a bridal boutique and was a prodigy at pinochle. Benny, the eldest, was incarcerated regularly and upon being freed would promptly resume stealing until he got caught again. This had gone on for twenty-seven years in jurisdictions stretching from Jacksonville to Naples. Benny had been tagged with the nickname "Blister" after backing into a pot of hot chowder while burglarizing the kitchen of a homeless shelter in New Smyrna. His parboiled, abscessed buttocks had drawn raucous and mostly unwelcome attention in the showers at the Volusia County lockup, and from then on "Blister" was listed as a primary AKA on his rap sheet. The judge in the New Smyrna case, unmoved by the defendant's second-degree disfigurement, slapped him with eighteen months.

Like many career criminals, Benny Krill suffered from a deficiency of ambition that left him content in midlife to be slim-jimming cars and looting mobile homes. That is, until the night he went to see Buck Nance's show at the Parched Pirate.

When his idol bolted in panic from the bar that night, Blister's only thought was to rescue Buck and comfort him. It had turned into a kidnapping only after Buck acted surly and unappreciative. His claim that he and his brothers were actually accordion players from Wisconsin was so lame that Blister felt insulted. He and Captain Cock were plainly cut from the same Deep Southern cloth—why would the man deny it? And why the hell would he hide his Cajun accent? What was he ashamed of?

Equally upsetting was Buck's apathetic response to Blister's tribute tattoos and treasured collection of Nance-feathered trout flies. The disavowing attitude displayed by the leader of the Nances disappointed Blister, and gave rise to the boldest criminal scheme ever to spring from his stunted imagination: He would trade his two high-value hostages, Buck and Buck's manager, for a role on *Bayou Brethren* as a newfound Nance brother named Spiro.

For all its daring, the plan was also laughably, fatally absurd. Later his mother would tell reporters that it proved she was right about living downwind from the paper mills—all those toxic vapors obviously stewed poor Benny's brain cells. A goddamn squirrel had more sense.

"This is a cool-ass ride," Blister commented, lounging in the back of the Cadillac limousine.

Buck Nance said, "You shouldn't have chased off Mr. Windsor. That wasn't too bright."

"Is that how you talk to the man with the gun?"

"That's how I talk to the man that just wiped his ass with my future."

Lane Coolman told them both to chill. "I left a message for Amp telling him to get here as soon as possible. Long as we stick together, we'll nail this deal. But if you guys keep stomping each other's nuts, it's game over. Amp will tell you the same thing. These network people can smell weakness."

"Know what I smell?" Buck said. "I smell that fuckin' briefcase in the trunk."

Not even Coolman had volunteered to wipe the shit off Cree Windsor's letter so they could review the terms of the contract proposal.

Blister said, "Don't you boys forget—I'm the only one here ever killed a ISIS."

Coolman advised him to never again mention what happened on the Conch Train.

"We need a new ride," Buck said grimly.

The black stretch Cadillac was drawing stares at every intersection. Blister seemed to be enjoying the attention. Coolman was glued to his cell re-reading a text from Smegg, his divorce lawyer. Rachel's team had told the judge that her husband skipped town; she was demanding a contempt order and an arrest warrant.

"I'm in deep shit back home," Coolman fretted to no one in particular.

Blister cackled as he snatched another Jack Daniel's miniature from the limo's minibar, illuminated by an inset string of violet LEDs. "This car's a total pussy magnet," he said. "Let's just drive 'round and see what happens."

Buck stared at this degenerate ambassador for his own popularity wondering how many other *Brethren* fans were homicidal nut-job stalkers. *Maybe it's time to quit the show and go fishin',* he thought for the first time since Blister had removed his handcuffs. *Dump the family. Move into the condo with Miracle.* He wasn't sure how much money he had in the bank—five, six million bucks? Krystal would grab half, but so be it. An unhurried, unexamined existence looked pretty sweet to Buck. A life free from soggy collard greens, rooster shit and all those fucking TV cameras in his face.

He heard Blister Krill tell the limo driver to stop the car. "I gotta piss."

The driver, a Cuban man with salt-and-pepper hair, began looking for a gas station.

"No, man, pull over now," Blister told him. "I can't hold it no more."

They ended up on a narrow street, the limo pulling over in front of a plain one-story house with Bahama shutters. From the outside they could see the wall of one room pulsing with colors from a massive flat-screen.

Blister stepped out of the Cadillac. He leaned against a fender to balance himself while he urinated, holding the gun in one hand and his pecker in the other. Inside the limo, Buck elbowed Lane Coolman, testing his interest in making a run for it. Coolman didn't respond; he was busy trading texts with Smegg.

Buck slid himself up the long bench seat until he was right behind the driver.

"Let's go," he whispered.

"Excuse me?"

"Take off. Hurry."

"But, sir—"

"It's all right. Go!" Buck said.

The evening stillness was broken by a flame-blue flash and an ear-splitting pop. Buck dove to the floor of the car. Coolman landed beside him, shielding his head with both arms and squeaking like a hamster.

The car door flew open and Blister Krill dove inside. He ordered the driver to hit the gas.

Buck sat up beet-faced and ranting.

Blister said, "Chill out, bro. I shot the damn mailbox is all."

"Why in the name of fuck would you do that?"

"To see what it's like. Pullin' a live trigger."

Buck stared incredulously. "This is the first time you ever fired a gun? And you live in *Florida*?"

Coolman scooted to the opposite end of the limo, as far as possible from the pistol in Blister's hand. Framed in the rearview mirror was the stoic Cuban driver, assessing his disorderly passengers. The driver's lips moved and Blister yelled, "What'd you say, Pablo?"

"*Están grandes pendejos*," the driver repeated cordially.

"What? Talk American, goddammit."

The driver, who of course spoke perfect English, said, "Where to now, gentlemen?"

Rogelio Burton hung around until the other cops were gone. "The truth, please," he said wearily to Yancy. "For old times' sake."

"Like I said, it was a random home invasion."

The detective gestured at the splintered remnants of the for-sale sign. "You were attacked by marauding realtors?"

Yancy shrugged. "It's a cutthroat business, Rog."

"You're full of shit. They're bouncers from South Beach."

"I knew it! Pinheads," said Merry Mansfield.

"And where were you when mild-mannered Mr. Yancy flipped out?" Burton asked her.

"Soon as we pulled up to the house, Andrew spotted somebody inside. He told me to drop him off, wait ten minutes and dial 911. I only waited five."

Burton went to the kitchen and came back with a beer. "One for the road," he said. "I'm going home to work on my memo for the sheriff."

Yancy said, "Okay, Rog, you win. Sonny doesn't need to know about this."

"Then keep talking."

"That slimy TV lawyer who bought the land next door—name's Richardson—now he wants me to sell him *my* house, and I said no way. Apparently the Calusas had a dental clinic on his property five thousand years ago. There's sacred Indian teeth all over the place, so now Richardson can't build on the lot. What are the odds, huh?"

Burton said, "Your neighbors always have the worst luck."

"Seems that way."

"So you think this lawyer hired those two fuckwits who broke in tonight."

"They didn't deny it. I intend to press charges, too."

"That would make my year," Burton said.

"I sure don't want a guy like Richardson living next to me."

"You don't want anybody living next to you, Andrew, except lizards and land crabs."

"I like the deer on the island."

Merry said, "That's true. He's very fond of the deer."

Burton opened the beer. "Did you rip your stitches whaling on those bozos?"

Yancy pointed at his shirt. "You see any blood? I'm doing just fine."

Burton turned to Merry. "It's probably good that you're here."

"Well, I'm leaving tomorrow. Andrew won't sleep with me."

"He's not being noble. That's just an act."

"About tonight," Yancy said to Burton, "what do you plan to tell our excitable sheriff?"

"As little as possible. He's got a big fundraiser tomorrow at the San Carlos."

"Put me down for a dollar."

After Burton left, Yancy hitched the boat trailer to his car. When he handed Merry's fleece to her, she said, "Wait. We're seriously going fishing in the dark?"

"Not fishing."

Yancy drove to the Old Wooden Bridge lodge and put the skiff in the water. He'd brought the handheld spotlight though he didn't need it; a bright half-moon hung in a clear deep sky. He steered with one hand and rested the other on the throttle. Merry's hair was flying everywhere so she pulled it into a ponytail. It occurred to Yancy that, in the time they'd known each other, he hadn't once seen her look at her cell phone. She never texted, tweeted, Facebooked, Instagrammed, or posted a single picture when they were together. He found this behavior alluring.

The breeze was light but cool, the tide rising. No other boat was in sight. After a short ride he staked the skiff in the shallows at Porpoise Key, a place he'd never taken Rosa. A honey glaze from the sodium lights of Miami rimmed the northern horizon.

Merry said the sky was amazing. "Where are we, Andrew?"

"Church. That's how it feels to me."

"Then we need music." Finally she appraised her phone, scrolling through the playlists. "I vote for Charlie Parker."

"You're unbelievable," Yancy said. "Come sit here."

"What, you don't like Bird?"

"Bird's the best. Come here, please."

Merry settled beside him on the poling platform. Due east a stream of cars and trucks flickered on the long bridge at Bahia Honda. When Yancy was buzzed, the headlights looked like regimental fireflies, but tonight he was dead sober, adrenalized from his run-in with the bouncers.

"You miss Rosa. That's allowed," Merry said.

"Yet here I am alone with you."

"Hey, I've been missed by guys, too. Trust me—I've broken the hardest of hearts, dudes way tougher and hotter than you. Though I will say this: You're a good kisser even when you're not cooperating."

"Tell me why you got that tattoo."

"The 'A.Y.' is what's got you worried, I bet. Well, guess what. It doesn't really stand for Andrew Yancy. It stands for 'All Yours.' For when I meet the right man."

She stood up to take off the fleece. Next to vanish was her blouse and then the cutoffs. Yancy found himself eye-to-eye with the perky bumblebee.

"Hello cutie," he said.

She turned and lowered gently onto his lap until their faces were inches apart, and she slipped both arms around him. "How's the boo-boo on your tummy?"

"Cured. This is better than a trip to Lourdes."

"Wait, I don't want to poke you." She unfastened some sort of ring from one of her nipples and flicked it overboard.

Yancy said, "This is the first time those pelicans ever heard a jazz saxophone." He recognized the tune as "Dexterity," manic and carefree.

"What pelicans, Andrew?"

"They're roosting up in the mangroves. I can show you with the spotlight."

"No, let 'em sleep. Tell me what's on your mind."

"Nothing. Except I haven't heard a word from her in four days."

"I know," said Merry. "I go through your phone at night while you're in the shower."

Yancy was annoyed at himself for not being more annoyed. He realized he was about to do the very thing that Merry had been predicting since the day she'd turned up at his house. It was tempting to blame Charlie Parker and the starry moment, but Yancy couldn't cut himself any slack. The romantic boat ride had been his idea, not Merry's. Nor could he pretend to be shocked that she'd wiggled out of her clothes. In his love life Yancy specialized in devising scenarios that could lead only to unwise decisions.

It was hard to picture an even-keeled relationship with a person who took her last name from a dead movie star and crashed automobiles half-naked for a living. Yancy himself was no paragon of dependability, as he was keenly aware. Ninety-six hours of radio silence from a faraway girlfriend wasn't a green light to stray, yet his hands felt perfectly at home cupping another woman's bare ass. He couldn't rule out the possibility that he was a hopelessly shallow horndog.

Merry said, "I predict Rosa calls tomorrow. She's probably just skiing—the cell service is suck-y in the mountains."

"You've been to Norway, have you?"

"Sugarbush. Same difference." She shifted in a significant way on his lap.

"That feels nice," he said.

"No, a puppy licking your toes feels 'nice.' What you're experiencing, mister, is transcendental contact."

A goner, he kissed her on the mouth. "Now you can say you told me so."

Merry laughed softly. "Men. I swear."

"You want me to stop?"

"What do *you* want to do, Andrew?"

"Rock the boat."

"Then hang on," she said.

TWENTY

The sex lasted a long time.

Forty-three minutes, according to Deb's Fitbit. Forty-three minutes and 167 calories.

Afterward she hit the nail salon, Starbucks and Whole Foods. When she returned home, she was surprised to see Brock Richardson's newest Carerra still parked in the driveway. He was supposed to be at the office taping a new Pitrolux litigation commercial.

Deb carried the grocery bags into the kitchen, where she found him wearing a long-sleeved shirt, cross-striped necktie and no pants. With clenched buttocks he stood in front of a blood-pressure monitor, the portable type sold at drugstores. He had placed his cock inside the compression cuff, which was emitting a deep hum.

"Wow," said Deb, "this is new."

"Something's wrong down there. It's still hard as a rock and I can't make it go away."

"So, you aren't actually boning the . . ."

"God, no! I just want to make sure I'm not having a damn heart attack." He showed her the flashing numerals on the machine. "One-thirty over eighty. That means everything's okay."

"Listen to me, Brock. If you're taking your blood pressure with your wiener, you are the opposite of okay."

He unfastened the Velcro strap and carefully withdrew from the inflated sleeve. Deb put him under a cold shower for ten minutes, yet his erection failed to flag. Next she made him dunk his junk in a bucket of ice cubes, with the same result.

She said, "For God's sake, how much of that crap did you use?"

"Same as always." Richardson's teeth were chattering.

"Tell the truth."

"It's all for you, babe. I did it for you."

Deb refilled her e-cig with nicotine syrup and took a drag. After the humiliating accident she'd switched to a brand of vaporizer that was advertised as fireproof. Meanwhile Richardson had contacted a lawyer pal and gotten her name added to a brewing class-action against the manufacturer of the first device. As a gesture of devotion he'd offered to waive his usual percentage of the settlement.

"You're not going to the office with a stiffy," Deb said. She suspected he was cheating on her with one and probably both of his brunette assistants.

"I'll wear bicycle shorts under my pants. Maybe it'll all fit."

"Don't be gross." She grabbed a bath towel and tossed it across his groin, where it waggled like a crippled kite. She proposed a trip to the emergency room.

"Has it been four hours?" Richardson checked his watch. "Four hours is when they say to panic."

"Then we'll wait here together." Deb opened a book and vaped on her plastic ciggie. If not for her own clandestine escapades—the kayak instructor, the Tantric landscaper, her stepsister's podiatrist, and so on—she would have pressed more aggressively the issue of her fiancé's infidelity.

"Swear to Christ, I'm gonna quit cold turkey," Richardson vowed, referring to the Pitrolux. "This is getting freaky."

Getting? Deb thought.

She had mixed feelings about the potent gel. It was indisputably harmful, as evidenced by the weird baby schlongs sprouting in her lover's armpits. On the positive side, his performance in bed had become so stellar that it served to counterbalance the repellent facets of his personality. She could envision a medium-length marriage—say five to seven years—based solely on the attractions of sex and money. She feared the future might not be so tolerable if Brock kicked the Pitrolux habit. He had spoiled her.

"You want to do it again?" she asked. "Just for fifteen, twenty minutes?"

"I'm in. Never waste good wood!"

At that moment his phone rang. He answered it and soon started pacing, still comically engorged. By the time the conversation ended he was storming through the kitchen shouting, "Shitheads! I'm dealing with useless, worthless, brainless shitheads!"

Deb closed her book and waited.

"Those two clowns I sent down to Big Pine," Richardson said, "the whole thing went to hell."

"What happened now?"

"What happened is they fucked up and got thrown in jail, but that's not the worst part," he railed. "Your engagement ring? That asshole Yancy had it all along. The mob guys took it from him, the guys Trebeaux sent. Martin told me they didn't find it, but Rick says that's not true."

"Rick is . . . ?"

"One of *my* guys."

"Who's now locked up? Classic," Deb said.

"Point is, those Mafia goons grabbed the ring at Yancy's house and kept it."

"Speaking of the house—he's going to sell to us, right? They smacked some sense into him?"

"Are you even listening? Those goddamn guineas stole my two-hundred-thousand-dollar diamond!"

"You mean *my* diamond," said Deb.

News of the six-figure ripoff had done what frosty testicles couldn't do—deflated Brock's boner. He stuffed himself into a pair of boxer shorts saying, "Don't worry, I'm gonna get that fucking rock back."

"We're talking about the same Mafia, right? The one that kills people and hangs them on meat hooks."

Brock put on some slacks, tucked in his shirt and fixed his tie. "Trust me, baby, I know how to deal with these mopes. I can totally get down and talk their language."

"Okay then," she said, thinking: *I'm engaged to a dead man.*

In an interview with a Brooklyn newspaper, the widow of Abdul-Halim Shamoon said the authorities in Key West weren't trying hard enough to find the tattooed white man who had fatally assaulted her husband on the Conch Train. Mrs. Shamoon implied that institutional prejudice against Muslims was to blame for the lack of urgency. The article was reprinted in the Key West *Citizen* and brought to the attention of Sheriff Sonny Summers, who regarded any controversy as a threat to his re-election. Nobody on his staff seemed to know how many Muslims were registered to vote in Monroe County, but Sonny Summers didn't wish to alienate a single one. Regardless of his or her religious leanings, any deceased tourist was bad for tourism, and anything that was bad for tourism was also bad for incumbents.

The sheriff summoned Rogelio Burton, his top detective, for an update on the Shamoon investigation. Burton reported that the main suspect, Benjamin "Blister" Krill, was still at large and possibly traveling with Buck Nance, the wayward television star. The men were said to have left the island on a private jet the night before, a report that turned out to be false. The aircraft in question had carried only one passenger, Mr. Credence Windsor of Los Angeles.

"So Krill's still in town? Then get busy and catch the bastard," Sonny Summers said. "We'll push the Conch Train thing as a hate crime. You deal with the media."

Burton wasn't optimistic. "It's not a slam-dunk case. The eyewitness accounts from the scene are inconsistent, to put it kindly. Not one of 'em could positively ID Benny Krill from his last mug shot. The only thing they agreed on is the tattoo across his back."

"Hell, that's almost as good as a fingerprint."

"We checked the social media—Facebook, Instagram, Twitter. There are at least thirteen other white males in the country with Captain Cock tats."

The sheriff said, "You're shitting me."

"It's a very popular TV show."

"So we'll have to prove all thirteen of these numbnuts weren't in Key West on the afternoon Mr. Shabeeb was killed."

"His name's Shamoon," Burton said. "But, you're right, we'd have to nail down thirteen different alibis. Major project."

"And flying them all in for the trial—that'll cost a damn fortune," Sonny Summers muttered, "even if we put them at the Best Western." He picked up a sterling silver letter opener that had been given to him for no reason by the governor. Idly he tested the sharpness of the point on his thumb. "Rog, did you talk to Dickinson? What's his mindset?"

"We might get Krill on a manslaughter," said Burton, "if we're lucky."

State Attorney Billy Dickinson shared the sheriff's allergy to negative headlines. Losing a high-profile homicide trial wasn't on Dickinson's bucket list.

"He says the Captain Cock tat might be enough to convict," Burton said, "unless Krill gets a halfway competent lawyer. Billy's afraid the other train passengers will get shredded on cross-exam. Tourists, as you know, make terrible witnesses."

Sonny Summers tapped the silver letter opener on a corner of his desk to see if it sounded like a tuning fork. It didn't.

"Rog, someone should speak to the dead man's family. Make sure they know we're busting our balls to catch this guy. Or whatever the Islamic word for balls is."

"I'll make the call, no problem. They're American, by the way."

"Meanwhile explain to me why Buck Nance, a TV star, would be hanging out with a third-rate scumsucker like Benny the Blister. Where did you hear that, anyway? I thought Nance was gone from the Keys, rehabbing at a desert spa somewhere. That's what he told me when he called."

Burton said, "An informant says otherwise."

"Well, fuckeroo."

"One other update. It's about your favorite restaurant inspector."

The sheriff seemed to slump. "This campaign party at the San Carlos tonight—all these folks are bringin' their checkbooks and I need to charm the shit out of 'em, meaning I need to be at my personal best. Keep that in mind before you say another word."

Burton assured him that the new Yancy situation was manageable. "A couple meatheads broke into his house. He put 'em in the hospital. The arrest report will call it a home-invasion robbery. Both suspects are in the medical wing at Stock Island."

"Did Yancy do anything, you know, *weird* to them?" Sonny Summers asked. "If he did, the media will go apeshit."

"No vacuum attachments this time. He clocked the intruders with a real-estate sign."

"That makes it less of a story, right? Maybe no story."

"Simple self-defense. Probably won't even make the papers."

The sheriff sighed pensively. "Why would robbers target Yancy of all people? You're his friend, but you get what I mean. What has he got worth stealing? Hell, never mind. Can you please not tell me any more about this?"

"My pleasure," said Burton.

"Be honest—what do you think of this suit for the party tonight? A hundred sixty-five bucks at Men's Wearhouse."

"They say seersucker's making a comeback."

"Don't bullshit me, Rog. I look like fucking Matlock," the sheriff said. "You'll call the Muslims?"

"Right away."

"Make sure they know this case is my *numero uno* priority, same as if poor Abdul was a Christian or a Buddhist. Tell 'em Key West is a place that loves everyone equal, and we want everyone to love Key West."

Burton said, "Have fun at your fundraiser."

"There's an open bar, thank God."

Jon David Ampergrodt looked across his desk at the stylish though drained figure of Cree Windsor and said, "Summation?"

"It's a shit show, Amp."

"Tell me something I don't know."

"No, I mean literally a shit show. The man wiped himself with the deal papers."

Amp leaned back studying his fingernails for nicks. *Bayou Brethren* was still doing spectacularly well without Buck Nance, the younger brothers having bloomed into fully realized redneck caricatures. Miracle's illicit affair with Junior had added a magic spark of toxicity. During the most recent taping, Buddy had thrown a Dewar's bottle at Junior while Clee Roy had stolen Junior's iPhone to leer at a picture of Miracle's bare ass that Junior had snapped in the outdoor shower. Meanwhile the Nance wives were in a frothing riot of jealousy and spite. It was magnificent television.

"We don't need another damn brother in the cast," Amp said.

Cree Windsor agreed. "This whole thing was Lane's idea?"

"But we also don't need Buck Nance in the same time slot on another network, being represented by another agency." Amp was thinking out loud.

"You're the only one this psycho 'Spiro' wants to talk with," Cree Windsor said.

"That's what Lane told me. Who, by the way, has not distinguished himself."

"Rule Number One: Never lose control of your client."

Amp looked up from his nails and nodded. "Or a shit show is what you get."

"Spiro's a bad dude, and not in a good way. He's scary crazy."

"You mean crazy scary."

"Right," said Cree Windsor. "You're seriously going down to Florida to meet him?"

Amp said it was the only way to get control of the situation. "Lane's working out the details."

"Bring some security. The biggest dude we got."

"Way ahead of you," said Amp.

"Oh, and don't forget—your aunt just died. That's why you sent me down there the first time."

"Right, right. What was her name? Did we even decide on one?"

"I don't know—Carol?" Cree Windsor said with a shrug.

"That works. Dear old Aunt Carol."

Judging from Cree Windsor's description, the man who called himself Spiro Nance would be terrible on the show—dull-witted, mean and uncoachable. Amp's idea was to keep him around for a couple of episodes, expose him as a fraud and then fire him for breach of contract. The script would call for Buck to be shattered by the revelation that Spiro wasn't actually his long-lost twin; there would be tears and humiliation at the weekly barbecue, but the hardy patriarch would rally and move forward.

The network had reluctantly agreed to double Buck's salary, as Lane Coolman had demanded, but Amp foresaw a walkout by the other Nances if they didn't receive comparable pay hikes. In theory that could be a windfall for Platinum Artists, which represented all the family members individually. However, Amp expected the network to dig in its heels if the entire cast staged a mutiny over money. Television executives loved reality programming only because it was cheaper to produce than sitcoms and cop shows. If the *Brethren* payroll jumped too high, the network would simply let the Nances' contracts lapse and replace the whole greedy clan with a fresh collection of goobers.

Once he was on-scene in Florida, Amp planned to elbow Coolman offstage and take charge. Buck Nance would be steered aside and given a bracing dose of straight talk. The man calling himself Spiro would be humored and led to believe that prime-time glory awaited. Amp also aimed to uncover Spiro's real name and feed it to a private investigator for a criminal background check that promised to be bountiful.

"The maniac walks around with a gun in his pants," Cree Windsor reminded Amp.

"So do half the crappy actors in Hollywood."

For a lunch break Amp met Rachel Coolman at the Wilshire, where he was crushed to hear that for once she wanted only lunch. Room service delivered two coho salmon Caesars and a bottle of white wine. Amp and Rachel sat on the edge of the king-sized bed in front of the food cart, which was draped with a linen tablecloth. Rachel kept most of her clothes on and out of nowhere began to complain that Amp appeared to be taking Lane's side in the divorce. She implored him to make Lane return to Los Angeles, so that court proceedings could resume.

To salvage his chances for a quickie, Amp assured Rachel he would speak with her husband as soon as he got to Key West.

"And you'll tell him to do the right thing? Promise?" She unfolded her legs.

"Baby, I will *order* him to be on the next flight home," Amp said.

Rachel smiled and took a pursed nibble of salmon. "Nobody wants a long, drawn-out trial. Be sure and tell him that, too, okay? Hurry back to L.A. and let's get this thing settled, then both of us can go our separate ways."

"That makes total sense." Amp assumed the judge had refused to issue a contempt order against Lane, forcing Rachel to try a new strategy.

"A trial would be completely exhausting," she went on. "I wouldn't have the energy for anything else, I'd be so burned out."

Amp got the message, and accepted his role in the Coolmans' court fight. He didn't want to give up his lunchtimes with Rachel. She was so damn hot.

"Going to trial would be crazy," he agreed. "A total nightmare for everyone except the goddamn attorneys. I'll get Lane on board, don't worry."

"I knew you'd understand." Rachel put down her fork and with her bare heels pushed the food cart away from the bed. "How about some dessert? You still look hungry."

After Blister shot the mailbox they sped back to the house on Fleming Street and turned off the lights. The next morning Lane Coolman ordered a different limo. When a white super-stretch arrived, he sent it away. "We're not going to a prom," he said to a downcast Blister. "Let's get something shorter than a city block."

They ended up in a standard black Yukon with non-pimp rims. The new driver was another Cuban, which elicited from Blister a vile monologue on America's self-destructive immigration policies. He got bummed when Buck wouldn't chime in.

Eventually the driver had enough, and spoke up: "Sir, I was born in New Jersey. I'm a U.S. citizen just like you."

Blister hurled himself halfway over the front seat snarling, "Hey, Pablo, you ain't just like me! And your people sure as hell ain't like my people. Tell him, Buck!"

"Quiet," said Captain Cock.

"What?"

"Just shut up."

Blister sat back fuming and confused.

Buck was no fan of Hispanics, but he couldn't bear listening to Blister berate the driver. When Buck was a boy he'd overheard his father speak to a Puerto Rican auto mechanic the same way, and he remembered feeling uneasy and possibly ashamed. True, he and his brothers had grown up to be racist dickheads like their old man, but they weren't in-your-face racist dickheads. Had Buck not been so flustered that night onstage at the Parched Pirate, he would never have blurted those crude jokes, not with muscular gays and Negroes in attendance.

"What'd you say your real name was?" Blister asked him gruffly.

"Matt Romberg."

"Is that Jewish? You a Jew?"

"German Lutheran," Buck replied.

"Sure about that?"

Buck wondered how Blister Krill had survived to middle age in a place as ethnically diverse and gun-crazy as Florida. He was confronted with the possibility that Blister had been a different person before becoming obsessed with *Bayou Brethren*. It was one thing to market a television program to attract low-class shitkickers; it was another thing to *create* them. Buck surmised that the pirated outtakes of his sermons were an inflammatory factor, and he felt fairly shitty about whatever Blister did to the Muslim on the Conch Train. It was no better than murder. According to the newspaper, the victim had a thriving business and loving family back in New York. That didn't prove he wasn't a closet jihadist, but the article said he was carrying souvenirs at the time he was attacked. There was no mention of the police finding any weapons, a suicide vest, or even one crummy ISIS recruiting flyer.

"Get Amp on the phone right now," Buck said to Coolman.

"We've been texting. He promises to come."

Blister said, "Hold on. I wasn't done talkin' about the Jew thing."

The stolen pistol came out, once again. Buck was over it.

"Shoot me or anybody else in this car," he told Blister, "and you fail the world's easiest IQ test. Instead of a TV deal you get life in prison."

Coolman said, "Come on, Spiro. Put the gun away."

"Then stop messin' with me!"

The driver interrupted to ask if they wanted him to turn around and do it again. They'd been riding back and forth on the Seven Mile Bridge because Blister was entranced by the ocean hues. This would be their seventh crossing of the morning. Buck put a halt to it, saying he was starving. The driver pointedly took them to a Cuban joint for lunch. Blister didn't complain, because he was hungry, too. They stuffed themselves with *arroz con pollo* and *picadillo*. Coolman brought a sandwich to the driver in the parking lot.

On their way back, traffic on the famous bridge slowed to a halt when an Airstream coach blew a tire. Buck and Coolman remained pegged to the backseat while Blister got out of the Yukon and leaned over the bridge rail, trying to see if there were any hammerheads swimming around the pilings.

Stopped in the opposite direction, blocked from Blister's view by the broken-down Airstream, was a nondescript Subaru driven by a Sanitation and Safety Specialist for the state Division of Hotels and Restaurants. Andrew Yancy was on his way to Marathon for a walk-through of a Tuscan-style bistro that had a spotless inspection record, so he was in a good mood despite the delay. He turned up the radio and rolled down the windows to catch the gusts off the ocean.

A cop finally showed up and laid out a pylon path for the northerly traffic to squeeze past the disabled RV. Yancy was moving no more than ten miles an hour when he passed by Benny Krill, sprawled witlessly on the hood of a black southbound Yukon. In the backseat sat two figures that looked very much like Lane Coolman and Buck Nance.

There was nothing for Yancy to do but keep driving, for there was no place on the long bridge to turn around. He was basically stuck on a conveyor belt going the wrong way. He didn't grab his phone and call Detective Rogelio Burton, although at some point he would. Maybe. Yancy was irked that Burton hadn't told him that Blister and the others were not aboard the gray executive jet that had departed the night before; by now the detective surely had obtained the passenger manifest from the pretty silver-haired woman at the airport.

Yancy rushed through the bistro inspection (one rusty dumpster plug, one dead gecko on a windowsill) and headed home to Big Pine. He wasn't sure Merry Mansfield would still be there but she was, lying out in a killer chrome tank suit and a floppy hat.

"This is the stupidest thing a redhead can do, try for a tan," she said when Yancy joined her. "It's your fault, Andrew. All that crazy boat sex scrambled my senses. Was it unforgettable? Possibly. Did it mean anything? Do *not* haunt yourself with that question."

"Guess who's still in the Keys. The *tres* a-hole amigos we followed to the airport, they never got on that jet."

"Tricksters, eh?" Merry said. "Here, Mr. Sensitivity, rub some of this age-defying potion on me. Clear zinc, a zillion SPF. Like it matters anymore."

Yancy did her arms, neck and shoulders. He confided that he couldn't stop thinking about the man that Benny Krill scared off the Conch Train. "There was an interview with the widow in the paper. Jesus, it's so sad."

"Let it go. The cops'll catch up with Blister."

"But, see, I'd like to be the one. He put a knife in me, don't forget."

Merry flicked him on the nose. "Here we go again, Andrew—this is where I remind you what Burton said, that the sheriff wants you out of the headlines. Unless deep down you don't really care if you get your badge back."

Yancy was coming around to Rosa's view that Sonny Summers wasn't going to bring him back on the force, no matter what. "I should clean the twelve-gauge," he said, "just in case."

Merry tore off her hat and slapped him with it. "What is it with guys and their guns? No wonder your brainiac doctor girlfriend ran off to Norway."

"Harsh," Yancy sighed.

"I'll get dressed. Then we should go."

The house on Fleming looked empty. Blister's common-law wife sat on the front step rolling a beer bottle in her palms. Her sad little bicycle lay in the front yard.

She looked up and said, "Not you people again."

"Where are Benny and the boys?" Yancy asked.

"I'm sorry he stabbed you, but that don't mean I owe you a conversation."

"Clee Roy ended up on Stoney's menu, just so you know."

Mona held up her chubby arms, crosshatched with claw marks. "Take a good look and tell me why I should be all boo-hoo sad."

Merry said, "Benny didn't tell you where he was going, did he? Now he won't even pick up his phone, I bet."

"How'd you know?" Mona asked glumly.

"Been there, honey."

To Yancy, Mona said, "I gotta ask you somethin'—is that the real Buck Nance my husband's hangin' out with? Without the beard it could be any damn jackoff."

"No, that's Buck. The one and only."

"Okay, but the fifty grand a week—that's total bullshit, right? Benny was lyin' 'bout that part, for sure."

"Fifty grand a week for doing what?" Merry asked. She sat down beside Mona. "Hey, I like your flips."

"Thanks," said Mona. "You a cop, too?"

Merry patted her hand. Sheepishly Mona related Blister's wild yarn about joining the cast of *Bayou Brethren*.

"He said they was gonna pay him fifty thousand for every show, and he was gonna be worldwide famous. I tole him he had shit up to his eyeballs, so then he says, 'I can prove it, Baby Buns!' Few days later he calls to say his Hollywood 'agent' rented a 'bungalow' on Fleming, I gotta come right away. So I hump over here on my bike, and there's Benny and his so-called agent man and the dude they said was Buck Nance. And the three of 'em sit here all serious-faced givin' me a rundown on the big TV deal, how rich we're gonna be—and now, today, they're all gone." She sucked a gloomy breath through the gaps in her teeth. "What's a normal woman s'posed to think?"

Merry said, "Benny's not going to be a television star. He's going to prison."

"With 'Captain Cock' wrote in giant ink all over his back. Dear God Almighty."

"No kidding. You need to put that man in your rearview."

"If only I could," said Mona.

Yancy went through the house and saw that the men had cleared out. The kitchen trash revealed that Buck remained faithful to the faves on his Green Room rider—empty PBR cans, a Jack Daniel's bottle, crumpled Fritos bags, Reese's wrappers and handfuls upon handfuls of discarded non-green M & M's. The only sign of Blister was a grimy red bandanna on the floor.

"They've definitely vacated," Yancy said to Mona when he emerged. "What are your plans?"

"*He* was my plan. Benny."

Merry said, "He'll call eventually. There's no way he won't reach out to his Baby Buns."

"Yeah, but then what?"

"Tell him the ride's over, honey. Tell him to give up."

"Better yet," said Yancy, "tell him to call me."

Mona heaved the beer bottle into some shrubs, righted her bicycle and pedaled away. Merry drove Yancy to Mel Fisher's treasure museum, where she impressed him with her knowledge of shipwreck booty. She said she'd studied up on the Spanish fleets in preparation for a bogus artifacts hustle that she later scuttled: "It was a boyfriend's idea. Not Chip but a different one. I was on quite a streak for a while. The dude scored a bunch of fake doubloons online from China and sold them as the real deal at these 'investment seminars' in West Palm. But his favorite target was old retired couples, so I bailed on the scam—and on him, too. I hear he's into reverse mortgages now."

Yancy said, "You want to go make out somewhere?"

"Well, aren't you the frisky one."

He found a secluded parking spot under some trees near the cemetery. The car's backseat wasn't spacious enough for a horizontal fit, and the result was Yancy kicking out an armrest during a strenuous sequence of moves. Merry said she'd take it as a compliment. Afterward they went to the Turtle Kraals for ceviche and boiled shrimp. Merry was in rare form, funny and flirty, keeping it light. To Yancy she seemed happy—but then so had Rosa.

Later, looking back on the afternoon, he couldn't think of anything he did or said that might have spooked Merry off. At the restaurant she laughed so hard at one of his raunchy cop stories that her eyes were streaming. And she was definitely still smiling when she kissed him and told him she was going for a walk on the waterfront. She promised to meet him in an hour at Mallory Square. She told him to look for the Iguana Man.

Yancy drove to the Stock Island jail to chat with the two South Beach bouncers, but they'd already made bail. He swung by Blister's duplex and wasn't surprised not to see the black Yukon. His final stop was a drop-in at Stoney's Crab Palace, where a wake of sorts was being held for a local biker who'd bought the farm at Mile Marker 19. Yancy wasn't cold-hearted enough to disrupt the ceremony with a kitchen inspection. He went back to town and left the car on Front Street.

The original Iguana Man had died years earlier, but there was always at least one crusty imitator on the scene. He was easy to find, not only because he was cloaked with green lizards but also because he was flocked by tourists who perceived the scaly creatures as exotic. In reality, South Florida was so overrun with the damn things that homeowners used high-powered pellet rifles to thin the herd. The local unpopularity of the reptiles was due to their appetite for delicate garden flowers and also their habit of prodigiously shitting in swimming pools.

Yancy tracked down the Iguana Man *du jour* and scanned the selfie-snapping throng for Merry's face. Something poked him bluntly below the waist, and he looked down. An Irish setter was sociably nosing his crotch. When Yancy reached for its leash, the animal bolted with an air of goofy elation toward Whitehead, and heavy traffic. Heedless of his stitches, Yancy ran after the dog. When he was a boy, he'd owned a golden retriever named Bowie that got run over by a delivery truck. Yancy still choked up whenever he thought about it. He sprinted as hard as he could after the footloose setter, which zigzagged crazily between honking taxis and tour buses. The chase went on until the fugitive veered down a dead-end alley, where Yancy was able to corner and calm the animal. He beheld a pleasing vision of himself strolling through Mallory Square with a red-haired dog and a red-haired woman.

But when he returned, there was no sign of Merry in the Iguana Man's crowd. Yancy called her phone but she didn't answer. From behind him rose a cement-mixer voice: "Yo, that's my fuckin' mutt."

Yancy turned and saw a burly neckless figure carrying a suede shoulder bag. The man wore a new pastel fishing shirt and khaki hiking shorts that displayed to no one's benefit a bowed pair of pallid, hairy legs.

Yancy handed over the leash. "That's a good-looking dog. What's his name?"

"John."

"Just plain old John?"

"I didn't fuckin' come up with it. That's what he answers to." The man sounded weary of defending his pet's bland name. "He must've took off while I was in the toilet. Thanks."

Yancy said, "No problem. I needed the exercise."

The man had a New York accent. He said he was visiting Key West on business. "This park is where everybody comes, right? To see the freaks and the sunset."

"You're in the right place."

"My girlfriend's floatin' around here somewheres."

"Mine, too," said Yancy, adding: "A girl who's a friend."

"They got phones, they know how to find us. You look like you could use a cold one."

Yancy was glad to leave the square, which had filled with meandering cruise-ship googans. He told the man there was a pet-friendly bar on Simonton.

"Fuck that. John goes where I go." The man opened his shoulder bag and removed a blaze-orange vest emblazoned with the words WORKING SERVICE ANIMAL. He snapped the garment on the Irish setter and said, "Now you're legal, dumbass."

Yancy started laughing. "I thought those dogs were trained not to run away."

"John's got what you call impulse issues. Thank God I ain't blind, he'd drag my ass in front of a train."

Yancy took the man with the dog to the top of the La Concha. Merry still wasn't picking up her phone. After a couple of Heinekens the man with the dog told Yancy that his name was Dominick, and that he owned a document-shredding business in Miami. It might have been true, though Yancy was doubtful. He told the man he was a health inspector. The rest was more small talk, two guys killing time. Despite the meatiness of his fingers, Dominick showed himself to be a nimble texter. He was visibly irritated because his girlfriend wasn't responding. Yancy changed the subject by inquiring if Dominick's family was involved in the shredding business. Dominick said only his son, Dom Jr., had shown any interest.

"He's gettin' married in a few months in Staten Island," Dominick said. "Great girl. He lucked out big-time."

On his phone Dominick proudly scrolled up a photograph of the couple, young Dom a wide-bodied spitting image of his old man. The raven-haired bride-to-be was all bosom and teeth, impossibly happy.

"Check out the rock on her finger," said Dominick, enlarging the screen image with his salami thumbs.

Yancy looked closely at the engagement ring in the photo. He smiled and said, "I'll be damned."

"I gave it to Dommie to give to her. Take a guess what that thing's worth."

"Two hundred grand?" said Yancy.

The man named Dominick sat back, surprised. "Motherfucker, you're good."

"Funny story about that diamond." Yancy told Dominick how it had come to end up in his refrigerator on Big Pine.

Dominick slapped a hand on the bar and said, "Small fuckin' world!"

"Can I ask how you know that lawyer in Miami? Richardson."

"Never met him. It was just a favor for a guy I'm sorta in business with."

Yancy said, "Look, I don't want the ring back. It's not mine, anyway. But, can I say, the gentlemen you sent to my house really didn't have to kick me on their way out the door."

"They told me you was a real smartass."

"Man, I'd just gotten out of the hospital." Yancy lifted his shirt to show Dominick his belly wound.

"Who the hell did that to you? Was it my guys?"

"No, not them."

"They don't like the smartass routine, my guys. But, tell you what"—Dominick glanced crossly at the dog, farting in its sleep between the barstools—"you saved me some world-class poon by catchin' that runaway retard right there. My *goomah,* she'd never let me touch her again if I lost poor dumb adorable John. So I owe you one is what I'm sayin'." He handed Yancy a business card for a company called Rocko Gibralter Document Disposal. "You ever need somethin', here's where to call."

"Thanks for the beer," Yancy said.

He felt better about the ring situation knowing that Brock Richardson's diamond was a source of romantic joy for Dom Jr.'s fiancée, more joy than it had brought to either of the lawyer's fiancées.

Yancy said goodbye to the mobster and walked to the elevator. When the doors opened, a woman who could only be Dominick's girlfriend emerged. Her lips were cardinal red, her bleached platinum hair was trimmed severely short, and the cheeks of her formidable ass appeared to have been shaped with a helium nozzle. Despite her forward presentation the woman seemed preoccupied as she brushed past Yancy on a high-heeled track to the bar. She was hurriedly repositioning a papaya scarf, though not before Yancy glimpsed upon her neck a florid mouth-shaped mark that was too fresh to have been made by Dominick.

Yancy stepped into the elevator and mashed the Lobby button half a dozen times. Back at Mallory Square he couldn't find Merry anywhere; her phone went straight to voicemail. On a whim he walked down to the treasure museum. She wasn't there.

At dark he drove back to Big Pine knowing what he'd find. Merry's clothes and sandals and travel bag were gone from the house. Same for her toothbrush and scrunchies and the one-piece chrome swimsuit that drove him wild. He checked the refrigerator and saw that she'd also cleaned out her stash of energy drinks.

Yancy felt worse about her leaving than he'd expected. He put on some Charlie Parker, smoked half a fattie and fell asleep on his new couch. Early the next morning he got up to go fishing, and that's when he found the square pink envelope she had placed on the casting deck of his boat.

The note inside said, "I'm going to miss you, A.Y. Now quit dicking around and call Rosa."

TWENTY-ONE

Martin Trebeaux, recklessly seeking to impress Big Noogie's girlfriend, bragged about his epic scheme to corner the market on Cuban beach sand. "They'll jump all over this deal," he bubbled, sprawled on his bed at the La Concha. "They're going capitalist even faster than the damn Chinese!"

Juveline told him to lie still. She was using a black Sharpie on his nut sack. It felt like she was drawing little hearts.

"There's a big meeting down in Havana," Trebeaux said. *"Muy importante!"*

"Yeah? Take me with ya."

Trebeaux thought she was joking.

"I never been to a real island," she said. "I wanna go. Long Island doesn't count."

Looking down, Trebeaux saw only the tinted crown of Juveline's noggin. He heard the felt tip of the Sharpie squeaking on his skin.

"Don't it tickle when I do this?" she asked.

"Sweetie, listen to me—Big Noogie will get suspicious if you're gone. This would never work. He'll kill the both of us."

"You serious? I been on lotsa trips and the Noog don't care. Two, three days sometimes he don't even call. Hey, what's that weird mark down here? That little purple V."

"Ouch! Hey, careful."

"What is it, Marty? Tell me."

"That's where the Noog pinched me with hemostats."

"Hemo-what?"

"Pliers. The kind they use in surgery."

"Holy shit, Marty. I bet that really hurt."

"That's the whole point of torture. Ask your boyfriend."

"Well," Juveline said, "if this don't cheer ya up, nuthin' will."

She stood Trebeaux in front of a full-length mirror and lifted his pecker to display her scrotal artwork.

"What exactly am I looking at?" the sand man asked.

"Emojis, ya big dork."

"You mean like smiley faces?"

"One for each ball. See, they're blowin' kisses," said Juveline. "Don't ya ever text with emojis?"

At that moment a more circumspect man might have paused to review the train of bad decisions that had brought him to such a precipice—screwing the girlfriend of a homicidal gangster while the gangster was out walking her dog. Trebeaux, however, wasn't one to beat himself up. He truly believed he was cunning enough to snake through any brand of trouble; regret was for suckers. Of course it was foolhardy to fall for the crude charms of a high-maintenance flake like Juveline. Yet now that the dangerous line had been crossed, Trebeaux was growing excited about the logistical challenges of long-term deceit. Dominick Aeola didn't seem like the brightest bulb in the chandelier.

If I want to, thought the sand man, *I can pull this off.*

A wolf began howling—Big Noogie's ring tone on Juveline's phone. He left another message saying he was waiting in the hotel bar. Juveline played it back while she hurriedly put her clothes on. When Trebeaux pointed out a florid hickey that he'd imprinted on her neck during love-making, she gave an airy shrug and reached for a scarf.

Trebeaux said, "Maybe you should cover that suck mark with makeup."

"Do I look like the fuckin' Avon lady? All I got in my bag is lipstick."

"You're right, you're right. The scarf works."

Halfway out the door, Juveline turned and said, "Text me tomorrow about Cuba, Marty. I need to know what to wear."

Trebeaux had booked a seat on a charter flight from Miami to Havana by presenting himself as a renowned sculptor whose medium was, naturally, sand. He stated his trip to the communist country would be strictly educational, and on his application he attached photographs of elaborate Gothic castles, languid mermaids and a medium-scale likeness of the space shuttle Atlantis. All these sand creations had been made one Saturday morning by fifth-graders competing in a "Floridays" contest on Cocoa Beach. Their proud schoolteacher had posted the photos online without the precaution of watermarking, which allowed Trebeaux to steal them and claim the sculptures as his own work. No one at the agency that booked his Cuba trip had displayed the slightest suspicion or, for that matter, interest.

He called the company and said he'd decided to bring an assistant— would that be possible? The assistant, he added, would be traveling on a different flight.

"But put her ticket on my credit card."

"We'll have a taxi waiting for her at the airport, Mr. Trebeaux."

"Very good. What's the best beach on the island? I mean *numero uno.*"

"Oh, they are all lovely," replied the woman on the other end.

"Come on. There must be one special place that knocks your knickers off."

She admitted there was. "Playa Ramera," she said fondly.

"Never heard of it. What does that mean in English?"

"I'm not sure," the woman at the agency lied. "It's just a local name. Would you like me to arrange a van to take you there from Havana? You and your assistant?"

"That would be fabulous," Trebeaux said.

He looked forward to cavorting openly with Juveline in Cuba, which the Mafia had abandoned when Fidel seized power. The fact that Big Noogie had no eyes or ears there made it a safe zone of betrayal for both pleasure and business. Of the dual schemes that Trebeaux was hatching, the beach-sand project was less problematic because it was he who controlled all the key information. Big Noogie would have no choice but to take the sand man's word about his dealings with Cuban officials—and the monetary split.

The tryst with Juveline would be trickier, Trebeaux knew, because he wouldn't be able to supervise her once she returned to Queens after their tropical adventure. One offhanded remark, one careless slipup—a matchbook from Hotel Nacional falling out of her handbag, for instance—could be fatal for both of them. Based on Juveline's nonchalant reaction to the swollen hickey, Trebeaux believed she needed more guidance in the art of discretion.

He was right.

Yancy dialed Rosa's number and she picked up on the first ring. She asked if he was finished with the case, really finished, and he said yes.

"Then you can come," she told him. "Bring a parka."

He didn't have a parka. He also didn't have enough money for a flight to Norway, but he had plastic.

The layover in Newark was murder; six hours and change. Yancy read a wild Harry Crews novel about a man who eats a car. After that he walked to a Hudson's, where he bought fishing magazines and the New York papers. The *Daily News* featured an update about the case of the Muslim tourist from Brooklyn who'd been killed in South Florida. The widow of Abdul-Halim Shamoon said police officials were now classifying her husband's death as a hate crime. A statement issued by Monroe County Sheriff Sonny Summers said that a "person of interest" had been identified, and that a joint city-county task force was combing the islands in search of the individual. The sheriff said he was confident the case would soon be solved.

As Yancy read the story he heard his jaws popping.

The *News* ran a picture of Abdul-Halim Shamoon and his family standing in front of an electronics shop. The caption said the store was in midtown Manhattan on Seventh Avenue. In the photo Shamoon was a smiling young man, unrecognizable from the bloodied corpse on Frances Street in Key West. Yancy counted five kids—three boys and two girls—posed on either side of their father. The children would all be grown now. Shamoon's wife wasn't in the photograph, probably because she was the one who took it. Yancy felt he knew what she looked like.

He put down the newspaper and jogged back to the main terminal, where he told a man at the SAS desk that he was canceling his Oslo trip due to a personal emergency. An hour later the airline brought him his luggage, which he rolled all the way to the Delta counter. There he purchased a ticket to Miami. After boarding the plane he called Rosa, not the warmest conversation they'd ever had. She made several strong points, the first being that nobody (including Sheriff Summers) wanted Yancy's assistance in pursuing Benny Krill. Secondly, Yancy's detective skills, superior as they might be, weren't needed on the Shamoon case because Krill plainly wasn't clever enough to elude the cops for long. Rosa's final point, even more emphatic than the others, was that Yancy seemed to be losing focus of the big picture, meaning their future together as a couple. Yancy pointed out that it was she who'd abruptly quit her job and flown off to Europe alone. Such a move was not, he asserted, an act of unshakable devotion. The discussion grew sharper until a flight attendant told Yancy to turn off his phone because they were third in line for takeoff. He bit off half of an Ambien yet didn't sleep a wink on the plane.

The next day was spent scouring Key West for Benny the Blister, Buck Nance and Lane Coolman. Yancy located only one black Yukon, occupied by a white Baptist rapper who was in town for a concert benefiting the Pre-Teen Pioneers for Abstinence. The listing agent for the conch house on Fleming said it had been rented by a talent agency called Platinum Artists, which had paid for a month in advance. The agent was surprised when Yancy informed her that the tenants had already moved out.

A text from Merry Mansfield sent him speeding up the Overseas Highway:

> Saw blk Yukon on my way back to Miami. Parked at a bar at MM 82. But you're in Norway, so never mind.

Yancy drove like a berserk person and made it to Islamorada in less than two hours. The bar at Mile Marker 82 was in a sushi restaurant where his credentials actually carried some weight. The hostess remembered three customers arriving in a black SUV the night before. One of the men, skinny but rough-looking, became belligerent because the restaurant served only beer and wine. The hostess said the loudmouth got wasted on saki and started tossing spring rolls in the air, trying to catch them in his mouth. She said the two other men from the black SUV stuck with Kirin Light and more or less behaved themselves. Yancy asked to see the credit-card receipt for their meal. It was signed by Lane Coolman, Buck Nance's agent/manager/ass-wiper.

Yancy figured that Krill, Nance and Coolman beelined from the sushi joint straight to Miami Beach, but out of diligence he inquired at the nearby Moorings, a secluded spread of resort cottages popular with fashion models, musicians and actors who don't mind not being recognized. A camera crew was set up on the beach taping a commercial for a brand of guava-infused vodka. Strung between palm trees was a mesh hammock upon which lay a young blond woman wearing sunglasses and a banana-colored bikini. She was clutching the fifth of vodka to her cleavage in such a manner that fake condensation—supplied by a crew member with an eyedropper—dripped from the bottom of the bottle onto her tummy, trickling down the spray-tanned slope into a flawless navel. The journey of each glistening droplet was tracked at gyneco-logical range by a scruffy sweat-soaked cameraman kneeling in the sand with his Sony. Gawkers snapped pictures with their phones.

Unnoticed, Yancy made his way through the shaded property cottage-by-cottage. He rapped on the doors pretending to be looking for a guest named Rosa Campesino. The reactions were mostly genial until he approached a blue-trimmed villa where a croaky voice from inside told him to get lost. Yancy barged into the villa and right away noticed that Benny Krill had upgraded his weaponry.

"I thought you were a knife man, Blister."

Krill raised the gun. "Name's Spiro."

"That's a winner. I like it."

"Close the goddamn door."

Yancy said, "Tell me what happened on the Conch Train."

"He freaked out is what happened. The little A-rab dude. I didn't lay a finger on him."

"A couple witnesses say otherwise."

"They's fulla shit." Blister took a step back. He looked anxious. "All I did was tell the man he wasn't foolin' nobody, I know a damn sleeper cell when I see one. Then there was some Bible stuff I laid on him, all righteous and true. Next thing I know he jumps off the train car. Which is exactly what a damn suicide sleeper would do. What they call a ISIS synchronizer."

"Sympathizer. And that's not what he was, Blister."

"It's 'Spiro' from now on. Close the fuckin' door."

Yancy kicked it shut. "I hear you're going to be a TV star. That's truly . . . unimaginable."

Benny the Blister beamed. "Done deal, man! Ain't you or nobody else gone screw it up."

"And where's the famous Captain Cock?"

Blister's grin was a pageant of prison dentistry. "You mean my new brother Buck."

"No shit?" Yancy said. "What a heartwarming turn of events."

. . .

Brock Richardson had some time to kill before his flight to Key West, so he tried something he hadn't done in years: Read a legal document from beginning to end. It was fascinating—and harrowing.

The document was a deposition from a respected German endocrinologist named Harft, who'd recently completed a four-year study of a drug called testopheromenal, sold in nineteen countries under the trade name Pitrolux. The law firm of Truss, Hitch and Truss, to which Richardson referred many of his telephone clients, had hired Dr. Harft to review the frequency and severity of Pitrolux side effects. The findings rocked Richardson to his core. Being in theory a plaintiff's lawyer, he was accustomed to grotesquely creative exaggeration in product-liability cases. A tiny red bump on the skin became a "pernicious and disfiguring rash." Sore joints were automatically presented as "excruciating and debilitative." Every headache was a "blinding migraine," every bout of constipation a "toxic gastrointestinal impactment." And, regardless of anatomical location, each side effect was alleged in every lawsuit to cause "a loss of libido and a fear of intimacy" that shattered the victim's sexual relationships.

However, while studying Dr. Harft's neutral testimony, Richardson realized that for once there was no hype in the charges aimed at the drug's manufacturer. If anything, the printed warnings on the Pitrolux bottles underplayed the ghastly possibilities. The lawyer's bizarre experience with the substance wasn't an isolated incident; numerous male users had reported the appearance of strange skin growths in their armpits, groins, buttocks cracks and even between their toes. These soft stalks of flesh were typically described as "mushroom-like" or "penile-shaped."

Dr. Harft capped his testimony with a discussion of addictive reactions to Pitrolux—some men doubled or even tripled their dosages even as the unsightly side effects worsened. Richardson could totally relate. When the attorney from Truss Hitch had asked for a professional opinion on what should be done about the deodorant hormone gel, Dr.

Harft replied simply, "Remove it from the pharmaceutical marketplace, of course. As you Americans would say, it's really bad *scheisse*."

Richardson placed the deposition in his briefcase and vectored to the nearest bar on the concourse. Before boarding the plane, he removed the travel-sized bottle of Pitrolux from his carry-on intending to throw it away. Then he changed his mind, telling himself it would be careless to discard such a dangerous substance in a public place. What if a child found it in the trash can?

In Key West he was forced to rent a minivan because it was the last vehicle on the lot. He called Deb, who reiterated her opposition to the trip. Richardson replied: "I bet you'd feel different if it was your two hundred grand."

"Don't be such a stubborn ass. Just let it go."

"I know what I'm doing."

"Really? Then I've got one more question," Deb said.

"I can hardly wait."

"Cremation, or burial? Let me know now, so I can start making arrangements."

Richardson drove to Louie's Backyard and waited. Martin Trebeaux showed up an hour late, with no apology. Richardson was on his third scotch.

"I had a girl in my room. She wouldn't leave," the sand man explained. "What can I do for you, counselor? I hope it's not the Cuba trip 'cause I already filled your slot."

"No, it's about my diamond ring, the one your guys were supposed to steal back for me."

"The one they couldn't find. Big Noogie told me himself."

Richardson lowered his voice. "Afterward I sent *my* guys back to Yancy's place, and guess what? He says *your* guys took the ring."

"And you believe that a-hole?" Trebeaux giggled, as if the notion of gangsters pocketing a two-hundred-thousand-dollar diamond was preposterous. "A man'll say anything when there's pliers attached to his nuts."

"That's not how it went down."

The bartender interrupted them with a Creole shrimp appetizer that Richardson had ordered earlier. Trebeaux admired the spoke-and-wheel design of the crustaceans on crushed ice. When the barman left them alone again, Richardson said, "I want my goddamn rock back, Martin."

Trebeaux frowned. "Wish I could help, but I honestly don't see how."

"I'll tell you how: Talk to Big Noogie. Tell him how important that ring is to me. Tell him, hell, I don't know . . . tell him Deb's heart is crushed because she lost it. Make it sound like a sentimental situation."

"Are you fucking serious?"

"Listen, these Mafia types, they're romantics deep down. They've all got families and wives and girlfriends," Richardson said. "Big Noogie'll understand. Being from the Italian culture, he will totally get where I'm coming from."

"Do me a favor. That Google app on your phone? Type in the name Dominick Aeola and tell me if you see the word 'romantic' anywhere on his Wikipedia page. The one that lists all his felony arrests, and all the witnesses that mysteriously disappeared."

"So you won't talk to him about this?"

"Under no circumstances," said Trebeaux.

It was the answer Richardson expected. "Then I'll do it myself. Set up a meeting for me, okay?"

Trebeaux said that was an extremely poor idea. Richardson fidgeted.

"What aren't you telling me, Martin?"

"This is not a man you want to insult. If you accuse him of jacking your diamond, he might take it personally."

"What if he doesn't even know?" Richardson said. "Those two meat hogs he sent to Yancy's, what if they decided to keep the ring and told Big Noogie they couldn't find it?"

"That would take elephant balls."

"But still you can picture the scenario, right? It's not what you call far-fetched. A crook is a crook."

Trebeaux was skeptical. "Seriously, that's your pitch? You're gonna tell Big Noogie that his own guys double-crossed him?"

"I am, and I'm not."

"Christ, this isn't a game."

"The word thing is what I do best. Trust me, Martin, the reason I write all my own TV commercials? Because I know how to connect with people, all kinds of people. I have the gift of instant empathy."

"You cannot fuck this up. This is my business partner we're talking about."

"And it's my two-hundred-thousand-dollar diamond."

Trebeaux swiped a shrimp from Richardson's platter. "I can't promise Big Noogie will see you. In fact I'd be amazed if he does—but I'll ask."

"And you'll come with me to the meeting? You don't have to say one word. Just sit there like, you know, the mutual friend."

"Not a chance in hell," said the sand man, licking a dot of cocktail sauce from his lips. "You go see Big Noogie, you're on your own."

TWENTY-TWO

Buck Nance walked out of a back room glowering at Blister Krill. Yancy noted a scraggly resemblance, close enough to pass themselves off as TV brothers. Both were thin, sallow and had brown hair shot with gray. Once their beards grew out, they might as well be blood.

"Hello, Buck," Yancy said. "Or is it Matthew, like the old times?"

"Who the hell are you?"

"He's the one that said he's a cop but he ain't," Blister interjected.

Buck snorted. "How do you know he's not?"

"Thank you," said Yancy.

Blister turned on the flat-screen and told everyone to sit on the couch. He said it was time for *Bayou Brethren*. Yancy was wedged in the middle, Blister gouging him in the rib cage with the barrel of the handgun. Buck drank Jack Daniel's while Blister popped an IPA called Grizzly Snot. They both quickly got swept up in the TV show, for different reasons. Buck was incensed to learn that Junior was sleeping with Miracle, and that she was now an open topic for all America. Blister's chief concern was his future seating location at the family table; he declared he wanted a chair between Clee Roy's wife and Buddy's wife, because they looked hot and do-able.

"I thought you were married," Buck snapped.

"Just common-law, which don't even count outside Florida."

"But homicide does," Yancy pointed out.

"Shut up and watch the damn show," Blister grumbled. When a commercial came on, he said, "I didn't mean to hurt that little Mooselum dude, but for all I knowed that bag in his hands was a damn suicide bomb."

"It was gifts for his family." Yancy looked over at Buck Nance. "Souvenirs, Matthew. That's all he was carrying."

"Hey, I had nothing to do with it."

"Sure you did. Blister idolizes you—those sermons on YouTube."

Blister said, "Amen, brother."

He raised his non-gun hand to quiet the talk, for on television Buddy Nance had snatched up a half-full Dewar's bottle and heaved it more or less at Junior's head. "Awesome!" Blister cheered at the slow-mo replay.

Lane Coolman walked in the front door, his face clouding at the sight of Yancy.

"There he is—my Hollywood agent!" Blister boomed.

Yancy said they'd already met. "What are you geniuses up to?" he asked Coolman. "I can't wait to hear the big plan."

Blister ordered Yancy to stand, lift his shirt and show the others where Blister had stabbed him—"in case they think I ain't a serious individual."

The sight of Yancy's sutures properly alarmed Buck and Coolman. Blister seemed satisfied.

Buck asked Coolman for an update on Amp.

"He's flying in to meet with us," the agent said, "as promised."

"When?"

"Soon."

Blister said, "Soon ain't fast enough."

"Who's Amp?" asked Yancy.

Somewhere Blister came up with boat rope and duct tape. He bound and gagged Yancy before sliding him under a bed. Yancy was impressed by the cleanliness of the floor—not even a dust bunny. The polished pine planks felt cool against his cheek. He shut his eyes and strained to hear the conversation of the carping fuckwits in the adjoining room.

Coolman was telling Blister it was a really bad move, tying up a possible cop. Blister asked if anyone had a better idea. Buck said he couldn't wait to get the fuck out of Florida.

Yancy rolled from beneath the bed thinking it was a good thing that Rosa couldn't see him now. He struggled to his feet and tumbled himself through an open window, his fall cushioned by a row of lush greenery. Once upright, he advanced pogo-style to the nearest cottage, where he used his forehead to bang on the door. The woman who answered was the blond model from the vodka commercial being filmed on the beach. Yancy blinked and grunted beseechingly. Miraculously the woman let him hop inside, where he toppled sideways onto a divan. After she peeled the tape from his mouth, he said, "You have the golden heart of an angel."

"Dude, who did this to you? I'm gonna call the cops."

Her name was Miso and she couldn't find her phone. Yancy asked her to get a knife and cut the ropes from his wrists and ankles. She hurried to the kitchen but returned emptyhanded saying, "Sorry, but I'm really stoned."

"Please go look again."

"I like you. What's your deal?"

"Any sharp object will do the job," Yancy said.

"I don't know. Maybe you're a serial killer."

"This would be an odd way to stalk my victims."

"That's true." Miso shrugged. "Look, I was supposed to meet up with some people. You know, from the crew?"

Yancy said, "I really need your help."

She went back to the kitchen, returned with a steak knife, and commenced sawing on the ropes. Because of her loopy condition, Yancy feared for his veins and arteries. The sash on her robe came undone, presenting a caramel flash of skin that distracted him from her bladework.

Once freed, he positioned himself by a window with an unimpeded view of the cottage occupied by Blister and the others. Yancy lowered and cracked the blinds. Miso sat beside him. He told her she'd looked great on the set of the vodka commercial.

"I totally don't even drink that crap," she said. "What is a guava, anyway?"

"You're on your way to something bigger. That's all that matters. Your life trajectory."

"Dude, I'm twenty-one and a half."

"Hang in there," Yancy said.

"What's your story? Why don't you call the cops on those assholes?"

"I left my phone in the car. Also, I *am* a cop."

"You are not!" She laughed and frogged his arm. "I said I was stoned, not stupid."

"Respect, *por favor.* I used to be a hotshot police detective, for real. Now I'm just a humble hardworking health inspector."

"Yeah, right. I totally know what you inspect."

"I'm Andrew, by the way. Andrew Yancy. I'd show you my ID, except—"

"It's in the car with your phone, right? I'm so sure."

Yancy smiled. She smelled like pot and coconut butter. "You who are so quick to judge," he said, "let me point out that 'miso' is a Japanese soup."

"It's just plain old Jane on my driver's license."

"A perfectly lovely name."

"Not for modeling it isn't," she said. "You want a drink? If I can even find the damn liquor. I totally smoked the last doob, so don't ask."

Yancy put a finger to his lips as he parted the blinds. "Take a look," he whispered.

Benny Krill, Buck Nance and Lane Coolman had emerged from the nearby cottage. They stood conferring on the porch, in no discernible state of panic, which meant they were unaware Yancy had escaped from the bedroom.

"Those three fellows," he said to Miso, "aren't exactly master criminals."

"Uh, yeah, I get that, *Andrew*. Why'd they tie you up?"

"I'll tell you everything later. Would you mind getting dressed?"

"Where are we goin'? Are jeans okay?"

"Jeans are excellent."

She stood up and shed the robe saying, "This is crazy. What am I doing?"

"You'll have a good story to tell your friends."

"Promise?"

"Totally," said Yancy.

Vance Banks stood on the slender balcony of his apartment wishing he had a view of Biscayne Bay instead of the Miami Beach public-works garage. He wore a Hurricanes hoodie and dark glasses to hide his face—an act of prudence, not paranoia. Vance Banks was only thirty-one, but he'd accumulated more enemies than most men twice his age. This was the result of failing to repay certain debts associated with a roaring appetite for cocaine, gambling and high-end escorts. One such obligation had in only a few brief weeks mushroomed with interest from $6,000 to $22,500, a sum currently unavailable to Vance Banks. Being not entirely dim-witted, he understood that the men from whom he had borrowed the $6,000 were more humorless and violent than any of his other creditors. His divorced sister in Jacksonville was unsympathetic, Vance Banks having tooted away a sizable inheritance. His brother in Gulf Shores had long ago stopped returning his calls, while his mother communicated seldom and only through attorneys. Having few options, Vance Banks accepted the fact that, once again, it was time to leave town.

So, late that night, he vacated his apartment, placed his gray tabby cat in the car, drove across the MacArthur Causeway and moved in with his cocaine dealer in Coral Gables. The men to whom Vance Banks owed $22,500 had never seen such a lazy attempt at evasion. They felt insulted.

In return for providing Vance Banks a place to crash, the coke dealer asked him to drive a 2008 Toyota Camry from the Port of Miami to a motel in Hialeah. Vance Banks had no experience on the supply side of drug transactions, but the coke dealer assured him that none would be needed for this job. If he'd known that Vance Banks was in debt to the Calzone crime family, he would not have handed him the keys to that particular vehicle.

The instructions given to Vance Banks were simple: obey the speed limits, observe all traffic signals, and do not open the trunk of the vehicle unless ordered to by a uniformed police officer. Leaving nothing to chance, or so he thought, the coke dealer selected on MapQuest the simplest route of travel and placed a printout in the hands of Vance Banks. Upon arriving at the motel, Vance Banks would simply back the Camry into a parking spot and walk away. There would be no verbal or visual contact with the individuals awaiting the delivery.

Vance Banks hoped to be well paid for this risky chore, but that didn't happen. He never made it to the motel. On Northwest 62nd Street, only five blocks off the interstate, the Camry was struck from behind by an old black pickup that had been following him unnoticed since he'd left his cocaine dealer's apartment. The crash didn't injure Vance Banks or his cat Sawyer, which he'd brought along to calm his nerves. With Sawyer safe in his arms he got out of the Camry and observed with dismay that the impact of the accident had sprung the trunk lid. Frantically Vance Banks tried to close it, but the crumpling was too severe.

Upon approaching the pickup truck he saw behind the wheel a red-haired woman in a tan low-cut sweater. When she rolled down the window he became aware of a disposable razor in her right hand. A dark skirt was bunched around her waist, and there was no outline of panties. The driver's long creamy legs led to feet adorned by gem-encrusted flip-flops.

"Super-duper sorry," she said.

"Are you seriously *shaving* your . . . ?"

"Bikini zone? It's worse than texting, I know. Completely took my eyes off the road."

"Freak city," muttered Vance Banks, nervously eyeing the passing traffic.

The woman tossed the razor and lowered her skirt. "I was on my way to Rocky's. That's my boyfriend. He likes a smooth landing zone, if you know what I mean. Your kitty's quite handsome, by the way. He's got what they call a noble countenance. What's his name?"

"Sawyer. And it's a she."

"I'm Merry," the woman said. "Spelled like Merry Christmas." She held her hand out the window so Vance Banks could shake it. "Honest, I'll pay to fix your car."

"It doesn't belong to me, unfortunately."

"Well, let's have a look-see at the damage." She reached to unbuckle her seat belt.

"No!" Vance Banks blurted. "Stay right there."

The red-haired woman wore a sexy perfume, which further diminished the chances of Vance Banks making a wise decision. What he should have done was get the hell out of there, before a cop drove up, but a pleasant sort of paralysis had set in.

She said, "Now my dumb truck won't even start. I've got some cash at home if you'll give me a ride. That way we don't have to call the police or insurance company. Please?"

"I guess. Sure." He figured he could use a shoelace to tie down the trunk lid of the Camry. "How far away is your place?"

"Oh, just a few blocks."

"You should text your boyfriend and tell him you'll be late."

She smiled. "You think he doesn't trust me? You're right."

"My name's Vance Banks."

The woman reacted with wide eyes. "Dude, are you feeling okay? Did you hit your head in the accident?"

"What makes you say that?"

"Because you gave me your real name," she said. "Most guys lie."

"Wait—what? Do you know me?"

"Poor baby," she said.

A white Lincoln coupe rolled up and a stocky well-dressed man got out. He had an ivory toothpick in his mouth and a small silver revolver in one hand.

Vance Banks said, with belated perception, "I am so fucked."

"My suggestion? Give 'em whatever they want."

"But I don't have their money! I'm tapped out!"

"Get creative," the redhead said. "Come on, Vance, step it up."

She offered to take care of his cat, but the transfer was vetoed by the man with the toothpick. Within moments the Lincoln departed at high speed carrying Vance Banks, the purring Sawyer and a gym bag holding forty-eight one-ounce bags of premium cocaine that had been removed from the Camry's trunk. Merry Mansfield abandoned the black pickup on 62nd Street and Ubered back to her hotel on the beachside. She did forty minutes on the treadmill, took a shower and then sat down with a book called *Treasures of the Spanish Main,* which she'd checked out of the library on Alton Road.

At half-past six she put on blue-jean overalls and clogs. Her hair was still wet so she opted for pigtails. A yellow cab dropped her at the News Café, where the man with the ivory toothpick was already waiting. When Merry sat down at the table, he passed her an envelope containing eleven one-hundred-dollar bills, more than she expected.

"You did real good. That's how come there's extra," the man said. "The dope in the car was a bonus."

"So you and I can talk direct from now on, right? No more Zetos in between."

"Jesus, what a retard. He really fried himself to death with a Prius?"

"It was a Tesla," Merry said.

"Is the voltage higher on them?"

"That's a darn good question."

The man took a drink of coffee, the toothpick still lolling in his mouth. He said, "Swear to God, long as I been in this business, it still blows my fuckin' mind."

"The stupidity, you mean."

"You never been to prison, but let me tell you this for a fact: Every new generation of these shitheads is dumber than the last. It's harder and harder to find good people."

Merry pushed the envelope full of cash back across the table and said, "The job I did today is free if you promise not to hurt the cat."

The man with the toothpick chuckled. "Keep it, babe. One call to momma and Mr. Banks came up with our money. Really it was more like eight, nine calls. Point is he got to keep his kitty and his nuts. You up for another gig?"

"Depends on when and where."

"Boca. Tomorrow afternoon. West Boca, actually. The guy's a major pussy hound, so it should go easy. He drives a gray Audi. I'll text you the tag."

Merry said, "Not tomorrow. I'm going out of town."

"What for?"

"Friend of mine down in the Keys—it's a long story. He's in over his head."

The man with the toothpick said, "Can't he wait a day, this friend?"

Merry shook her head. "I've got a feeling he can't."

The three men walked across U.S. 1 to a restaurant called Morada Bay. They took a table outside, supposedly to watch the sunset.

Benny the Blister announced he'd changed his mind; he no longer wished to be called Spiro when he joined the cast of *Bayou Brethren*.

"I come up with somethin' way better," he said. "Deerbone."

"Deerbone. Deerbone Nance." Coolman repeated it several times. "I think I'm loving it."

Buck said, "What does it even mean? Besides that deers have bones." Listlessly he stared out at the mangrove islands. Coolman could tell he was thinking about his ex-mistress, Miracle, grinding on his brother.

"Make sure it's fixed in the legal papers," Blister went on. "Call your damn boss and tell him Spiro's out. Deerbone's in."

"Great name, bro. Authentic," Coolman said. He didn't care what the cocksucker called himself when he got to jail, which is where he was going as soon as they nailed down the deal memo for Buck's contract. Coolman had stored on his phone the number of the local Crime Stoppers hotline.

A more immediate worry for Coolman was "Inspector" Yancy, hogtied under a bed in the bungalow. Conspiring in an abduction was not in the Platinum Artists agents' playbook. Even if Yancy wasn't a cop, he probably had cop connections. Coolman decided to offer him some money to forget about what happened. The payoff could be layered into Buck Nance's deal, as a one-time "consultant's fee."

Blister continued yammering throughout dinner, while Buck spoke barely a word and snubbed his broiled lobster.

Coolman finally said, "Look, I had nothing to do with Miracle switching to Junior. That wasn't my call."

"So it was Amp?"

"The bitch was pissed off at you, dude. Vengeance-wise, she had worse things in mind, trust me. This was a compromise."

"What about the condo? I want her out of my goddamn condo."

Blister piped, "Hell, I'll take it. Is there a hot tub?"

"Jacuzzi," said Buck through clenched teeth.

"What's the motherfuckin' difference? I'm gone hang a big-ass Rebel flag and blast Molly Hatchet all night long."

The Pensacola condominium was titled in Miracle's name, and there was already a Confederate flag on the bathroom wall.

"Legally she owns the place," Coolman said to Buck. "That's how you wanted it, remember?"

Buck slammed a fist on the table, which was so heavy it barely moved. Tears pooled in his eyes as he nursed his throbbing hand.

Blister was sympathetic. "You was blinded by the pussy, that's all. I been there, brother. Say hi to pussy, say bye-bye to common sense."

"Just shut up," Buck groaned.

A pair of ibises landed nearby and began walking the beach side-by-side, probing here and there with their curled beaks. Coolman wondered why he and Rachel could never get in sync like that.

Blister was now babbling about the iconic significance of the Stars and Bars, how the proud white race shouldn't let those damn Northern faggots and communist Negroes tear down that sacred old flag. Having minored in American history at UC–Davis, Coolman was tempted to pop a Civil War quiz on Mr. Krill; the moron probably didn't know Manassas from Manitoba. However, since the moron had a loaded gun and no sense of irony, Coolman kept quiet. As a manager of so-called talent he was demoralized to find himself in such low company, sitting between an armed crackpot and a fake chicken farmer known to millions as Captain Cock. Back home in Beverly Hills, rival agents were dining with classy A-listers like Javier Bardem and the Coen brothers, or so Coolman bitterly imagined.

If I ice this deal, he thought, *I should start my own agency.*

After sunset the three men walked next door to Pierre's and took seats at the elegant wooden bar. Coolman began feeling more positive about his professional situation. At one end of the room a curly-headed guitarist played killer flamenco, applauded by a couple sitting together behind a potted palm. A tall brunette who had mistakenly dressed for St. Barts emerged from a thrumming cluster of women and approached Buck Nance. She handed him a cocktail napkin and asked for an autograph, which he signed "Jerry Jeff Walker." Her request for a selfie was denied, but still she was beaming as she rejoined her friends.

When Blister called out for a Pabst, the bartender looked at him as if he were speaking Togolese. Coolman ordered Jack-and-waters for all of them.

"Where are we meeting Amp?" Buck asked, the Cajun accent still exiled.

Blister said, "Someplace safe. Those fuckin' Key West cops is still lookin' for me."

Coolman put a hand on his shoulder. "No worries, Deerbone. I've got this."

Blister smiled at the sound of his new name. Buck sullenly scratched at the thickening stubble on his chin.

The bartender came over and said, "That gentleman back in the corner says you boys owe him a drink."

Coolman worriedly scanned the room. "What gentleman?"

"The tan dude with the hot blonde. They're sitting near the guitar player."

Andrew Yancy rose and parted the fronds of the potted palm, so that the men at the bar could see his face.

"You gotta be shittin' me," Blister said. "I'm gonna kick that mother's ass."

Buck Nance muttered, "Nice job on those knots, *Deerbrain.*"

Yancy saluted the trio with an erect middle digit, raised high.

"What's he drinking?" Lane Coolman asked the bartender. "Get one for the girl, too."

TWENTY-THREE

Martin Trebeaux told Juveline he was meeting Big Noogie at Higgs Beach.

"Just don't show him your prize jewels," she said.

They were in the bathtub, Juveline soaking on her back. Trebeaux was curled like a comma on top of her, his head pillowed by her breasts. There was water all over the floor. Gentle scrubbing had failed to remove the kiss-blowing emojis from his testicles.

"Are you positively *positive* he doesn't know about us?" Trebeaux asked.

Juveline flicked his soapy earlobe. "The Noog don't have a clue. You must think I'm dumber than a mud fence. Is that whatchu think?"

"What about the hickey?"

"I told him it was a love nip from John."

"The dog? And he believed that?"

"'Course he did. I could make you believe it, too."

The sand man climbed out of the tub. "Where are you supposed to be right now?"

"I dunno. Shoppin'."

"Then that's where you need to be."

"I already bought two new hats for Havana," she said, "and panties with little green parrots all over—but you're not allowed to see 'em till we get there."

"Sweetie, I can't wait."

The weather had warmed so Higgs Beach was crowded. Trebeaux searched awhile before he located Big Noogie, enthroned under a rainbow-striped umbrella with John the First. Exuberantly the setter began sniffing Trebeaux, who backed off in fear that his clothes bore incriminating scents.

Big Noogie said, "Juveline lets him sleep in the same bed as us—you believe that? Dog hairs all over the goddamn duvet."

Trebeaux couldn't change the subject fast enough. "Great news!" he said. "Cuba approved my visa."

"You set up that meeting with your connection?"

"The deputy minister's very pragmatic, for a socialist. I wish you could come with me." Trebeaux held his breath, praying that the federal judge who had confiscated Big Noogie's passport hadn't suddenly changed his mind.

"Another time," said the mobster. Having never seen the second *Godfather*, he knew next to nothing about Havana. Scooping a handful of sand, he asked, "Is the shit over there as good as this?"

"Way better." Trebeaux smiled. "And it's pink, Dominick."

"No fuckin' way."

"The beach at Playa Ramera, you bet your ass. Miles and miles of it."

"You mean pink like . . ."

"Oh yeah." Trebeaux offered a knuckle-bump that went unreciprocated.

Big Noogie was watching the grains drizzle through his fingers. "Your oceanfront hotels here in the States, your four-star properties," he mused, "they'd pay a goddamn fortune for pink."

"We're gonna kill it, Dominick. Kill. It."

Two lanky young women walked up and asked if they could pet Big Noogie's service dog. John the First rolled over, reveling in the sweet-smelling attention. The women said they were visiting Key West on spring break with their college sorority. They said they were playing a volleyball match with some off-duty firefighters. From the way the women looked at him, Trebeaux sensed they were trying to figure out whether it was he or Big Noogie that needed a special canine companion. The women said they attended Washington and Lee, which sounded like a serious school.

"What do you think of this beach?" Big Noogie asked. "On a scale of, like, one to ten."

"Eleven!" the women answered together, laughing.

"Okay, what if the sand was pink?"

"Bullshit," one of them said. "Pink sand?"

"I'd give that a fifteen!" the other one chortled. "No, twenty!"

They hugged John the First and called out goodbye as they scampered back to their sorority gathering. Trebeaux clapped and said, "This Cuba deal's gonna be mega-mega. We ought to change the company name to *Global* Sedimental Journeys."

"I think those two girls were tanked."

"Who cares, Dominick? We don't need a damn focus group to tell us pink beaches kick ass."

Big Noogie opened a sports canteen and poured some water into a plastic bowl. He placed it in front of the fake service dog, which commenced slurping like a horse.

"When are you going back North?" Trebeaux asked with a nonchalant lilt.

"Why do you give a shit? I like it here. Today is forty-seven fuckin' degrees back home." Big Noogie flapped his flimsy tank top to demonstrate how comfortable he felt in South Florida. "Now, what's this other favor you want from me? The first bein' not feedin' your ass to the hammerheads."

"It's nothing, really. No pressure."

"Do I look fuckin' pressured?"

"So, it's the dude whose girl lost that big diamond ring. The Miami lawyer. He wants a sit-down to talk about what happened when your guys went to his crazy neighbor's house."

"I told you what happened. My guys didn't find no rock."

"He's got a theory. What can I say?"

"A theory. That's rich."

"More like a scenario," the sand man said. "Listen, Dominick, you don't need to bother with this. I'll tell him you're too busy to meet, end of story. What's he going to do?"

Grunting like a hog in quicksand, Big Noogie dragged himself from the shade of the beach umbrella into the sunlight. He rose up, squinting behind his sunglasses and brushing off the seat of his tent-sized board shorts.

"Now you got me curious," he said to Trebeaux. "Go on. Set it up."

"Seriously? Just you and him?"

"Tell me again the name of this douche."

"Brock Richardson."

"The one on TV does all the dick deodorant cases. I seen his commercials."

Trebeaux said, "You don't put the stuff on your dick. It goes under your arms."

"How the fuck does *that* get you hard?"

"I have no clue, Dominick. But from what I hear, that shit will definitely mess you up."

"Tell the lawyer to come tomorrow morning. Ten sharp, same place."

John the First started barking at a trio of tourists hanging from a fluorescent parachute being towed by a speedboat offshore. Big Noogie stepped on the setter's leash to prevent another manic breakaway.

"That's a sharp vest he's got," the sand man remarked. "How much?"

"Twenty-nine bucks off Amazon."

"Did I not tell you it was easy?"

"It's still a scum move. Only reason I did it, Juveline don't want her little buddy catchin' pneumonia down in cargo. She wants him sittin' on the plane with us."

"Hey, that doggie vest also got you onto this beach. It says right there that only service animals are allowed." Trebeaux pointed at the sign. "You should thank me!"

Big Noogie closed the rainbow umbrella and tucked it under one arm. "Be that as it may," he said, "John and me are gonna go watch a volleyball game."

Rosa emailed a photo of herself carving a reindeer shank at the butcher shop in Oslo. A few minutes later, Merry Mansfield sent a picture of a gold earwax spoon recovered from the wreck of the *Santa Margarita*, a treasure-laden galleon that sank off the Marquesas during a hurricane in 1622. Yancy wasn't sure how to respond to either of the women, so he didn't.

He was back in Key West, parked at the cemetery waiting for Irv "Clippy" Clipowski. The restaurant owner had made him promise to come alone.

Yancy sent him a text: "Could you pick a creepier place to meet?"

"Be there in 15," Clippy texted back.

In the meantime Miso the vodka model called to thank Yancy for a fun time the night before. She'd been a very good sport. Yancy had given her contact info to Lane Coolman, Buck Nance's manager, during an impromptu meeting on the porch at Pierre's. Miso had remained inside at the wooden bar, expertly mesmerizing Buck Nance and Benny the Blister.

Outside, Coolman was offering Yancy seventy-five thousand dollars to forget Blister had pointed a loaded firearm at his head, tied him up and shoved him under a bed. When Yancy had turned down the payoff, Coolman got aggravated.

"Then what the hell do you want from us?"

"I want Benny Krill," Yancy had replied, "soon as you're done with him."

"Are you going to kill him? Because here's the thing: We prefer him to be in jail, not deceased. The story line we have in mind, jail would work better."

"That's where he'll be."

"And we can be assured of that . . . how?" Coolman had said.

"Because I keep my word, which I realize is freak behavior where you come from."

"Why don't you just take the damn money? We'll do the wire transfer first thing tomorrow."

"I'm not going away," Yancy had said. "When you guys finish with Blister, call *me*—not Crime Stoppers. If that's not how it goes down, meaning he ends up somewhere other than my custody, I'll be submitting a sordidly detailed affidavit describing what you and your deranged clients did to me inside that cottage at the Moorings. The whippings and fondling and so forth."

"Oh, come on!"

"I don't think you appreciate my ragged state of mind."

"Fine. Whatever. We'll give you Krill."

"When?"

"Two days. Three tops," Coolman had said.

"Here's my phone number. One more thing."

"Jesus, I fucking knew it—"

"My beautiful companion at the bar, she wants to be an actress."

"Imagine that."

"Find her some work," Yancy had said.

His state of mind was, in fact, not good. Watching *Bayou Brethren* in the company of Buck Nance and Blister had been a setback, morale-wise. Yancy might have found humor in the bourbon-soaked TV version of rural Southern life if Buck was just another harmless stooge, but he wasn't. He was a septic inspiration to impressionable mouth-breathers such as Benny the Blister, who had accosted an innocent Muslim man only because he imagined that's what his hero Captain Cock would have done.

Yancy looked forward to handing over Blister Krill to Sheriff Sonny

Summers, though he knew the Conch Train case was weak due to the conflicting witness accounts. The odds were at least fifty-fifty that Blister would get acquitted, leaving unpunished the death of Abdul-Halim Shamoon. As for the stalker-style kidnapping of Buck Nance and his manager, Coolman had informed Yancy that neither he nor his star client planned to cooperate with prosecutors. Once Buck returned to the *Brethren,* there would be no window in his hectic shooting schedule for a lengthy—and embarrassing—trial.

Even if delivering Blister to the sheriff got Yancy reinstated, it would be sickening to see the man walk free later. Yancy felt sick now, thinking about it. The best hope for sending that crazy dirtbag back to prison was to prosecute him for the stabbing. As the victim, Yancy would be compelled to take the witness stand, where his character would receive a battering by Blister's defense lawyer. There was rich material to work with.

Rosa emailed Yancy another picture—snow flurries, bare trees and glowing street lamps. It made Yancy want to drive home, gas up his boat and go fishing in the sunshine.

But first here was Clippy, arriving in a dingy truck that belonged to a carpet company. He pulled up next to Yancy's Subaru, lowered a window and said:

"I put in a good word for you at Sonny's fundraiser, Andrew. Just so you're aware, Neil and I forked out the max for his campaign. Meaning we had his full, undivided attention when I told him he should hire you back on the force. I said you were a solid guy, a brilliant detective."

"I sincerely appreciate that. Thank you."

"Happy to do what I can. Happy to help."

"Clippy, why are you driving that truck?"

"You'll see."

"And why are we here at the graveyard?"

"Get in, Andrew. Please."

Stacked behind the front seats of the truck were rolls of Berber carpet and foam padding. Yancy heard something move and wondered if a person was tied up in the back. Perhaps Clippy and Neil were having a falling-out.

"I know I can trust you," Clippy said. "Right?"

He drove without elaboration to the landfill on Stock Island. The porcelain sky was full of buzzards and seagulls. A sickly tang rose from the steep hill of garbage, where Yancy and Rogelio Burton once spent seven wretched hours searching for a carrot peeler that had been used as a murder weapon. They never found it, but the experience bonded the two for life.

At the top of the mound lay the ripest waste, bagged and unbagged, awaiting the county backhoes. On windy afternoons you could almost breathe without covering your face, but today there was no breeze off the Gulf. The smell was awful, even with the truck windows rolled up.

"Oh dear God Almighty," gasped Clippy, pinching the bridge of his nose.

"Please tell me we're not here to bury the mayor."

"What a hideous thing to say! The two of us couldn't be happier, Neil and I. Are you kidding? We're getting married on June 23. That's Clarence Thomas's birthday!"

"I'll save the date," Yancy said. "What's in the back of the truck?"

Clippy shakily uncapped a bottle of Valium and gulped two pills. "You don't understand how difficult this is for me," he said.

Yancy got out and opened the rear doors, Clippy posted behind him.

"Holy shitfire," Yancy said. "A doubleheader."

"They're not hurt. They're just fine."

"Yes, I can see that."

"It's a live-catch trap," Clippy explained. "The same kind they use on coyotes."

"I would greatly prefer coyotes."

"They must be boyfriend and girlfriend, right? The way they're acting."

"Their relationship doesn't interest me," said Yancy. "It's their size."

They were the biggest fucking rats he'd ever seen. Inside the wire caging, two Gambian pouchies copulated frenetically, oblivious to their audience.

"I caught 'em last night behind the main bar," Clippy said.

"On what?"

"Cantaloupe slices drizzled with organic peanut crumbs."

"Heart-healthy," Yancy murmured.

"Two at once! I almost freaking peed my pants. Afterward, Jordie, the busboy, helped me load the trap into the truck. His step-uncle has a carpet store."

The rats looked to be solid six-pounders. They finished screwing, disengaged and rose inquisitively on their hind legs. Eyes aglow, whiskers twitching, they seemed intoxicated by the sweet reek of the dump.

Clippy said, "You *cannot* tell Tommy Lombardo about this. If news gets out, they'll shut us down so damn fast. Please, Andrew, TripSwami will destroy us! We might as well just give the restaurant to the bank."

"You're putting me in a tough spot."

"Hey, it's not like you found them during a regular inspection. For all you know, these animals could be personal pets of mine, just two rats in a truck."

"I see where this is going," Yancy said.

"And don't forget I did you a major *major* solid, talking to Sonny."

"Indeed you did."

"Bottom line," Clippy said, "I don't have the heart to euthanize these two. I figured this was the best place to let 'em go. Rat heaven, right?"

"Okay, but why'd you call me?"

"A, because I trust you. And B, are you kidding? I can't do this alone! These things are huge. You're the rodent guy, Andrew."

"I am *not* the rodent guy. Don't ever say that."

"You know what I mean." Clippy admitted he didn't want to touch the trap. He claimed to have a pathological fear of hantavirus. "Goes back to when I was a kid up North. One summer my brothers locked me in a horse barn—"

"Know what? I believe you," Yancy said.

"So, I'll just stand back while you do your Rat Whisperer thing."

"I can't just turn 'em loose, Clippy. They're from West Africa. They don't belong here."

"This is a landfill, for Christ's sake, not a nature preserve."

"The word biologists use for them is 'invasive,' Clippy. Want to know why? Because one female pouchie pops out a new batch every five weeks. By summer, Stock Island will be covered up with these fuckers. Think Old Testament."

"Tell me the worst that can happen. What—they chase off all the regular rats? I say good riddance."

Yancy observed both animals tinkering with the hinges of the trap, trying to spring the door. Their bony pallid paws were as nimble as a monkey's.

"So, what're you going to do with 'em?" Clippy asked pitifully. "I think they're kind of cute together."

"They've got jowls," Yancy said. "There's nothing cute about rats with jowls—"

"You're right, you're right."

"—especially when they're galloping through the rafters of your bistro. Remember that night?"

Clippy nodded somberly. "Do what you must. I'll wait in the truck."

Yancy rummaged through the carpet-laying gear until he came across a cordless nail gun. *This can't really be my life,* he thought. *I couldn't possibly have screwed it up this bad.*

The lovestruck pouchies were going hard at it again, this time with high-pitched pornographic audio. Yancy picked up the nail shooter, which was fully charged. Overhead the gulls scolded and the buzzards circled in silence. To the west, the Gulf waters glinted like green crystal, as far as the eye could see. It was a glorious day to be doing almost anything else.

Yancy planned to burn his clothes when he got home.

TWENTY-FOUR

The Gulfstream jet leased by Platinum Artists touched down at Key West International carrying Jon David Ampergrodt. He was accompanied by his occasional "security assistant," a man called Prawney, who was tall, bald and African American. These characteristics were practically mandatory at the security firm that employed Prawney; many of its celebrity clients were white, and white celebrities always wanted big, shiny, black muscle. It was a status thing. Prawney was introduced to clients as ex-NFL or ex-military, when actually his background was the culinary arts. For years he was a salad chef at Morton's before opening his own Mediterranean restaurant in Long Beach. Despite a well-reviewed debut and excellent word-of-mouth, Prawney's lively taverna shut down abruptly after only two months. A shipment of spoiled Greek octopuses is what put him out of business, incapacitating in one disastrous night Sarah Silverman, Josh Brolin's tax accountant and half the cast of *Empire*. Crestfallen and broke, Prawney was steered by a Jamaican weightlifter friend to the security company, which hired him after a thorough background check. He shaved his skull, hit the gym and soon thereafter began work as a bodyguard. Never in his life had he thrown a punch.

"Prawney, where the hell is my ride?" Amp asked when they stepped off the plane.

"Right there, sir."

"No, that's a Hummer. Nobody rides in Hummers anymore, not even the Russians."

"Nothing else was available on the island," Prawney said.

"Make it go away."

They ended up cabbing it to the Pier House, where Platinum had booked a top-floor suite for Amp. He waited at the door while Prawney inspected the rooms. From the windows you could see the main harbor channel, a mad derby of yachts, Jet Skis and fishing boats. It was Prawney's first trip to Florida.

"Why isn't Lane answering his goddamn phone?" Amp griped.

He was so worried about the meeting that he'd asked Prawney to bring a gun. The security firm expected every "in-country" employee to have a California concealed-weapons permit, which Prawney was able to obtain only because marksmanship skills weren't required. He was a lousy shot, and avoided practicing on the pistol range because the noise hurt his eardrums. Prawney believed his height, girth and stony demeanor were adequate deterrents to trouble; the firearm was just a prop. He rarely bothered to clean the secondhand Glock that stayed snapped in the plastic holster under his suit jacket.

"Maybe Mr. Coolman left a message at the front desk," he said to Amp.

"Call down there and find out. Tell 'em to send up some sushi, too."

During the flight Amp had briefed Prawney about the deal meeting. Lane Coolman would be there with Buck Nance, a redneck TV personality who was a valuable Platinum client. Prawney had never watched *Bayou Brethren* because reruns of *Hell's Kitchen* aired at the same time on another channel. Amp described Buck as a harmless poser, no threat whatsoever.

The wild card in the group—and the reason Amp brought Prawney for protection—was a middle-aged white male who would be introduced as either Spiro or Deerbone. Amp described him as breathtakingly stupid, hotheaded and armed. So far the only thing he'd shot was a mailbox, but Amp wanted Prawney to confiscate his weapon before the meeting.

"How big is this dude?" Prawney asked while they waited for room service.

"Cree says he looks like a freaking scarecrow. He keeps that pistol in the waist of his pants."

"Not a problem."

"Lane says the man is racially intolerant."

"Intolerant, or insensitive?"

"A full-on drooling bigot," said Amp. "Just a heads-up."

"I appreciate that."

The sushi rolls were made with local yellowfin. Prawney admired the presentation, the frisky choice of radish sprouts instead of alfalfa. Amp ate two rolls and left one for Prawney.

Coolman called while Amp was taking a shower. Prawney answered the phone.

"I thought Mr. Ampergrodt was coming alone," Coolman said in a low voice.

"Is there a problem? I'll have him get back to you right away."

"Tell him Deerbone wants a ride in the G5."

"Where to?"

"Doesn't matter. Just circle the Keys for a while. The yahoo's never been up in a plane."

"I understand."

"One more thing . . ." Coolman was practically whispering now. ". . . he's carrying a gun."

"Me, too," said Prawney.

"Good. Can I sit next to you?"

Deb was driving the cherry-reddest of Brock's Porsches when he called to tell her about his upcoming meeting with the mob boss at a place called Higgs Beach.

"And you think he's going to return the diamond? Incredible," she said.

"Have some faith, for once. Don't be so goddamn negative."

Deb didn't tell him she was on her way to the Keys. She planned to surprise him at the hotel later, if her plan worked out.

Yancy was hosing down a small boat on a trailer when she pulled up to his house. From the glove box of the Porsche she removed a bag of potent reefer, which she waved under Yancy's nose as she breezed up the steps, through the front door.

He trailed her inside, where she opened with: "Can you please change the music? Or at least turn it down?"

"The answer would be a hard no. That's Mr. Sonny Landreth on the slide guitar." Yancy beelined for the couch.

"God, what's that smell?" Deb said.

"I was burning something in the backyard."

"Not a body, I hope." She stripped down to her bra and a spidery thong selected for the occasion. The heels she left on while she rolled a joint from her stash. She took a hit and joined Yancy on the couch.

"I know I came on way too strong the night we met, but I was so freaked about losing my diamond that I was ready to do whatever, basically *anything*, to get it back. Most guys—to be honest?—wouldn't say no to a free BJ. Still, I shouldn't have gotten so mad."

"So, you've returned to make amends. In your underwear."

She said, "Tonight I intend to do a proper seduction. Give me a chance to show off a little, okay?"

"Your timing's not great. Also, I don't have your engagement ring anymore, as you surely must know. It was removed from the premises by two gorillas."

Deb took Yancy's left hand and placed it between her legs. His free hand reached up and plucked the joint from her lips. "So this isn't about the diamond," he said.

"No, that's Brock's project. Tomorrow he's meeting with an actual gangster to ask for the ring back, if you can imagine."

Yancy smiled. "You must mean Dominick."

"I don't know the guy's name. I don't care to know."

"No offense, Deborah, but my arm's falling asleep."

"I drove all the way from Miami," she said, "to persuade you to sell us your house. That is, if Brock survives his Mafia beach party."

Yancy said he'd heard about the hassle with the archeologist over the Indian teeth found on their property. "But, Deborah, I'm not selling you my house as a backup."

She tightened her thighs and offered him twenty percent above market value.

"I can't move my fingers," he said.

"This place is a total tear-down. Get yourself something bigger, with a pool."

Yancy yanked his hand free. "I like it here. I'm not leaving."

She stood up trying to tug him toward the bedroom, but he didn't budge.

"It wouldn't feel right," he said. "I'm already in a relationship—possibly two—and you're engaged to the man of your dreams."

"Oh please. This is a fucking real-estate deal."

He stubbed out the doobie. "Did you honestly think this approach would work? I mean, knowing what you know about me—this is what you came up with?"

"It's my go-to move," Deb said, popping out of her bra.

"You don't want to live in this neighborhood, trust me."

"The view from your lot's way nicer than ours. I was thinking Cape Dutch architecture."

"Sorry to interrupt, sweetie, but we've got company. No sudden moves, please."

She turned her head and let out a cry of fright. Two twitchy bat-eared intruders stood upright on the glass coffee table. They swayed slightly sniffing the air, using their long white tails for balance. It appeared to Deb that the creatures were preparing to leap.

"Gambian pouched rats," Yancy whispered. "They must've chewed through the drywall. This whole damn island's crawling with 'em."

Deb tensed up, trembling. She folded her arms across her chest.

Yancy told her to be cool. "They can smell fear. Also brie. They go beast-mode over brie."

"I fucking hate rats. And, Jesus, they're so big!"

"Don't piss 'em off, just stay calm. Here's what we'll do—I'll distract 'em while you make a run for the car. Count of three, okay?"

"Are they f-f-fast?"

"Whatever happens, Deborah, don't look back. Even if you hear me screaming, begging, weeping, do *not* look back. Ready? One . . . two . . ."

She kicked free of her Jimmy Choos and flew out the door. The keys were in the Porsche, thank God.

Mona had taken a job at Stoney's, walking distance from the duplex. Brennan gave her a fifteen-minute break to speak with Detective Rogelio Burton, who was at a four-top by himself. Mona sat down saying, "I ain't seen him since the last time you asked."

"Has he called?"

"No, and you can tap my damn telephone, I don't care. Benny's gone."

Burton had ordered a fish sandwich, which he pushed aside after one bite. "That's not mahi," he said. "That's fried vinyl."

Mona shrugged. "I bring my own lunch."

"There's no warrant out for Benny yet. We just want to speak with him about what happened on the Conch Train. Get his side of the story."

"Bullshit. You wanna haul his ass to jail."

"He knifed a man, as well," the detective said, "a crime you witnessed with your own eyes."

"You married?"

"Sixteen years."

"A million bucks says you wouldn't never snitch out your wife, no matter what she done." Mona tapped two fingers sharply on the table. "'Cause she's everything to you, right? Your whole world."

Burton laid a twenty on the table and stood up. "If you really care about Benny, tell him to come see me."

Mona appreciated that the detective didn't refer to Benny as Blister. It showed he respected her as Benny's wife. Still she said, "I got no clue where he's at."

"Think about it, please. Unless he does the right thing, his future is grim."

"I ain't so sure that's true," said Mona. "You want change back?"

After work she went home, got dressed up and rode her bike to a Chevron station on the main highway. Minutes later a steel-blue van with tinted windows pulled up. The doors slid open and Benny's head popped out. "Hop in, Baby Buns!" he said.

As soon as Mona sat down, he placed a cold rum runner in her hand.

"I thought you said limo," she said.

"This *is* a limo. A limo van—made by Mercedes-Benz! It came from a place on Miami Beach."

"Do I look like a fool, Benny Krill?"

"No, this is the new hot thing. They call it a Sprinter. Right, boys?"

Benny's Hollywood agent was in the back of the van along with the man they said was Buck Nance. Mona asked the agent if Benny was still going to be on the *Bayou Brethren* show.

"Absolutely," Lane Coolman said. "I'm thinking we might have a place in the cast for you, too."

"Doin' what?"

"Just being yourself, Mrs. Krill."

"Would I get fifty grand a week same as Benny?"

Benny cut in: "Don't worry, Mr. C. She ain't serious."

"Screw you. What if I am?" said Mona.

Buck started coughing and told the driver to open the windows. "Somebody put on too much damn perfume."

It was the fanciest van Mona had ever ridden in. The seats were soft tan leather and the carpet smelled brand-new. There was a bar and a flat-screen, like in the real car limos that movie stars used. Mona felt underdressed in her blue-jean skirt and cowgirl shirt with snap buttons.

"My TV name is Deerbone," Benny told her. "Best you start callin' me that."

"What on earth does it mean? *Deerbone.*"

"It's just a name. Same as Buck or Clee Roy."

"Where'd you get them clothes?" she asked.

All three men were wearing untucked tropical shirts and khaki-style pants. Mona felt like she'd stepped into the Tommy Bahama at the outlet mall.

Benny said, "Mr. C took us all shoppin'. Gotta look fly for the meet-up with the boss man." He winked at Mona. "On his private jet plane."

"Oh, no way," she said.

"Oh yeah. I tole you these people were serious."

After a lifetime of being disappointed by men, Mona felt herself longing to believe that this time was different, that Benny was really truly going to be a cable TV star. She asked if she could come onto the plane, too, but Buck didn't seem okay with that.

"Maybe next time," said Benny.

She sniggered. "Oh sure. What next time?"

Coolman said, "Of course you can join us on the jet, Mrs. Krill. Things are happening pretty fast, aren't they? Big things. Good things."

The van accelerated suddenly and made a neck-twisting turn. Coolman scooted forward and spoke under his breath to the driver.

"He thinks we're being followed," Coolman reported to the others, Buck nodding ruefully.

"It's those goddamn tabloids. They ride my white ass all over creation," he said.

The group turned to watch out the back window. There were no cars behind them on the road now, but the driver hadn't been imagining things. It wasn't a tabloid photographer who'd been tailing the Sprinter; it was Andrew Yancy.

He was so baked he shouldn't have been driving a lawn mower, much less a car. He should have stayed home to recapture the Gambian pouchies that he couldn't bring himself to shoot. The mega-rats had escaped by deftly unlatching the door of the trap, which Yancy had hidden in a closet before he went outside to burn his clothes. Now the animals were roaming his house, raiding his cabinets, gnawing his baseboards, fucking in his laundry basket, shitting up a storm. It was a health inspector's nightmare.

And while he had not staged the creepy rodent tango on his coffee table, Yancy had shamelessly taken advantage of the spectacle, to speed along Deb's departure. Later, on the drive to Key West, he'd passed her bright red Porsche stopped on Summerland Key. She appeared quite animated in the driver's seat, probably trying to explain to the state trooper why she was speeding topless in thong panties down the Overseas Highway. On the plus side, she'd left her bag of primo weed at Yancy's place.

His destination was Stock Island because he wanted to keep an eye on Blister Krill, in case Lane Coolman lost control of the nitwit. Expecting Blister to return for Mona, Yancy staked out the duplex, parking the Subaru behind a shrimp truck at the end of the block. To kill time, he sorted through the jumbled contents of his billfold searching for the business card of Rocko Gibralter Document Disposal. It was stuck between two five-dollar bills, the highest denomination in Yancy's possession. He dialed the number, a Miami mobile exchange, and left a message. He honestly didn't expect a callback from the mobster with the rowdy service dog.

Mona emerged from the duplex and climbed on her bicycle. Yancy followed slowly in the car, hanging back a few blocks. She pedaled to the Chevron, locked her bike to a newspaper rack and went to stand by the diesel pump. Yancy was spying from a nearby parking lot when she climbed into a blue Mercedes van, which proceeded at a suspiciously lawful speed toward Key West. Although Yancy felt reasonably alert, the pot definitely had affected his rolling surveillance skills. The van driver figured out they were being tailed, and made a wild-ass turn off Flagler

Avenue. Yancy continued straight in hopes of appearing uninterested and no threat, just another set of headlights on the road. His idea was to pull off at Habana Plaza and wait for the van to reappear, Flagler being one of the main drags into town.

Yancy spotted the shopping center and changed lanes, but at that instant an oncoming car veered across the center line speeding directly toward him. He yanked the wheel hard and boot-heeled the accelerator, trying to squirt out of the other driver's path. The lunatic missed him by inches, Yancy's Subaru jouncing over a concrete curb and rattling to a stop in a dense row of bougainvilleas. He wasn't hurt, although a hot twinge in his abdomen reminded him of the stab wound. Not wishing to attract first responders, he swiftly backed out of the shrubbery, thorns screaking on the paint of the Subaru. Meanwhile the other vehicle, some generic sedan, sat perfectly aligned on the shoulder of the road, comfortably clear of traffic. The car looked like either a Dodge or a Chrysler, metallic gold. The door was open and Yancy heard music blaring—"What Kind of Man," by Florence and the Machine.

I should've guessed, he thought.

Merry Mansfield stepped out of the sedan and waved.

"Miss me?" she called.

"Are you insane!"

"Look who's talkin'. Let's go for a spin."

The car was an eleven-year-old Chrysler 300. "A marvel of engineering," Merry said. "Comes with its own chiropractor. Somebody gave it to me for a bang job in Boca next week. They already yanked the airbags."

Yancy turned down the radio and buckled himself in. "You almost killed me," he said.

"Not even close!" She was amused to see him so rattled. "Andrew, I knew you'd turn right and not left, because that's how your logical little man-brain works. This is what you get for having starlight sex with me on a boat. Now I'm totally in tune with the way you think."

"Then what am I thinking right this second?"

"You're thinking how smokin' hot I look," she said. "You're thinking you're really super-happy to see me, even though you won't dare admit it."

"I'll admit I'm glad to see you, if you'll admit that running me off the road is an extremely fucked-up way of saying hello."

"So what happened with Rosa?"

"I never got on the damn plane. I came back for Blister."

"And *that* is why I came back for you," Merry said.

She was cruising up Flagler in the opposite direction of Old Town. The Chrysler had at most five good cylinders, and perhaps one functioning shock absorber. Yancy asked Merry if she'd seen a blue Mercedes van with tinted windows.

"You mean the Sprinter you were tailing while I was tailing *you*? I'm pretty sure they were on their way to the airport," she said, "which is where we're headed, too—unless your cock's hijacked your guidance system, and now you want to get a room because sitting so close to me is driving you freaking crazy."

She reached over and touched a fingertip to his lips.

"Airport," he said.

"Well, aren't you the hardass."

They found the Sprinter outside the check-in office used by private aircraft. Merry parked the Chrysler in the pay lot and took a stroll in her rhinestone flip-flops. She came back to report the van was empty, and the driver was getting coffee in the main terminal.

"He told me his name's Pete and he's divorced," she said. "Two lies in two minutes. Men are the worst."

"Where's Blister and the others?"

"Probably cracking a bottle of Cristal." She pointed out a big Gulfstream, waiting at the end of the runway.

Yancy cussed and beat on the dashboard—Coolman, the fuckweasel, was taking Buck Nance and Benny the Blister back to California.

Merry said, "Easy, Rocky. Don't hurt yourself."

"Fuck the stitches. Fuck this case."

"One of these days," she said, "we're gonna get here *before* the plane leaves the gate."

They stayed long enough to watch it take off. Then Yancy grumbled, "Let's go."

"Where to? I know you're hungry. What about Clippy's? I like that place."

Yancy said he wasn't up for the Clippy's experience. Merry suggested grabbing a pizza and going back to his house.

Thinking of the escaped pouchies, he said, "I changed my mind. Let's get a room."

"What a slut puppy! I love it." Merry gunned the Chrysler out of the airport, peeling rubber on Roosevelt.

They were checking in at the Doubletree when Yancy's cell started ringing. It was a Miami number.

To Merry he said: "Sorry but I need to grab this."

"I'll be waiting upstairs. Get ready, young man—whips, chains, condiments."

Yancy hurried out of the lobby to take the phone call in private.

"Whassup?" asked the voice on the end of the line. "I bet I know."

"Hello, Dominick," Yancy said.

TWENTY-FIVE

Mona and Blister were enchanted by the Gulfstream. Each of them claimed a window seat. Mona thought the plane was bigger and fancier than the one Dr. Nekrotos used on *Learjet Vet*. The flight attendant took drink orders and brought tiny bowls of warm pecans. When Mona asked why she couldn't see anything but darkness below, the flight attendant explained that they were over the ocean.

Blister kept his nose to the glass and was barely listening when Jon David Ampergrodt rolled out the dead Aunt Carol story, apologizing for sending Cree Windsor to the first meeting.

"No prob," Blister mumbled.

Buck Nance inquired about the large bald Negro on board.

"He's an air marshal," Amp said. He opened a brushed-leather briefcase and handed the deal memo to Lane Coolman, who leafed through it intently.

"Where's my producer credit?" he asked.

Amp's left shoe started tapping. "That wasn't part of the package we agreed on. I'm the producer, Lane, same as always."

"Nothing's going to be the same as always. Don't you get that?"

Amp was stunned. His protégé was behaving like a soulless, backstabbing cockhead, which would have been fine if he'd been backstabbing someone other than Amp, who said, "Associate producer. That's the best we can do for you."

Coolman frowned. "Two words: *Bayou Blood.* I could do the pitch in my sleep. 'Betrayed and rejected by his family, Buck Nance and his long-lost twin start their own chicken farm a few miles down the road.' It would take me—what?—maybe two minutes to find another network that would buy that show. You think I'm bullshitting? Two more words: William Morris. That's my next stop, and I'm taking Buck with me."

The cabin of the luxury jet suddenly felt very small. Amp said, "All right, Lane. You're producer. I'm *executive* producer."

"Not happening. Wake up."

"You're ready to blow up this whole deal over something so petty? Maybe we should check with the client first. Hey, Buck, you really want to leave Platinum Artists after everything we've done for you and your brothers?"

Buck had been munching nuts, waiting for his shot. "Was it your idea, Amp? Tell the damn truth."

"Was what my idea?"

"Giving Miracle to Junior."

"It was the other way around, man. *She* picked *him.*"

"But whose idea?"

"You went AWOL, remember?" Amp said impatiently. "The show was in trouble. We had to come up with something major."

Buck reached across the aisle for Amp's throat, but the muscular Negro intercepted his arm and twisted it into an unnatural, somewhat agonizing configuration. Buck's feral moan caught the attention of Blister, who whipped out the semiauto and aimed it at the so-called air marshal.

"Tell your nigger to let go my bro!" Blister hollered at Amp.

Mona spun around saying, "Hey, I thought this was s'posed to be a fun trip. Benny Krill, you put that goddamn gun away!"

Prawney let go of Buck, who uncrimped his arm and continued moaning. The silver-plated pistol remained in plain view, now on Blister's lap. To Amp the barrel looked like it was pointed in Lane Coolman's direction, which seemed only fitting.

"Deerbone, just so you know? We don't use the n-word on television," Amp said, "or in our company meetings. It's totally not cool, not smart—and that's all I'm going to say about *that*. So if you'd be kind enough to apologize to Mr. Prawney, we can get on with our work."

"Are you shittin' me?"

Buck, still grimacing, raised his head. "Go on, man. Tell him you're sorry."

"When hell freezes over," sneered Blister.

"Then that's when you'll get your TV contract, *brother*. When hell freezes."

Blister turned for support to Coolman, who said, "In this business, first impressions are key. So far? Not too good."

"Okay, fuck it. Sorry I called you nigger, dude. But, listen here—nobody lays a hand on Captain Cock long as I'm alive. He's blood now."

Prawney said nothing. He was scoping out the redneck's gun while trying to appear as if he wasn't. The Gulfstream began a wide turn. Mona spotted something bright on the water, and the flight attendant said it was the lights of a cruise liner. Blister popped his seat belt and jumped to the other side of the plane, so that he could see the ship, too.

"Let's buzz that motherfucker!" he exclaimed. "Go tell the pilot."

Amp's foot started tapping again. Coolman knew what he was thinking—that "Deerbone Nance" was even more flaky and brain-dead than he'd been led to believe.

Buck said, "I want to go back to the airport. I'm pretty sure my arm's broke."

Prawney spoke up. "Sprained elbow. Ice it tonight and wrap it tomorrow."

"Oh, now suddenly you're a doctor. I see."

"Just trying to help."

The flight attendant brought another round. Buck and Blister were doing bourbon on the rocks. Mona had a second hurricane, this time with a floater. Coolman sipped Diet Coke, while Amp drank clam milk from Gwyneth Paltrow's favorite organic market in Brentwood.

"You and me," Amp said to Coolman, and the two men headed for the galley in the rear of the plane. The topic of discussion was Coolman's divorce. Amp counseled him to return to California as soon as possible and begin settlement negotiations with Rachel.

"Is she still balling that dickface Drucker?" Coolman asked.

"I heard she's moved on."

"To who? Tell me she's still not using the Wilshire."

"What's the difference? Come home and get proactive," Amp said. "You don't want to end up in a trial, which would be ugly for you *and* the agency. Rachel's legal team has been talking to some of your female acquaintances. They're lining up for a chance to throw you under the bus, and then drive it back and forth over your head."

Coolman grunted. "Smegg told me."

"Point is, your marriage is history. When I fly back to L.A. tomorrow, you're coming with me. This judge is hardcore. You need to show up."

They returned to the front of the cabin, where Amp again tried to start the meeting. "All right, troops, no more drama and bullshit. Can we please focus on our deal points and get this sucker in shape for the network? That means, Deerbone, that it's time to put your piece away. But only if you're interested in getting rich."

Blister lifted his shirt to insert the pistol into his pants, and that's when Amp noticed the striking ink job.

"It's a kick-ass rooster," the redneck boasted. He stood up and unbuttoned. "That's the evil fuckin' eye," he said, circling a fingertip above his glaring greasy navel.

Coolman unnecessarily explained to Amp that the tattoo was a tribute to Captain Cock.

"Epic," Amp said tepidly.

"Yo, check this out." Blister spun around to display the legend inscripted on his back.

From the prim-looking flight attendant: "Oh yeah, baby!"

Mona wanted it known that she disapproved of the tats. "Low-rent biker ink is all that is," she said. "Hey, girl, what's all them lights down there?"

"Miami Beach," the flight attendant replied.

"No shit?"

"Where?" cried Blister, lunging again for the window.

Amp looked at Coolman. "This is fucking hopeless."

"I agree."

"Tomorrow then."

"I'll call you at the Pier House," Coolman said. "They've got a business center there, I'm sure."

"Why?"

"So you can print up a new deal memo that includes my producer credit."

"Right. How could I forget." Amp flagged down the flight attendant and whispered, "The sightseeing tour for these retards is over. Tell the pilots we're going back to Key West."

Dominick "Big Noogie" Aeola got up, took a leak and returned to bed. He was dozing off again when he heard something that made him open his eyes. It also roused John the First, curled between Big Noogie and his girlfriend. Soon the Irish setter fell back to sleep, but Big Noogie remained wide awake. He lay there thinking, listening in the dark. The room now was still but for Juveline's mewling snore and the occasional dog fart. Although the time was well before sunrise, roosters started crowing outside in the courtyard. Big Noogie had never seen a town with so many goddamn chickens running loose. Of course Juveline thought the fuzzy yellow babies were adorable.

The mobster put on some shorts and led the setter downstairs for a walk. He and Juveline were staying at a new bed-and-breakfast on Eaton Street. The towels were soft and the cuisine was first-rate. Everybody who worked there seemed happy. One night, in the lobby, Juveline had spilled a screwdriver on John the First's bogus service vest. Within an hour it had been spot-cleaned, pressed and delivered back to Big Noogie's room.

He'd gotten used to strangers stopping to tell him what a good-looking dog he had. Once they realized he wasn't blind or deaf they would extend the conversation, trying to figure out his disability. Often Big Noogie responded with a blank smile or a woozy nod, which seemed to satisfy them. Humming a nonsense tune was effective, too.

The morning twilight was full of joggers, young and old. Big Noogie walked John up to Margaret Street and cut over toward the old shrimp wharf. He hadn't expected to like Key West as much as he did. The air was somehow salty and sweet at the same time. He didn't really mind the traffic or the tourists; everyone worked hard to act laid back. Likewise the gay scene was no problem, though Big Noogie had dug in his heels when Juveline tried to take him into one of the dance clubs. All during their trip he'd been telling her to dial down her makeup and wardrobe, but she wouldn't do it. As a result, she had been mistaken more than once for a drag queen.

A humongous yacht was moored at one of the docks but Big Noogie was more interested in the sailboats, the older ones with teak trim. They looked so sleek and pretty. He thought about chartering one for a guys trip to the Bahamas, but nobody was awake for him to ask. Later he hit Harpoon Harry's for breakfast, ordering extra bacon strips for John. From there it was a schlep across the island to Higgs Beach. Ordinarily Big Noogie would have flagged a cab but today he had plenty on his mind, and the time spent alone would be welcome. With the sunlight warming his neck and the dumb mick setter surging joyfully on its leash, Big Noogie thought what the hell. The weather app on his phone reported forty-two fucking degrees and sleet at JFK.

By the time the mobster made it to the beach, he was sweat-soaked and huffing. Having left his umbrella at the B and B, he bought one for ten bucks from an elderly German couple armed with an extra. The man and woman seemed embarrassed to take his money but Big Noogie insisted. He walked along the shore to his favorite spot and looped the dog's leash around the stem of the umbrella, which he speared into the soft sand. Wearily he flung himself into the shade and guzzled a blue raspberry Slurpee that he'd purchased on his trek. John the First lapped at a kiwi strawberry.

At ten on the button the Miami lawyer showed up in crocodile loafers, a thousand-dollar suit and no tie. He smelled like an apple orchard. Big Noogie motioned for him to sit down in the sand.

The lawyer hesitated saying, "I'm not really a dog person."

John the First was elated to have company under the umbrella.

Big Noogie said, "He spazzes out but he don't bite."

Brock Richardson positioned himself so that Big Noogie's body mass served as a barrier between him and the wriggling, slobbering, shedding canine.

"I seen your ads all over TV," said the mobster. "I never tried that shit. What's it called again?"

"Pitrolux."

"Never needed it, knock on wood." Big Noogie snorted at his own joke. "How does it make your Johnson hard if it goes in your fuckin' pits?"

"Bad stuff," Richardson said solemnly. "Really bad."

"I saw the one where you said you was a victim, too. Is that for real?"

The lawyer looked edgy. "Yes, unfortunately."

Big Noogie was curious about what had happened. Richardson said he'd rather not talk about it. His hands were closed and his elbows were pressed to his sides, as if he was jammed into a phone booth.

"Guy I know tried that goo," Big Noogie said, miming the underarm application, "but he told me the boners hurt like hell. Is that true? His girlfriend made him do it. Angelo's his name. Went to Mount Sinai and got a shot in the tip of his pecker, to make the hard-on go down. That's how much it hurt."

The anecdote made the lawyer wince. "Really bad stuff," he reiterated. "Any day now the feds'll yank it off the market."

"I'll give him your number. My friend Angelo. Maybe you can get him some money."

"For sure," Richardson said gamely. "Sounds like he's got a helluva strong case."

Big Noogie pulled the straw from his Slurpee and sucked the icy dregs from the cup. John the First had lost interest in the lawyer and was yapping at some kids tossing a Frisbee. Big Noogie told the dog to shut up.

Then he turned to Richardson and said, "I heard you got a theory 'bout your diamond ring."

The lawyer nodded, scooting closer. "First of all, thanks for taking the time to meet with me. Is it all right if I call you Dominick?"

"Just talk."

"So we're clear, I'm not one who throws random accusations around. Misunderstandings happen in any business—mine, too—honest misunderstandings. I don't *know* exactly what went down at Yancy's house, Dominick, because I wasn't there. But here's what I do know: Deborah, my fiancée, is devastated about losing that ring. Inconsolable. Sometimes I get home from the office, she's sobbing into her pillow. Can't eat, can't sleep. The diamond just fell off her finger, did you know that? She didn't even notice it was missing till later—but by then Yancy had already found it, is what I think. It was hidden in his house. Deb blames herself, and she's a total wreck. To see her this way would absolutely break your heart. Imagine something like that happened to your wife, how shattering that would be."

Big Noogie said, "My wife lives in Red Hook. I see her, like, twice a year."

"Your daughter then," Richardson pressed on. "Imagine your daughter losing her engagement ring right before the big wedding. You can't put a price on something like that, Dominick."

"You can put a price on anything, is my experience. And I don't have any girls, thank God. All boys."

It wasn't the reaction Richardson had been hoping for. "I've got information," he said, "fairly solid information that the men you sent to Yancy's house? They *did* find the diamond. Now, maybe they were under the misimpression they could keep it, and that's why they didn't tell you, but they definitely walked out with that ring."

"How come you think so?"

"I sent guys of my own, Dominick. They were awful rough on Yancy. He spilled everything."

"You must mean the guys that ended up in the medical ward at the jail. The guys Yancy beat the holy shit out of." Big Noogie was grinning like a moray eel. The wind had kicked up, fluffing the ocean with whitecaps.

"But Martin said you told him your guys didn't find the rock—"

"Thing about Marty and me," Big Noogie said, "I don't tell him what he doesn't need to know, and I'm sure there's things he don't tell me. Fact, I'm positive."

The lawyer appeared uneasy and not nearly so crisp. His cheeks were flushed, his forehead shiny. "Dominick, I certainly hope Martin told you how grateful I was that you sent those men to see Yancy. How much I value the favor."

"Your theory, it's horseshit. My guys do what I tell 'em to do, always. They don't have your rock."

Big Noogie pulled out his cell phone and showed the photo to Richardson.

"My future daughter-in-law," he said. "Take a good look at her hand, counselor."

Richardson wilted when he saw what the mobster wanted him to see. John the fake service dog began whining and fidgeting on the leash.

"He's gotta pee again," Big Noogie muttered.

"Know what? Forget I said anything. I'll just buy Deb another ring."

"This time get one that fits."

"Pleasure meeting you, sir. Thanks again for your time." Richardson held out his hand.

The mobster laughed and said, "You think we're done? We ain't done."

The Doubletree was near the airport but Yancy didn't hear the Gulfstream land. He was in the bathroom, talking on the phone with Rosa. She still wanted him to meet her in Norway, only now with the possibility of moving there. He listened patiently while she extolled the mountains and fjords, the civility of the culture, the infrequency of violence, and also (as a low-blow teaser) the spectacular salmon fishing.

Yancy didn't bite. He reminded her that the Vikings practically invented rape-and-pillage.

"That's my point. These people have evolved in a positive way," Rosa said. "Americans are heading the other direction."

"Way too cold over there for me."

"You get used to it, Andrew. Please keep an open mind."

When he came out of the bathroom, Merry was asleep. He turned off the television, pulled the covers to her chin and lay down on the other bed. In the morning she took him to get his car on Flagler and followed him up the main highway back to Big Pine.

Before entering the house he warned her about the Gambian pouchies. Merry said it was no big deal.

"They got rats in the palm trees on South Beach," she said.

Yancy shook his head. "Not like these."

He had baited Clippy's trap with banana slices and Nutella. When he opened the door, Merry said, "Ho-leeee shit, Andrew."

"They're pretty chill, but I'll go first, just in case."

One pouchie was inside the trap. The other stood on top, a chocolate sheen visible on its whiskers. It was munching a chunk of Chiquita.

"Look! She's feeding him through the wires," Merry said. "I love the commitment!"

Yancy tugged her toward the kitchen, saying, "I'm gonna need your help."

After a harried pursuit using a laundry basket, they cornered and captured the escapee, which they put in the trap with its mate. Yancy was pleased that neither he nor Merry was bitten during the transfer. The trap barely fit in the back of his car. Merry insisted on cutting up a peach to feed the animals on the drive back to Key West.

"Are we taking 'em to the pound?" she asked. "We can say they're gerbils with a thyroid problem."

Yancy wouldn't tell her where they were going. In town he stopped at Fast Buck Freddie's and bought a straw shopping basket with dolphins drawn on the sides. Next he parked outside a laundromat and sent

Merry to swipe a pillowcase from one of the dryers. The pouchies were drowsy and cooperative.

Two blocks away, a divorcee from Dallas was prowling Duval Street in search of a skanky swimsuit. Nicole Braswell wanted something that would excite her new cruise companion, a Plano road contractor named Jared who was overweight though nimble in the sack. Currently he was sleeping off a savage hangover on Premier Deck number eleven of the *Azure Countess Royale*. Nicole had met him two nights earlier at the floor show, "Les Misérables on Ice," an ambitious reimagining of the venerable Broadway hit. Thrilled to find a Texas man who loved both skating and musicals, Nicole planned to ditch her schoolteacher friends and move into Jared's spacious cabin for the remainder of the voyage.

As a shopper she was tireless though undisciplined, returning to the docks with a fishnet bikini, an orange one-piece that unzipped from cleavage to crotch, two bottles of coconut schnapps, numerous raunchy tee-shirts, nine reggae-themed beach towels, at least four cowrie necklaces manufactured in Shanghai, an ashtray made to look like a baby hawksbill turtle, sunglasses for every member of her book club, and a $29 conch shell that called you a "sucker" when you held it to your ear.

Nicole was aware that she sometimes got carried away. After lugging her purchases up the long ramp, she was chased down by a uniformed attendant whose accent she couldn't place. Filipino, maybe? She recognized him as the same nice kid who'd helped her find the advanced spin class on the first day of the cruise.

"Excuse me," he said. "A gentleman down there, he told me you dropped this."

It was a straw bag with leaping dolphins on the side. Nicole didn't remember buying it, but that occasionally happened when she was in one of her souvenir frenzies. She thanked the attendant and wiggled a free finger upon which he could hook the straw bag, which was surprisingly heavy.

He said, "Let me take all these things to your cabin."

"Aren't you a sweetheart? Tell me again who found this one."

"He's right down there. That's him in the hat."

Nicole saw a man in a Panama hat at the foot of the boarding ramp. He looked tall, very tan—and taken. At his side stood a pretty ginger-haired woman.

"How nice of him to do that," Nicole said, waving.

"Let's take the elevator," the attendant suggested as she piled the purchases in his arms. He detected movement among the shopping bags and thought it was the woman's hand, perhaps reaching for her purse.

Walking from the docks, Yancy didn't look back. The *Azure Countess Royale* was boarding for departure. A crewman had told him the ship was heading to Galveston. Merry asked Yancy what that meant for the stowaway rats.

He said, "They're together. What else matters?"

"Too bad they're not doing Nassau. They'd rock Nassau."

"Galveston's fine. Vermin make their own fun."

"You could get your ass fired for what you just did, right?"

"Yes, but I can still look myself in the mirror."

"You are," Merry sang out, "so full of shit!"

"I really am. I absolutely am."

They stopped at an upscale fly-fishing shop because Yancy wanted to show her a tarpon streamer made with hackle feathers from a genuine Nance rooster. "As Featured on *Bayou Brethren*!" promised a sticker on the plastic sleeve.

He said, "It's a thing of beauty, you've got to admit."

Merry sighed. "Once again, Andrew, you've opened my eyes. To what, I'm not sure."

After purchasing three of the flies, he took her to the harbor for oysters and beer. She kept him smiling while he waited for Lane Coolman, the lying sack of scum, to call back.

"Why didn't you pounce on me last night?" she said. "At least cop a feel. I even took my bra off."

"I thought you were sleeping."

"Well, I wasn't. It was a test. Maybe you need Bird music to put you in the mood."

"Are you ever going to tell me your real name?"

"I bet I'm your first redhead. Is that right, Andrew?"

His phone rang. It was Coolman.

"What the fuck? We had a deal," Yancy snapped.

"Still do."

"What've you done with Benny the Blister?"

"Nothing," said Coolman.

"I'm coming to L.A. to get him. Next flight out."

"That's a brilliant idea, except we're not there."

"I watched the goddamn jet take off last night."

"Deerbone and his lady wanted an airplane ride."

"Who and what is a Deerbone?"

"Your boy," Coolman said. "It's his *nom de TV.*"

The band at the restaurant was mauling Neil Young, so Yancy was having trouble hearing the other end of the conversation. Merry motioned for him to go out on the patio. After finding a quiet place, he angrily laid into Buck's cocky manager.

"You think you're safe in California? What you and those peckerwoods did to me at the Moorings, starting with false imprisonment, that's an extraditable felony. Which means all of you get a free ride back to Florida, in handcuffs."

"What on earth are you talking about?"

"Just tell me where you are."

"Key West," Coolman whispered, "in the parking lot of the Pier House."

Yancy took a slow, very deep breath. "Okay, give me a timeline."

"One more hour, and he's all yours."

"I'm counting the minutes. No more games."

"Aw, shit . . ."

"Now what? Coolman, are you still there?"

"The fuck are you guys doing? Stop!" the agent cried out, before the line went dead.

Yancy took off running. Merry watched curiously through the window, an empty oyster shell in each of her hands.

TWENTY-SIX

Prawney was confident he could disarm the tattooed redneck, whose behavior was increasingly erratic. "Deerbone" had demanded to do the meet inside the Sprinter van instead of the hotel, because he didn't want to be seen in public. The Key West cops, he kept saying, were hunting everywhere for him.

Jon David Ampergrodt told Prawney he wasn't comfortable bargaining with a paranoid bumblefuck who had a loaded pistol on his lap. Prawney promised to take care of it. He outweighed the dumb cracker by a hundred pounds.

Nobody in the group had gotten much sleep. After the Gulfstream landed, Amp and Prawney had returned to the Pier House while Blister Krill ordered the driver of the Sprinter to top off the gas tank. He said there was a roadside motel way up in Key Largo where they'd be safe for the night. When Buck Nance objected, Blister said tough shit.

And this was his idol he was talking to.

Along the way they stopped on Stock Island to drop Mona at the duplex. Ninety-two miles later, Blister was still pounding the bourbon and Reese's Cups, and rhapsodizing about the plane ride on the G5 and the new Ford dualie he was going to buy with his TV money. Buck had tuned him out early in the trip. Coolman had stayed busy answering emails on his phone.

The motel Blister chose hadn't been renovated since the Nixon presidency. Coolman rented four rooms, including one for the driver, who was swayed by a thousand-dollar tip to stay for the night. At three a.m. Buck knocked on Coolman's door complaining that Blister was howling like a bobcat in a stump grinder.

"It only gets worse when I bang on the wall," Buck said.

"Christ, don't do that! He's so wasted, he'll start shooting everywhere."

With a slump Buck paced back and forth in Coolman's room. He was holding a bag of ice cubes on his sore elbow. "This whole damn plan," he said, "what a nightmare."

Coolman promised it was almost over. "By this time tomorrow your phony twin bro will be in jail, and you'll have a deal that's going to make you crazy rich. Soon as Amp signs off, we're golden."

"Even though the Deerbone thing isn't real? Amp's gonna figure that out."

"Buck, he already knows the guy's not your brother. The part he doesn't know, that Blister's going to jail, trust me—Amp will thank me later for getting that dickweed out of his hair. So will the network."

"Why are you so sure he's getting busted?"

"One phone call and it's over," Coolman said. "This is what I do, okay? Calm the waters. Now please go get some rest."

"What about Miracle?"

"You want her back?" Coolman's tone was forebearing. "All right, let me work on that, too."

"Never mind. I'd have to be insane."

"Sad but true."

"It's Krystal I want," Buck admitted dolefully. "I want us to be Rombergs again."

"Get a grip. Please."

In the morning they made the slog through high-season traffic back to Key West, where Blister refused to leave the Sprinter because he thought he heard police sirens. Negotiations with Amp commenced inside the vehicle at the Pier House parking lot. Every time Amp turned hardass, Coolman played the "Bayou Blood" card. It worked. Buck got his salary doubled, a bigger cut of the *Brethren* reruns and guaranteed helicopter service back and forth to the chicken farm. Coolman would be crowned "senior executive producer," Amp grudgingly accepting a standard producer credit as long as his name came first in the opening scroll.

The trouble in the van erupted while Coolman was on the phone with Andrew Yancy, moments after Amp had initialed and signed Buck's deal memo. Amp was skimming through the terms of Blister's contract when Blister suddenly declared he wanted more than fifty thousand an episode, and also 24/7 access to a jet. It didn't have to be the Gulfstream, but it had to be the same color.

"Those green stripes are sick," he said.

Amp never lifted his gaze from the document. "No jet, Deerbone. Not even Buck gets a jet, and he's the bloody star of the show."

Out came Blister's gun and Prawney went into action, hurling himself upon the stringy redneck. In the cramped confines they tangled clumsily, Prawney unable to separate Blister from the weapon. The driver hopped out and bolted.

"Aw, shit," Coolman said.

Amp and Buck clambered to the rear of the van ducking behind the seats. Prawney drew his Glock, setting up a taut stare-down with Blister. Neither looked exceptionally steady.

"The fuck are you guys doing? Stop!" cried Coolman, who correctly perceived he was in the presence of two rank amateurs with firearms.

Blister was the first to pull the trigger, with inconclusive results. The slug entered Prawney's open mouth and exited his left cheek before demolishing the phone in Coolman's hand. Prawney's long-neglected Glock misfired twice, so he employed it as a mallet on Blister's midsection, replicating the same compact stroke he had mastered pounding beef for the Thai salad at Morton's. The redneck's pistol fired again and Prawney felt a searing pain in his shoulder, the Glock falling from his fist.

He passed out while Amp was yelling, "Knock this shit off, Deerbone, or the deal's off!"

Buck and Coolman were yelling, too. Everyone in the parking lot would have heard the men, had they not been inside a vehicle with superior soundproofing. They fell silent when the sliding door of the Sprinter was flung open.

Yancy looked inside and took a cop-style head count.

Buck Nance was cowering in the back of the van. Beside him crouched a glossy white male in his thirties. Lane Coolman sat pale and shaken in one of the middle rows. Out cold on the floor: a heavyset African American male bleeding from the mouth and upper body.

Finally, there was Benny the Blister—disheveled and gasping, though erect on his feet. The buttons of his absurd tropical shirt had been torn off, the rooster tattoo on his belly pulped to a crimson gargoyle. Gripped crookedly in one of Blister's hands was the semiautomatic.

"Just in time!" he yukked at Yancy, and waggled the gun barrel toward the front seat. "Drive, asshole. Me and my team got a plane to catch."

The sand man also had a plane to catch, an American Airlines charter from Miami to Havana. Juveline was ticketed on a later flight, a precaution at which she'd scoffed. To tease Martin Trebeaux she arrived early at the airport flaunting Tropicana-worthy cleavage. In flame-colored heels she clacked into the gate area and sat down beside a startled Roman Catholic priest. Soon they were engaged in earnest conversation, Juveline shooting a smoky glance at Trebeaux while her painted fingernails feathered a sleeve of the old cleric's cassock.

It was more than Trebeaux could endure, and he signaled heatedly for Juveline to switch to the chair beside his. She did, saying, "Do I know you, mister?"

"Behave yourself, okay? Until we get there."

"Guys in black really turn me on. Plus he talks like a cute old leprechaun."

"That would be Irish," Trebeaux said thinly. "Sweetie, what'd you tell Big Noogie?"

"He thinks I'm goin' to see my sister Kimmy. She lives in St. Louis."

"But what happens when he tries to call and you don't answer? Your cell phone won't work in Cuba."

Juveline said, "The Noog won't call 'cause he can't stand Kimmy. Plus he'll be too busy. Some of his New York peeps are comin' down to hang at the Pyrenees—so thank God you put in that sweet new beach, right?"

The morning *Herald* was open on Trebeaux's lap. Juveline slithered a hand beneath the newspaper and favored him with an intimate tickle. At this point he became immune to rational thought. She showed him her neck saying, "See? I made it so you can't even tell there's a mark."

"My bad. I got carried away," he said.

"Well, I think it's kinda hot. They got Internet where we're goin'?"

"Here and there. But you can't post any pictures, okay? Havana doesn't look anything like St. Louis."

"Marty, I hate it when you talk to me like I'm just a stupid piece a ass."

He didn't think she was stupid, yet in his experience even worldly, hard-edged women went overboard with the social media. Juveline was likely the first in her circle of girlfriends to visit Cuba, and it would require extraordinary self-restraint not to share her tropical experience online. Even if Big Noogie didn't follow his mistress on Facebook, the mistresses of his Mafia cohorts might be keeping tabs. Trebeaux plotted to disable Juveline's phone once she arrived on the island, in case they wandered into a Wi-Fi hotspot.

Otherwise he was excited about their exotic assignation. Up to now the relationship had existed only in a hotel room, brief trysts made more thrilling by the danger. That first night in Havana would be their first together with no hurried departures. Although there was much Trebeaux didn't know about Juveline, he wasn't concerned. Having gotten past the fact her boyfriend was a murderous gangster, the sand man couldn't imagine any other revelation that would scare him away. He didn't care if she was bisexual, bipolar or biohazardous. He didn't care if she wanted to draw Mike Huckabee's face on his balls.

She rocked his sleazy little universe. That's all that mattered.

Unfortunately, as Trebeaux later discovered, Juveline did have one particular habit that would have iced his ardor and panicked him into primal flight. In his defense, it was nothing he'd overlooked; rather it was something he couldn't possibly have known about her, since the two of them had never spent more than an hour in bed, always awake.

Which left him unaware, catastrophically unaware, that Juveline talked in her sleep.

And that the previous night she had unconsciously blurted three words, repeating them loudly enough to awaken the man lying beside her, an individual known to state and federal authorities as Dominick "Big Noogie" Aeola.

The three words exclaimed by Juveline in slumber were: "Harder, Marty, harder!"

Had he known of this occurrence, Martin Trebeaux would have traded his ticket to Cuba for a seat on the next flight anywhere else. Haiti. Paraguay. Fucking Yemen. The farther away, the better.

But the sand man, unaware, proceeded toward his secret island rendezvous.

Thirty minutes out of Miami, as the plane began to descend, Trebeaux was at peace. He smiled to himself at first sight of the island—miles and miles of white-ribbon shore. Somewhere below, in some drab cubicle of that leaden communist bureaucracy, sat an enterprising bureaucrat who would hook him up with all the sand he could barge, for the right bribe. Trebeaux was sure of it.

After clearing Immigration he changed his dollars to Cuban currency, collected his suitcase and hopped in a two-toned taxi, a '52 Chevy convertible. With a couple hours to burn he asked the driver for a road tour of Old Havana, which was spectacular but also a little depressing. The whole place cried out for a pressure-washing, and many of the magnificent grand old buildings were falling apart in chunks. Laundry was strung everywhere across the balconies, while the peeling walls bannered faded revolutionary slogans. The taxi took Trebeaux speeding along the legendary Malecón, under a spray of crashing waves, and then through a tunnel to the other side of Havana Bay. From there the city looked timeless and unworn. He did a selfie at the Morro Castle, and another in front of Che Guevara's house.

On the trip back the driver stopped on the Prado, where Trebeaux bought a handful of Cohibas from a chatty street vendor. The loose-fitting bands betrayed the cigars as counterfeit but the sand man didn't care; he simply liked the way they looked in his breast pocket. He planned to give one to Big Noogie back in the States.

At a café near Parque Central, Trebeaux ordered a *cubata* made with seven-year-old Havana Club. It went down silky so he ordered another. The place was packed with foreigners, including many Americans. In English the barman complimented Trebeaux on his attire, a bone-colored linen suit. The café featured many photographs of Ernest Hemingway at play. Trebeaux said he'd read every single one of the great man's books, a line of bull the bartender heard no less than a dozen times a day.

Another antique cab—a blue Dodge Royal Lancer—carried Trebeaux back to the airport, where he waited with a carnal buzz for Juveline. When her flight landed, he stationed himself at the forefront of the throng outside the terminal building. A half-hour passed, then an hour. Arriving passengers, tourists and Cubans, streamed out the doors—but where was Big Noogie's mistress? The way she was dressed, she'd be impossible to miss. Trebeaux was more irritated than worried. Maybe there was a problem with her paperwork at Immigration. Was it possible she lost her damn visa? He'd watched her place it in her handbag before they said goodbye in Miami.

Unfuckingbelievable. The sand man checked the time on his watch.

As he looked up, the last passenger from the Miami flight walked out of the airport. It wasn't Juveline.

It was, however, somebody Trebeaux recognized. He wished he didn't.

"Hello, Marty," said the man with the ivory toothpick. "Let's you and me take a ride to the beach."

Brock Richardson lunched alone at the Casa Marina, then drove back to Miami Beach. The warm and pretty day was wasted on him. Even the muscle-whine of the newest Porsche in his fleet failed to raise a smile; on Card Sound Road he hit a mirthless one-thirty-five with no spike in his pulse.

Upon arriving home Richardson stalked into the bathroom and clawed free of his suit. The shirt flew off next, revealing a rampage of acne across his chest and back. While examining the cock-like skin tag under his arm, he was shocked to observe the bluish downward trail of a vein. In true junkie form he scrambled for more Pitrolux.

By the time Deb walked in, violet gunk oozed from every crevice and Richardson stank like a truckload of rancid Granny Smiths. Deb snatched the Soft-Glide applicator from his fist and said, "Brock, we need to talk."

"Bad news, babe. My meeting in Key West, it didn't go too well."

"Shocker," she said. "Want to hear what happened to me last night?"

"How about a quick one? I'm a wreck."

"Clean yourself up and put on some clothes, for God's sake."

They reconvened later in the dining room, at opposite ends of the rosewood table.

Richardson went first: "The diamond ring's history. Dominick took it. He gave it to his son's fiancée."

"And you couldn't change his mind? You with your legendary powers of persuasion."

"That I don't need, the sarcasm and snark. It took bull-sized *cojones* for me to brace this dude. You should look him up on Google. He's badass, squared."

Deb chuckled coldly. "And his name's actually Dominick?"

"What'd you expect—Rory? Sven? He's in the goddamn Mafia!"

"So this means you'll be buying me a new rock, right?"

"I guess so," was Richardson's barren reply.

The boner under his bathrobe throbbed, oblivious to his melancholy. He knew of no other big-time TV lawyer in such a sorry predicament—hooked on the very substance that was the target of his own commercials. If the truth got out, Richardson would be sensationally discredited, if not disbarred. The legitimate law firms to which he farmed his Pitrolux clients would cut off all contact, creating a savage drop in his cash flow. Potentially it could cost him millions. By comparison the loss of the engagement ring was negligible, a blip on Richardson's bank statement.

Deb said, "Well, here's *my* news: Forget about that vacation place in Big Pine, 'cause I'm not going back there. Not ever."

"Really? All right."

"Don't you want to know why? I didn't tell you this 'cause I didn't want to piss you off, but yesterday I drove down to see that a-hole Yancy. About selling us his place? I was ready to make him a better offer—"

"Let me guess what that was," said Richardson.

"—but his house is full of monster rats, the nastiest things you ever saw. All the way from Africa, swear to God, and they've got like zero fear of humans. It wouldn't matter if we bulldozed everything, Brock, those hairy bastards would come back. See, they live in the woods. Yancy says they're all over the islands. Two of the damn things were chillin' in his living room, okay? Like they owned the place. And big enough to carry off a baked ham! I got so freaked, I drove straight home, took two Valiums and crashed—and still I had the worst dreams. Bottom line, I am so done with the Keys."

Richardson was stunningly calm. "Actually, I'm relieved to hear you say that, because I've decided to sell our lot."

"Wow. Really? Wow." Deb's mind raced ahead. She'd heard good reports about Captiva, on the west coast. Boca Grande, too. Supposedly there was a five-star spa at the Gasparilla Inn. She asked Brock how much they could get for the Big Pine property.

"I'll be taking a hit," he replied, a miserable understatement.

"How big a hit? You paid what for it—ninety?"

"A hundred and ten, Deb."

"And we're listing it for how much?"

"I'm not listing it. There's already a buyer."

Deb was happily amazed. "When did all this happen? Do they know about the Indian teeth? That they can't build on the land?"

"Not a problem. Not for this guy."

"Unbelievable. Who is he?"

"A friend of Dominick's, apparently." Richardson wore a smile of sickly resignation.

"You mean like a good friend?"

"Dominick wants me to close the deal as fast as possible."

"For how much?"

"Twenty-five hundred dollars."

Deb felt like throwing up. "What the fuck! He *cannot* be serious."

"He most definitely is."

"But what about your mortgage on the lot?"

"Oh, I'll be paying that off next week with a cashier's check to the bank."

"This isn't a sale, it's a robbery! Just tell the man no, Brock. What if you said no?"

"You're a bright person. Use your imagination."

She tipped her head into her arms. "So who is this creep," she said, "that's getting our dream lot for practically free? Another gangster probably. You ever heard of him?"

"He's not a gangster, Deb. It's worse than that."

"What are you talking about? How could it be worse?"

.   .   .

The Sprinter handled like a coupe. Yancy purposely chose the slowest, most convoluted route to the Key West airport. Benny the Blister sat up front in the passenger seat. His window was open, and the gun was still on his lap.

Yancy used the rearview to keep an eye on the others. The wounded bald bodyguard sat upright and glum, a bloody handkerchief pressed to his cheek. Lane Coolman remained hunkered in the last row conferring in low tones with the man called Amp. Buck Nance appeared ashen and deflated, for good reason; Blister was his creation, the ultimate white-trash nightmare.

As the van passed a Hassidic family on Elizabeth Street, Blister leaned out and screamed something horrible. Buck's reaction was instant and scalding, though Blister's ensuing tirade sounded to Yancy like a spoof of Buck's own YouTube sermons at the First Chickapaw Tabernacle of Hope and Holiness.

Blister's next target was two men holding hands on Truman Avenue. Coolman and Amp pleaded with him to stop yelling, though for some reason they called him "Deerbone" instead of Benny. Yancy didn't bother to ask why. Buck's stubbled chin had dropped to his chest and his breathing had become heavy, as if he was willing himself into a stupor.

"I can't wait to get my white ass up to that bayou," Blister seethed, "where they ain't no Jews or faggots!"

Yancy said, "You are quite a specimen."

"Yo, this ain't the right way to the airport."

Yancy said he was taking the back roads to steer clear of the cops. They ended up trailing one of the slow-moving Conch Trains, which gave Yancy an opening to bring up the death of Abdul-Halim Shamoon.

"Doesn't it bother you even a little bit?" he asked Blister. "I should show you some pictures of him and his family."

"Shut the hell up right this second."

"What's the matter, Benny?"

"Turn here. Get offa this street!"

From the rear of the van, the man called Amp asked if they could stop to get medical aid for Prawney the bodyguard. Blister said no way,

José, but Yancy made a few slick moves and minutes later they were on Stock Island, rolling up to the hospital. Blister was going ballistic until Yancy pointed out a police cruiser idling in the lane behind an ambulance. Clutching his shoulder, Prawney got out of the Sprinter and trudged toward the emergency room.

"I'll email a plane ticket!" Amp shouted after him.

Hiding low behind the dashboard, Blister ordered Yancy to hit the gas. "I don't see the airport in five minutes," he rasped, "I'm gonna blow your damn brains out."

"Can I ask where you wild and crazy guys are going?"

"Los Angeles." Coolman's voice, from the back of the van.

"On a private jet plane," Blister added, "but first they droppin' off me and Buck at the chicken farm. Clee Roy and Buddy and Junior, they gotta meet their new kin."

Yancy said it was safe to get up. Blister hopped back in the passenger seat and positioned the semiautomatic between his legs. Amp reported a text from his pilot—the Gulfstream was fueled and ready to go. Yancy was struggling to come up with a plan that wouldn't end with more gunshots. He knew Coolman and Amp would be useless in a group struggle for Blister's weapon, while Buck was totally out of the game, listless and glassy-eyed.

They were on South Roosevelt, maybe a mile from the airport, when Yancy said, "Benny, you're not leaving Key West. I'm just telling you up front. I can't let you go."

"You don't see this *pistole* aimed right at your ear hole?"

"Yes, it's a concern."

"Then what the fuck?" Blister's face twisted like a dirty mop. "How you gonna stop me from gettin' on that goddamn jet plane? Tell me how, motherfucker?"

Yancy shrugged. "Whatever it takes."

"Dude, I already stabbed you. Now you're gone make me shoot you, too? And all 'cause of one skinny dead Moose-lum."

"This is difficult for you to grasp, I know."

"What—you sayin' *I'm* the stupid one?"

"That's how you're acting," said Yancy. "It would be the opposite of smart, for instance, to shoot your driver. Why? Because a driver with a gunshot could easily lose control and crash. This van's going forty-nine miles per hour and you, Benjamin Krill, aren't wearing a seat belt."

"Then stop right now, so I can put a bullet in your skull and get it over with."

Yancy in his doom-state almost cracked a smile—in the mirror he saw Amp and Coolman scrambling to buckle up.

"I said pull offa this goddamn road!" Blister roared.

"Now *that* would be stupid," said Yancy, slapping at the gun barrel.

There was a bang. The van spun sideways and rolled a full 360.

There was a louder bang when it struck a palm tree. A coconut fell from the branches spidering Yancy's side of the windshield.

He knew instantly that the first loud noise wasn't the semiautomatic, because his ears weren't ringing and he didn't smell gunfire. It was only a traffic accident. Nobody appeared to be injured except Blister, who was spitting raw chunks of tongue. His nose was mashed, his jawline gashed from ear to chin. Bright blood dappled the stud rooster inked on his belly. The pistol, knocked loose by the impact, was nowhere to be seen.

Yancy unbuckled, stepped from the van and managed to slide open one of the doors. Blister was the first to clamber out, charging toward the car that had caused the crash. It was an old gold Chrysler 300. He saw that the driver was a good-looking woman with dark red hair. Her skirt was hitched up around her waist.

Blister quit ranting and gaped.

"Super-sorry," the woman said sheepishly. "I'm late for a date. Are you okay? You don't look so okay."

He stepped closer, his eyes riveted on one special zone. He didn't notice the razor in the woman's right hand. Not a cheap disposable, either—a shiny old-fashioned barber's blade.

Blister's mangled mouth said, "Jethuth Chritht, you are *hot*." He took two more foggy steps before Yancy roughly yanked him away, saving him from a more serious laceration.

Amp and Lane Coolman stood on the side of Roosevelt inspecting themselves for injuries. Buck Nance stayed back, leaning almost casually against the rear bumper of the damaged van.

"Hey, Bob!" the redheaded driver shouted to Coolman, who raised his arms incredulously.

"You?" he called back. "Seriously?"

To Yancy the woman said: "I bumped you guys too hard, didn't I? It wasn't supposed to be a rollover, swear to God, but this was my first time doing a Sprinter. The center of gravity on those suckers is ridiculous."

Yancy took the blade from her hand. "You probably ought to get out of here."

"I don't believe in leaving the scene, Andrew. That's not my style."

He bent down and kissed her.

She grinned. "But you were surprised, right? Never saw me coming."

"I'm truly blown away. You can pull your dress down now."

"Like you're not loving the view."

They heard a siren in the distance; somebody who'd seen the accident had called 911. Yancy kicked Merry's razor underneath the Chrysler.

Another car pulled over. The driver, a muscular young Hispanic man, said he was a paramedic. His wife and two small children were with him, a beach trip. He grabbed a medical bag from his trunk and ran to Blister, who shoved him away bellowing, "Ain't no goddamn beaner gonna thtick a needle in me!"

Yancy walked over and knocked Blister flat. He flashed his roach-patrol ID at the paramedic and said, "The man attacked you for no reason. That's what I just witnessed, and that's what I intend to tell the police. He was completely delirious, a menace to everyone. I'd appreciate it if you back me up on that."

The paramedic said okay, though he was unnerved. Yancy put an arm around his shoulder saying, "We're good here. Enjoy the rest of the day with your family."

"But, dude, he's really fucked up," the man said, watching Blister wheeze and thrash on the pavement.

"There's an ambulance on the way. After that he's going to County."

As soon as the paramedic left, Yancy dialed Rogelio Burton's number. He was leaving a colorfully detailed message when he heard Merry honking the horn.

Blister was back on his feet, barreling toward the van.

Yancy thought: *Not that fucking gun again.*

But that's what Blister went looking for—and found. He flew out of the Sprinter clutching the pistol with both hands and steaming headlong toward Yancy, who could already hear Rosa's heartsick I-told-you-so.

The two frayed Californians, Amp and Coolman, turned and ran. Yancy didn't blame them. He shouted for Merry to get down as he positioned himself between Blister and the Chrysler. The vision of a deranged dumbass waving a firearm scattered the gawking crowd of non-heroes that had been drawn to the crash site.

Yancy widened his stance and braced for a bullet. The prospect of being killed in such a public place was depressing—all these goddamn tourists, posting snapshots and videos. What a lousy way to go viral.

Maybe the gun will jam, he thought, *like in the movies.*

The gun didn't jam. It fired one last shot, which missed its target and lodged in a clown-themed SnoCone truck across the street.

This happened at the instant when Buck Nance, of all people, jumped Blister from behind and snapped his neck, like he was a damn chicken.

TWENTY-SEVEN

Playa Ramera was a well-known place for foreigners to connect with prostitutes until the Castro regime cracked down. These days the beach was quiet, one of the loveliest in the Caribbean. On maps the government had optimistically changed the name to Playa de Amor. All the sex cabanas were torn down.

The honeymooning Tumbrells—Daniel and Melodie—walked holding hands along the dreamlike shore. They were excited to be together, far from their families and the gray Canadian winter. Neither of them had ever been to the tropics, so they took pictures of practically everything, even their own footprints in the sand.

Daniel was thirty-two, Melodie twenty-nine. They'd met in the beer line at a Blue Jays game and wed six months later. As a gift Daniel's mother offered them first-class tickets to the sunniest destination they could think of. The newlyweds chose Havana over Miami because they'd heard the crime rate in dictatorships was much lower. Melodie aimed to get pregnant on the honeymoon, a family tradition. Daniel hadn't yet told her about his privately schooled child from a previous relationship, and this would be the focus of many future quarrels.

For now, though, the Tumbrells were close and carefree.

"Is this amazing or what?" Melodie said, skipping clear of an incoming wavelet.

Daniel kicked at the water shouting, "Let's not ever go home! *Adiós,* Toronto!"

Farther up the beach Melodie spotted a half-buried seashell that looked even pinker than the sand. She bent to pick it up, but it wouldn't budge. Daniel came over to help. They noticed two dark circles on the pink shell's surface.

Melodie said, "Look, Danny, somebody drew on it. Are those smiley faces?"

The shell felt tough and rubbery when Daniel tried to pry it loose. He wondered if it was some exotic species of barnacle.

"Maybe it's attached to something under the sand," his bride said. "Leave it there, honey, we'll go find another one."

"No way." Daniel stoutly dropped to his knees. "I'm going to dig this sucker up!"

The policemen who arrived later were as shocked as the Tumbrells, for tourist murders are extremely rare in Cuba. The pantless victim, who'd been strangled and buried, carried a U.S. passport and two soggy Cohiba knockoffs in the breast pocket of his linen suit jacket. The youngest of the Cuban police officers identified the artwork on the dead American's scrotum as emoji characters.

The following day, on a different beach 257 nautical miles away, a man walking an unruly Irish setter received a phone call informing him that the body of Martin Trebeaux had been found.

"That was quick," said Dominick "Big Noogie" Aeola.

He was annoyed though not surprised to learn that Trebeaux had lied about having a high-ranking connection inside the Cuban government, that there was no secret source of sand that could be barged back to Florida for lucrative re-sale.

"Scum of the scum," Big Noogie said. He hung up thinking: *At least the jackoff fixed my beach.*

The Royal Pyrenees Hotel and Resort was rebounding toward a

banner season. Big Noogie surveyed the cheerful crowds at the water's edge and wiggled his hairy toes in the sugary lushness of Trebeaux's final delivery. Nearby, a bunch of kids scrambled to build a sand castle, racing the tide.

A man war-painted with zinc sunblock ambled up to the mobster and asked, "What's your dog's name?"

"John," Big Noogie said. "Just plain John."

"He must be smart. Where'd you get him trained?"

"Harvard."

"No, really."

"He's dumb as a turd," said Big Noogie, "really."

Farther down the beach lay Juveline on a garish floral print towel. She was rocking to Flo Rida and catching some rays. When Big Noogie sat down beside her, she plucked out her earbuds and said, "Don't stay mad, okay? Marty didn't mean shit to me, Noog. I just wanted to see Cuba."

"Next time call a travel agent. Don't bang a stranger."

"Jesus, I said I was sorry like a thousand fuckin' times."

"Shut up, I gotta make a call. Then we'll grab some lunch."

Brock Richardson was home, watching Deb pack her bags, when his phone rang. He assured Big Noogie that everything had been taken care of.

"Also, your friend Angelo has been added to our plaintiff list," he said.

"I was just about to ask."

"Dominick, when is your son's wedding? I'd like to send a gift."

"Not necessary," Big Noogie said. "We're all square. His girl's still creamin' over that diamond."

"I'm sure she is. It's a beauty."

Richardson said goodbye to Big Noogie and went outside for Deb's grand departure. She was taking one of his Porsches, so her bags didn't fit. A limo service had sent a Suburban to serve as the cargo escort.

Deb had on the same hot Jimmy Choos that she'd worn to Yancy's house the day the mutant rats scared her off. Yancy had mailed the shoes back with a note saying: *"You'll need these in your next life."*

To Brock, standing expressionless in the driveway, Deb said, "I'm sorry about this, but I really need some time alone to think."

She wasn't dressed for thinking. She was dressed for cocktails at the Delano.

Richardson kissed her goodbye saying, "I understand completely."

She was in a sulk because he hadn't dashed out and bought her a new engagement ring. It wasn't that he refused to do it; he just wasn't in a hurry.

Her face was unstreaked by tears as she got in the Porsche and sped away, trailed by her luggage courier. Richardson went back inside and flopped onto the bed. The voice coming from the television was his own, cool and persuasive, cataloging the many gruesome side effects of Pitrolux armpit gel.

"And remember," the voice said, "I'm not just your lawyer, I'm a fellow victim!"

"Fucking A!" Brock Richardson cheered.

On the nightstand was the portable, battery-powered blood pressure cuff. With a hungry grin he reached for it.

His housekeeper found him five hours later. He should have quit after four.

They named their new agency Ampergrodt Coolman Legends, ACL for short. The square footage of the two side-by-side offices was identical, as was the window space. It was a starter suite on the third floor, overlooking a drab stretch of Beverly Drive. Each of the partners had hot Asian assistants with marketing degrees from Southern Cal and no patience for grab-ass.

ACL lost its marquee client the very first week, when Buck Nance announced he was quitting television. Lane Coolman and Jon David Ampergrodt begged him to reconsider. The network even offered to rip up his hefty new *Bayou Brethren* contract and double the money. Inconceivably, Buck said no.

By killing his armed stalker—a violent street felon known as Benny the Blister—the Nance patriarch had been transformed in the public's eye from a rehabbing racist to a selfless civic hero. The media was delighted to forget about his repugnant performance at the Parched Pirate and the toxic YouTube diatribes. Buck was suddenly, according to *People* magazine, the most-admired man in America. He had courageously attacked and overpowered a trigger-happy maniac, saving the lives of God knows how many innocent bystanders—bystanders of all races, creeds and sexual inclinations. A New York publisher offered him two million dollars to do a book about what had happened in Key West.

Buck was the big story. Buck was the bomb.

And Buck was done.

Hundreds of thousands of anguished fans circulated a "Come Home, Captain Cock!" petition on social media, yet he remained unswayed. In an interview with Polka Radar Online, he disclosed that he was moving to Milwaukee and opening a music shop. He said his dream was to introduce young people to the joys of the accordion.

To his credit, Buck never ratted out his brothers as Rombergs. Buddy and Clee Roy inked new management deals with Amp. Junior and Miracle talked at length with ICM and CAA, but they ended up signing with Lane Coolman. Krystal Nance spent a week meditating under hot stones at Canyon Ranch before declaring that she, too, was quitting the show. Her replacement would be the crusty common-law widow of Buck Nance's psycho-peckerhead stalker.

Signing Mona Krill was Coolman's brainstorm, though he hadn't been able to track her down and get the deal nailed. For help Coolman reached out to Andrew Yancy thinking their mutual life-threatening adventures with Benny the Blister had forged some sort of man-bond. He was mistaken.

"Why won't you help me find her? Come on, bro," he pleaded.

"I'm a busy guy," Yancy said.

"Busy with what?"

"Busting a sushi bar that's serving salmonella rolls, for starters. Then tomorrow it's a bagel joint where the sourdough smells like mangrove mud. This happens to be my job." Yancy spoke with no rancor.

Coolman said, "Did I forget to mention we intend to pay you?"

"In that case, I'll do it—for twenty-five hundred bucks."

"Whoa."

"That's my freelance fee these days."

"And you seriously won't cut me a break?"

"Twenty-five is what I need," Yancy said. "Yes or no, *bro*?"

"Fine, whatever. Lock it in."

"One more thing. My friend Miso—you promised to find her some work."

"She didn't tell you? I got her in that new Seth Rogen movie, the one they're shooting in Lauderdale," Coolman said. "She even has a line."

"Let's hear it."

"'What's your problem, asshole?' And then she slaps Seth's face. Only it's more like, 'What's *your* problem, asshole?' Seth says she totally kills it."

"I'd be stunned if she didn't."

"And FYI, it's not 'Miso' anymore. It's Jane."

Yancy laughed and said, "A perfectly lovely name."

Mona had quit Stoney's and was tending bar on Big Coppitt. Every so often Yancy saw her riding that droopy little bicycle along the highway. He drove down to the island at midnight and caught her at the end of her shift.

As he anticipated, the news of Coolman's offer unofficially ended Mona's mourning period for Benny Krill. There was a bayfront condo waiting in Pensacola, and premium roosters to be groomed. "Sign my cracker ass up!" she said.

The following afternoon Yancy dropped her at Miami International and texted Coolman, who didn't respond immediately because he was at Square One in East Hollywood, having a civilized breakfast with his future ex-wife. He and Rachel had actually settled on a digestible number for the divorce payout. Their lawyers would pitch a hissy, but screw 'em. The informal negotiation was made possible because Rachel had landed a rich new boyfriend—an actor, not an agent, Coolman was relieved to learn. She promised him that she was done with payback nooners at the Wilshire, and he apologized for being a lousy unfaithful husband.

Later, watching his future ex-wife slide into a yellow Lambo driven by an impossibly buff young airhead, Coolman could only marvel at the durability of stereotypes. On the way back to the office he called Yancy to thank him for locating Mona Krill, who with so many rough edges seemed destined for glory on *Bayou Brethren*.

Yancy said, "I'm thrilled for all of you. Now please send me my money."

He wanted to pay back Merry Mansfield, who'd loaned him the cash to close on Brock Richardson's lot. Yancy planned to re-title the property with a conservation easement so that nobody could build anything on it, not even a tiki hut, for all eternity.

Rogelio Burton had told him that he was crazy, that he could resell the land for at least a hundred grand.

"Sell it to who—another shitweasel like Richardson?" Yancy said. "I'd rather just plant some buttonwoods and watch 'em grow."

The detective pressed his friend to explain why a savvy Miami attorney would unload a prime lot in the Florida Keys for a ludicrous fraction of its true value.

Yancy failed to exude innocence when he replied, "Panic sale, Rog."

"And what would be the cause of Mr. Richardson's panic?"

"Possibly the Calzone crime family. But that's only a guess."

Burton said, "Oh fuck. Forget I asked."

"Specifically, a man named Dominick Aeola. His associates fondly call him Big Noogie. One day his service dog got loose at Mallory Square, and I brought it back to him. He seemed keen on repaying the favor."

"Andrew, this subject is now closed forever. Don't say one word about this to *anybody*, not a fuckin' soul, unless you want to spend what's left of your pitiful career scrapin' dead roaches and mouse shit off your shoes."

Yancy wanted Burton to know it was Dominick Aeola who'd set the property's purchase price at the absurd figure of $2,500. "Hell, I would've jumped on it even at fair-market," he said. "That's the truth, Rog."

"And paid for it how?"

"I don't know. Sell my Picassos?"

"Sonny wants to see you for lunch. Try not to let it slip that your new BFF is a *mafioso*."

The sheriff set the meeting at Stoney's Crab Palace, of all places, which Yancy had shut down once again due to cavorting bacteria. Tommy Lombardo had overruled the closure, allowing Brennan to reopen the dining area on the condition that all tuna entrees were eighty-sixed until the lab reports came back from the CDC.

When Yancy arrived, Sonny Summers was at a two-top morosely scanning the menu.

"What looks good?" Yancy joked.

"The door."

"This isn't a restaurant, it's a fungus factory. Why'd you pick this god-awful joint?"

"Because I knew there wouldn't be a crowd," answered the sheriff, who preferred not to be seen with Yancy.

Out of gastric caution they ordered bottled beer and scorched chicken. Yancy commended Sonny Summers for his poise at the press conference announcing that the Conch Train case had been solved, and that the assailant of Abdul-Halim Shamoon was the same dirtbag who died at the hands of Buck Nance in the melee on South Roosevelt.

"Strange," the sheriff said to Yancy, "but I never got the whole story about that traffic accident."

"Meaning how I happened to be driving the Sprinter? It was all in the report—Benny Krill snatched me at gunpoint from outside the Pier House. Coolman, Ampergrodt, the bodyguard, they all back me up on that. Didn't you read their statements?"

"Andrew, I honestly don't want to know how you ended up in the middle of this particular goat fuck. All I care about is that your name was all over the goddamn media. Again."

"I'm not getting my badge back, am I?"

"This can't possibly come as a shock to you."

The food arrived, and Sonny Summers tentatively bit into a drumstick.

Yancy flailed onward: "You had a dead tourist, tons of bad press and nobody in custody. Now the homicide's solved, the bad guy's deceased, and the victim's family is sitting there with Matt Lauer thanking you, personally, for closure. Meanwhile your only opponent in the sheriff's race dropped out, which means the election's a done deal. Sonny, you've got the damn job locked for another four years! What do you have to lose by hiring me back on the force?"

The sheriff took a hasty slug of beer and swished it around his mouth.

Yancy waited until he was done. "Sonny, this case got closed because *I* found Benny Krill. It was me on his dumb redneck ass—not your guys."

"But see, unfortunately, you ended up in the dumb redneck's custody—not the other way around. If it wasn't for Buck Nance, Krill would've shot you dead in the street."

"Point is, I was ready to take a bullet from that shitbird." The words came out with an edge of futility that Yancy had hoped to conceal.

Brennan slunk up to the table to ask if they were enjoying their meals. Yancy told him to go away.

The sheriff gave up on lunch saying, "This could be buzzard meat for all I know."

"Be straight with me, Sonny. Is there something else in play here?"

"The woman driving the other car. The one who hit the Sprinter van."

"I remember, sure. What about her?"

"The driver's license she gave was a fake. We still don't know her real name."

Yancy felt an icy twisting in his gut.

"That junker Chrysler she had," Sonny Summers went on, "it came from a repo yard in Liberty City. The registration in the glove box was forged."

"Okay, but what's that got to do with me? I was in the vehicle that got smashed, remember? The one that flipped."

Deep breaths, Yancy was telling himself. *Stay cool.*

"Do you know the other driver, Andrew?"

"What are you talking about?"

"Three of the witnesses at the scene said they saw you kiss her."

"Oh, that." Yancy offered a penitent nod. "We're talking about an exceptionally good-looking woman, Sonny. I mean overpoweringly attractive. Still, I get that it wasn't a smart move."

The sheriff's expression made clear that his doubts about Yancy's fitness for duty had once again been validated. "I assume you got her phone number," he said dryly.

"Nope. Just a kiss."

"Hope she was worth it." Sonny Summers signaled for the lurking Brennan to bring the check.

Yancy asked, "What do I need to do to get another chance?"

"Stay away from trouble, for Christ's sake. It's really not that hard."

The drive home made Yancy feel better. At every bridge the water seemed a different shade of blue. The winter sky was bright as an egg, and spangled with birds. Yancy loved the evocative roll call of the lower Keys—Big Coppitt, Sugarloaf, Cudjoe, Ramrod, Little Torch. Here was one blessed stretch of the highway that hadn't yet been blighted by fast-food chains, box stores and strip malls. That shit was coming, though. Everybody said so.

When he reached Big Pine he turned down Key Deer Road, and from there to his house he counted one deer and seven damn iguanas. Merry's rental, a new Accord, was parked beside his skiff. She was sunning in a beach chair beside a tall frosty drink. Her tank suit flashed like a chrome streamer from the rail where she'd flung it.

"You're burning your little bumblebee," Yancy said.

She reached behind her and patted the tattoo. "All yours, mister. As advertised."

It still flustered him a bit, the "A.Y." on her butt cheek. He went inside for a beer. When he came out she was sitting up, legs locked yoga-style.

"Can we officially call this place an estate," she said, "now that you've got all this land?"

"I'm going to pay you back, don't worry. There's a check coming from California."

"So I can cancel your beat-down? Good. I'll tell my guys."

He said, "Rosa called today. She's taken up with the butcher's apprentice."

"Get! Out!"

"It's borderline quaint. Better than a ski instructor, at least."

Merry wrapped herself in a towel. "You sad? Of course you are, Andrew. Stop pretending you're not."

Sad he was, though not blindsided. He'd known that Rosa wouldn't come back to Florida, just as he'd known that he could never move somewhere as cold and tame as Oslo. Their conversation had been painful but not shattering. She said the butcher's apprentice was named Ole, rhyming with roly-poly, which conjured an image Yancy could live with.

"Let's go out in the boat," he said.

"Oh, I know what *that* means—wild rebound sex! Men are so freakin' predictable."

"It'll be chilly on the water. Where's your fleece, Merry?"

They trailered the skiff to Bahia Honda and set out on the gulf side. The wind was westerly and mild, so Yancy steered for the Horseshoes. He backed off the throttle because he wanted the ride to go on and on.

"Wouldn't it be cool to find a shipwreck?" Merry said.

"You already did."

"Shut up, Andrew. You're gonna be fine."

"There's something I've got to ask. Was your plan to kill Benny Krill with that razor blade?"

Merry shook her head. "The plan was to stop him, that's all. It was time for everybody to move on."

"Will you please tell me your real name?"

"I should kick your sorry ass for asking me that."

She leaned close, holding on to him with both arms as the skiff bumped through a choppy patch of waves. Her long red hair blew wildly in the breeze, tickling his neck. He could see his own reflection in her sunglasses.

That's how he knew he was smiling.

Carl Hiaasen was born and raised in Florida. He is the author of thirteen previous novels, including the best-sellers *Bad Monkey, Star Island, Nature Girl, Skinny Dip, Sick Puppy* and *Lucky You,* and five best-selling children's books, *Chomp, Hoot, Flush, Scat* and *Skink.* His most recent work of nonfiction is *Dance of the Reptiles,* a collection of his columns from *The Miami Herald.*

A NOTE ON THE TYPE

This book was set in a modern adaptation of a type designed by the first William Caslon (1692–1766). The Caslon face, an artistic, easily read type, has enjoyed more than two centuries of popularity in the English-speaking world. This version with its even balance and honest letterforms was designed by Carol Twombly for the Adobe Corporation and released in 1990.

Composed by North Market Street Graphics,
Lancaster, Pennsylvania

Printed and bound by Berryville Graphics,
Berryville, Virginia

Designed by Soonyoung Kwon